ANTHONY CELANO is a former detective and detective squad commander who served 22 years in the NYPD. His assignments included the Queens District Attorney's Office Squad, the Colombo Organized Crime Task Force, the Organized Crime Control Bureau, the DEA Joint Task Force and several detective squads in Manhattan and Brooklyn. The author also served as a special investigator for the Office of the Special State Prosecutor-Nursing Home Investigation. Mr. Celano was the Co- Founder/ Owner/ CEO of Full Security Incorporated, a Midtown Manhattan based investigative firm, for seventeen years. After his retirement from FSI, Mr. Celano began writing a series of Sergeant Markie Mystery novels. He is currently working on The Case of the Missing Sole, his eighth offering in the series. In 2019, Mr. Celano began hosting monthly Author-Wordsmith Networking Lunches in Manhattan with Carl Gambino, Peapack Private, to assist authors, aspiring authors and businesspeople to establish mutually beneficial relationships.

Author's Website: anthony-celano.com

This book is dedicated to two people who are very special to the Celano family:

Angelina Parisi
Chris Gambino

THE CASE OF THE DEADLY DIARY

ANTHONY CELANO

1

The Obligation

SIXTY-ONE-YEAR-OLD COSMO THE FLORIST stepped out of the shower and into a white terrycloth robe. Once dried off, he went to his bedroom to get dressed for work. He paused for a moment to look at himself in front of the full-length mirror. Cosmo shook his head unhappily as he looked at the once-toned body that now sagged.

It being his birthday, one would think that Cosmo would be grateful for having reached the age he was while still in good health. He wasn't. The bags under the florist's eyes and the blue veins that protruded from the back of his hands presented a grim reminder that old age was creeping up.

Cosmo ran his hand through his hair. He took a few seconds to stare at the silver threads captured between his fingers. *Ahh, look at this crap,* he thought, *there is no winning when you're up against Father Time.*

Other than the typical minor aches and pains that accompany aging, Cosmo really had nothing to complain about. For a man of his years, he remained robust. The manual labor aspect of his occupation ensured that.

Financially, Cosmo was equally fortunate. Aside from owning his own florist shop he also owned the multistory building that housed the enterprise. Being a greedy man by nature, the florist's thirst for money was at times unquenchable.

To supplement his income Cosmo entered into a pact with the devil, who appeared in the form of a ruthless Bronx mobster. Their agreement entailed Cosmo taking bets at his florist shop on behalf of the gangster in return for a weekly cash payment. It wasn't long before Cosmo realized that the gangster was the sort of man who paid little attention to detail. As long as his gambling operation was steadily fruitful, the mobster asked very few questions.

For many years Cosmo took advantage of the hood's lackadaisicalness by regularly skimming money for himself from the gambling enterprise. This was truly a risky business, but one that came with great financial reward.

Cosmo's childhood friend was Johnny Bronco, a retired NYPD police captain. Bronco, a degenerate gambler, entered Cosmo's florist shop regularly to say hello and place his wagers. Besides being a gambler, Bronco was a notorious womanizer. Being a bachelor, the former captain was a bon vivant who drifted from one romantic entanglement to the next without considering the consequences.

Cosmo, like Bronco, was also a lifelong bachelor. Both unattached men were at a point in life where they heard their leg joints crack every time they rose from a sitting position. Unlike Cosmo, who fretted over this, Johnny Bronco used the cracking sound to his advantage.

The former captain thought nothing of being untruthful with love interests. He'd attribute his joint issues to having been shot in both legs while on the force. This falsehood was impressive enough to gain him access to many a boudoir.

As usual, Bronco entered the florist shop to say hello to his friend and put in his wagers.

"What's doing, Cosmo?" Bronco asked with the jovialness he was noted for.

"What could be doing?"

"What's with the long face?"

"It's my birthday," answered the florist with little enthusiasm.

"Happy Birthday!" declared Bronco gleefully. "Why so glum?"

"What's it all about, Bronco? I mean, where are we going?"

3

"You want to go someplace?"

"Forget about it, Bronco. What's the use of talking to you? You're too clear headed to care."

"Maybe so, but I'm going someplace."

"You are?"

"I'm moving to Las Vegas. If you want to go someplace, why don't you come with me?"

"You know my situation. I got my obligation upstairs to deal with."

"C'mon, Cosmo, Esther's a grown woman for God's sake," said the retired captain, dismissing his friend's explanation. "You got plenty of money. Just dump this place and the two of us can get out of this town."

Cosmo frowned at the suggestion. "C'mon, where am I going?"

"Listen, Cosmo, you and me just don't belong in the Bronx anymore. Everything has changed. This neighborhood for instance, it's shot."

"So where do you want to go?"

"I already told you where, we can go out to Las Vegas."

"Vegas is no place for you," warned Cosmo, who was well aware of his friend's addictive nature when it came to gambling.

"What are you talking about, no place for me? I got my sister living in Vegas, so I won't be alone."

"What'll you do when your money runs out, Bronco?"

"I don't have to do nothing. My pension will carry me. Besides, if I ever need money, I'll get work in one of the hotel casinos. My sister's husband is a pit boss, he can always get me a job."

"I know how reckless you are with money when it comes to gambling, Bronco. You'll end up on your ass living in one of those underground tunnels they got out there."

"Don't worry about me, pal of mine. I'll always find a warm berth. So, do you want to come to Vegas with me or what? Between us we could rent a nice place, split expenses and live it up over there. We could be out there right now banging them two at a time." This remark managed to generate a slight upturn on one side of Cosmo's mouth.

"I can't, what's the matter with you? You keep forgetting about my obligation on the third floor."

"What obligation? Your daughter's a grown woman with a good job now. What are you waiting to do, die without spending your money?"

"Shhh, not so loud," warned Cosmo, who didn't want anyone to know the secret of his being a father.

"You're gonna end up dropping dead in this shop. You look ready to keel over on the roses right now."

"Thanks, Bronco, that's nice to hear."

"C'mon, take your money and collect your social security. Let's live it up while we still can. Think about the Vegas weather and smelling the pretty flowers that await our pollination!"

"I swear, you get nuttier every day, Bronco. Anyway, I can't turn my back on my obligation."

"What's the big secret with Esther being your daughter, Cosmo? It's only right that the kid knows."

"Jeeze, will you be quiet about that! While I'm alive I don't want her or anyone to know that I'm her old man, Bronco," said Cosmo, excitedly. "You're the only living person who knows the truth, and I'm sorry that you know."

"Alright, alright, don't blow a fuse. Your secret is safe with me," assured Bronco. "I'm good at keeping my mouth shut. So, what's the verdict? Are you going with me to Vegas?"

"You know, you're like a broken record sometimes, Bronco."

"Ahh, you're hopeless, Cosmo. Here, put this in for me," said the retired captain, passing the shop owner an envelope that contained money and a sheet of paper that reflected his wagers.

"You want to bet every race to win?"

"Yeah, send all my selections in to win."

"Well good luck to you, my friend....and do yourself a favor and forget about Vegas." Cosmo shook his head as he watched his friend leave the flower shop.

The business owner began working on a floral arrangement for a customer. He paused periodically to take wagers from gamblers as they entered the florist shop. A surprise came when

5

Gino Pagnetta came into the shop to place an order. Pagnetta, a soldier in the Long John Capezzo crime family, was the gangster Cosmo had an agreement with.

At forty-nine years old, Gino could be described as a man with his finger in many pies. Having vast interests, the prominence he enjoyed in the crime family was attributable to the healthy envelopes of money he turned over to Long John, the family boss.

The diminutive Gino suffered from a small man's complex that caused him to resent anyone taller than he was. Feeling cheated by his lack of stature, early on the gangster arrived at a successful formula to level the playing field with those of a larger presence. His willingness to pull a trigger caused people to fear him. It also served as his entrée to the Capezzo organized crime family.

Gino soon became part of the enforcement arm of the family. His proficiency as an assassin was what earned him induction into the family. Gino's resume of dead bodies was cause for Bronxites to remain on the good side of Gino Pagnetta. Those who knew of his reputation walked on eggshells whenever they were around him. This suited Gino just fine. His ability to humble people was an ego booster that elevated the altitude challenged thug.

After attaining the status of soldier in the family, Gino began dressing the part of a successful made man. He favored custom made suits and open collared shirts that revealed the thick gold chain that hung from his neck. Always clean shaven, Gino's generous mane was jet black and slicked back.

Gino drove a huge black Lincoln Continental that drew the attention of neighborhood residents. The locals found it a riot that Gino's head was barely visible over the steering wheel.

"Hey, Gino, how is it going?" Cosmo asked, greeting his gangster associate.

"Good," replied Gino. I need a floral arrangement sent to where Two-Buck Philly is being waked."

"That's too bad about Philly, I had heard that he was sick."

"Yeah, it is too bad. I never made much off of him, but at least he bet regularly. What have you got for me, Cosmo?"

Cosmo removed a brown paper bag from beneath his counter. Inside the bag were gambling records and cash.

"Here you go, Gino," said Cosmo, handing over the bag.

As the two men spoke, the shop telephone rang. As Cosmo fielded the call, Gino was able to see how busy the florist shop could get. This caused him to think that Cosmo could use full time help.

"Why don't you bring in somebody fulltime to help you with the flower work, Cosmo?"

"I got the two kids working parttime, that's enough. I had fulltime help once. No more."

"It didn't work out?"

"In one way it worked out too damn good!"

"I don't follow you."

"In all due respect Gino, I'd rather not talk about it."

"Suit yourself."

Cosmo didn't want to reveal that he had an illicit affair with a married woman that once worked for him at the shop many years prior. The relationship produced a daughter. At the time it was decided that it would be best if the true father of the child remained a secret. The baby girl, Esther, assumed the name of the woman's husband, Trumbell. As far as people knew, with the exception of Johnny Bronco, Cosmo was just a dear friend of the Trumbell family.

For whatever faults Cosmo had, he did feel a sincere obligation to look after his illegitimate child. His monitoring was always conducted from afar. His protectiveness was magnified after the unfortunate death of Mr. & Mrs. Trumbell in a road accident. Esther was in nursing school at the time of the accident.

Unbeknownst to anyone, the florist took a hefty insurance policy out on himself, naming Esther the beneficiary. When Esther began working as a nurse in a Bronx hospital maternity ward, Cosmo rented her an apartment over his flower shop at a discounted rate. Whatever money the florist received from Esther he put aside for her. The safety deposit box where

7

Cosmo banked contained a sealed letter that was addressed to Esther. The contents of the letter revealed where Cosmo stashed his cash and a list of his assets.

Cosmo never intended to let on that he was Esther's father. That was a secret he intended to take to the grave with him. The florist's reason for this was something that Cosmo never explained to anyone.

Since Cosmo himself lived in one of the apartments above the florist shop, it was convenient for him to keep a watchful eye on the unmarried Esther. While he disliked seeing boyfriends pass through her door, Cosmo respected Esther's privacy. He was afraid that appearing overly inquisitive might lead to questions as to why he was so interested. As a result, Cosmo never got to meet any of Esther's boyfriends.

After Gino left the shop, Cosmo stepped outside to sweep the sidewalk. As he pushed his broom Cosmo wondered why he continued to toil at the florist shop. Financially secure, he certainly didn't have to do so. Any notion of retirement was quickly abandoned once Cosmo glanced at the names on the mailboxes after he finished sweeping. Seeing the name of his obligation reminded him that he was staying put.

2

Dear Diary

CLEANING HER APARTMENT WASN'T one of the most enjoyable things for Esther Trumbell to do. Once she finished tidying, she dusted. The real chore came when, armed with a scrub brush, she toiled to make her bathroom sparkle. The reason for such diligence in making her apartment presentable was to impress her most recent love interest, who was scheduled to visit her.

Upon completion of her tasks, her attention was drawn to one of the two framed photos that rested on a shelf over the mantel piece in her living room. She paused for a moment to focus on the image of her mother. Esther let out a deep sigh as she thought of how stunning a woman the late Mrs. Trumbell had been. The daughter could only wonder what part beauty played in her mother's life journey.

So beautiful a woman must have had many beaus, Esther thought. *I can only imagine the number of unwanted advances she had to fend off.*

The daughter viewed her own comeliness as both a blessing and a curse. The blessing was obvious in that her appealing looks garnered her much attention from those who desired her. The downside was her being hounded by pursuers she had no interest in.

Esther then turned to the framed photo of the man she believed to be her father. Mr. Trumbell projected in the photo exactly how he was, a stern unsmiling disciplinarian. Esther recalled the mustachioed public-school science teacher as being a dour looking oval-shaped patriarch who waddled when he walked. The glasses he wore did little to soften his image. The daughter bitterly recollected how, when in his presence, both she and her mother tread lightly.

It was mind boggling to Esther how such an unappealing man as her father could have ever gotten her mother to marry him.

He must have been different then, thought Esther, *although he did have a little money.*

A taskmaster, Mr. Trumbell was fast to criticize people. His wife and daughter were no exception. Any error they made, regardless of significance, was met with unforgiving chastisement. This shabby treatment had an adverse impact on Esther's confidence.

A feeling of being unloved left Esther susceptible to exploitation. Men of her father's ilk, who were astute enough to recognize Esther's need to feel wanted, were able to take advantage of her. Subsequently, Esther entered into a pattern of getting involved with a series of questionable paramours.

Esther took each of her dalliances seriously, believing each lover to be the one she was destined to spend her life with. A series of unfruitful romances inevitably led to scars. With no close friends to confide in, Esther turned to keeping a diary as an outlet to vent her innermost thoughts. The chronicle served as a friendly ear. There were no scolding or punitive reprisals coming from her treasured journal.

When between relationships, Esther would often stare at the unoccupied space next to her in bed. She tortured herself with speculation as to what she had done to derail her past romances. Her final thoughts prior to entering the land of slumber were always the same. She'd groan and wonder if she would ever find Mr. Right.

Esther struggled to remain resilient in her effort to stay positive. Unfortunately, the challenges she faced began to overwhelm her. Each romantic disappointment chipped away at her mental stability, until eventually Esther's melancholy began gaining the upper hand.

There was a pattern to Esther's romantic entanglements. Each new love came with a high that washed away a prior heartbreak. Esther always thought that she finally scored a touchdown with each new love interest. Her elation over her current romantic partner caused her to write happily about her great joy in her journal. The diary entries flowed with the excitement of a schoolgirl's fairytale coming true.

FRIDAY

Oh, Diary, I can hardly wait for tomorrow to come! I just want to love Frankie to death! I'm so anxious to tell him the wonderful news of my pregnancy. I can't find the appropriate words that would accurately express my joy!

Perhaps simple is best....things are marvelous! My ship has finally arrived! Tomorrow can't come soon enough! My yearning demands the hours to fly by. I'm hoping Frankie will marry me long before the baby comes.

After making her final entry Esther placed the end of her pen in her mouth. Her eyes pointed upward as she began thinking happy thoughts. Sighing deeply, she then returned both pen and diary to the nightstand drawer beside her bed and shut off the lamp. With closed eyes she thought of Frankie, hoping that he would appear in her dreams. As usual, he did.

Esther's nocturnal video couldn't have been more perfectly choreographed. It was all moon, June and spoon. The dream concluded with her walking on the beach beside Frankie near their seaside home on the Jersey Shore. Their child was cradled in her arms.

Esther was attracted to Frankie the very first time she saw him performing at a supper club in Westchester. He was a guitarist and vocalist for the trio he headed. Attracted by Esther's beauty, the singer flirted with her from the stage.

Esther was transported to cloud nine that night as she listened to the sounds of the Frankie Flamarian Trio. Frankie maintained eye contact with Esther as he warbled his songs of love.

After his set was completed, Frankie followed up with the confidence that makes a musician successful with groupies. After a brief conversation the singer acquired Esther's phone number. Within a week, a heated romance was underway.

In truth, Frankie Flamarian wasn't the wonderful person he seemed to be. In actuality he was a self-absorbed fast living serial seducer with a penchant for narcotics. To make matters worse, the singer had a wife and two children residing in Putnam County. Frankie's marital status was something that never stood in the way of his romantic pursuits.

The deceitful singer had no qualms about resorting to cocaine to win over those he had designs on. The white powder served as one of his key seductive tools. With Esther, no drug was necessary. All that was required was his attention.

Esther's plan for their big evening was to have drinks, eat and then retreat with Flamarian to the bedroom for their usual intimacy. During a timeout, Esther intended to share the news of her pregnancy. The following day, Esther turned to her diary before Frankie's arrival to record her thoughts:

SATURDAY

He'll be here soon! Oh, Diary! I'm so bursting with joy that I

could scream! These remaining minutes seem to pass slowly as I watch the clock.   I have to admit that my desire for Frankie is

shameless. When he gets here I want him to....

Unable to find the right words, Esther paused to think. She wanted to express herself properly, and not with common vulgarity. But it was vulgarity that best described how she felt. She concluded her diary entry with:

fuck my brains in! Oh, I'm just dying to tell him the wonderful

news!

With her entry completed, Esther thumbed back the pages of her diary to look at past submissions. She paused when she came to Georgie Pride. Her mind reflected back on the pharmacist as she read the earlier diary entries that pertained to the past love.

Georgie took more pills than usual tonight. He said he needed it

after standing all day at the pharmacy. He really isn't a very

strong man physically, Diary, so I find myself always worrying

about him. What Georgie lacks in strength, he more than makes up

for intellectually.

Georgie called me a dumb cluck because I got an answer wrong

to one of his silly quiz questions. I have to do better! When he

talks I find myself always learning something new.

I do worry about Georgie taking those pills. He gets so, so agitated sometimes! That probably goes with his being so highly intelligent.

MONDAY

This evening was a disaster, Diary! I write this with a broken heart. Georgie accused me of cheating on him, when all I was doing was talking to someone. I'm sure that Georgie's mood swings have to do with those pills he takes. He got so angry that I thought he was going to strike me!

Georgie refused to even let me explain. He just stormed off in a rage. He said that it's over between us diary. I know Georgie well enough to know that he'll never come back. His pride was too hurt for reconciliation. I messed up again!

TUESDAY

Oh, Diary, still no word from Georgie. Why, Diary, why? We were so right for each other in so many ways. He never called, and I know he never will. Can he really not care?

Oh, Diary, why can't I seem to do anything right? I've lost Georgie, forever. I don't know what I'll do!

WEDNESDAY

Still nothing from Georgie, Diary. I just have to call him at work.

Georgie told me he never wants to see me again! I've ruined yet

another relationship, Diary. What is wrong with me?

I know Georgie meant it when he said that he's done with me. I

begged his forgiveness, but he just hung up on me. All of my

subsequent calls have all gone unanswered. What am I to do,

Diary?

After she tired of reading the Georgie entries, Esther delved further back through the pages of her diary. She paused when she came to Owen Selby.

Esther recollected the firefighter's aptitude at pleasuring her. A broad-shouldered hunk of a man, the smoke eater's impressive physique had once graced the pages of a firefighter themed calendar. She paused to read a couple of the entries she made at the time of their torrid affair.

TUESDAY

Oh, Diary, I've never been with a man like Owen! Only he can

bring me to such heights! He performs with an insatiable appetite

for me! He's coming over tonight…. I can't wait!

WEDNESDAY

No one has ever taken me to the pinnacle of pleasure as Owen does! Two, three, four....the count continues to rise! When I close

my eyes and allow him, he never fails! Owen overwhelms me. And

I love it! Oh, why must he be married, Diary?

Esther continued to leaf back through her diary. She stopped at a page that referenced the oldest man she had ever been romantically involved with. Her recall of the retired police captain caused her to shake her head as she wondered what possessed her to get involved with Johnny Bronco. Her diary entry told the tale.

SUNDAY

Oh, Diary, how can I be so stupid? Bronco is a hopeless

gambler, and he's old enough to be my father! What I find

perplexing is his secretiveness. Why on earth is he that way?

I do make allowances, but only because the poor man was shot

in both legs. I know Bronco needs me. That's probably why I'm

drawn to him so. I see no future with such a man, but what can I

do? He needs me.

MONDAY

I don't understand why Bronco refuses to come to my apartment,

Diary. His reluctance is a complete mystery to me! I always

have to meet him at his apartment. Why is that?

Is he ashamed of me? When I ask him about it, he gets angry.

But that passes. When he is nice, Bronco can be so persuasive!

When Esther finished reading excerpts from her diary she closed the book and grew pensive. She wondered what Frankie Flamarian would think if he was privy to her innermost thoughts as reflected in her writings. The very idea of a judgmental Frankie was upsetting to her.

Esther briefly contemplated destroying the diary out of fear that the book could potentially undermine her relationship with her lover. She had become so accustomed to turning to her journal as a vehicle to release her feelings that she couldn't bring herself to do it. In a nutshell, Esther's diary remained a best friend in which she could confide in.

Esther turned her thoughts in a more positive direction. She began to concentrate on the babies in the maternity ward where she worked. She smiled happily as she recalled the infants that she tended to. The wee ones came in all ethnicities, colors and shapes, each representing a beautiful new entry into the world. *I hope my baby, if a boy, looks like Frankie*, Esther thought.

Esther sat by the window that faced the street. From her upper floor perch, she watched below attentively. She began having last-minute thoughts on how to break the news of her pregnancy

Maybe I should be direct and just tell him, she thought. *But when? Would it be best to do it after we eat. Or should I let him know when we're in bed?*

***

FRANKIE FLAMARIAN ARRIVED at Esther's house in a taxicab. When Esther saw the singer step out of the car her heart began to flutter. She hurried to her front door to greet him. In her haste, she never got to see him staggering on the sidewalk in front of her house.

It took time for Flamarian to finally climb the steps that led to Esther's front door. The odor of alcohol explained why he was unsteady on his feet. When Esther asked him if he was okay, he failed to offer a response to her question. The singer simply ignored his host as he walked past her.

Once inside the apartment Flamarian proceeded directly to the bathroom. When he finished there, the singer entered the living room where he took a seat on the couch. He stared blankly ahead as if stupefied.

At this point Esther entered the bathroom to inspect it. She was taken aback at what she saw. Seeing the discarded hypodermic needle atop the bathroom sink made it evident that Flamarian just shot up.

When Esther approached Frankie, he was nodding. When she spoke to the singer loudly, he abruptly awakened, the jolt causing him to sit up straight.

"Are you okay, Frankie?" Esther asked.

"Uh….yeah, I'm good," he replied clearly.

Soon after, Flamarian once again began nodding off. Each time the singer seemed about ready to fall on his side, the concerned Esther spoke to him. The sound of her voice magically caused Flamarian to abruptly straighten up.

Having only made love in the dark with Frankie, Esther had no idea that he was hooked on heroin. To satisfy her curiosity, Esther raised the sleeves of Frankie's shirt in order to check the singer's arms. Seeing the ugly track marks clarified things. In his present condition the singer was useless. Esther turned to her diary for solace as Flamarian remained in whatever world he was in.

SATURDAY

Oh, Diary! What am I going to do now? I knew that Frankie drank and took pills, but I never realized that he was shooting dope!

18

Did I do something that drove him to this? Was it me again, Diary? Whatever his issues are, I'll be here for him when he normalizes. He truly needs me now, Diary.

When the singer came down, he entered into a series of mood swings that fluctuated between apathy and anger. Esther was careful not to alienate Frankie by questioning him. She'd wait before doing that. However, she couldn't have chosen a worse moment to announce her pregnancy.

Flamarian found nothing wonderful about the blessed event he was informed of. He just stared at Esther for what seemed like extremely long seconds. This proved to be the calm before the storm. When the singer finally spoke, he did so explosively. He engaged in a merciless tirade against the pregnant woman, calling Esther every vile name he could think of. Terms such as harlot, whore, tramp and scheming gold digger were hurled mercilessly.

The pathetic sight of the sobbing Esther did nothing to quell the verbal onslaught. Esther took Flamarian's venom without defending herself. It was almost as if she felt deserving of such cruel treatment.

Esther's tears didn't defuse the singer. The cruelty in Flamarian demanded more. To achieve satisfaction, he ramped things up by professing his love for his wife and their children. In effect, he twisted the knife to achieve his desired outcome.

Esther collapsed emotionally. She was practically immune to further verbal persecution. The one thing that did resonate harshly with Esther was Flamarian insisting that she go for an abortion. This proved to be the most devastating blow.

Esther's adamant refusal to comply with Flamarian's demand to end her pregnancy was met with physical violence. After slapping Esther, the angry singer stormed out of the apartment, declaring that all was over between them. Once alone, the bruised Esther began weeping uncontrollably. After being drained of tears, she turned to her diary.

Another love is lost, Diary. My heart is broken to where there is no point in going on. What have I to live for now? I can no longer cope with disappointment.

The only avenue to take, for my baby and I, is the path of the coward. I sign off a broken and incomplete woman, Diary....it's best this way.

Esther left the diary on the kitchen table where it would be sure to be found. She left the book open to her last entry. The distraught woman then walked slowly to the sink where she picked up a long sharp kitchen knife. Being a nurse familiar with anatomy, she knew where to strike. After taking a deep breath, she plunged the blade into her heart with force enough to end her sadness forever.

3

Chess Playing

COSMO THE FLORIST LOOKED FORWARD to the first of every month. It was the day that the rent was due. In return for charging a modest rent, Cosmo required that Esther's payment be made in cash. The other tenants wrote checks that reflected the going rate.

Requiring cash from Esther had nothing to do with money. It was all about giving the landlord a chance to spend a few minutes of face-to-face time with his daughter.

Cosmo's routine was to drop by Esther's apartment to collect his due. These visits allowed him to see if Esther was taking care of herself. Under the impression that the landlord was a longtime family friend, sometimes Esther would invite Cosmo into her apartment for a cup of coffee. These private moments with Esther were innocent and came without strings, which was fine by the landlord. The last thing Cosmo wanted was to be obligated in terms of parental responsibility.

Cosmo would sit at the kitchen table and listen attentively to whatever Esther decided to talk about. He was careful to resist the temptation to volunteer any advice that would suggest he was something more than a family friend. His wisdom was imparted only when requested. This relaxed approach caused

Esther to view her landlord as good company when she was in the mood.

The florist long noted the fluctuations in Esther's personality. There were times that his tenant was upbeat, and times that she was gloomy. When happy Esther was quite the chatterbox, discussing her work, her social life and so on. When things weren't going well, she remained uncommunicative. During these blue moments Esther would simply turn over the rent and close the apartment door on Cosmo, leaving him in the hall to wonder. While Cosmo was naturally curious as to what troubled his daughter, he resisted prying.

There were brief moments, especially around the holidays, when Cosmo thought about revealing that he was Esther's biological father. Such honesty was short lived. In the end Cosmo's phobia against assuming responsibility always won out. Any discussion about his past involvement with Esther's mother was something he wanted to avoid. *It makes no sense for me to open a can of worms when I can avoid it*, he thought.

***

COSMO WAS DISAPPOINTED WHEN Esther didn't come to the door when he appeared to collect the rent. Since there was no indication of activity inside the apartment, the florist assumed that Esther was out and about.

Cosmo returned to Esther's apartment several times throughout the day and evening. Finding no response to his door knocking, the florist figured that his daughter was away for a day or two. Since he wasn't asked to water Esther's plants, Cosmo found it doubtful that Esther would be away for an extended period of time. What he found unusual was that Esther did not leave him payment for the rent.

After the passing of several more days, Cosmo grew concerned. Prepared to use the pretext of inquiring about the rent payment, the landlord began reaching out to Esther on her cell phone. When his calls and messages went unanswered, real worry set in.

Thinking that Esther might have taken seriously ill or had an accident that rendered her incapacitated in her home, Cosmo rushed upstairs to Esther's apartment to investigate. Using his master key, Cosmo entered Esther's apartment and received the shock of his life.

The father found his daughter on the kitchen floor amid a pool of blood. It didn't require a formal examination for him to know that his daughter was gone. Having been a veteran of war, Cosmo knew what death looked like. But this wasn't the kind of death in which you looked at a body and moved on. This was Esther. Overcome with emotion, Cosmo took a seat at the kitchen table to collect himself.

From his seat the landlord stared at the bloodied Esther as she rested on the floor in front of the sink. Once settled emotionally, Cosmo rose to inspect his daughter's body. The florist stooped down over his daughter for a closer look at her wound. Part of him wanted to pull the kitchen knife from her chest. He didn't.

Cosmo found it difficult to look at the dead woman's face. Seeing Esther's open eyes eerily staring up at the ceiling was too graphic a sight for him to withstand.

Why would anyone want to murder Esther? Cosmo thought, thinking his daughter was a homicide victim.

Cosmo went through the apartment looking for signs of ransacking. Finding none, he checked the front door. Finding no tool marks on the door, he turning to the windows thinking a perpetrator crept up the fire escape. Finding the windows locked, the theory of a break-in was quickly dismissed as a possibility.

She must have known the son of a bitch and let him in! Cosmo thought.

When the florist recollected that the front door had been locked, he amended his conclusion. There was now only one logical explanation.

"SUICIDE!" Cosmo suddenly bellowed.

Cosmo took out his cell phone with the intention of calling 911 to report Esther's death to the authorities. He ceased dialing when he noticed Esther's open diary resting on the kitchen table. Curious, he began to leaf through the pages of the journal. What he found made clear the reason why his daughter took her own life.

Cosmo's teeth were clenched as he read about Frankie Flamarian and Esther's other lovers. His ire reached a new plateau when he came to learn that one of Esther's romantic partners was his childhood friend, Johnny Bronco, the former police captain.

"SON OF A BITCH!" Cosmo shouted loudly. This outburst was following by a second thundering of, "SON OF A BITCH!"

Cosmo slammed the diary closed and pounded the table with his fist. After a brief pause, he held the book close to his heart. Cosmo then took a solemn oath of vengeance. He looked toward the heavens and with the greatest of intensity declared his commitment with a clenched fist raised upward.

"Every last one of these bastards are going to pay for this, Esther. You'll be avenged!"

Cosmo took charge of the diary and Esther's address book. Before he notified the authorities he removed these items to his own apartment for later inspection. Then, after dialing 911, he went outside to await the arrival of the police.

The uniformed officers who responded to the call for service took one look at Esther and requested the presence of the patrol sergeant. The supervisor, after viewing the body, then notified the precinct detectives.

Cosmo, out of respect for his daughter's reputation, made no mention of the diary to the law
enforcement officers. The responding detectives, as expected, concluded that Esther took her own life.

***

COSMO THE FLORIST EXONERATED HIMSELF of all responsibility in how things turned out with Esther. Looking inward left him feeling not a scintilla of culpability. In Cosmo's mind he did the right thing by removing himself from all involvement in raising Esther.

I wasn't going to damage the reputation of Esther's mother, thought the florist.

Cosmo's justification for his absence in Esther's life rested in his belief that a child was better off living under the roof of both a father and mother. However flawed this perspective may or may not be, it was a position that absolved Cosmo of guilt. In this, the florist found comfort.

The grieving father refused to reflect on certain telling aspects of his relationship with Esther's mother. The mother's complaints of her husband's cruel dictatorialness and physical abuse didn't fit well into the narrative Cosmo crafted. At the time Cosmo dismissed the accusations lodged by Esther's mother by claiming that all married men were entitled to rule the roost.

Comfortable in his position of blamelessness, Cosmo the Florist felt it to be his duty to avenge his daughter's death. An advocate of an eye for an eye, the florist saw revenge as the only way to square the account with those he believed collectively caused Esther to take her own life.

With the payback bar raised to maximum altitude, Cosmo began to plot. He knew that in order to accomplish his mission he would need support. This translated into the necessity of entering into a murderous pact with the devil.

Once Esther was put to rest, Cosmo let no grass grow under his feet in starting out on his unholy undertaking. He isolated himself in his apartment, where he masterminded a strategy of liquidation. The plot the florist orchestrated was akin to a clever chess player who uses his queen to achieve victory. Cosmo's queen was a soldier in the Long John Capezzo organized crime family.

Cosmo knew that the price tag would be substantial if he were to gain the cooperation of the mobster he knew. Although it was painful for the florist to even think of giving away anything, he accepted that he'd have to if he wanted Gino Pagnetta to kill for him.

***

COSMO THE FLORIST FOUND GINO PAGNETTA sitting alone at a table in a small Bronx restaurant that the gangster had an interest in. Gino, who was early for their meeting, was drinking a scotch on the rocks when Cosmo approached his table.

Gino pointed to a chair, indicating that Cosmo should take a seat at the table. The gangster then wiggled his index finger to summon the waiter to his table. The waiter, a slightly built man of middle age, hurried over.

"Bring us two salads, oil and vinegar," said the mobster. "Give me the veal the way I like it, just lemon. And bring my friend here the exact same."

"Yes, Mr. Pagnetta," said the waiter.

"And a bottle of red."

"Most of the waiters here are Irish," commented Gino, once the waiter walked off.

"Why is that?"

"They make a clean appearance," replied the gangster. "Pretty smart, right?"

"Yeah, very."

"You're okay with what I ordered, right?"

"Sure, I eat anything."

"Don't worry, you're gonna love the veal here."

"Veal is fine, thanks."

"Did you bring me my money?"

"Yes," replied Cosmo, passing Pagnetta an envelope containing proceeds from the gambling operation being run out of the Bronx flower shop.

"How did I do?"

"Okay, but you did have a big winner."

"Who was it?"

"Lee."

"Who is Lee?"

"The guy who used to work in the Chinese laundry a couple of doors down from the florist shop."

26

"Him again?"

"He'll go on a losing streak, he always does," assured Cosmo, who fabricated Lee's win to cover up his pilfering from the gambling proceeds. The florist regularly rotated bogus winners who were either difficult to trace or were invented.

Gino made a quick count of the money in the envelope. He then removed some of the cash and handed it to Cosmo. "Here is your end."

"Thanks, Gino," said the florist who received a weekly salary for his role in Gino's gambling operation.

"So, what is it that you want to discuss with me, Cosmo? If you're looking for more money from me for using your florist shop, that ain't happening."

"No, it's nothing like that. I'm satisfied with our arrangement."

"So, what is it then?"

"I'm in need of a favor, Gino," replied the florist. "And you're the only guy I know who could deliver on what I need."

"What kind of a favor?" The vain gangster asked, as he began combing his hair at the table.

The florist leaned forward when speaking. In a whisper he communicated to the mob soldier that he wanted to have Johnny Bronco murdered.

"You want to me to ice a cop?" Cosmo nodded. "And a captain no less!"

"This is important to me, Gino. I'm willing to pay you. Besides, Bronco isn't on the force anymore."

"Do you really think that I'd prostitute myself for a buck and kill for you?" Gino asked, shaking his head.

"I didn't mean to insult you, I just thought…."

"Well, you did, Cosmo," barked Gino, cutting off the florist.

"What did Bronco do to warrant you wanting him dead?"

"It's something really personal, Gino. I'd rather not say."

The florist's reluctance to convey why he wanted the murder committed didn't faze Pagnetta. It made no difference what the reason was, because Gino had no intention of accommodating Cosmo.

"Listen, Cosmo, forget it. I don't really care what Bronco did to you. Did you forget that I'm taking Bronco's action? It ain't in my interest to go bumping off one of my own good customers.

"I can make it in your interest, Gino."

"How do you propose to do that?"

"I'm prepared to leave you my florist shop in return for what I'm asking. It'll be all yours when I die, you'll own the whole shooting match."

Since Pagnetta liked the idea of ownership in a thriving legitimate business, the proposition put forth now merited consideration. After pretending to be thinking it over for a minute the cagey gangster responded.

"What kind of money are you pulling down in the florist shop, Cosmo?"

Cosmo communicated the financials. Finding them impressive, Pagnetta expressed that he might be willing to reverse his initial position.

"You got no family that might put in a claim on the business, right Cosmo?"

"There is nothing to worry about there, Gino. There is no family to interfere with our deal. It's just me and you."

Gino now saw greater opportunity. "Since you got nobody, what happens to the building you own after
you cash in your chips? It's worth a pretty penny." The crime family soldier was angling for the property.

"I haven't really decided, Gino. I was thinking that maybe I'll leave it to the church."

Pagnetta frowned at the answer provided. "Is a priest gonna knock off Johnny Bronco for you? Besides, how can you expect me to own a business and not the building? I'd be at the mercy of the landlord."

Cosmo saw the point. "Okay, Gino, I'll throw in the building if you grant me this favor. It all goes to you when I cash in my chips."

"Yeah, well that's another thing, Cosmo. What if you live to be a hundred?"

"That ain't likely, besides I'm a lot older than you."

"Use your head, my friend. What do you think will happen if I get tired of waiting for you to croak?"

The florist quickly got the point being made.

"So how can we come to terms, Gino?"

"Tell you what, you give me ten percent of the flower shop take every week. That'll hold me until the trumpets start playing your tune. I get the business and the building on the day you croak. That'll make me patient. Have we got a deal?"

"Okay, you got it," said the florist, with a wince. Although he got what he wanted, parting with anything was always painful for Cosmo.

"We got a deal. Now here is how we're gonna work things, Cosmo. I'm gonna bring in somebody to work at the florist shop with you. Whoever that is will learn the business and keep an eye on my end."

"No problem," replied the florist, who had been planning on this.

"And I'll come up with somebody to front for me on the inheritance. I don't like nothing in my name."

"Who do you have in mind to work in the florist shop, Gino?"

"I haven't thought about that yet. It'll be someone capable of learning the flower business and handling the gambling action for me."

"Don't you want me to keep handling the gambling?" asked the florist, thinking that his thievery in the gambling enterprise was in jeopardy.

"Yeah, that won't change. You and the guy I put in there will work it together."

"That works fine, Gino," replied Cosmo. "How about bringing in Louis to work with me?"

"You want my imbecile cousin Louis? Why?"

"I always liked Louis. I think that he could be a good fit in the florist shop, besides, you know you can trust your cousin....and he already understands the gambling aspect."

"Yeah, maybe bringing in Louis is a good idea."

The florist favored Louis because he was known to be a strongarm man for the Capezzo crime family. Cosmo also knew that Louis resented living in the shadow of Gino, who had a tendency of flaunting his authority over his cousin.

By getting close to Louis, Cosmo believed he could compromise him. He would then have access to someone who could perform the additional executions he needed at a more moderate rate.

"I'm sure Louis will work out fine, Gino," advised Cosmo.

"Okay, you got him. Oh, and one other thing, Cosmo. Both you guys are gonna have to do a little work."

"Of course, me and Louis will both be working in the business," answered Cosmo quickly.

"I'm talking about my kind of work," clarified Gino. "You and Louis are gonna be helping me knock off the cop."

"Me?"

"Yeah, you're gonna share in the heavy lifting on this by setting up the pigeon."

"That's not my thing...."

"It is now, my friend," insisted Gino. "You want the piece of work done, so you ain't above participating."

Cosmo's passion for revenge was strong enough for him to go along, although with some reluctance. In retrospect he found a way to feel ahead of the game. *At least he didn't ask me for any cash*, he thought, looking at the bright side.

***

GINO'S COUSIN LOUIS WAS AN olive complexioned man devoid of emotion. His hair was black with traces of gray running through the sides. Everything about Louis seemed sinister. It was said that he looked though people rather than at them.

Louis disliked his cousin Gino since childhood. The first cousins were the sons of two brothers, with Gino's dad being the older sibling. The Pagnetta brothers worked together in a small landscaping business owned by Gino's father. Landscaping was what first connected Gino Pagnetta to Cosmo the Florist.

Growing up, Louis was accustomed to seeing his father defer to his uncle on all issues. The pecking order set by the brothers carried on to the next generation, with Gino considered more

30

important than Louis. This unfairness was even more evident once Gino gained official admittance into an organized crime family.

Exasperating the friction between the cousins was a quirk in Gino's makeup. Gino, who was quite short, suffered from a small man's complex. The fact that Louis was much taller bothered Gino. The organized crime soldier made Louis pay for his allotment of inches by rudely treating his cousin publicly.

Louis welcomed the offer to work in the florist shop. At this juncture in his life, the strongarm man felt he was going nowhere careerwise. Gino's assurances that his cousin would one day be inducted into the family had begun to lose credibility. Gino actually had no intention of proposing Louis for membership.

Louis had grown tired of seeing Gino reap great rewards while taking fewer risks. What Louis failed to realize was that his cousin Gino had been undermining him with the family bosses behind the scenes for years. The last thing the Capezzo soldier wanted was his cousin Louis out from under his thumb.

4

Bronco Busting

IT WAS SUNDAY AFTERNOON and Louis Pagnetta was in his studio apartment having coffee. He was reading the sports section of the newspaper when his cellphone began ringing. Seeing that the call was from his cousin Gino, a serious look came over the face of Louis as he answered the call.

Gino was brief and to the point, ordering Louis to drop everything and be at his home in an hour. After acknowledging these instructions Louis shook his head in disgust. It irked him that the only time he ever received an invitation to Gino's house was when his cousin needed him for something.

When the two men got together, Gino shared limited details regarding his plans to commit murder. Being kept in the dark as to why someone was targeted for death was another thing that made Louis bitter towards his cousin. Louis perceived the lack of transparency as being Gino's way of showing off his superior position in the crime family they were a part of.

Louis was instructed to go to Funzi's Auto Salvage, located in a remote section of Greenpoint, Brooklyn. The salvage business was just one of the many businesses Gino held an interest in. Gino, who went to grammar school with Funzi, provided his former schoolmate with the startup money to open his business. Gino's generosity came with his receiving half interest in the new entity.

Aside from the financing, what made the partnership attractive to Funzi was his knowledge that Gino came with a multitude of connections that ensured profitability. Funzi also knew that the partnership would demand that he comply with any request made by Gino.

When Louis pulled his car into the salvage yard, he was met by Funzi. Gino's partner was an unshaven chunky man of average height, who spoke with a scratchy voice that was annoying to hear. Funzi's unpleasant sound stemmed from his once being struck across the throat with a stickball bat as a youth. Smoking three packs of cigarettes a day only exasperated Funzi's vocal unpleasantness.

"I got the car ready to go," said Funzi, who was hoping that he wouldn't be asked to do something too far out of his comfort zone. When he learned what was expected of him, Funzi appeared visibly relieved.

"So now you know what to do," declared Louis, after having briefed Funzi.

"I got it, Louis," stated the yard owner, "the car will be there. But tell me, what's this all about?"

"Do you really want to know?" asked the stone-faced Louis. The iciness that accompanied the question left no doubt that being inquisitive was an error in judgment.

"No, it's none of my business."

"Okay, Funzi, now run through what you're gonna do."

"I drive a car to the front of the Bronx flower shop and wait outside with the car running. When I see you, I get out of the car and go home. At that point I'm finished for the night."

"What kind of a car did you get us?"

"One with a big trunk. It's a white Oldsmobile."

"Good. Now what time are you supposed to be there?"

"I gotta be there exactly at midnight because that's when the cops change shift."

"Once you give up the car, how are you getting outta the neighborhood?"

"One of my guys will be parked two blocks away by a subway station. After I drop off the car, I walk to the train station and jump in the car with him. He'll take me home."

"And your man knows nothing, right?"

"Not a thing. He thinks he's picking me up from a girlfriend's house."

"Okay, now remember to wear gloves. We don't want no prints."

"No problem, Louis. Tell Gino that they'll find no prints."

***

GINO PAGNETTA HAD COSMO LURE JOHNNY BRONCO to a high-stakes poker game to be held in the rear of Cosmo's florist shop. The retired captain was told that those participating in the game were out-of-town yokels with poor poker skills. As expected, the seasoned card player found the invitation to play in a rigged Gino Pagnetta game too good an opportunity to resist. When told that he would have to split his winnings with Gino, Bronco had no objections, seeing this as only fair.

Cosmo was told to arrive early in order to familiarize himself with the marked cards that were to be used in the game. He was also supposedly there to gather intelligence on the habits of the other card players. Tidbits such as what it meant when a particular player fingered his money, lit a cigarette or covered his mouth were valuable insights.

The back room of the flower shop was big enough to accommodate a large circular card table with chairs, a small portable bar, a refrigerator and a couch. A long rectangular folding table for food stood against a wall. A backdoor led to a small outdoor area where a white marble religious statue was visible. A grape arbor ran along one side of the yard and across the back of the building. When in season the grapes were boxed by Cosmo and turned over to Gino, who gave them to his father for making homemade wine.

When Bronco arrived at the flower shop he was greeted by Cosmo, who then escorted him to the back room where the treacherous Pagnetta cousins were waiting. Gino smiled broadly as he rose from his chair to greet the unsuspecting former police captain. The gangster's smile was deceptive. The display of Gino's perfectly aligned pearly whites had always been an effective tool in lowering people's guard.

"Captain Bronco!" said the gangster with great enthusiasm.

"Are you ready to make some money?"

"That's why I'm here, Gino," replied Bronco.

"Louis, go and fix us some drinks," directed the mob soldier.

"Scotch or beer?" asked Gino's cousin, who began taking drink orders.

As the drinks were being fetched, Cosmo began to converse with Bronco. While the former lawman was distracted, Gino circled to his rear. The gangster produced a handgun from under his sport jacket and fired once, striking Bronco in the back of the head. The force of the bullet caused Bronco to jump forward, landing him face down on the floor, where he remained motionless.

"He done for," announced Gino casually after examining the dead man. "Louis, forget the drinks. Go get the drop cloth, blankets and rope."

When Louis returned, he and Cosmo spread the drop cloth on the floor. They then placed Bronco atop the cloth. Once the dead man was centered, Gino handed the murder weapon to his cousin, ordering Louis to put a bullet into the already dead Johnny Bronco.

Louis shunned the gun. Instead, the cousin produced a Jagdkommando twisted tri-blade dagger.

"I'll use this," said Louis, asking, "okay with you?"

"Go on," said Gino.

Louis stabbed the dead man in the heart with his pet weapon.

"You happy now?" asked Gino, with a trace of annoyance. "Now take this damn gun and put one in him like I said," ordered the mob soldier, in an authoritative tone. This time Louis followed instructions and fired a round into Johnny Bronco.

Gino then ordered Louis to pass the gun to Cosmo. "You're up, Cosmo. Put a slug in the roof of his mouth." After taking a deep breath Cosmo mustered up the resolve to fire the round as directed.

The homicide victim was packaged in the drop cloth and placed inside blankets that were then snugly held together with duct tape.

"C'mon, let's clean up," announced Gino.

At the allotted hour Louis stepped outside the flower shop to make sure Funzi was there in the car waiting for him. Seeing that he was, Louis went back inside the flower shop. He and Cosmo then carried their victim's body to the running vehicle and placed the dead man in the trunk.

As per Gino's instructions, Louis drove the vehicle to the Split Rock Golf Course. He was followed by Cosmo, who trailed behind in his own personal vehicle. After abandoning the car containing Bronco's body they departed the scene in Cosmo's car.

After Gino received word from his cohorts that their mission had been accomplished, he glanced at his watch. By his standards it was still early. He telephoned a girlfriend to inform her that he'd soon be stopping by her apartment. After hanging up with his mistress, Gino called his wife to let her know he wouldn't be home.

"Why not?" asked the wife.

"Something came up," was the answer she received.

***

AFTER LEAVING THE GOLF COURSE, Cosmo and Louis took a slow drive back to the flower shop. Since homicide was nothing new to Louis, he remained unfazed by the murderous act he had engaged in. He sat on the passenger side of the car casually smoking a cigarette.

"I'm hungry," announced Louis. "Wanna get something to eat?"

"You can eat?" asked Cosmo, finding it hard to believe that Louis had an appetite after what they had done.

"Yeah, I'm starved. Let's go to a diner."

"I don't feel like eating in any diner."

"What's the matter, Cosmo? No stomach for this kind of work?"

"I have no regrets, Bronco deserved what he got."

"I have to eat something," repeated Louis. The florist saw this as an opportunity to further the devious plan he devised.

"If you want, come upstairs to my apartment," suggested Cosmo. "I'll make you something."

Once inside his apartment, Cosmo put on a pot of coffee. The men chatted casually as the host prepared a Swiss cheese omelet for Louis.

"You got any red peppers, Cosmo?"

"Yeah, I do. Do you want pancakes too?"

"Sure, why not?"

As Louis ate, Cosmo studied him. In Louis, Cosmo saw a cost-effective alternative to Gino. Since things were cordial, the florist began laying groundwork that would ultimately lead to his propositioning Louis.

"You know, Louis, I've noticed something."

"What's that?"

"Your cousin doesn't seem to treat you too nice."

"You picked up on that, huh?"

"Yeah, it's none of my business, but the way he orders you around isn't right."

"Gino has always been like that. His old man is the same way."

"That's too bad. I mean, after all you do for him."

"My cousin is a one-way street."

"To be honest with you, I kind of find his behavior a little embarrassing."

"What do you mean?"

"I mean the way he bosses you around in front of me, it embarrasses me."

"Gino's a made man. That button gives him all the authority in the world. There isn't a thing I can do about it."

"Do you think you'll ever get proposed for membership?"

"To tell you the truth I don't even know anymore," said Louis.

"Let me tell you something, Cosmo, if I were to get my button things would be very different. My getting inducted into the family would mean that me and Gino become equals."

"And if that don't materialize?"

"Then I'm stuck where I am."

"You know, Louis, there may be another way to level the playing field."

"Yeah, right," said Louis, with great pessimism. "What way is that?"

"With money."

"I don't follow you, Cosmo."

"If you had enough money, you wouldn't need to jump every time Gino calls you, right?"

"I have to, I earn money with him."

"But if you had money, you wouldn't have to rely so heavily on your cousin."

"I suppose, but what are you driving at?"

"Look, Louis, let me be blunt. I need somebody like you to take care of some things for me," said Cosmo, his tone dead serious. "If you help me, I'll help you."

"How can you help me."

"I can make you financially independent."

"How? By buying me Lotto tickets?"

"You're looking at the winning ticket right now, Louis."

"You're talking in riddles, Cosmo. Speak plain."

"Look, I got a bundle tucked away and plenty in the bank. You do what I ask, and your worries are over. I'm talking real money here."

"How much?" asked Louis, with no concern over what Cosmo wanted done.

"I got a half million in the bank that can go to you when I cash in my chips. It'll all be legit and spelled out in my will. When I croak, you'll be guaranteed to collect the money."

"Where did you get that kind of money?"

Cosmo hesitated before answering the question. "What I'm about to tell you could get me killed, Louis. But since we're going to be working together, well, I want to be fair with you."

"Shoot, I know how to keep a secret."

"I've made a fortune skimming money from your cousin's gambling operation," admitted Cosmo.

"Are you nuts telling me that?"

"I don't think so Louis, because I'm holding the ticket that gets you out from behind the eightball. I'm offering to go partners with you in the skimming. It'll make you a rich man."

"What do you think will happen when Gino gets wise?"

"He'll never get wise. I've been raking it in for years. I got ways of doing things worked out that he'll never catch on. You'll have plenty of money coming your way."

"And you'll still be leaving me a half million in your will?"

"I got nobody else in this world to leave it to, Louis. It'll be all yours. Are we good?"

Louis let out a deep breath before replying. "I got to think about this," he finally said.

"Do you want out from under your cousin's thumb or what?"

"I do."

"Then roll the dice with me, Louis. You'll be a wealthy man. Once you got enough, you can walk away from your cousin."

"If Gino ever figures things out, forget about it."

"Don't worry so much about Gino. As long as he gets his, he's not looking at anything beyond what I turn over to him. Besides, I'm leaving him my end of the florist business and the building when I check out, so he loves me."

Louis began to rub his jaw, thus making it clear to Cosmo that he had his attention.

"Okay, Cosmo, we're in business. What needs to be done?"

"I want you to kill three people who deserve killing."

Louis was taken by surprise at hearing this. "You aren't kidding, are you?" asked Louis, noting the intensity in Cosmo.

"I'm dead serious."

"Is Gino one of the three?"

"No, of course not, Louis."

"If Gino ever finds out that I'm taking out people without his okay, he'll go ballistic."

"This has nothing to do with your cousin or anybody he knows. It's strictly a private vendetta that involves just me. Gino doesn't have to know anything about it."

"What you're asking me to do is against the rules."

Sensing a renewed reluctance, Cosmo knew he had to make his offer more appealing. "I can make the pot sweeter for you, Louis." This got the killer's attention.

"How sweet?"

After negotiating a number for each killing, Cosmo reminded Louis of what he would be inheriting and his cut of what could be pulled out of the gambling operation."

"What if you spend the money before you croak, Cosmo?"

"Me, spend money?" Cosmo asked with a chuckle. "I've lived a frugal life, so I got more than enough for me without touching what I promised you."

"You really got me thinking," acknowledged Louis.

Seeing that Louis was warming to his proposition, Cosmo became more self-assured.

"Eat your pancakes, Louis. We got a lot to talk about."

***

COSMO WORKED LOUIS into his florist business slowly. Learning about flowers and the preparation of simple floral arrangements was challenging for Louis. Gino's cousin was better at taking customer orders, working at the register and dealing with vendors. Since Louis was familiar with gambling, that aspect of transitioning into the florist shop came easily. Louis left the skimming formula to Cosmo, who shared with Louis the money stolen from Gino.

Cosmo waited until the interest in the Johnny Bronco homicide seemed to die down before embarking on his murderous agenda with Louis. When alone in the confines of his apartment the florist kept his animosity alive by continually reading through Esther's diary. The focus for his next act of revenge centered on the singer Frankie Flamarian.

As far as Gino Pagnetta was concerned, the mobster was a content man as long as money kept coming his way. He didn't think Cosmo or Louis would ever have the nerve to betray him. Gino's sense of security removed any notion of his micromanaging the gambling operation taking place at the florist shop. In this, Gino was short sighted.

5

Tied Like A Rotisserie Chicken

DETECTIVE HOWARD KIRBY WAS AN investigator assigned to a Bronx police precinct. Kirby, an old-timer, was a union delegate. His role in the union consisted of representing peers whenever they found themselves in trouble. Kirby was clever at extricating his fellow detectives out of troublesome predicaments. In accentuating his union position, the detective did so at the expense of performing his investigative duties in earnest.

The delegate was a less than a stellar mentor to young investigators, who he trained to be less than ambitious. The cautious Kirby was an ardent believer in self-protection. Years of jousting with management over procedural miscues and/or questionable behavior influenced the detective's outlook.

"You can't get in trouble doing nothing," was the misguided veteran's motto, "so only do what the book requires you to do."

To prove his wisdom Kirby was fast to cite examples of detectives who had gotten into trouble over their being too conscientious. After conveying a sad tale or two, he'd conclude his point by emphasizing how no one wanted to hear about good intentions if you screw up.

42

"The bosses will write you up sure as shit," Kirby would remind novice sleuths. He was referring to a formal written complaint.

The veteran detective's book cover was impressive. His silver locks lent credibility to his words. Kirby, blessed with an ample mane that gave no sign of thinning, wore his hair back with a high part. He exemplified what many people believed a detective should look like. He was conditioned, tall and well-groomed. His cleft chin gave him a model-like appearance. When wearing a suit, white shirt and lowkey tie he was a poster boy for the detective division.

Hidden behind Detective Kirby's polished veneer existed traces of his urban roots. This translated to a philosophy that mandated that a person had to look out for himself first. In short, if it came down to Kirby or the other guy, it was always going to be the other guy getting the short end of the stick.

Even though Kirby was a union delegate, he still was obligated to catch cases. When summoned by the patrol sergeant to respond to where a dead man was discovered in the truck of a car, Kirby reacted by displaying a pained look.

Kirby, who was working alone, drove to the scene in question. Upon seeing the body in the car trunk, he immediately called for a forensic team to respond to the location. He then notified the covering detective supervisor. The detective supervisor, aware of the experienced Kirby's ability to cover all the bases, informed the detective that he would go to the scene only if absolutely needed. This was fine with the delegate, who preferred to work without oversight.

After the crime scene unit performed their forensic work, they gathered the personal belongings of the homicide victim and turned these items over to Kirby. When the detective found a police identification card in the victim's wallet, he winced. The added twist of a dead retired captain on his hands translated into more work for him.

"This guy is Captain Bronco," announced Kirby aloud, who after a closer look at the homicide victim's face, recognized Bronco. This new wrinkle was ample reason for Kirby to again call up the covering detective supervisor.

"Now I'll have to swing by the scene," advised the detective supervisor. "Do what you need to do, I'll catch up with you shortly."

"Do you want to notify the chief of detectives, boss?" asked Kirby.

"I'll take care of that. You do the unusual report and put me down as present.

***

DETECTIVE KIRBY WAS talking to the covering detective supervisor when Detective Sergeant Al Markie and First Grade Detective Oliver Von Hess arrived at the precinct squad room. Kirby and the covering supervisor both recognized the visitors as men from the chief of detective's special headquarters squad.

Markie announced that he and Von Hess were dispatched to the precinct by the Chief of Detectives to assist in the homicide investigation of the retired police captain.

Kirby had uncertain feelings over the presence of Markie and Von Hess. He wasn't sure if the involvement of the headquarters team would mean more work for him or less. The covering detective supervisor welcomed the presence of Markie.

"If you're on this, there is no sense of me sticking around," stated the covering supervisor to Markie. "I might as well take off."

"Not a problem," said Markie, "I got it."

"So, what's the story with this?" asked Markie, turning to Kirby.

"We found the captain in the trunk of a car located in the parking lot of the Split Rock Golf Course. From what we know so far, he was shot and stabbed. Whoever did this tied Captain Bronco up like a rotisserie chicken."

"How many bullet wounds were there?"

"He took at least three slugs, Sarge, one in the back of the head, one in the mouth and one in the torso."

"Somebody said he was stabbed too...."

"Yeah, and according to crime scene the cut was made with an unusually nasty blade."

"Was the family notified yet?"

"I haven't gotten that far, Sarge," replied Kirby. "Crime Scene is still out there working. I want to know a little more before I start calling family members."

"Did you run the plate on the car?"

"Not yet, Sarge, it's on my list of things to do," replied Kirby.

"What are you doing now?"

"I'm going through the captain's belongings. He's got a lot of Atlantic City casino cards in his wallet. It looks like he was fond of gambling."

"Is that the captain's gun?" asked Markie, pointing to the Smith & Wesson detective special that was on Kirby's desk.

"Probably, Sarge, it was on his hip."

"Didn't you check the serial number with the license division to confirm that it was his piece?"

"Not yet, boss. That's on the list of things to do."

While Markie and Kirby conversed, Von Hess looked through a small address book that had been recovered from the body of the homicide victim. One entry in the book caught his eye.

"Looks like he's related to a Janice Bronco Masterson who lives out in Las Vegas," announced Von Hess.

"When I get to the address book, I'll start making some calls," advised the squad detective."

"Is there a home address for the captain in that book, Ollie?" Markie asked.

"Yeah, according to this he lives on Belmont Avenue."

"Are those his house keys?" asked the sergeant, addressing Kirby.

"Probably, they were in his pocket, Sarge."

"You do what you have to do here, while we go do some leg work," said Markie. "We'll go to Belmont Avenue and see what we can dig up. I'll take the keys with me."

"No problem, Sarge, I appreciate any help I can get. Does your office want to do the research on the car and gun?"

"No, you can take care of that. We'll take care of the field work."

"Okay, Sarge."

"What is your name again, detective?"

"Kirby, I'm the delegate here."

"Where is your squad commander?"

"He's out sick with the chickenpox."

"Isn't he kind of old for that?"

"It can happen at any age."

"Apparently. When you prepare the unusual report, add me as being present."

"Here is my card," injected Von Hess, addressing the delegate. "My cell number is on there if you need us."

When Markie and Von Hess were in their car the sergeant telephoned his office at headquarters to notify his boss that he'd be covering for the ailing squad commander. Markie and Von Hess then headed to the Belmont Avenue address.

***

JOHNNY BRONCO LIVED IN A MODEST ONE BEDROOM apartment, located over a butcher shop. Markie used the dead man's key to access his apartment. After entering he and Von Hess began snooping around. Inside a dresser drawer in Bronco's bedroom the sergeant found a loaded police service revolver, a box of .38 caliber bullets, handcuffs and a blackjack. He closed the drawer without touching these items.

In another drawer Markie came across a stash of condoms. The sergeant called out to Von Hess, who was poking around in another room, asking him to join him in the bedroom.

"The captain has been a busy boy," said Markie, pointing into the drawer with the condoms.

Von Hess looked into the drawer, nodded and remained silent.

The detectives resumed their examination of the apartment. An envelope containing a letter from a woman named Bunny was found in a desk drawer by Von Hess. The contents of the communication revealed that Bunny was angry due to the captain's involvement with a woman named Esther.

"It looks like the captain was involved in a love triangle, Sarge," advised Von Hess after reading the letter.

Markie read the letter himself. "It looks like this Esther threw a monkey wrench into Bunny's rabbit habit," commented Markie.

"It would seem that way, Sarge."

The detectives found nothing in the apartment that provided them with a solid clue. This left only the letter to look into.

"C'mon, let's get this place safeguarded, Ollie."

Once back on the street Markie called for the patrol sergeant to respond to the apartment. After explaining the reason for their being there, Markie made it appear that he and Von Hess hadn't already been inside the apartment. The patrol sergeant called for a squad car to conduct an official search of the apartment. This resulted in Johnny Bronco's weapon, some cash and other items of value being confiscated for safekeeping.

At the conclusion of the search, the patrol sergeant took steps to seal the apartment for the purpose of protecting the remaining property. As this was being done Markie and Von Hess went to the store-front butcher shop to determine who the landlord of the building was.

The investigators were informed by the butcher shop owner, a gray-haired man in his early fifties, that the landlord was a snowbird who was spending the winter months at his home in Jupiter, Florida. The butcher was stunned when informed that Johnny Bronco was found in the trunk of a car murdered.

"Bronco was murdered?" asked the butcher in disbelief. "Why would somebody want to kill him?"

"That's what we're trying to find out," advised Von Hess.

"My God, what a terrible way to die. He must have pissed off somebody."

"Somebody who was pissed off enough to put three slugs in him," added Markie.

"What do you think the problem was, Sergeant?"

"All we know," said Markie, "is that he was clipped gangland style."

Markie's remark put an end to the butcher's questions. The word gangland reminded the butcher that he lived and worked in a neighborhood controlled by Gino Pagnetta, and that meant he had to keep his mouth shut if he valued his health.

"What can you tell us about Captain Bronco?" asked Von Hess.

"What do you mean?"

"We want to know about his habits. Who he hung out with, stuff like that," clarified the detective.

"All I know is that he'd come in here to buy meat. Sometimes he'd buy veal, sometimes chicken and sometimes baloney. It all depended on how he was doing with the ponies."

"He gambled?"

"There was talk of that."

"You said it depended on how he was doing with the ponies like you knew."

At this point the butcher wanted to distance himself to avoid having to answer any other questions. He decided to steer further questions to one of his workers.

"Why don't you talk to the guy who works for me, he would know more than me."

The butcher called his worker over to join in the conversation. A man in his mid- thirties, the employee proved to be more forthcoming. He indicated that Johnny Bronco had a reputation as a gambler and a womanizer.

"Where did he place his bets?" asked Von Hess.

"I wouldn't know about that," answered the worker, he too was being cautious.

"Was the captain the type who borrowed money?"

"Johnny Bronco never asked me for money. The guy was a police captain, so he had a big pension."

"Do you know who his lady friends were?"

"I would see him with this one woman all the time. She hangs out in the Slender Fox pretty regularly. Then there was this other younger woman. One time I caught him bringing her up to his apartment. This one was a lot younger and a looker. They were both pretty bombed that time."

"When was that?"

"A while back, I guess. I was coming in to work when I caught them stumbling in. The older one, like I said, I would see him with more often at the Slender Fox."

"Where is the Slender Fox?"

"The place is only a couple of blocks from here."

"Do you know the name of these women?" asked Von Hess.

"Just the one from the Slender Fox, her name is Bunny."

"Can you describe her for us?"

"She's tall with blondish hair."

"How old is she?"

"In her forties, I'd say."

"And what's the story with the other woman?"

"Like I said, she was a honey. I've seen her around the neighborhood, but I got no idea who she is."

After thanking the butcher and his worker, the detectives headed over to the Slender Fox. The bartender over at the Slender Fox knew exactly who Bunny was. He directed the investigators to an apartment over a pizzeria located across the street from the bar. Seeing that the bartender was being cooperative, Von Hess put forth questions about the dead captain.

"Why sure, everyone around here knows Johnny Bronco," advised the bartender. "What happened, did he do something wrong?"

"He's dead, we found him in the trunk of a car," informed Von Hess. "Did he have any enemies that you know of?"

"Jeeze, I'm sorry to hear that."

"Did he have any enemies that you know of?" repeated he detective.

"No, as far as I know, he got along with everybody. He was an easygoing guy."

"What about bad habits?"

"No more or less than anyone else, I guess."

"No vices?"

49

"Who don't have vices?" asked the bartender. "I mean, he liked the women. But what he really loved to do was gamble. He'd bet on the color of the next car passing by."

"What kind of gambling?"

"Numbers, horse racing, cards….you name it."

"Do you know if he was into any loan shark?"

"I don't know anything about that," replied the bartender, not wanting to go there.

"When he bet the numbers, do you know where he placed the bet?"

"I got no idea," answered the bartender untruthfully. He, like many in the area, placed his bets at Cosmo's florist shop. Like everyone, his fear of incurring the wrath of Gino Pagnetta prevented him from being more forthcoming.

"You said that the captain liked the ladies…." voiced Markie.

"Maybe you should go and talk to Bunny across the street. She could tell you more than I can about Johnny Bronco."

"I guess maybe we should," agreed Markie.

6

The Detectives
Start Digging

VERONICA WALDEK HAILED from Cut and Shoot, Texas. Raised
with four brothers, she grew up a tomboy with an affinity for
the outdoors. She was particularly fond of hunting and fishing.
Her skill at rabbit hunting caused the brothers to nickname her
One-Shot Bunny, a sobriquet that was eventually shortened to
simply Bunny. It was a handle that stayed with her into
adulthood.

Bunny worked as a kitchen worker in a home for veterans not
far from Cut and Shoot. It was there that she met a self-
employed Scotland born painter who often worked at the
facility. Sniffing around the kitchen, the vendor took a shine to
Bunny, who was good for an occasional free tuna salad
sandwich and soda.

Having an interest in Bunny, the painter began asking her to
join him for a "wee heavy" after work. Unfamiliar with the term,
she asked him for clarification. "Scottish Ale," advised the
painter.

After several declined invitations, Bunny finally relented. She
agreed to accompany the stout painter to a beer garden one

evening. The evening turned out better than expected.

With the aid of the drinks consumed, Bunny began to find the Scot amusing. When she began to roar whenever he uttered the word "nae" instead of no, the painter knew he was making headway. As things worked out a spark was ignited in Bunny which eventually led to the two becoming sweethearts.

The painter suggested to Bunny that she should allow him to move into her apartment. Being less than truthful, he explained that he had to give up his own apartment because his landlord needed the rooms for a family member.

The painter emphasized how they could save money by splitting expenses. Bunny found this to be a sound argument that merited consideration. After some contemplation, Bunny consented to their living together.

It wasn't long after the painter settled into Bunny's apartment that their relationship began to spiral downward. At the heart of their difficulty was Bunny's realization that the painter was a lazy user with little ambition. Further straining their relationship was the painter's lack of funds. His failure to contribute financially left Bunny assuming the cost of their living arrangement. With Bunny meeting the bills, the painter took on just enough work to give himself money to keep him in wee ones.

Once Bunny got tired of the freeloading, she terminated the relationship. Her demand that her boyfriend find lodgings elsewhere was met with complications. In answer to the painter's reluctance to move out, Bunny went to the courts for legal intervention. Not receiving the prompt satisfaction she desired, Bunny turned to her brothers to expedite the painter's exit.

Three of Bunny's brothers, who were all of broad back, tried explaining to the painter that the time had come for him to move on. This effort failed, with the user scoffing at the suggestion he move out. Two seconds after the painter voiced the word nae, Bunny's brothers hoisted him in the air and carried him off to the bathroom. Holding the painter upside down by his arms and legs, the brothers stuffed his head into the toilet bowl. Two flushes later the wet painter agreed to gather up his things and leave the apartment.

Once removed from the residence the ousted lover embarked on a vindictive campaign of harassment aimed at Bunny. Fearing what her brothers might do, Bunny opted to relocate rather than deal with a situation that would likely get her brothers in big trouble. Believing that a change in scenery would do her good, she moved east.

Bunny found employment at an all-night Bronx diner. It was there that she first met Johnny Bronco, who was then the commanding officer of the precinct that covered the diner. Impressed by a big city police captain taking an interest in her, Bunny took up with Bronco. She even wrote letters to her family back in Cut and Shoot about her new law enforcement flame.

Bunny's involvement with Bronco was an enduring one that continued long after the captain's retirement from the force. Due to Bronco's gambling addiction, and her past unpleasant experience with the painter, Bunny expressed no interest in marrying. In this, both she and the police captain were on the same page.

However, Bunny did expect her relationship with the captain to be strictly monogamous, even though both maintained their own apartment. Restricting himself to being a one-woman man was a covenant easier verbalized than adhered to by Johnny Bronco.

Bronco's repeated infidelities led to a pattern of separations and reconciliations. Each reuniting lasted only until the next infidelity was discovered. Bronco took these periods of separation as part of their relationship. There were times he welcomed the break.

As for Bunny, she drew the line when Bronco took up with a beautiful younger woman. Esther was someone Bunny knew she couldn't compete with in terms of beauty and youth. Of all their breakups, this was the one that left the bitterest taste in Bunny's mouth.

***

MARKIE AND VON HESS FOUND the door that led to the apartments over the pizzeria open. Making their way up the stairs they knocked on doors until someone directed them to Bunny's apartment.

The sound of a vacuum cleaner could be heard coming through the door. Bunny, who was unable to hear the knocking over the humming generated by the cleaning device, continued with her work undistracted.

"Give it a good rap, Ollie," instructed Markie.

This time, Von Hess began smashing the door with his open hand. Bunny, startled at the sound of the door being traumatized, realized someone was at her front door. She shut off the vacuum cleaner and went to see who was there. Bunny opened the door a crack and peeked through the space granted by the chain lock. The two men in suits standing outside her door looked like cops to her.

"Detectives," announced Von Hess, holding up his gold shield to the partial face visible through the opening.

Bunny undid the chain lock and opened the door to her apartment. When coming face to face with Bunny the detectives realized that they had interrupted her housework. The rolled-up sleeves on her red and black flannel shirt and worn jeans made that evident. Strands of Bunny's blond hair could be seen jutting out beneath the lavender head wrap she wore. Bunny's shoulders were broad, developed along the lines of a swimmer.

"Bunny?" asked Von Hess, politely.

"Yes, I'm Bunny. What do you want?"

"We'd like to ask you a few questions, Ma'am."

"About what?"

"Johnny Bronco."

"Oh, him," commented Bunny with a frown. This being an off period in her relationship with the former captain, Bunny's feelings for Bronco were at a low point.

"We were told that you're a good friend of his."

"Well, once maybe. But not anymore."

"What happened, if I might ask?" queried Von Hess, sensing hostility.

"Let's just say that we parted ways."

"Would you mind telling us why?"

"Go and talk to his new girlfriend," said Bunny, sounding peeved.

"We can't," injected Markie, bluntly adding, "Bronco is dead and we don't know of any other girlfriend."

"Bronco is dead?" asked the shocked Bunny, her lower lip dropping. "Oh no!" she blurted with emotion. "What happened?" she asked, as she began leaking tears.

"May we come in, Ma'am?" Bunny stepped aside to let the detectives into her home.

"Tell me what happened, please, Detective. Was there some kind of accident?"

"I'm sorry to have to inform you that the captain was murdered," said Von Hess.

"Bronco was murdered?"

"He was found in the trunk of a car with three bullets holes in him."

The news caused Bunny's legs to buckle. She supported her balance by grabbing onto a piece of furniture. Von Hess took the shocked woman's arm and guided her to the couch. Once seated the detective asked her if she wanted a glass of water. Bunny declined, opting for brandy. After swilling down a healthy allotment of Christian Brothers, she poured herself another.

"Bronco can't be dead!" she suddenly blurted out.

Once the distraught woman exhausted herself with grieving, she settled down to where she was capable of answering questions. Bunny revealed all she knew about Johnny Bronco. She explained how they met and what ultimately led to the latest disintegration of their relationship.

"Do you have any idea as to who may have killed him," asked Markie.

"None. Everyone liked Bronco. Sure, he had his faults, but everyone liked him."

"Bronco was supposed to be a gambler, right?"

"Yes, Bronco was a big gambler," confirmed Bunny.

"Was he into any loan sharks?" queried Markie.

"I doubt that. He always had enough money."

"How can you be sure of that?"

"Because he never once asked me to loan him any money. Actually, he was a lot of fun when he'd win money," Bunny recollected fondly. "I never knew what he'd do next. He was full of surprises."

"And when he lost?"

"He was okay, Bronco wasn't a sore loser. He took his losses in stride. He saw losing money as a downside faced by all gamblers."

"Where did he place his bets? Did he go to the racetrack, a casino or what?" Markie asked.

"We'd go to the racetrack once in a while. Sometimes he'd take me to a casino."

"No place local?"

"I know he placed bets at the florist shop."

"Where is that?"

"On the avenue here, there is only one."

"Do you know who owns the florist shop?"

"Cosmo the Florist owns it. Cosmo and Bronco grew up together. They're best friends."

"This Cosmo is the guy who takes the action?"

"Yes, I believe he does. But as far as I know, Cosmo just owns the florist shop, not the gambling
portion. At least that's what Bronco told me."

"But the bets are put in with Cosmo?"

"That's right."

"So, who controls the gambling operation?" asked Von Hess. "Somebody has to be taking care of Cosmo."

"That could only be be Gino."

"And who exactly is he?

"Bronco told me that Gino Pagnetta is a member of the mafia."

"You know Gino?"

"I met him once or twice when I was with Bronco. Bronco would say hello to him."

"So, tell me about Cosmo."

"I don't really know how involved he is with Gino."

"Did they get along?"

"I suppose so."

"What about the captain and Gino?"

"Bronco got along with everyone. Sometimes he got along too well with people….and that caused us problems."

"What do you mean?"

"Bronco and I broke off because I caught him fooling around with a young girl who lives in the neighborhood."

"Would you mind telling me who she is?"

"No, I don't mind. Her name is Esther. She lives in one of the apartments over the flower shop."

"So, as far as you know Bronco was having no problems with anyone?" Markie questioned.

"Other than me, he never fought with anyone."

***

LOUIS PAGNETTA HAD JUST TAKEN a bet from a local gambler just as Markie and Von Hess entered the florist shop. Louis did a double take after seeing two serious looking men in suits enter the shop. He immediately suspected the visitors to be members of local law enforcement. They had that unmistakable look of detectives with something on their mind.

A couple of bulls, Louis thought. His mouth was turned downward, making it apparent that he was unhappy to be visited by members of law enforcement.

The detectives sized up Louis with the same alacrity that Louis sized them up with. In Louis, the detectives saw a thug right out of central casting. The tough guy look, the snarl and the gold chain around his neck made Louis a walking billboard that advertised what he was.

Holding an envelope containing gambling records, Louis discreetly dropped the evidence in the wastepaper basket beneath the counter he stood behind. He then slid the basket forward with his foot to further conceal it from view.

When the detectives formally identified themselves, Louis tried to cloak his apprehensiveness. His fret was for a good reason. He was carrying his pet weapon, the unique dagger he used in the Johnny Bronco homicide.

Opting for a strong offense, Louis bolstered himself by standing to his full height. He tossed his shoulders back and inflated his chest. He was hoping that a forceful appearance would reduce the chances of his being searched.

Louis wasn't fooling anyone. Markie and Von Hess had dealt with his ilk in the past. Both investigators had noticed Louis drop something behind the counter. Since the investigators had been alerted that the florist shop was taking gambling action, they correctly assumed that Louis was trying to conceal gambling records.

What Markie and Von Hess didn't know was that Louis was on parole after having served time in jail
for the felonious assault of a man who got in the crosshairs of his cousin Gino.

"Are you Cosmo?" asked Von Hess.

"No," replied Louis.

"Where is Cosmo?"

"He's not here."

"Where is he?"

"How should I know, I'm not his babysitter."

"Look, friend, there is no reason to get cute," Markie said, sounding practical.

"I ain't getting cute, all I'm doing is trying to work over here."

"So, answer the question, where is Cosmo?"

"I already told you, I don't know."

"How about I turn this dump upside down until I find something to pinch you on?" asked the sergeant.
"We can start with what you dropped behind the counter."

"Look, boss," replied Louis, now remembering his parole status, "I'm not looking to get in a beef with you guys. Cosmo didn't say where he was going."

"What's your name?" questioned Markie.

"I'm Louis."

"Do you have a last name, Louis?"

"Louis Pagnetta."

"Are you related to Gino?" asked Von Hess.

"Gino is my cousin."

"So, Gino's connected to what goes on in this joint?"

The mouth of Louis began twitching as a result of the question. For the detectives, this physical reaction was all the indication they needed to suspect that Louis was worried over more than gambling charges. The law enforcement officers suspected that Louis was either holding something illegal like a gun or narcotics, or perhaps he was even a wanted man.

Markie was left with a decision to make. He could look to bust Louis for something or simply continue to question him. To avoid complicating matters by having to explain probable cause to make an arrest, the sergeant opted for the latter.

When queried in relation to Johnny Bronco, Louis claimed to have never heard of him. Questioned pertaining to the identity of a tenant named Esther, who was believed to reside over the flower shop, Louis communicated that he did not know any of the building tenants. When pressed, Louis referred the detectives to Cosmo, the landlord.

"Okay, so now we're back to Cosmo," said Von Hess. "Are you ready to tell us where he is so we can get out of here?"

"Okay," said Louis, finally relenting. "He's on jury duty."

"Why didn't you say that in the first place?"

"It slipped my mind."

"When did he start jury duty?"

"Today was his first day."

"Go check the bells, Ollie," directed Markie.

"No names, Sarge, just apartment numbers," reported back Von Hess a minute or two later.

"What time does the mail get here, pal?"

"There is no set time."

"Was there any mail for the tenants yesterday?"

"None."

"Where does Cosmo live?"

"He lives upstairs."

"We'll be back," advised Markie, realizing that he was making no headway. "C'mon Ollie, let's go."

"What do we do now, Sarge?" asked Von Hess, once they were outside.

"Let's try talking to a few neighbors," advised Markie.

***

MARKIE AND VON HESS gathered no insights with their canvass until their encounter with a longtime neighborhood resident who happened to be a steady customer of the florist shop. She was a clear complexioned stylish woman of seventy-five with fine features. She wore her silvery hair up in a bun. It wasn't the everyday bun ordinarily worn by typical senior citizens, but rather a modern messy bun with bangs that gave her a more youthful appearance. Even her preference in clothing had a chicness to it. A casual, long sleeved two button apricot sweater and jeans won out over the boring clothing favored by others at her stage in life.

The senior had just finished cleaning the litter box of her beloved white-haired cat. The cat was named McMillen, after a long-lost married love. The charm of McMillen the cat and McMillen the two-timer rested in the striking blue eyes each was blessed with.

"Now hold it a second, McMillen, you be patient," said the woman, as the cat followed her into the kitchen. She was pushing McMillen's nose away from the bowl she was pouring milk into when her bell rang. *Now who could that be?* She wondered.

When she opened her door, the detectives produced identification and introduced themselves. After doing so they were invited in. Once inside, Von Hess explained their purpose before the questioning commenced.

"Did you know John Bronco? He lived around here, Ma'am," said Markie. "He was a police captain."

"No, I'm afraid I don't. I used to know a cop from this neighborhood very well' Officer McMillen, but he would be retired and probably dead by now. He was almost twenty years older than I am, you know."

"He must be, Ma'am," said Von Hess. "What about a young woman named Esther who lives around here. Do you happen to know her?"

"Do you mean the girl who lives over the florist?"

"That's right, what can you tell us about her?"

The old woman's upper lip stiffened. "Oh, her," said the senior citizen. "She was a beautiful girl in her way I suppose."

"Was?" asked Von Hess. "What happened to her?"

"Why, don't you know?"

"No."

"It was a terrible thing. The poor girl killed herself."

"Do you have any idea why she would do something like that?"

"No, nobody seems to know. I asked the florist why such a young girl would do such a thing. Not surprisingly, he was quite abrupt with me."

"How so?"

"Let's just say that he made it quite clear that he didn't want to talk about it."

"Are you talking about Cosmo the Florist?"

"That's right. I've been going to his store to buy my potted plants for many years. He's expensive but conveniently located for me. Cosmo owns that whole building, you know."

"Why do you think that Cosmo didn't want to talk about Esther's suicide?" Markie asked, bringing the senior citizen back on track.

"I don't know for sure of course, but I have my suspicions."

"And what might they be, Ma'am?" asked Markie.

"You can fool some of the people some of the time, Sergeant, but no man ever saw the day he could fool me. Maybe Officer McMillen fooled me once, but I learned my lesson well."

"I don't follow you, Ma'am. Could you explain what you mean by that?"

The senior citizen became pensive in response to the request for her to elaborate. "You really want to know about Officer McMillen?"

61

"No, Ma'am, we only want to hear about Cosmo and Esther," clarified the sergeant.

"Whatever you tell us will remain confidential, Ma'am," assured Von Hess.

"Well, I always had my suspicions about that girl and Cosmo," the senior citizen said. "Are you sure this goes no further?"

"Whatever you say won't be attributed to you."

"Well, I remember Esther's mother. She worked in the flower shop many years ago. It was quite clear to me what was going on."

"And what was going on?"

"Why, the woman acted like she owned the flower shop, rather than just being an employee. She really thought who she was. You know how it is, sometimes when you give people a little authority, they think who they are."

"That's true in some cases," agreed Von Hess, conceding the point. "Go on, Ma'am, please continue."

"Esther's mother was a good-looking woman, in a cheap sort of way, you know the type. Esther took after her mother, as far as good looks went."

"And what about Cosmo?" questioned Markie, who was beginning to lose patience.

"Well, I always wondered how Esther's mother got away with being so bossy. I mean, it seemed as if she was in charge. They'd bicker like husband and wife, her and Cosmo. It was clear to me that they were involved, if you know what I mean."

"They were an item?"

"Oh, absolutely they were. Esther's mother was a married woman, you know, so they had to be careful. But still, the husband must have been asleep, or he just didn't care."

"Did they ever get caught?"

"Who knows? Once Esther was born, I never saw the mother again. But I know the true story."

"What story is that?"

"If you saw the way Cosmo used to look at Esther, you'd know."

"You think he had designs on her?"

"No, no, no. His looks were nothing like that. He was like a hawk the way he watched over that girl. Sure as rain, I know who the real father of that poor girl was."

"So, you're saying that Esther is Cosmo's daughter?" asked Markie point blank. The old woman only committed to a shrug. "Is that what you think?" pressed the sergeant.

"I can't say for certain one way or the other of course, but you can go see for yourself."

"See what?"

"Look at their teeth. The father and daughter have the same type of teeth."

"What do you mean?"

"Cosmo's two front teeth have a slight separation. Esther had the same spacing."

"A lot have people have that," injected Von Hess.

"But are a lot of people saw-toothed as well? Cosmo and Esther have the same exact teeth, I'm telling you."

"Do you know what Esther's last name was, Ma'am?" asked Markie.

"Her mother's married name was Trumbell."

"So, Esther is Esther Trumbell, is that correct?"

"Yes."

"What kind of cat is that you have there?" the pet loving Von Hess asked, changing the subject as he and Markie were preparing to leave.

"McMillen is a Khao Manee," answered the elderly woman. "Isn't he a darling?"

"A real beauty," agreed the detective, thanking her as he prepared to leave her home.

"Ahh, so was Jim," said the old woman reflecting back on the fun times she had with the two-legged McMillen. "Officer McMillen was a liar and a rascal, but he was a lot of fun. I have to give him that."

"May I ask what you did for a living, Ma'am?" asked Markie.

"I was a model," she replied, quite proudly. "I was in many of the magazines, Life, Look, all of them."

The investigators returned to the local precinct to confer with Kirby, the detective who caught the Johnny Bronco homicide. Kirby was seated at his desk typing reports. The detectives from headquarters learned from Kirby that the sister of the murdered former captain would be flying to New York from Las Vegas the following day to make funeral arrangements for her late brother.

Markie informed the squad detective that he and Von Hess were off the following two days and would be unavailable. He added that they would resume their assistance on the case when they returned to duty.

"I'm swinging out myself," said Kirby. "I guess I'll have to get together with the sister when I return to work…. unless something else comes in that takes priority."

"How did you make out with the car they found the captain in?" asked Markie.

"I didn't get to it yet, Sarge."

"What about the gun you recovered at the scene?"

"It was legit. It was registered to Captain Bronco."

"What are you doing now?"

"I'm typing the necessary reports on the homicide."

"That's a pretty thick folder you have there. What are you writing, *War and Peace*?"

"A fat homicide folder is a good one, Sarge."

7

Farewell Frankie

COSMO THE FLORIST SAT QUIETLY in a huge room among the remaining prospective jurors. All were waiting for the next announcement, each hoping their name wouldn't be called. It being late in the afternoon, and his not having been summoned to service as of yet, the florist was hoping that his luck would hold out. It did.

Devoid of civic pride, Cosmo was delighted after being notified that he was dismissed. This meant that it would be years before he'd again be called for jury duty. Once released from his obligation the florist scooted out of the government building. Although not usually an expressive man, the look on his face was one of undeniable happiness.

When Cosmo arrived at his florist shop Louis wasted no time informing him that two detectives had been around looking for him. While this came as a surprise, it was even more surprising to learn that the visiting detectives had inquired about Esther.

"What did they want with Esther?" Cosmo asked.

"The cops didn't say," replied Louis.

"Did it seem like they were looking into what we got going here?"

"Nobody knows what a bull has on his mind."

"If detectives came here, they had a reason," said Cosmo, sounding concerned. "Do you think it could have had something to do with Bronco?"

"Relax will you. If anything, they were just fishing around for information. They ain't got nothing to go on regarding Bronco."

Cosmo wasn't as optimistic. Not being one to underestimate the authorities, the florist was taking no chances. He made up his mind to step up his murderous agenda while he was still at liberty to do so.

Later that evening, when alone in his apartment, Cosmo revisited Esther's diary. Re-reading the contents of the journal reinforced Cosmo's resolve to murder those he held responsible for Esther's suicide. The references pertaining to Esther's last paramour, the singer Frankie Flamarian, went far in fueling Cosmo's desire for revenge.

To get a line on the entertainer Cosmo turned to Esther's address book. Tucked within the pages of the book, he found a The Frankie Flamarian Trio business card. Beneath the name of the group, in parenthesis were the written words:

(Call Me. Frankie)

When Cosmo telephoned the number on the card a recorded male voice identified himself as Frankie. The voice advised the caller to leave a message. Also provided on the recording was the trio's scheduled appearances.

Among the venues mentioned on the recording was Mel's Westchester Supper Club. Cosmo telephoned the supper club to confirm when the trio would be performing there. Once armed with this information, Cosmo turned matters over to his hired assassin, Louis Pagnetta. When informed that the time had come for him to take action, Louis didn't flinch.

"It's about time," said Louis, who was anxious to be put into service so that he could reap the cash bounty he was to receive. "I was starting to think that you changed your mind."

"Not a chance," replied Cosmo coldly.

As luck would have it, Louis had an uncle who owned a plumbing business located close to Mel's Westchester Supper Club. The uncle, who everyone called Leaky due to his profession, was on the mother's side of the contract killer's family. Since his father's family and his mother's family weren't particularly friendly, Louis was confident that it would be unlikely that word would reach Gino regarding what Louis was up to.

Louis telephoned his uncle to advise that he had business in Albany. He indicated that on his way to Albany, he'd like to stop by his uncle's home to say hello and catch up. In truth, Louis was looking to gain insights on the area. The uncle, who lived alone in a large house, insisted that Louis stay the night when he came.

Louis arrived at Leaky's house late in the afternoon. The overnight bag he carried contained a pair of socks, fresh underwear, a clean shirt and a toothbrush. The twisted tri-edge dagger Louis favored was also inside the bag, as was a .44 caliber magnum handgun.

The uncle and nephew spent time catching up over glasses of wine. As they traveled memory lane, Louis steered their conversation to the supper club where Flamarian was appearing. As it turned out, the visit was fortuitous in that the supper club was a client of the uncle.

"I heard that's a great place to eat," said Louis, referring to the supper club.

"Oh, it is," confirmed the uncle. "Mel has been a client of mine for years."

"Is it a big joint?" asked Louis.

"It's a good size. I can tell you this, when there is music there Mel crams the people in like sardines."

"What's it like inside?"

"They have a nice fully stocked bar. In the back where the tables are is a small stage. People around here go there to have dinner and get entertained. "Years ago, they had comedians playing there. I saw Dick Capri and Leonard Barr appearing in that place."

"Is everything on one floor?" asked Louis, who was unimpressed by the names dropped.

"They got a small lounge on the second floor that the entertainers use. I've been up there lots of times."

"You have?"

"Oh sure, I'm Mel's plumber. I know him for years, so he lets me go upstairs to meet the talent."

"Could you get me upstairs?"

"Sure, anytime you want."

"So, you know the people good then?"

"Didn't I just say that I know Mel for years? He's the owner of the place."

"How about we go there for dinner?"

"What for?"

"We'll eat and check out the music. It'll be my treat."

"What's the big interest in the supper club?"

"C'mon, it'll be fun," said Louis, failing to address the question posed.

"Does Mel have a problem?" asked the uncle, who was now suspicious. The plumber was well aware that Louis worked for Gino.

"No, of course not," came the reply of Louis. "Mel's got nothing to worry about."

***

THANKS TO HIS UNCLE's influence at the supper club Louis was able to secure a table not far from the stage. From his vantage point he was able to get a good look at the trio's singer. Once Frankie Flamarian was identified, Louis sat back and relaxed. *This is gonna be a piece of cake*, thought the killer.

"You like the way this guy sings, Louis?" asked Leaky.

"He's no Sinatra," replied Louis.

"C'mon, there ain't nobody like Sinatra. This mook ain't even close."

"How's your food?" Louis asked, changing the subject.

"The food in here is always excellent."

When the trio took their break, Louis asked his uncle if he could get him upstairs to the second floor where the entertainers were resting. The uncle spoke to the club owner, who granted his friend's request.

Once upstairs, the uncle and nephew were introduced to the group. Louis took the opportunity to complement the trio. During general conversation, Louis came to learn that the trio was slated to perform in Maryland the following evening.

Louis discreetly got around to asking one of the trio members how they were able to trot about to gigs at various locations without getting burned out. The musician indicated that they found being on the road to be fun. Further conversation resulted in Louis learning that the trio intended to leave for Maryland the following day around noon. Pretending that he was familiar with Maryland, Louis inquired as to where they would be staying in Maryland. He was informed that the trio was stopping at the Half Horse Hotel, located a short distance from where their gig was.

The following morning Louis left his uncle's house early in order to arrive at the Half Horse Hotel before the trio. Upon arriving he parked his car in the hotel parking lot. He lit a cigarette and commenced his wait for the trio to arrive.

The musical group arrived in a 1987 Nissan van. Louis watched as the trio members carried their belongings into the hotel. Seeing no opportunity at this point to get to Frankie Flamarian, Louis had to wait. After about forty minutes the group members left the hotel. They got into their van and drove to a diner a short distance away. Louis followed, parking his vehicle where he could observe the trio's van without drawing attention to himself.

Once the musicians were seated inside the eatery Louis casually walked over to the Nissan. After looking about, he quickly removed the dagger that was concealed within his coat and punctured a rear tire. He then swiftly returned to his own vehicle.

Once inside his car Louis began to chain smoke cigarettes as he waited for the trio to exit the restaurant. When they did, Louis watched their movements closely, as he waited for an opportunity to corner Flamarian alone.

The members of the trio were clearly upset at the sight of their cut tire. Judging by what he saw, it seemed to Louis that Frankie Flamarian was the most perturbed of the threesome. Flamarian was flailing his arms in the air and seemed to be barking at the other two men angrily. When he was done venting, the singer returned to the restaurant while the others remained occupied changing the tire on the van.

This is it, thought Louis. The assassin emerged from his car and entered the restaurant in the hope that he would find Flamarian sitting in a booth. His intent was to slide in next to the singer and discreetly stick him with the dagger.

As it turned out, Louis followed his prey into a small restroom. When Flamarian entered a stall, Louis pushed the dead bolt on the bathroom door to the right, locking it. When the assassin opened the door to the stall, he found the singer sitting on the toilet bowl preparing to inject a hypodermic needle into his arm.

As Flamarian was mainlining the heroin he suddenly felt a hard tug on his hair that lifted his head upward. The singer then felt something tear into his throat. The dagger's noiseless penetration cut deep and was effective. Louis closed the door to the stall and slipped out of the restaurant without incident.

The murderer casually walked to his vehicle unnoticed by the other members of the trio, who were still struggling to put the spare tire on their van. As Louis embarked on his journey to the florist shop, he put on some easy listening music. After stopping at a rest stop for a cup of coffee and a buttered roll to go, he happily ate and drank as he made his way back to the Bronx.

Cosmo did a double take when Louis entered the shop. "So, how did it go?" asked the florist, anxious for an update.

"Mission accomplished," replied Louis, without elaborating.

"You got my money?"

* * *

LATER THAT EVENING, when alone in his apartment, Cosmo once again turned to Esther's diary. Finding the entry in which his daughter referred to Flamarian, he removed a red pen from his shirt pocket and drew a line through the singer's name wherever it appeared.

That makes two down, thought the florist.

Cosmo perused the memorialized thoughts of his daughter. When he came upon Esther's referencing of Georgie Pride, he bit down on his lip.

A freaking pill popping pharmacist, he thought, shaking his head. *They should give me a medal for giving this motherless bastard what he's got coming to him.*

8

Prescription For A Pharmacist

GEORGIE PRIDE WAS THE SON of well-meaning parents who emphasized the importance of a good education. Indoctrinated from an early age to embrace intellectual things, his idea of a hero was the Greek philosopher Aristotle, who was arguably the world's greatest thinker ever.

As a devotee of all things cerebral, Georgie was considered by many to be something of an oddball.

He was an avid reader that was more apt to be found in a library rather than a ballfield in his youth. His recreational preferences were restricted to board games rather than physical activities. Although, while in high school he did try his hand at bowling. This was a short-lived diversion, with Georgie shunning the game after someone filled the holes in his bowling ball with chewing gum.

When in college Georgie became fascinated with a lecture given by a brilliant professor who went on about quantum physics. When he voiced his admiration for the professor to classmates, he became the recipient of teasing by classmates who were less than happy with a rigid professor who put forth hard tests.

Higher education did little to reduce Georgie's social awkwardness. He remained a loner who threw himself deeply into his studies. Georgie's academic diligence ultimately earned him a Doctor of Pharmacy degree from an accredited institution.

The newly minted pharmacist took a job working evenings at a twenty-four-hour Bronx drugstore. Prone to periods of depression, Georgie found relief from his melancholy at the pharmacy. Easy access to pills proved to be too great a temptation to resist.

With a diet of amphetamines to bolster him, Georgie navigated life. Unfortunately, his acquired habit came with mood swings. In Georgie's case, his emotional shifts were at times mercurial. When agitated the pharmacist morphed into someone capable of terrible acts of aggression.

Georgie and Esther Trumbell first crossed paths purely accidentally. Esther was on her way to work at the hospital when her attention was drawn to a man having difficulty tying his shoelace. Judging by the white wrapping on his hand, the stranger appeared to have broken his thumb. Georgie had his foot atop a fire hydrant and awkwardly juggled his balance while trying to tie his shoe. When Esther approached him to offer her assistance, the pharmacist gladly accepted the help.

After securing the shoelace, a conversation ensued as to how Georgie injured his thumb. The pharmacist told of how he had gotten his thumb caught in a car door. As the tale unfolded Esther began to broadly smile. She found it amusing that Georgie's explanation included a detailed narrative on the vehicle's shortcomings. It was soon clear that the two were happy to have met.

From Esther's perspective, she appreciated meeting someone who made her feel needed. Also appealing to Esther, who was accustomed to being pursued by aggressive men, was Georgie's seeming backwardness. The pharmacist represented a change of pace for Esther. In short, Cosmo the Florist's daughter found someone to mother.

For Georgie, he was thankful to have a beautiful woman look at him twice. Georgie was bright enough to know that there had to be more to it. The pharmacist recalled reading in a psychology journal that there were some people who were drawn to those they could take care of. George recognized that Esther fit into this category. Whether it be pity, his profession or whatever the motivating factor was, it made no difference to Georgie. He welcomed the attention Esther was willing to bestow on him.

Over time Esther came to learn of Georgie's substance abuse. The pharmacist's addiction actually enhanced her commitment. She now felt more needed than ever. Georgie's mood swings were viewed as challenges that smacked of cries for help.

The love connection took a downward turn when Georgie saw Esther engaging another man in conversation on the street. Feeling threatened, Georgie's insecurity reared its ugly head. When he questioned Esther in her apartment as to what she was talking to the man about, she offered an explanation that Georgie refused to accept. For the first time Esther saw that Georgie had a dark side.

In the midst of their argument, Georgie began belittling Esther for what he referred to as her lack of intelligence. The words he chose to insult her with were the cruelest known to him. Once he completed his harsh verbal assault he left the apartment in a huff, never bothering to look back at the sobbing woman he abandoned.

When Georgie arrived at his home he found solace in his pills. As for Esther, her diary was the only place to turn to. With pen in hand, she began writing to help ease the pain. The entry in her diary was smudged with ink that was dampened by her tears. This soiling did not escape the attention of Cosmo when he later had access to the journal.

***

AS FAR AS COSMO THE FLORIST WAS CONCERNED, Georgie Pride was a lower than dirt nut case. To a product of the old school like Cosmo, the pharmacist's treatment of Esther warranted the payback he intended to administer. Cosmo, serving as both judge and jury, had no hesitation in rendering a verdict that called for capital punishment.

Esther's diary contained enough information for Cosmo to gather that Georgie was a pharmacist working somewhere in the Bronx. By going down the list of Bronx pharmacies and making phone calls, the florist was able to establish that Georgie worked at an all-night store located on City Island. He passed this information on to Louis, reminding the hit man of the payoff that would come with Georgie's elimination.

The assassin wasted no time. He drove to City Island the following evening. Louis was happy to see that the pharmacy was located on a main drag that led to a dead-end where there was a beach. It being winter was also to the advantage of Louis. The right weather conditions would ensure that the area would be desolate.

Louis entered the pharmacy to identify Georgie. Spotting the name tag on Georgie's white jacket, Louis was pleased to see that his intended victim didn't look like someone capable of giving him much trouble physically. Subsequent visits to the pharmacy enabled Louis to establish that Georgie finished work at 11 P.M. When Georgie's shift was over his routine was to walk to his car, which was always parked not far from the pharmacy. All Louis needed to do now was wait for a rainy night.

***

AFTER WATCHING THE WEATHER forecast on television Louis Pagnetta looked out the window of his Bronx apartment. Unshaven, with a cigarette dangling from his mouth, he watched the raindrops bounce off the cars parked in front of the store he lived above.

This is perfect, thought Louis.

As reported on the televised weather forecast, the rain was predicted to come down heavy with no indication of letting up anytime soon. Having plenty of time before heading out, he returned to his favorite chair and began to channel surf.

Louis paused his search for something to watch when he came upon a lawyer advertising his services as a defense attorney. Louis recognized the lawyer who was pitching to the viewing public. It was someone the organized crime associate knew well.

"Get a load of this bullshit artist!" said Louis, addressing the television screen.

Louis had zero respect for the attorney because he viewed him as a hypocrite. Louis knew the lawyer beyond the expensive suits he wore, his suave delivery and portrayal of a man of high moral fiber. He knew him to take cash payments under the table for the purpose of fixing mob prosecutions with judges willing to be compromised.

Now thinking of money, Louis pondered the payout he was going to receive after taking out Georgie. *This is just the tip of the iceberg*, thought Louis. *When Cosmo checks out, I get the mother lode that comes with the inheritance. Gino is gonna drop dead when he sees what I got coming to me.*

Two questions then came to Louis that disrupted this pleasant thought. *What if Cosmo lives for another twenty years? Or, even worse, what if Gino expects a piece of what I inherit?*

Louis forced himself to think optimistically. *If Cosmo is destined to stick around to an outrageously ripe old age, I could always fast forward his demise.* This solved one issue.

As far as paying tribute to his cousin, there was little Louis could do about that. This being the case, he resigned himself to the reality that he'd likely have to share some of what he received. Once he got past this thought, Louis again focused on his mission to kill.

When the time came to ready himself Louis took several deep drags from the cigarette he was smoking before putting it out. He donned dark jeans and a black turtleneck shirt. Over the turtleneck he wore a black V-neck sweater. For shoes, he selected his oldest pair since he would be out in foul weather. He then went to his closet, where he decided to don a black double breasted raincoat.

Lastly, Louis removed a hat box from the top shelf of his closet. Contained within the well of the hat was a handgun. Since Georgie Pride wasn't a very strong looking man, Louis actually felt that the dagger was all he needed. Nevertheless, he took along the gun just in case the intended victim turned out to be more formidable than anticipated.

***

GEORGIE PRIDE WAS BEGINNING TO GET antsy as he neared the end of his shift at the pharmacy. He went to the restroom to check the number of pills that remained in the orange vial that he carried in his pants pocket. Satisfied that he had a sufficient amount of the controlled substance, he returned to his workstation. While it took some self-control, Georgie managed to finish his shift without having to pop one of his pills. It would be the first thing he'd do when he reached his car.

When Georgie emerged from the pharmacy, he stood at the entranceway for a moment to look at the rain coming down from the sky. Seeing no letup in sight, he wasn't waiting for the downpour to ease up. His hunger for a pill wouldn't allow that.

Georgie raised his sport jacket over his head to protect against the rain. In doing this he left his stomach area exposed. Georgie held his breath as he darted to his vehicle, which was located about twenty car lengths away from the pharmacy.

Louis, who was waiting in his car with the engine off, had spotted Georgie standing in the entranceway of the pharmacy. In exiting his vehicle, Louis was careful to gently close the car door to avoid attracting attention. His look was one of murderous intent. With a tight grip on his twisted tri-edge dagger he advanced toward his unsuspecting victim.

Georgie was fully focused on getting to his vehicle during the downpour. His head was down to avoid heavy drops of rain striking his face. The pharmacist stared at his feet as they pounded the pavement, neglecting to see what was ahead of him. The chill of the rain bouncing off his body caused Georgie to mutter curses under his breath. He was angry at himself for having left both his overcoat and umbrella in his car.

The pharmacist was just a few steps away from his vehicle when he collided into the business end of the dagger that was thrust into his gut. The entry of the twisted steel came with such sharp pain that Georgie let out an agonizing groan that echoed in the night. Doubled over, the stabbing victim wrapped his arms around his belly as he slowly sank to his knees. Louis held the wounded man up by his collar as he again punched the blade into Georgie's midsection. The third poke that was intended to be the finisher was unnecessary.

Louis wiped the blade clean against his victim's shoulder before releasing his grip, allowing Georgie to fall to the ground. Louis looked in all directions to see if there was anyone around. With all being clear, he placed the dagger in his pocket and hurried to his car. He drove off without bothering to take a final look at the pharmacist he left in the puddle of blood mixed with rainwater.

The following morning Louis met with Cosmo at the florist shop. Cosmo, having heard nothing on the news regarding the City Island murder, sought answers from his paid assassin.

"So, when are you getting around to taking care of that thing for me?" Cosmo asked.

"It's done," replied Louis, without going into any details.

"It is?"

"Yeah, when do I get my money?"

Clearly impressed, Cosmo appeared delighted. "You'll have it by this afternoon, Louis," he assured.

"Who is next to go, Cosmo?"

"A fireman named Owen Selby."

9

The Detectives
Keep Digging

MARKIE AND VON HESS, fresh from being off for two days, reported to their office at headquarters. After taking their vehicle for maintenance at a department shop, they were free to resume their inquiry into the homicide of the retired captain. They responded to the Bronx precinct where Detective Kirby was stationed, arriving after having something to eat at a diner.

Kirby explained that he interviewed Bronco's sister and her husband at the precinct earlier that morning. The family members of the murdered captain had flown in from their home in Las Vegas. The detective recounted that the interview went smoothly.

"How upset were they?" asked Markie.

"I've seen worse," replied Kirby.

Kirby described the captain's sister, who was in her mid-fifties, as a true Bronxite. By this he meant that the sibling spoke confidently, with an assertiveness that conveyed she was no one to be taken lightly. An office manager at UNLV, Johnny Bronco's sister wanted to know what was being done about the death of her brother.

"She was okay with everything?"

"Yeah, Sarge, I was able to handle them."

"What was the husband like?"

"He was missing a finger."

"Missing a finger?"

"Yeah. He said that he used to be a carpenter. I suppose he got careless and snipped off a finger when using a table saw."

"What is he doing now?"

"He's a dealer in Vegas."

"Did they have anything relevant to add to the case?"

"The sister did all the talking. She wears the pants."

"And?"

"She said the captain had intentions of moving to Las Vegas."

"Did she indicate that he was taking anyone with him?" questioned Von Hess.

"She said Bronco was trying to convince his friend to join him in relocating to Nevada."

"What friend was that?"

"A guy named Cosmo," answered Kirby, adding, "she said that he owns a florist shop in the precinct here."

Detective Kirby went on to advise that Johnny Bronco was described by his only sibling as the happy go lucky sort who never seemed to worry about anything.

"She said that her brother was the kind of guy who rolled with the punches," said Kirby. "She said that he had no enemies that she knew of."

"What about vices?" asked Markie.

"The sister said that Bronco liked to gamble."

"Did he look to borrow money from her?" asked Von Hess, thinking that the captain might have run afoul of loan sharks.

"I asked her that. She didn't think he gambled to that extent."

"Any mention of a girlfriend?"

"She said her brother had lots of girlfriends," answered Kirby, adding, "the sister said her brother, and his friend Cosmo, were both confirmed bachelors."

"When the sister questioned you regarding the progress of the case, what did you tell her?" asked Markie.

"I told her that there were no prints of value lifted from the vehicle her brother was found in," replied Kirby.

"That's it?"

"No, I further advised her about the car her brother was found in. I told her the vehicle plates were registered to a deceased person at a bogus address and that the vehicle identification number (VIN) had been altered. I had to explain exactly what that meant."

"How did you leave off?"

"I closed the conversation on a positive note. I told her the investigation was ongoing and that we were out there questioning people. I piled it on thick about how respected her brother was. I think that made her feel good."

"She was okay with everything?"

"Yeah, she bought it."

Markie was actually impressed at how Kirby conducted himself with the dead man's relatives. The precinct detective, in voicing his account of how things went, showed the sergeant something.

This Kirby may be an empty suit, thought Markie, *but he* definitely *knows how to stroke people.*

The three detectives further discussed the case. They agreed that the only evidence they had was ballistics related. However, without a recovered gun to use for comparison purposes, the ballistics evidence was of no help at this juncture. The same could be said of the stab wound received by the victim. While the knife wound was unique, the actual weapon was needed.

"How are you making out on your end, Sarge?" asked the precinct detective.

"We're still questioning people," was the sergeant's reply.

Markie decided that, in the name of efficiency, Detective Kirby should return to working on his other cases until some new information came to light on the homicide in question.

"I'll keep the homicide open and mark it pending further developments. Okay with you Sarge?"

"That's good. Me and Ollie will continue digging for as long as we can."

This was fine with Kirby, who was happy that the detectives from headquarters would continue to beat the bushes for him.

***

MARKIE AND VON HESS RESUMED their investigation at Cosmo the Florist's Bronx shop. After parking suitably for surveillance, they remained in their unmarked vehicle, vigilant to the activities taking place at the business. They noted that there seemed to be two types of people entering the shop.

Some visitors, mostly women, entered the shop for relatively short periods, only to leave carrying flowers, plants or some other related item. Others, predominantly men, mostly went inside and either stayed for extended periods or exited after a minute or two empty handed. In the opinion of the detectives, these men were stereotypical gambler types identifiable by their appearance. They smoked, carried newspapers and appeared to be the knockaround sort one would see at a racetrack.

"These people gotta be putting in bets, Ollie," said Markie.

"I think so. They don't seem the type that would be scoring drugs, Sarge," agreed Von Hess.

"This is no drug location. These people popping in and out of this place are just regular guys putting in bets."

"How about we go inside and see if Cosmo is around, Sarge?"

"Yeah, let's do that, Ollie."

Cosmo the Florist was immediately suspicious of the two men in jackets and ties that entered his place of business. Louis, who was standing beside him, confirmed what Cosmo was thinking.

"These are the two bulls I told you about," whispered Louis. Cosmo nodded at Louis as the detectives approached him.

"Can I help you?" Cosmo asked.

"We're here to speak to Cosmo," said Von Hess, holding out his gold shield for examination.

"I'm Cosmo," acknowledged the florist. "What do you want with me?"

"You own this building, right?"

"Yes, I do, is there a problem?"

"Not really," injected Markie, "we just want to know about a tenant of yours."

"Which tenant?"

"A woman named Esther."

Cosmo winced. His reaction made it clear to the detectives that the mere mention of Esther's name had an effect on the business owner, who was unable to cloak his feelings.

"She killed herself," said Cosmo, after taking a second.

"Have you any idea why she would do something like that?"

"I got no idea what gets into the head of my tenants."

"Did you know a guy named Bronco?"

"Are you talking about Johnny Bronco?"

"Yeah, that's right."

"Sure, I know him, we grew up together. What about him?"

"He's dead."

"Yeah?" asked Cosmo, feigning surprise. "What happened to him?"

"We found him in the trunk of a car. Somebody put a few slugs in him."

"WHAT? Oh, that's terrible! Bronco was my dearest friend."

"You didn't know about that?"

"This is news to me," lied Cosmo.

"Did you know if the captain had any enemies, or maybe a problem with somebody?"

"Not that I know of," replied Cosmo, shaking his head in the negative.

"Did he have some kind of connection to your tenant?" asked Von Hess.

"Which tenant?"

"Esther."

"Not that I was aware of," fibbed Cosmo.

"So, you never saw him with Esther?"

"No," snapped Cosmo, now appearing annoyed. "The only woman I ever saw Bronco run around with was some twist named Bunny. She's from the neighborhood."

Cosmo slipped. His reply was revealing.

"Who said anything about Bronco and Esther running around together?" asked Markie.

"That's what you were implying, right?"

"So, were they involved in that way?"

"Look, fellas, I got no interest in knowing who runs around with who. I mind my own business."

"Do you know if either Bronco or Esther had any enemies?"

"All I know is that I run a florist shop over here, not an information center."

"Okay, Cosmo," said Markie, ending his inquiry. "Thanks for your time."

Once outside, Markie and Von Hess compared perceptions.

"The old lady was right, Sarge," expressed Von Hess,

"Right about what?"

"She was right about his teeth."

"I didn't notice. Cosmo is definitely not telling us all he knows, Ollie," said the sergeant.

"Yeah, that's the impression I got too."

"We have to get these guys by the short hairs if we're ever gonna get them to open up."

"Are you looking to pinch him, Sarge?"

"Let's do some research first and see what we can find out. After that, we can decide if it's worth zeroing in on the flower shop. We just may end up having to knock over the joint."

"Look, who's coming, Sarge," said Von Hess, after noticing that the mailman was in the process of delivering mail.

The investigators looked through the mail that was about to be delivered to Cosmo's building. They noted that among the delivery was a letter addressed to Cosmo from a bank, and another from an insurance company.

Armed with this information, Von Hess contacted a retired detective he knew who now worked as an insurance investigator. The insurance investigator discovered, via his network, that Cosmo listed Esther Trumbell as his beneficiary on the policies he held.

With the insurance information gathered, Von Hess contacted a second receptive retired member of the service he knew. This second investigator now worked in the security department of a bank. This connection led to learning that Cosmo's bank records once reflected Esther as receiving everything in the event that something was to happen to Cosmo. The current beneficiary on record was Louis Pagnetta.

Having acquired this information, it seemed reasonable to assume that Cosmo was more than likely the father of Esther. The connection between Cosmo and Louis left the investigators curious.

"Let's concentrate on closing in on that flower shop, Ollie. Maybe a pinch will get us someplace."

"Righto, Sarge."

***

MARKIE EXPLAINED TO HIS SUPERIORS at headquarters that the Johnny Bronco homicide gave all the appearances of an organized crime hit. This was news they already knew. The sergeant indicated that he suspected the key to solving the homicide might rest with an illegal gambling operation believed to be run out of a Bronx florist shop. This was something the higher ups didn't know. Markie made a convincing argument which resulted in his receiving the authorization to focus on Cosmo's florist shop for the purpose of building a case.

Markie and Von Hess began surveilling the shop. They were sipping coffee in their car and engaging in small talk as they scoped out the location. Markie mentioned to Von Hess that he was still interested in proving that Fishnet Milligan's death wasn't a suicide. Fishnet was retired NYPD rogue detective who had been found hanging at the end of a rope off the side of a staircase in the Manhattan townhouse he inherited. It never made sense to the sergeant that the crooked former detective would hang himself.

"You know something, Ollie," said Markie, "that slippery prick Fishnet would never hang himself. He was carrying a gun on him, for God's sake. Why wouldn't he just shoot himself?"

"That would have been simpler, Sarge," answered Von Hess.

"And another thing, I don't buy that wife of his and her girlfriend dying accidently in that Pennsylvania quarry. Fishnet came into a bundle with her gone."

"She was a very famous actress, Sarge," noted Von Hess. "So, she had plenty of money."

"Not just an actress, Ollie, she was an heiress."

"That's right, I forgot that."

Markie rehashed their unofficial probe into Fishnet's death. The detectives discussed the results of their interview of Fishnet's girlfriend, a young actress. The girlfriend had informed the detectives that Fishnet secured her a role in a play and in an upcoming movie being produced by Enzo Baffi, a very well-known producer. She had explained that Fishnet arranged these opportunities through the Maestro, an octogenarian musical virtuoso who was tight with Baffi. Fishnet had met the Maestro through his late wife.

"You know what doesn't sit right, Ollie? How a guy like Fishnet ends up in a business partnership with a big shot like Enzo Baffi."

"And what about the Maestro turning up dead," Sarge?

"That's another thing. The guy he played house with, Pascal, gets in the wind without leaving behind a forwarding address."

"The whole thing stinks from A to Z, Ollie," said Markie, "and what about us seeing Fishnet with that conman. What was that all about?" Markie was referring to Fishnet having been spotted in the company of a conman posing as a priest.

"Maybe Fishnet really was strung up by somebody, Sarge," said Von Hess, "and his death made to appear as a suicide."

"The first chance we're gonna dig up this guy Pascal and see what he can tell us about all this, Ollie."

10

The Pain Of Juliana Swain

A FABULOUSLY SUCCESSFUL FILM PRODUCER, Enzo Baffi was known as a man capable of building the career of aspiring actors. He was also noted for not being above impeding the professional progress of those who fell out of favor with him.

Baffi split his time between the east and west coast, while his wife and children were restricted to their home in Malibu. Influenced by the good life she led, and the prestige that came with her being Mrs. Baffi, the producer's wife was fine with this arrangement.

When it came to her husband, she was able to justify his freedom.

Why not? Enzo has been supportive of me in whatever I do, she thought. *So, he can do what he wants in New York.* In time Mrs. Baffi became a power on the west coast in her own right.

Enzo Baffi prided himself in his sophistication. On the surface the producer was a soft spoken, well-mannered man who seemingly oozed of good breeding. Baffi was the sort who balanced his teacup by keeping his pinkie up when dining in public.

Baffi dressed in the style of an elegant dandy. His clothing was customized and age appropriate. His monogrammed shirts came with French cuffs that he secured with expensive cufflinks. The cigarettes Baffi favored were housed in a gold-plated case with diamond studs positioned to display his initials. His manicured fingernails came with high gloss. His after shave was expensive and pleasant to smell. All of this contributed to his ability to conceal that he was a maniac.

Throughout the years Baffi managed to prevent his dark side from surfacing publicly. Since he was affluent, he had the wherewithal to keep his warped sexual preferences cloaked. Those involved in his romps were silenced via generous compensation in the form of money or career opportunity. Complicit in Baffi's big secret was Rochelle Parrish, his loyal personal assistant/secretary.

Baffi's great success spoiled him. The steady diet of homage he received over the years ultimately led him to believe that he was entitled to do whatever he wanted. He came to feel invincible, a man immune to repercussions. This mindset is what eventually caused the producer to venture into the darkest waters imaginable.

Baffi's decline began with dalliances with wannabe starlets. These trysts usually took place at his Manhattan penthouse apartment. Since his conquests were looking to further their careers, they accommodated the producer's desires willingly. Baffi saw it as a safe practice to deliver on whatever promises he made to his romantic partners. This went far in keeping his aberrant behavior in the shade.

The producer acquired a taste for simulating homicidal activity. Having adopted this new preference, his Manhattan penthouse became an obsolete venue. The producer built a two-story log cabin in Dutchess County that was situated on acres of land. The upper left wing of the cabin was turned into what Enzo Baffi referred to as his dungeon in the sky. Behind the cabin, farther back on the property, was a large outdoor incinerator that came with the purchase.

Baffi's interest in death scenes came about in an unusual way. It began as a result of his being shook down by a former detective named Fishnet Milligan, a man well known to Markie and Von Hess. To repel the extortionist, Baffi joined forces with two associates who shared his hatred for the retired detective. Acting collectively, the trio cleverly murdered Fishnet, making the death appear as a suicide.

Once Baffi got a taste of committing an actual murder, there was no turning back. The thrill of taking a life gave the producer sexual satisfaction that surpassed all else. The experience left him with an ugly desire for more of the same.

Baffi was mentally stable enough to realize that his newly discovered predilection to murder was an unsustainable long-term activity. Yet, his craving was too powerful to totally ignore. The producer, unable to suppress his need completely, tried to appease his want by returning to simulated death scenarios as a substitute for the real thing. This was easier said than done.

***

THE PERFORMANCE CLUB, a private entity located in Midtown Manhattan, boasted an impressive membership of celebrated people. Most club members made their living primarily in the entertainment industry. The fraternity was also home to a number of high-level businessmen who liked the idea of rubbing shoulders with the film, stage and media crowd.

Juliana Swain couldn't have been happier when hired as the club's lobby receptionist. The starstruck eighteen-year-old was thrilled to have the opportunity to interact with the entertainment personalities she idolized. The few words she got to exchange, even if only a greeting, overshadowed any concern over the modest monetary compensation she received.

No amount of money could be placed on the thrill Juliana received when telling friends and family how she was on a first name basis with actors, directors, producers and captains of industry. These associations were empowering. It made the receptionist important to those lacking such access. This gave Juliana a good feeling about herself.

The affable Juliana was tall and slender. She possessed an infectious personality that enabled her to conversationally strike the right chords with many club members. Being a knowledgeable movie buff, she was able to identify on sight many of the actors who appeared in both classic and current movies. This ability led to fun exchanges with club members who enjoyed chatting with her.

Juliana was so taken with the world of entertainment that she'd often dreamily envisioned herself living the life of a lead player in one of the flicks she saw. When she closed her eyes at bedtime, she injected herself into her favorite movie scenes. These nocturnal escapes always saw her playing the lead role.

Juliana, a buzz cut strawberry blond, was the daughter of a working-class single mom from Washington Heights. Her late father, a factory worker, had been felled by pancreatic cancer shortly after his daughter finished grammar school. The loss of her dad placed a strain on the family finances. The resulting economic hardship derailed whatever higher academic aspirations Juliana may have had.

Juliana's mother, who recognized her financial limitations, never encouraged her daughter to pursue a higher education. To alleviate the difficulty in keeping up with their expenses, Mrs. Swain encouraged her daughter to go to work. Juliana's financial contribution to the household, however meager, was helpful.

Juliana projected a youthful impishness. Some club members equated this with innocence. This, and her attractive figure, made her romantically desirable to members with an active libido. Those of a more wholesome nature looked upon the receptionist as a parent would look upon a daughter. There were also club members who Juliana was totally invisible to. Enzo Baffi fell into the first category.

***

90

ENZO BAFFI TOOK ADVANTAGE OF his Performance Club membership when staying in Manhattan. He'd mostly use the club for business meetings over lunch or cocktails. He enjoyed the club atmosphere because it gave him a chance to see acquaintances that he had done business with over the years.

The producer immediately took notice of the new club receptionist. He found the youthful Juliana Swain to be an interesting study. At first, the producer saw the receptionist strictly in professional terms. He viewed Juliana as a potential talent who, if properly brought along, might appeal to movie audiences. This eventually changed.

Baffi had also seen Juliana as a resource that could provide insights into the way people of her age thought in terms of likes and dislikes. Baffi had been worried that, with his aging, came a certain disconnection from younger movie goers. Through Juliana, Baffi saw a way to keep his finger on the pulse of the youth. The producer believed such intelligence gathering would enable him to rework screenplays so that his movies would have a broader appeal to a younger audience.

Baffi began innocently smiling at the young receptionist whenever he saw her. The purpose of this was to gauge her reaction. Juliana's return smile came with a certain polite shyness. This impressed the producer, who now saw Juliana's tenderness as something potentially appealing to movie goers.

Baffi began escalating matters with prolonged eye contact when speaking to Juliana. This was followed by a playful banter. These mild flirtations made by the much older producer were well received by the receptionist, who was quite flattered by the attention she was receiving from someone of great prominence.

As Baffi grew closer to Juliana, a fondness developed. When the producer learned of her being enamored by the lure of the theater, he wasted no time in delving deeper into her suitability for the screen....and his bed.

"Do you have a favorite play, my dear?" asked Baffi, one afternoon at the club.

91

"Not really," replied the receptionist, "I love plays, but I've only actually seen one."

"That won't do at all. My personal favorite is *Phantom of the Opera.*"

"I've never seen it," admitted Juliana, hoping to receive an invitation to attend a performance of the show. She wasn't disappointed.

"We need to broaden your exposure, my dear. You'll come as my guest to see *Phantom* tomorrow evening."

Juliana smiled happily as she accepted Baffi's invitation. The receptionist found their evening together to be a grand experience. The show, dinner and fine treatment introduced Juliana to a world she only previously experienced via the movies she watched. It only took a second round of theater and dinner for Baffi to move beyond the professional image he was presenting. Now having amorous designs, he invited the receptionist up to his Manhattan penthouse apartment for a nightcap.

Baffi, who often bedded the talent he planned to work with, made no exception with Juliana. The receptionist, desperate to gain the acceptance of the older man, offered no resistance to Baffi's intimate overtures. The fact that Baffi filled her with alcohol and promises of putting her in movies went far in gaining Juiliana's compliance.

Since Juliana's sexual experience was limited to a few abbreviated sessions in the back seat of a car with a boy of her own age, there was an excitement to explore unchartered waters with the producer. When Baffi requested that he be the recipient of a golden shower, Juliana was puzzled as to whether or not this was something normal. This hurdle was overcome with the producer's assurances that such activity wasn't all that unusual. Her wanting to please the producer caused her to accept this explanation as factual. As a result, she went along with his wishes.

The following morning the veteran seducer had his personal assistant/secretary anonymously send a
dozen long stemmed roses to Juliana at the Performance Club.

"Shall I sign the card the usual way?" asked the generously compensated Rochelle Parrish, who was long accustomed to doing such things for her boss.

"By all means, Rochelle," replied the producer. "By the way, order two ringside seats for the Royal Rumble, it's being held in Albany this year. Take your sister or whoever you like, it's my treat."

"Why thank you so much!" said Parrish enthusiastically. "My sister and I both love to attend the wrestling matches."

"I know you do, my dear."

Baffi didn't miss much when it came to things of a sexual nature. He instinctively knew that the unattached Parrish got her jollies seeing muscular hulks up close grappling. What Baffi didn't know about his employee was the enjoyment she derived from tussling herself.

When Juliana received her flower delivery at the performance club, the receptionist blushed at the attention she was receiving from those employees in close proximity to her workstation. Juliana found their remarks about her having such an ardent unidentified admirer to be complementary. A smile crossed the receptionist's face as she showed her co-workers the sender's accompanying note:

The fragrance of these roses pale in comparison to the scent of you, my dear.

YOU, Juliana, are by far the most precious jewel in the crown of passion!

Subsequent gossip among club workers as to the identity of the mysterious admirer abounded. One employee, a middle-aged woman who worked as a bartender in the club's main bar, immediately suspected Enzo Baffi as the flower sender. She too had once been the recipient of such attention from the producer. For her, the term, *my dear*, on the accompanying card was a dead giveaway as to who the author of the note was.

The jilted bartender was bitter for not having realized her theatrical ambitions. She monitored Baffi and Juliana from afar as they interacted at the club. When she noticed Baffi put his hand on the receptionist's rear end, the bartender decided to mail an anonymous letter to the club manager claiming that a hostile work environment existed.

Meanwhile, the receptionist's interest in Enzo Baffi only heightened. Juliana was there for the producer as long as he continued to talk about movie scripts for her. Unfortunately, this was just talk. Once, as a result of an audition, Baffi established that Juliana had no true acting ability, she was no longer a property worth developing. The receptionist was now reduced to being nothing more than another of Baffi's bedroom conquests.

Eventually Baffi introduced Juliana to the black room in his penthouse apartment, a venue in which the producer stepped things up when it came to his darker jollies. This zone of perversion had blackened walls, with bizarre red etchings. It was second in eeriness only to Baffi's Dutchess County upper floor dungeon.

The producer's assorted preferences were shocking to Juliana. Yet, her belief in the producer was a
powerful inducement to comply with his wishes. Exposure to Baffi's ways inevitably came to have an adverse effect on Juliana. Telltale signs that something wasn't quite right in her personal life began to become apparent to co-workers at the Performance Club.

Juliana began arriving at work with signs of bruising. The club manager, who was reluctant to delve into the personal life of an employee, eventually found himself having to do something. He had little choice in the matter once he received the anonymous communication alleging a hostile work environment.

The manager reached out to the club's labor lawyer who was spending the winter months at his Key West home. After having heard some of the particulars, arrangements were made by attorney Fred Klein to fly back to New York City the following week.

As things continued with Baffi and Juliana, the inevitable came to pass. The producer invited the receptionist to his Dutchess home for the weekend. It was here that the producer pulled out all the stops in satisfying his perverted cravings.

The simulated death scenario the producer orchestrated went too far, leaving Juliana seriously injured. She was curled in a ball on the floor of the dungeon writhing in pain. As she held her stomach with both hands she complained of internal injury.

"Oh, come now, Juliana, don't be so dramatic," said the still panting producer as he dressed. "Get up off the ground, you're just a little winded, my dear."

When Juliana wasn't able to rise to her feet Baffi got nervous. It soon became obvious to him that his house guest sustained injuries that required medical attention.

This could be a ruptured bladder, thought Baffi, now realizing that his frolic created a dire situation.

"Take it easy, my dear, all you need is some rest," voiced the producer.

"I'm really hurt inside, Enzo," Juliana uttered feebly. "I think that I need a doctor."

"Let's wait and see how you feel later. I'm sure you'll be okay."

A scandal like this could ruin me, thought the panic-stricken producer, who had grown frantic. All he could now think of was minimizing his exposure. In doing so he selfishly placed little value on the life of Juliana.

Baffi lifted Juliana off the floor and carried her to a bedroom. Once she was placed on the bed, he looked down at her. He tried not to appear worried as he assured the injured woman that she would be okay after some rest. In this he was wrong. The moans coming from Juliana grew increasingly fainter. Then there was silence. With Juliana dead the producer knew he had to take drastic steps.

Baffi removed the emerald earrings he had gifted Juliana from her ears. He placed them atop an end table where her purse was. He then waited until the wee hours before picking Juliana up off the bed and placing her over his shoulder. With a flashlight in hand the producer carried his victim outdoors to the incinerator on his property. He fired her up without a second thought.

The producer then hurried back to the house to gather Juliana's belongings, some of which were in the dungeon. He placed the receptionist's property into a green garbage bag. During the transfer he never noticed that one of the emerald earrings he gifted to Juliana had fallen onto the kitchen floor.

Baffi took the garbage bag and filled it with several bricks. On his return to Manhattan the producer disposed of the bag by dropping it into the waters of the East River.

11

Greasing The Wheels Of Justice

THE MANAGER OF THE PERFORMANCE CLUB telephoned the home of Juliana Swain to find out why Juliana didn't come to work. He was informed by the receptionist's mother that she had no idea why her daughter wasn't at work.

The mother explained that as far as she knew, Juliana spent the weekend with a friend who had a home somewhere in Dutchess County. The mother indicated that she was worried, noting that her own calls to her daughter were going unanswered. Both agreed that if they didn't hear from Juliana by the end of the day, it might make sense notifying the authorities.

During the early evening the receptionist's mother contacted the police to advise them that her daughter was unaccounted for. The response she received from the authorities was disappointing. Mrs. Swain was told that since Juliana was of age, and without a history of mental illness, there was little the police could do without some indication of foul play.

In need of support, the distraught mother passed this information on to her daughter's employer the following morning. During her conversation with the club manager Mrs. Swain communicated that as of late Juliana had been receiving expensive gifts from someone unknown to the mother. She indicated that this began after her daughter started working at the club.

The club manager sympathized with the distraught mother without commenting. Hearing the mother's statement made him unsure of the club's exposure in terms of liability. Since the manager was awaiting the arrival of the club's labor attorney, for guidance in the hostile workplace allegation, he finally advised the mother that he would make inquiries at the club and get back to her. Mrs. Swain found this acceptable.

Fred Klein, the club labor attorney, was a longtime club member. A bushy haired fit man of average height, the attorney briskly entered the office of his client. Klein was attired in a blue blazer, black tie, gray slacks and burgundy tasseled loafers. At first his client didn't recognize the clean-shaven attorney, who had shaved off his trademark beard.

"You clean up nice, Fred," said the manager. Klein smiled without saying anything. "How was your flight?"

"It was fine," replied Klein, adding, "but we should get down to business. We can chitchat later."

After taking a seat on the visitor side of the manager's desk, the lawyer removed a yellow legal pad from his briefcase. With pen in hand, the left-handed Klein crossed his legs and rested the pad on top of his knee. Once prepared to take notes he asked, "So talk to me. What's going on?"

With an ear out for headaches, Klein listened attentively as he was told of the anonymous handwritten letter that was received at the club alleging a hostile work environment.

"Was the allegation written on club stationary?" Klein asked.

"Yes."

"Who was named in the letter?"

"Allegedly Enzo Baffi. He's a long-standing club member that was seen inappropriately touching Juliana Swain, our receptionist."

"I know Enzo," commented Klein. "Did Juliana complain to anyone about this?"

"Not that I'm aware of."

"That's good. It's possible that he might have innocently brushed against her. Do you have any idea who may have penned this letter?"

"No."

"We could probably figure it out by doing a little homework. Anyway, let me see the letter."

After reviewing the communication Klein asked if the manager recognized the handwriting as belonging to anyone he knew. The answer received was negative. After conducting further questioning Klein immediately proposed a course of action to take. This included going through the receptionist's desk at the club.

"Do me a favor," said Klein, "go through the desk at the receptionist station. Sometimes people stick things in drawers. Maybe we can come up with something informative."

The club manager went through the open desk as directed by the attorney. To his surprise, the manager discovered the note that came with the roses that were sent to Juliana Swain. He immediately turned the note over to Fred Klein.

"You were right, Fred. I found this card that came with some roses that Juliana received. It was in the top center drawer of the reception desk."

"What's this note about?"

"Someone sent Juliana roses."

"Who?"

"Nobody knows, it came anonymously. Read the card."

Klein took the printed note and read it aloud, after which he commented, "Pretty smooth stuff." Klein again read the note, this time aloud and very slowly." The lawyer then closed his eyes in contemplation.

"What are you thinking, Fred?"

"I'm thinking that the delivered roses and the anonymous hostile work allegation might suggest a love triangle."

"I don't follow you."

"The person making the accusation of a hostile work environment may have done so for reasons of a personal nature," explained Klein.

In his mind's eye Klein was able to picture the words on the note flowing gracefully from the lips of fellow club member Enzo Baffi. Without revealing his suspicion, Klein advised the club manager to safeguard both documents until further notice.

"Okay," began Klein, for right now I want you to just hang on to these documents. Safeguard them in your office safe. I'll be back tomorrow morning at nine to conduct interviews. I'll probably start with the receptionist."

"I don't know about Juliana, she hasn't been coming to work."

"Is she sick?"

"Nobody knows."

"What do you mean?"

"I spoke to Juliana's mother, the two live together. The mother hasn't heard from her."

"Where did the mother say her daughter was supposed to be?"

"At a friend's house in Dutchess County," replied the manager.

"How old is the daughter?"

"Eighteen."

"Does the mother know about the allegation of a hostile work environment?"

"No, of course not."

"What about the roses."

"I don't think so."

"So, what's the mother saying?"

"I think she has it in her head that her daughter must have been involved with someone from the club.

"What makes her think that?"

"Apparently Juliana was receiving some expensive gifts. Do you want to speak to the mother, Fred?"

"No, not right now. Tell me something, is the mother naming anyone specifically as having some culpability in the daughter's disappearance?"

"No, Fred."

"Well, what exactly did she say?"

"I don't know," answered the frustrated manager. "All I know is that she's calling me up and busting my balls. She wants to know what we're doing about Juliana."

"When was the last time you telephoned the receptionist?" asked Klein.

"This morning," replied the club manager.

"This is strange," acknowledged Klein. "But we can't discount that Juliana is a grown woman. She's entitled to go where she pleases and do what she wants."

"You would think."

"Besides the anonymous letter mentioning Enzo Baffi, have there been any additional issues at the club regarding Juliana that you haven't told me?"

"Well, yes, I suppose. She had been coming to the club bruised up lately."

Klein was taken aback at hearing this. "What exactly do you mean by bruised up?"

"Black and blue…."

"This isn't good," said the lawyer, his voice now turning grave. "Did you ask her about it?"

"No, at the time I thought it best not to get into her personal business."

"Are the police actively working on finding her?"

"No, the mother tried to speak to the detectives with no luck. She said that the police don't consider Juliana a missing person."

"Okay, let me see if I can rectify that."

It has to be Enzo Baffi, thought Klein on his way to his office. *Baffi used these same exact words when he sent a note with flowers to that Brazilian woman who worked at the old Peacock Club on Second Avenue!*

Klein, who had been friendly with the human resources director of the Peacock Club, remembered that there were whispers of a cash payoff to hush that matter up. He also vaguely recalled that there was some talk that Enzo Baffi was a weirdo.

101

***

IN ANSWER TO THE JULIANA SWAIN disappearance, Fred Klein telephoned Police Commissioner John Randolph. Having the commissioner's private cell phone number practically guaranteed Klein that he'd get whatever favor he asked for.

Since the commissioner was known to be a man of many moods, the attorney handled Randolph tactfully. After explaining the details regarding the disappearance of the receptionist, Klein expected the commissioner to readily offer his assistance in finding her. When this didn't happen, Klein wanted to know why.

"Are you annoyed with me for some reason?" asked Klein. "If yes, why is that?"

"Frankly, I'm disappointed, Fred."

"What have I done?"

"I assigned people to help that plastic surgeon like you asked me."

"You mean Doctor Vanidestine, he was a member of my club."

"That's right," confirmed Randolph. "After I go out of my way to help him, he turned around and wanted me to pay him full freight to perform a small procedure."

"The plastic surgeon was murdered, you know," pointed out Klein.

"Yeah, well, I can see why, Fred."

The labor lawyer was stunned at the commissioner's callousness. Seeking to mend the strained relationship with the police commissioner, the attorney asked to meet Randolph for dinner at the Performance Club. Klein's invitation caused Randolph to thaw somewhat. The commissioner enjoyed, as Klein knew, being introduced to the celebrities and influential people who frequented the club.

Over a cordial dinner Klein was able to mend fences. He then went on to explain the situation concerning the missing club employee.

102

"I suppose I could have my people look into this for you, Fred," said the commissioner.

"Thanks, Commissioner, I appreciate that. The poor mother is distraught."

"Don't worry, I'll light a fire under the ass of the chief of detectives."

"Can I pass your assurance on to the mother?"

"Tell her that the chief of detectives is aware of her problem. Extend his assurances, not mine. The last thing I need is for her to start reaching out to me direct."

"No problem, Commissioner."

"Is that Pat Cooper who just came in?" asked Commissioner Randolph.

"Yes, that's Pat."

"He's a taller guy than I imagined. You know, I always found him to be funny as hell."

"He's a good guy. Would you like to meet him?"

"Sure."

12

Detoured

MARKIE AND VON HESS TOOK NOTICE when a city sanitation sweeper stopped in front of the Bronx florist shop. They watched closely as the civil servant gingerly jumped out of the cab of the vehicle and scooted into the shop. The sanitation man exited after a minute or two without appearing to have purchased anything. The detectives found this to be revealing. Having a trained eye, both sleuths had no doubt that the activity going on within the confines of the flower shop went beyond the sale of floral arrangements and potted plants.

"That guy either put a bet in or made a shylock payment," commented Markie.

"Do you want to talk to him, Sarge?"

"Yeah, stick with him, Ollie. Let's pull him over when he gets a few blocks away from here."

The detectives followed the sweeper until it stopped at a red light. Von Hess, who stopped directly behind the vehicle, exited his car and approached the driver's side of the sweeper. When the street cleaner looked to his left, he was greeted by the detective flashing his badge.

"Pull the sweeper over in that bus stop," instructed Von Hess.

"What's the problem?" asked the sanitation man.

"Just pull over when the light changes," ordered the detective, in his most authoritative voice.

"Okay, okay, don't get excited."

"Is this your regular route?" asked Von Hess, addressing the sanitation man once the sweeper pulled over.

"Yeah, what's the problem?"

"Let me ask the questions. What's going on in the florist shop?"

"What florist shop?"

"The one you just came out of."

"I don't know," replied the sanitation man. The driver of the sweeper was at a loss for further words. He just shrugged.

"You don't know what you went in there for?"

"I just went in to price some flowers," answered the civil servant, finally thinking of something to say.

"Look, cut the bullshit, will ya?"

"What's this all about? You guys are stopping me from working," protested the civil servant. "I got a schedule to keep."

"Listen, my friend, let's not make this about you," chimed in Markie, sounding annoyed. "Unless you want to be the star of the show, you better start cooperating."

"Star of what show? What are you talking about?"

"I'm talking about us following you around all day," answered the sergeant. "How would you like that?"

"Why would you do that?"

"To catch you off base."

"Off base doing what?" asked the sanitation man, now growing defiant.

"Stopping to see a squeeze maybe, scoring a little weed or how about placing a bet in that flower shop back there?"

"Why are you guys gunning for me?" asked the sanitation man, realizing he could be targeted. "What did I ever do to you?"

"Nobody is looking to hurt you. All you have to do is answer a couple of simple questions," explained Von Hess, using a softer tone. "Why jeopardize your job?"

After a second of thought, the sanitation man finally relented.

"Okay, what do you want to know?"

"We want to know what's doing inside that florist shop?"

"I just go in there to put a bet in once and a while."

"What kind of bet? Numbers? Horses? Sports?" asked Von Hess.

"Horses, but they take action on other stuff."

"Who takes your bets in there?" queried the sergeant.

"I put the bets in with either Cosmo, or Louis. I don't know their last name."

"Who is the boss?"

"It's probably Cosmo, he owns the flower shop."

"Okay, man, have a nice day," said Markie, before returning to his own vehicle with Von Hess.

Having confirmed that there was illegal activity taking place, the detectives returned to their surveillance position by the florist shop.

One parked, Von Hess made a notation of their conversation with the sanitation man. Included was the time, date and number of the city truck that was stopped. He then began recording the license plates of people entering and leaving the flower shop. The detective did this in order to later determine who the registered owners of the visiting vehicles were. If the vehicle owners were organized crime figures, that would provide an indication as to who may be controlling the gambling activity at the flower shop.

The interest of the detectives spiked when a large Lincoln Continental pulled up in front of the florist shop.

"Is that a kid driving that car?" asked Markie.

"I can't tell, Sarge. There is not much of him to see over the steering wheel. Hold on, he's getting out."

From the second Gino Pagnetta emerged from his Lincoln he gave off the appearance of being somebody of importance. The clothes he wore were sharp, far too sharp to be worn by someone of little significance. The well-groomed gangster was wearing a cream-colored double-breasted overcoat over a navy turtleneck. His gray slacks sported a prominent crease. Covering Gino's black socks were shiny black alligator loafers.

"Make sure you get this guy's plate, Ollie. He looks like a wise guy."

"10-4," acknowledged Von Hess, removing the binoculars from the glove compartment. "I'll call in the plate now."

Von Hess telephoned Detective Silverlake, who was at his station in the office of the chief of detectives. Silverlake was asked to run the plate in question. After a few minutes the office detective provided the requested information. The plate on the Lincoln was registered to a Bronx resident named Gino Pagnetta."

"Do you want me to have him checked for a criminal record, Ollie?" Silverlake asked.

"Yeah, do that."

A few minutes later Silverlake again reported back. He communicated that Pagnetta's record revealed prior arrests for gun possession, attempted murder, assault, gambling and loansharking. Based on this extensive record, Von Hess telephoned the NYPD Intelligence Division to see if they had anything on Pagnetta.

The folder on Pagnetta in the Intelligence Division told much. The records indicated that he was known to be a soldier in the Long John Capezzo organized crime family. The records further reflect that the gangster was headquartered out of a Bronx social club. Surveillance photographs taken when covering mob weddings and funerals placed Pagnetta in the company of prominent organized crime figures.

"So that squirt is a made man," commented Markie, after being apprised of the information gathered.

"Seems that way, Sarge," answered Von Hess. "The Capezzo family must be desperate for people."

"I doubt that, Ollie. This guy must be a big earner or a killer."

"Whatever the case is, he must have met their criteria. Intelligence documented him hanging out with the heaviest hitters in the family."

When Gino didn't leave the florist shop right away the detectives assumed that he probably had an interest in the gambling that was taking place.

"What do you think, Sarge? Want to give his car a toss when he comes out?"

"Yeah, let's do that."

While waiting for the gangster to return to his vehicle Markie received a call from his headquarters office. It was his supervisor, Lieutenant Wright. Wright informed the sergeant that, on the order of the chief of detectives, he and Von Hess were to immediately start a new assignment for the chief.

"The chief wants you and Ollie to go over to the Performance Club in Midtown and talk to the manager, Al," instructed Wright.

"What's it all about, Loo?"

"Something about a receptionist that didn't show up for work."

"Isn't that something for missing persons?"

"What can I tell you? This is a contract that came straight from the police commissioner to the chief of detectives. So Chief McCoy wants you to drop everything and get over there."

"What do you want us to do about the Captain Bronco homicide?"

"You'll have to find time to work both cases."

"No problem, boss," said the sergeant, who was used to juggling more than one priority at a time. Markie then turned to Von Hess and said, "We're gonna have to continue the Bronco homicide at another time, Ollie. Head over to Manhattan."

"Where to?"

"We're going to the Performance Club, it's in midtown someplace."

***

WHEN MARKIE AND VON HESS arrived at the Performance Club they met with the club manager, who explained the situation concerning the unaccounted-for club receptionist. After doing this the manager presented the detectives with a white envelope. Contained within the envelope was the card that came with the roses that were delivered to the club for Juliana Swain.

"You're pretty careful with that," said Markie, commenting on how delicately the manager was handling the envelope. "

"I was told to handle this with care by our attorney," replied the manager.

"This is fancy penmanship. Any idea who wrote this."

"It was possibly written by a club member."

The manager then showed Markie the letter complaining about Enzo Baffi creating a hostile work environment. The name of Enzo Baffi jumped out at the sergeant. Markie held out the letter for Von Hess to read.

"This is a different handwriting than the card, Ollie." Von Hess looked at the card without commenting.

"Do you have anything with Baffi's handwriting on it?" Markie asked, addressing the manager.

The manager produced a document from his records that reflected the handwriting of Enzo Baffi. After comparing the writing samples, the investigators concluded that two different people penned the documents.

"You hang on to these documents," said Markie, "we may want to check fingerprints down the road. We might also want to bring in a handwriting expert."

"Don't you want to do those things now?" questioned the club manager.

"In due time. Does Juliana Swain have any relatives that you know of?"

"She lives with her mother. The woman is quite upset over this."

"Understandably," acknowledged Markie. "Let me have her home address. Also, let us have a listing of the club members." As he perused the list the sergeant asked the manager a question to confirm the identity of Baffi.

"This is the Enzo Baffi that's the big shot producer, correct?"

"Yes. Mr. Baffi is a longtime member," replied the manager.

"Now this is something, eh, Ollie."

"What is, Sarge?"

"Baffi and Fishnet were supposed to be in business together, remember? Thats what Fishnet's girlfriend told us when we interviewed her."

"That's right, I remember."

Markie departed from the Performance Club with Fishnet on his mind. Getting to the bottom of Fishnet's death was more important to the sergeant than the missing receptionist and the homicide of Johnny Bronco. When he and Von Hess were in their unmarked car they rehashed the matter of Fishnet's death.

The whole thing is bizarre, Ollie," said the Sergeant.

"How so, Sarge?"

"Let's break it down. First, we have Fishnet, who is in business with Baffi. He turns up swinging from a rope like a salami in a deli window. The Maestro goes second of a bum heart, he's Baffi's good friend. So why is he exercising on a bike against the orders of his doctor? You tell me. And if that ain't enough to get you thinking, now we got a missing girl who Baffi's got designs on."

"What do you make of it, Sarge?" asked Von Hess.

"I don't know what to make of it. But I'll tell you one thing, Ollie. I can't help but smell a rat with this guy Baffi."

"I hear you."

"And another thing, what happened to the Maestro's significant other, Pascal? Where did he disappear to all of a sudden?" Von Hess offered no response. "Here's what we're gonna do, Ollie. First, we're gonna go see Fishnet's girlfriend and find out more about this producer Enzo Baffi. I want to know everything about him. After that, we shoot uptown to go talk to the missing receptionist's mother."

"What about the murdered captain, Sarge?"

"We'll have to get back to him, Ollie. And don't forget, we still have to dig up this guy Pascal."

***

THE DETECTIVES PROCEEDED to the apartment of Fishnet's actress girlfriend. They found that Cheryl's apartment was now occupied by roommates who didn't know who the prior tenant was. The investigators spoke with the building super, who advised Cheryl mysteriously abandoned her apartment. He conveyed that Cheryl left behind all of her belongings, which included her passport.

"Now what do you make of this, Ollie?" asked Markie.

"You have to wonder why all these people are turning up dead or missing, Sarge."

"I don't see it as any coincidence that they're all connected to Enzo Baffi, Ollie. Let's go see that receptionist's mother."

13

Meeting Mama

VON HESS PARKED IN FRONT of the Washington Heights apartment building. He and Markie entered the building when someone was exiting. They checked the mailboxes and bells for the name Swain.

"Ms. Swain is on the sixth floor, Sarge," announced Von Hess.

"Do you want to take the stairs up?"

"Stop kidding, just ring the bell and let her know that we are here," said the sergeant.

Mrs. Swain had been waiting for the detectives, who called ahead. When the door to her apartment opened, the investigators were surprised to see a younger woman than anticipated.

Mrs. Swain was of average size with fine features. Standing a bit stooped, her shoulders were slightly rounded. The dark circles under her eyes suggested fret. Having just worked an overnight shift, coupled with worry, contributed to her appearance. The deep lines on her brow further indicated stress.

After inviting the detectives into her apartment Juliana's mother politely offered the detectives coffee. They declined. Once seated in the living room, Mrs. Swain explained that she suspected her daughter of being involved with a Performance Club member. She had no idea as to who the member was.

Mrs. Swain communicated that she based her assumption on an expensive gift her daughter received. She described the gift as a pair of heart-shaped emerald earrings with gold siding.

"Those earrings had to come from someone with lots of money," expressed the mother. "The only people that Juliana would know with that kind of money would be someone from that club."

Ms. Swain conveyed that when she pressed her daughter for more details regarding the mystery man in her life she answered vaguely, saying only that her friend was an important man. Mrs. Swain noted that her daughter's secrecy was unusual.

The mother's narrative took on a grave tone as she revealed that her daughter had been showing signs of physical bruising. When she queried her daughter regarding the marks the mother said that Juliana was evasive. She noted that her daughter only behaved this way when she was concealing something.

"And you haven't heard from your daughter at all?" asked Von Hess.

"The last time I spoke to her she said that she was visiting a friend. She was dressed up and wearing those earrings. Do you think someone may have robbed her for the earrings?" the mother asked.

"That's a possibility, Ma'am," acknowledged Von Hess.

"But it's unlikely," injected Markie. "Bad news usually travels fast. We'd have heard something by now if she was ripped off or had an accident."

"I'm just sick over this, Sergeant. I've tried my best; it hasn't always been easy for me."

"Is Juliana's father around, Ma'am?"

"My husband's been dead a long time," answered the mother sadly.

"You did try calling Juliana on her telephone, correct?"

"That's all I've been doing."

"Did she happen to say what she was doing or where she was going?" Von Hess asked.

"She mentioned something about seeing where Franklin D. Roosevelt lived in Hyde Park. Juliana said that the house overlooked the Hudson River."

"That's up in Dutchess County," said the detective.

"Is it?"

"Yes, Ma'am. I know because my daughter did a paper on Roosevelt when she was in grammar school."

Before concluding their time with Ms. Swain, the detectives asked her for a recent photo of her daughter. Once they received Juliana's photograph, Markie assured Mrs. Swain that they would do their best to try and find Juliana. The distraught mother smiled weakly and thanked them.

After leaving Juliana's mother Markie thought the time had come to see what they could find out about the producer Enzo Baffi. Markie had Von Hess conduct a background check on Baffi. This comprehensive search revealed several addresses linked to the producer, his litigation history, his property ownership and his business interests.

"I think we hit upon something, Sarge," announced Von Hess after completing his research. "Baffi owns a house in Dutchess County."

"Where are his most recent addresses?"

"Dutchess County, California and Manhattan."

"Let's show Juliana's photo around Manhattan before we take a hike up to Dutchess County."

"Should we send Juliana's picture to the California cops? They could poke around for us out there."

"No, not yet, Ollie. We can do that down the road if we have to."

A canvass conducted in the vicinity of Baffi's Manhattan penthouse proved negative. The building doorman indicated that the woman in the photo looked familiar. He was unable to positively link Juliana Swain to Enzo Baffi with any certainty.

"It looks like we're taking a ride to Dutchess County, Ollie," said Markie. "Maybe we'll get lucky and find the girl there."

114

"When do you want to head up there?"

"As soon as I get the okay for us to make the trip."

When the sergeant called his office to secure approval for traveling out of the city on a matter that could result in overtime, he was informed by Lieutenant Wright that he first needed to confer with the Chief of Detectives before providing authorization."

"Isn't he around, Loo?"

"No, the chief is in South Carolina. He had a death in the family. He'll be back next week."

"Can't we call him?"

"I'm not bothering the chief over something that can wait when he's grieving the loss of a brother, Al."

"Can't you give the okay in the chief's absence under the circumstances?"

"Not a chance."

"But this has to do with the missing receptionist, Loo."

"Let it go, Al," said the lieutenant just before ending the call. "The chief will be back next week."

"How did it go, Sarge?" asked Von Hess.

"Not good, Wright derailed us. We have to put Dutchess County on hold until next week."

"So, what do we do now?"

"We go back to concentrating on Cosmo's florist shop."

14

The Producer's Proclivity

IT WAS OBVIOUS THAT ENZO BAFFI was highly successful in his chosen profession. He was, in some respects, brilliant. Early on, to gain recognition, he relied on sheer cunningness to see him through. No one realized just how astute Enzo Baffi was in orchestrating his rise to such great prominence.

Baffi recognized that in the namedropping world of entertainment, people thirsted to attach themselves to those in a position to further their careers. Attuned to this tendency, Baffi devoted himself to projecting an image of great achievement. He saw giving the impression of being a mover and shaker as a way to create opportunities for himself. In this strategy he was spot on.

Investing everything he had in himself, the moderately successful producer embarked on a campaign aimed at appearing to be someone of financial independence thanks to the movie deals he put together. Baffi felt by having others think that he had the magic touch, they'd want to invest in his projects. This proved to be a stroke of genius.

The false narrative Baffi crafted claimed he had a role in a host of highly successful overseas movie projects that were difficult to fact-check. He hired foreigners to accompany him when on the town, passing them off as people who appeared in screen credits.

Just as Baffi figured, the fancy car he drove, the penthouse he lived in and the stylish clothes he wore dissuaded people from challenging his veracity. The producer made it a point to dine at the best restaurants and leave big tips. His formula, while draining him financially, gained the traction he sought.

Baffi, once making big money, went on to open a small Manhattan office. He married, had children and purchased a home on the west coast for his family. He also held on to his New York City penthouse apartment.

As Baffi prospered, so did his social life. He established a routine which enabled him to sample aspiring starlets who viewed the producer as a conduit to stardom. With power, Baffi's attempts at humor were now funny, and his perversions accepted by those with ambitions.

As the producer's boudoir batting average rose, he began to develop a fascination with things considered taboo by most. With little difficulty in signing up willing partners, Baffi's curiosity led to increasingly darker behavior, and ultimately the purchase of the Dutchess County log cabin that was equipped to accommodate his nefarious side.

***

IT WAS DURING A VISIT TO SEE HIS family on the west coast that the producer first set eyes upon a young woman he took an interest in. He had been strolling along Rodeo Drive intending to purchase a gift for his wife. This was something he did whenever he returned home from the east coast. He believed that such largesse ensured domestic tranquility.

Paloma was selling bottled water on the street. Her black curly hair was cut short, giving her a boyish look. The producer saw something familiar in the young woman. After a minute he realized that she reminded him of the late dancer/singer Josephine Baker. The producer had been involved in a biographical project concerning Baker, who had been a huge success in France in the 1920's.

Having been fascinated by Baker, Baffi couldn't resist getting an up-close look at Paloma. To do so, Baffi approached Paloma to purchase a bottle of water. In making the purchase he peeled the necessary cash off the thick wad of bills he carried. This, along with the fancy watch the producer wore, his fine threads and designer sunglasses, greatly impressed the struggling young woman.

As he sipped the water, Baffi casually initiated a conversation laced with compliments. The producer's soft-spoken delivery alleviated any trepidation the young woman may have had. Influenced by Baffi's apparent wealth, Paloma was warm to the interest she was receiving. She began smiling broadly, revealing perfectly aligned teeth of the whitest variety.

Paloma, who had entered the country illegally with her boyfriend, saw in the older man a way to a better life. Tired of facing harsh economic challenges, she was open to doing whatever was necessary to disentangle herself from her challenging domestic situation. When Baffi suggested that they get to know each other better, Paloma welcomed the opportunity.

After receiving the producer's avid attention during his California visits, Paloma came to accept Baffi on his terms. She agreed to leave the man she was living with, a dishwasher without a promising future, and relocate to New York City.

Baffi paid the rent for a furnished studio apartment in the Hells Kitchen section of Manhattan for Paloma. Payments were made with the cash the producer allotted his lover. Baffi also took Paloma shopping for a wardrobe that he felt was presentable. All of this was in return for the producer's ability to see his mistress when in the mood. Paloma saw the price of giving Baffi what he needed romantically to be a small one in return for what she was receiving. Since the producer was still concealing his dark side at this point, Paloma had no reason not to continue to go along with her benefactor.

Paloma was awestruck the first time she entered Enzo Baffi's Manhattan penthouse apartment. Having never before been in such posh surroundings she felt as if she were living in a dream. Just as Baffi had figured, the view and general atmosphere of the penthouse overwhelmed Paloma to a point where she would comply with anything he wanted.

At one point the producer left Paloma alone in his apartment for a brief period. Free to explore the digs, she didn't let the opportunity escape her. A thoroughly honest person, thievery wasn't Paloma's motivation behind looking around. She was simply curious.

Paloma poked through Baffi's dresser drawers, went into his closets and stuck her head in his refrigerator and freezer. The producer's jewelry box was especially interesting to her, as were the celebrity autographed photos that were sprinkled throughout the penthouse. Paloma's inquisitiveness peaked when she found the door to the producer's black room locked.

There must be something very valuable in there for this door to be locked, she thought. *I wonder what it could be.*

Unable to control her curiosity, she later asked the producer why he kept the door to the room in question locked. A slight smile crossed the face of Enzo Baffi when the question was posed.

"Perhaps after we have dinner, my dear, you'll have your answer," stated the producer.

When Baffi got around to introducing the transplanted woman to his penthouse's black room her eyes widened in disbelief. Entry to the protected area meant that Paloma was going to receive her introduction to Baffi's world of perversion.

Participation in the activities the producer restricted to his black room came to be something that Paloma wasn't fond of. She only went along with Baffi's warped erotic orchestrations because she feared that if she failed to do so, the producer would turn his back on her. Paloma, now use to a better life, had advanced too far to return to selling bottled water on the

119

street. Her priority was to solidify her relationship with the producer, not jeopardize it.

Paloma, who was used to a hard life, managed to endure the time spent in the black room. She eventually came to look at these sessions with the producer as nothing more than working at a job for which she was well compensated. With acclimation came callousness.

Things began to sour with Baffi once Paloma began to have more of a voice. When she began making what Baffi perceived as demands, she had unknowingly entered dangerous territory. The producer reacted to what he saw as opposition by relocating Paloma to his Dutchess County log cabin. It was there that Baffi intended to administer the discipline necessary to keep Paloma in line.

"I have a surprise for you, my dear," said the producer, with a diabolical smile that a shrewder eye would recognize as pure evil.

"What kind of surprise? Paloma asked.

By this time Paloma knew that surprises coming from Baffi could mean anything. She hoped that he would be giving her something wonderful.

"I'm moving you into my home in Dutchess County."

"Why? I love living in my apartment."

"You'll love Dutchess County more. There are acres of land, fresh air and lots for us to do."

"What about my apartment?"

"You won't need that anymore. Tomorrow, I want you to pack your belongings. We'll drive up to Dutchess County together."

"But I won't know anyone there," protested Paloma.

"You'll make friends."

"But I don't want to go!"

In light of Paloma's adamance, the producer amended his offer. "I'll tell you what, my dear, let's do this. The apartment rent is paid for this month with the money I gave you, correct?"

"Yes, I gave the landlord cash like usual."

"Good. Let's just drive to Dutchess County and see if you like it there. If you really don't want to be there, we'll return, and you can keep your studio apartment. Now that's fair, isn't it, my dear?"

This proposition sounded reasonable. Paloma gazed at the ruby ring on her finger and felt the fine quality of the threads she wore. She nodded her agreement as she fingered the gold cross that hung from her neck. There was really little choice other than to agree to Baffi's terms.

While Paloma tolerated much, she wasn't amenable to what was expected of her in Baffi's dungeon in the sky. Her resistance led to an altercation that quickly got out of hand.

***

ENZO BAFFI STEPPED OUTSIDE his Dutchess County abode appearing to be a little tired. The smell of the incinerator's dirty work was still in the air. To offset the odor, he lit up a scented cigar. After drawing a deep drag he released the smoke slowly, watching it lose itself in the evening air. After a few minutes the producer grew uncomfortable due to the winter chill. He returned to his log cabin. Once inside he poured several ounces of Remy Martin into a water glass.

Baffi sat in front of a roaring fireplace drinking, smoking and thinking of the murder he committed.
While some remorse existed, he was hardly overcome with regret. He believed himself to be too important a man for that.

It was just a terribly unfortunate thing, he thought, minimizing his culpability. *I had no intention of killing her. Why would I?*

After consuming a second equally hefty drink the producer continued to go over the incident in his mind. However, this time he looked at things from a differing perspective. While acknowledging that his cravings were abnormal and subsequent actions despicable, he nevertheless appreciated the pleasurable aspect of his conduct.

"Ahh, what is the price to pay for bliss?" He asked himself aloud, slurring his words. As he drew deeply on his cigar Baffi contemplated the existence of hell.

My reservation in the inferno is guaranteed, he thought, *if such a place in fact exists*.

Yet, even with the threat of possible eternal damnation looming, the producer continued to recount the pleasure he derived from his depraved actions. The high spot came when he placed Paloma into the incinerator. The recollection of Paloma's body being gobbled up in the enclosed death chamber awakened a wickedness that wanted a repeat performance.

The producer's retrospection was interrupted by the annoying barking of a dog. The hound wasn't cutting forth with a singular arf. Instead, the animal let out a rapid series of woofs followed by a chilling wolf-like howl.

"That damn mongrel is impossible!" Baffi shouted.

His alcohol consumption fueled his anger over the disturbance coming from the neighboring property across the road. *That barking is maddening,* he thought. *It has to stop!*

Fortified by drink, Baffi removed one of the two antique swords that hung over the fireplace. Armed with the weapon he took along a flashlight to investigate the whereabouts of the noisemaking hound. The darkness of night prevented any sighting of the four-legged canine. "They'll be another day to deal with this mongrel!" Baffi said aloud, before returning to his log cabin in a huff.

The following day, a hungover Enzo Baffi walked to the mailbox that was located at the start of the road that led onto his property. After removing a couple of pieces of mail he again heard the barking of his neighbor's dog. The producer turned to where the noise was coming from. On the opposite side of the road, he saw a bearded man walking a floppy eared golden-brown bloodhound.

Baffi gave an unfriendly look at both the dog and its owner, a rotund man in his fifties. The whiskered neighbor and his dog, who had paused barking, both presented a look of curiosity. Both were wondering why their neighbor was glaring at them.

The producer was about to return to his log cabin when the bloodhound resumed his infernal barking and eerie howling. At this point Baffi reacted to the annoyance. He stomped over to the man with the dog. The dog owner took a step back as the producer neared him. Anticipating trouble, he wrapped his leash twice around his hand to secure a firmer control of his animal.

"My dear man, isn't there something you can do about that dog's infernal barking?"

"I'm sorry, but what do you expect me to do? Dogs are prone to bark you know."

"The noise that dog makes is terribly disruptive," advised Baffi, pointing accusingly at the dog. "Besides that, think of the birds. They have sensitive ears."

"Their sense of smell is also sensitive," shot back the dog owner.

"And what exactly is that supposed to mean, my friend?

"It means that the odor, noise and smoke coming from your property is very disturbing to me."

Not wanting to draw attention to his furnace by escalating matters, Baffi ended their discussion abruptly at this point. He returned to his log cabin in a huff. *They'll get theirs one day,* thought the producer.

Baffi was confident that there was no risk of his being arrested for murdering Paloma. He had been very careful in his dealings with his victim. He made it a point to travel from California to New York on separate planes. When in New York City, Baffi had Paloma deal directly with her landlord. Since all their transactions were on a cash basis, there was no paper trail leading to him.

In the unlikely event of the law arriving at his doorstep with evidence that could link him to Paloma, Baffi came up with a B-plan designed to counter all of his troubles.

15

The Fireman

THE HEARTBREAK REVEALED IN Esther's diary continued to provide Cosmo the Florist with the necessary incentive to continue on with his mission of revenge. Next on his death list was Owen Selby. Even though the florist generally held firefighters in high regard, Cosmo's respect for the profession failed to afford Selby a reprieve. The civil servant was destined to meet a violent end.

Cosmo turned to his late daughter's address book in the hope of finding contact information for the fireman. The florist telephoned the one number that was listed next to Selby's name. It was to the local firehouse. A robust voice picked up the phone at the hook and ladder company.

"Is this the firehouse?" asked Cosmo.

"Yes, it is. How may I help you?"

"Does Owen Selby still work there?"

"Who is asking?"

"A friend of his."

"He's out on a job, let me have your name and number. I'll tell him you called when I see him."

"That's okay, I call back."

***

COSMO DROVE TO THE BRONX firehouse where Owen Selby was working. When he got there, he began recording the license plates of the vehicles parked around the firehouse. He took the list of plates to a private investigator who subscribed to the DMV database. For a fee, the investigator ran the license plates through the database. Cosmo, now knowing the vehicle that the firefighter drove and his home address, passed this information on to Louis Pagnetta.

"Where do you plan to take him out, Louis?" asked Cosmo.

"I won't know that until I do a little homework. I have to figure out what hours this guy is working and where the best place would be to clip him."

"Do you need anything more from me?"

"I don't need any help, Cosmo," said Louis. "I know what I need to do. You just get my money ready."

"You'll have it," voiced Esther's father. "You're gonna get on this right away, right?"

"Don't rush me. People make mistakes when they rush."

"You're right, Louis. You need to be careful."

"When will you have the cash for me?"

"You'll get your money the day the fireman is history."

***

IT WAS LATE AFTERNOON WHEN MARKIE AND VON HESS arrived at the florist shop. They parked far enough away from the shop to avoid attention. With the help of binoculars, they maintained a good visual of the front entrance of the business. Things weren't very different from their last surveillance. Gambler types continued to enter and exit the business without having made purchases.

The detectives perked up when a sanitation truck double parked in front of the florist shop. Leaving the engine running, two sanitation men emerged from the truck. The men entered the florist shop, only to leave a minute or two later. They then

125

returned to their vehicle and drove off. As they did this an idea suddenly came to Markie.

"Do you know what we're gonna do, Ollie?"

"What's that, Sarge?"

"Next time we come here we're gonna have Silverlake with us.'

"What do we need Silverlake for?'

"This looks like where the sanitation men place their bets. We'll dress Silverlake up like a sanitation worker and send him into the shop to place a bet," advised Markie.

"Do you think the people working in the florist shop are gonna take a bet from someone they don't know, Sarge?" Von Hess asked.

"I think so, my guess is that they're accommodating the whole garage. They're bound to think Silverlake is a legit sanitation man."

"That'll probably work."

"Yeah, we'll have Silverlake put in a couple of bets and then get a warrant for the joint. Maybe putting handcuffs on somebody will net us some information about what happened to Johnny Bronco."

"They might not know anything, Sarge."

"Pinching them is the only way for us to find out if they know anything."

There came a point during the surveillance when the detectives noticed Louis leave the florist shop. He got behind the wheel of the Chevy Vet that was parked opposite the florist shop. After a minute he exited the car and opened up a pack of cigarettes as he returned to the flower shop.

"Take a pass by and get the plate number of that Vet," directed the sergeant.

After jotting down the plate number, Von Hess returned to his original position so that he and the sergeant could resume their surveillance. Von Hess called his office requesting that Silverlake ascertain who the registered owner of the Vet was. Silverlake reported back that the vehicle was registered to a Bronx resident named Louis Pagnetta.

An hour later Louis again came out of the shop, this time accompanied by Cosmo the Florist. The two crossed the street to where the Vet was parked. Louis opened the door to the car, allowing Cosmo to get behind the wheel. He later lifted the hood of the vehicle. As the two men checked out the engine, it was apparent that Louis was showing off the car to Cosmo, who was nodding approvingly. Once they finished examining the Vet, Cosmo handed something to Louis before returning to the florist shop alone.

Louis put down the hood of the Vet and walked to a second parked vehicle, a chocolate-colored Buick. Louis got behind the wheel of the Buick and drove off.

"Follow him, Ollie," instructed Markie.

During their rolling surveillance Markie copied the license plate of the Buick. A call to Silverberg revealed that the vehicle was registered to Cosmo's Florist Shop.

"Cosmo must have handed him the keys to that car, Ollie," said the sergeant. "Stick with him. Let's see where he goes."

The detectives followed Louis to the local firehouse. Louis slowed up as he passed the building, making it apparent that he was looking for something specific. Louis circled the block, this time pulling up alongside Owen Selby's car close enough to read the license plate. Louis again circled the block, parking in an empty space in front of a fire hydrant. He kept his engine running while eyeballing the vehicle he had been looking for. It was obvious to the detectives that he was waiting for someone.

"What's do you think he's up to, Sarge?" Von Hess asked.

"It beats the hell out of me," replied Markie. "He's waiting for somebody."

"It looks like a lot of firemen are going in to work, Sarge. It must be nearing the change of shift."

When Owen Selby exited the firehouse, he proceeded directly to his car and drove off. Louis pulled away from the hydrant and followed him. Markie and Von Hess followed suit. The three-vehicle procession ended up in the Riverdale section of the Bronx.

Selby parked his car on the street and entered an apartment house. Once the firefighter was inside the building, Louis drove off.

"What do you suppose he's got going with this fireman, Ollie?"

"I'm not sure, Sarge. Do you want me to stick with the Buick?"

"Yeah, do that. I'll have Silverlake run the plate of the fireman's car."

The detectives followed Louis back to the flower shop. Before they reached that destination, Detective Silverlake identified the firefighter's vehicle as being registered to Owen Selby. Markie had Silverlake check to see if Selby had a criminal record. He didn't.

"Something is doing with these guys, Ollie," said Markie.

"Yeah, but what?"" asked Von Hess.

"Maybe the firefighter is part of the gambling operation," conjectured Markie. "He could be taking action at the firehouse."

"I wonder if these guys are pushing a little blow, Sarge."

"That's another possibility. I think it's time to dust off Silverlake. I'm gonna use him in that undercover capacity I mentioned."

"Silverlake is gonna love hearing this."

"He'll probably squawk at first, but he'll be okay, Ollie. He did a good a good job for us last time we needed him."

"Are you talking about the case with the blind witness?"

"Yes."

"He did do a good job on that," conceded Von Hess.

"If Silverlake is successful putting a couple of bets in at the florist shop, we'll go for a search warrant."

"Do you really think a gambling charge will get one of those guys to roll over, Sarge."

"I'm hoping to find a loaded gun in the joint, Ollie. Or something else to use as strong leverage."

"I can see them having a gun someplace in there to protect against a rip off."

"That's what I'm banking on, Ollie."

"You know what I'm thinking, Sarge?"

"What's that?"

"If they're taking action at the florist shop, then they're probably doing some shylocking. That fireman could possibly have fallen behind on his payments."

"Good point, Ollie. They might be looking to lean on him."

16

Silverlake Shines

DETECTIVE SILVERLAKE HAD WHAT WAS CONSIDERED to be an enviable assignment at police headquarters. As Chief of Detectives Harry McCoy's gopher, the veteran detective had it good. His feathered nest was one of the softest landings possible in the department.

Silverlake fell into the category of a protected class that rarely had to engage in actual police work. Silverlake's role was an administrative one. His responsibility encompassed answering the phone and record keeping. Attendance, vacation picks, days taken off, overtime and the scheduling of training all fell within the scope of his job.

Silverlake was also responsible for reviewing incoming unusual reports generated by detectives working in squads throughout the city. Matters considered newsworthy were passed on by Silverlake to Chief McCoy without delay. This was an important duty. Nothing was more upsetting to the chief than being caught flatfooted when questioned by the police commissioner about an incident McCoy knew nothing about.

Silverlake's close proximity to the chief made him important to other detectives. His value lay in being in a position to leak information that wasn't yet released for public consumption. Silverlake was privy to who was getting transferred and when the transfers were happening. The same went when it came to promotions. Those anxious to know where they stood were more than willing to reward Silverlake with a bottle of his favorite whiskey in return for these insights.

It wasn't uncommon for Silverlake to be called upon to use his influence with the chief to arrange for a transfer to a desired assignment. This, commonly referred to in the department as a contract, also came with the expectation of a reward to the facilitator. In the world of the police department few would argue that it wasn't good to be Silverlake.

Experience taught Silverlake that the ideal time to approach the chief with a contract request was when McCoy, who didn't like to drink alone, had him in his office for cocktails. It was during these refreshment breaks that the chief was most amenable to granting favors.

While poring through the unusual reports one morning Silverlake noticed what appeared to be a pattern of stabbing homicides in the Bronx. After digesting the content contained in these abbreviated reports, Silverlake, a competent detective when he chose to be, took it upon himself to telephone the detective squads in question for additional information. He came to learn that each of the stabbing homicides involved what was believed to have been a twisted tri-edge dagger.

Detective Silverlake recollected that, in addition to ballistic evidence, such a weapon figured in the Johnny Bronco murder. He brought this to the attention of Chief McCoy, who was out of state tending to family business.

"That was a good catch, Silvie," said McCoy. "Stay on top of those unusual reports and keep me posted.
I want to know if there are any more of these."

"You don't want me to do anything other than that, Chief?"

"Just fill in Markie and Von Hess. They're working on the Bronco case. As far as the rest of the homicides, since they all took place in the Bronx, nobody is going to care. Just continue to monitor things in case somebody important ends up as a victim."

"What if more bodies start dropping as a result of getting

knifed, Chief?"

"Then we'll have to address it."

"Oh, by the way, Chief, one other thing. Sergeant Markie wants me to do some field work for him."

"What kind of field work?"

"He wants to use me to help out on the Bronco homicide. I told him that you needed me in the office, but he was adamant." Chief McCoy could see that Silverlake didn't want to step out of his comfort zone.

"What exactly does he expect you to do?" After learning what Markie wanted the detective for, the chief responded curtly. "Do what the sergeant asks."

Silverlake, not wanting to appear like a prima donna, put on a false front. "I got no problem, Chief. You know me. Whatever it is, you give me the green light and I'm ready to jump into action."

"I know Sylvie, you live for the chance to get in the game," said McCoy, facetiously. "How are we doing with the Red Breast?"

"You got plenty, Chief. I just picked up a fresh bottle for you."

"Good. I'll see you when I return to work."

***

MARKIE AND VON HESS stopped by a Manhattan sanitation garage to borrow an old sanitation uniform from a neighbor of Von Hess. The detectives were fortunate that the neighbor was around the same size as Detective Silverlake.

"Here you go, Ollie," said the neighbor as he produced the clothing. "These clothes are kind of dirty."

"Don't worry about that, these threads are going to work great. I'll get them back to you once we're finished with them."

"Keep them, Ollie. They don't fit me anyway. I got extras."

When Von Hess handed the uniform over to Silverlake at their offices in police headquarters, the chief's detective inspected the clothes. The odor coming from the well-used uniform was noticeable.

"These clothes stink," protested Silverlake.

"Garbage smells, Silvie, we can't do anything about that," Von Hess said. "Ratty clothes are in order for this job. You aren't supposed to be working in an operating room, you know.

"But the clothes smell lousy," insisted Silverlake.

"You're supposed to be a garbage man, not a perfume salesman," said Markie. "Do me a favor, just put the damn thing on and quit your squawking."

Markie's words were sufficient in hushing Silverlake up. After donning the uniform, he presented himself to the sergeant for inspection.

"The clothes fit you like a glove, Silvie," commented Markie.

"You're a natural," voiced Von Hess.

"Thanks," answered Silverlake, unenthusiastically.

"No kidding, Silvie, you look perfect for the job we need you to do," encouraged the sergeant.

"I just have to put a bet in someplace, right, Sarge?"

"That's right. All you have to do is put in a bet at a florist shop in the Bronx," advised Markie. "We're looking to make a pinch."

"Are we going out now, Sarge?"

"No, I'll let you know when. In the meantime, find yourself a broom and dustpan to take along."

When the time was right Markie and Von Hess, with Silverlake in tow, drove to the Bronx florist shop. During the ride to the location Silverlake was briefed as to the type of bet to place.

Cosmo the Florist nodded his greeting to Silverlake when the disguised detective entered the florist shop. Just as Markie figured, seeing Silverlake in a sanitation uniform and armed with a broom and standing dustpan, led to the assumption that Silverlake was just another sanitation man placing a bet.

"What happened?" Cosmo asked, "They got you walking around sweeping?"

"Yeah, I got my barrel around the corner."

"I didn't know they still do that."

"I got seniority, so every so often I get to do something easy."

Cosmo nodded his understanding. He then took the detective's bet.

The following day the same script was followed. When

Silverlake placed his bet with Cosmo, Louis Pagnetta was also present in the florist shop. The detective noticed that Louis was fiddling with a knife that appeared to be unusual. Before Silverlake left the shop he was able to ascertain that the knife Louis held was a twisted tri-edge dagger.

"How did it go, Silvie?" asked Von Hess, when Silverlake got in the backseat of the unmarked police car.

"No problem at all, Ollie."

"See, nobody cared that you stink," said Von Hess.

"You're a riot, Ollie."

"Now we can get a warrant and knock over the joint," announced Markie, interrupting the exchange.

"I guess I'll have to be a part of that, Sarge."

"Definitely, Silvie. You're the man."

"You don't need me to make the actual pinch after we execute the search warrant, do you?"

"No, Silvie, we'll handle that. But you'll have to be around to identify the perps after we raid the place and then later talk to the ADA."

"By the way, before I forget, you guys may be getting new work, Sarge," informed the chief's man.

"What kind of work?"

"I've been going through the unusual reports. I came across what may be a pattern of Bronx homicides involving a twisted tri-edge dagger."

"That's unusual," observed Von Hess.

"That's what I thought," said Silverlake, adding, "Johnny Bronco was stabbed with that kind of a dagger."

"Did you mention this to anyone?" questioned Markie.

"I did, Sarge. I informed Chief McCoy."

"And?"

"He wasn't too concerned."

"That's surprising," commented the sergeant. "I'll have to look at those unusual reports myself."

"Do you want to hear something funny, Sarge?"

"What's that, Silvie?"

134

"When I put that bet in just now, one of the guys working in the florist shop was cleaning just that kind of a dagger."

"A twisted tri-edge dagger?" asked Von Hess.

"I'm pretty sure it was."

"You did okay, Silvie," complimented Markie. "We got to get you out with us more often."

"Yeah, maybe we can have a three-man team, Sarge," voiced Von Hess.

"That's not likely, Ollie," voiced Silverlake. "I'm too vital a component in the chief's day to day operation. I'm more valuable to McCoy in the office."

17

A Fireman's Flame
Goes Out

OWEN SELBY HAD JUST finished working his tour of duty at the firehouse. Since it had been a quiet shift, he was well rested. The only taxing thing he did was to work out in the firehouse gym. The handsome six-footer was dedicated to maintaining his fine physique. He was so physically buffed that he was one of the firefighters featured shirtless in the fireman's wall calendar.

Being health conscious, Selby was an exceedingly careful eater. Adhering to a stringent diet he showed no signs of carrying excess weight. His balanced combination of muscle and low body fat gave off an appearance that was deceiving. When in clothes, Selby could mistakenly be taken for a man with a slight build.

The residents of the Belmont section, including the business owners, thought favorably of their local ladder company. As a result, the calendar featuring the bare-chested Selby hung from the walls of many Belmont stores. This exposure made the firefighter something of an area celebrity.

Selby's rugged handsomeness drew the attention of many of the local women. Adding to the firefighter's appeal was the colorful snake tattoo that ran from the top of Selby's shoulder to his elbow. The macho decoration provided a dangerous bad boy touch that drew the opposite sex to him like a moth to a flame.

Although happily married for five years, the firefighter wasn't above taking advantage of the availability of easy pickings. Soon he evolved into a serial philanderer who led a double life. Not above boasting, Selby carried a wallet sized photo of himself in a posing suit. This was a conversation piece he produced over drinks to anyone he was interested in romantically. This tactic was often a successful one.

Selby telephoned his wife to inform her that he wouldn't be home until the following day. He explained that he had to work overtime due to a couple of firefighters having called in sick. Selby's wife, who had become accustomed to such happenings, never doubted the truthfulness of this.

After showering, the firefighter donned one of the thongs he kept in his locker at work. The powder blue underwear was just one of several seductive gifts given to him by his current flame, the manager of a boutique clothing store. Selby first met his mistress at a supermarket when both were food shopping for yogurt and skim milk in the dairy aisle.

Since the saleswoman resided in the firefighter's geographical area of employment, the two proved to be ideally suited in terms of convenience. Her apartment served as their love nest. It was located across from Ciccarone Park, a small public venue which featured bocce courts and a playground.

Aware that his lover enjoyed doing a newspaper crossword, the firefighter on his way to his lady friend's apartment picked up the New York Daily News. Selby found that such thoughtfulness, however small, went a long way with paramours.

Selby had telephoned the saleswomen, who had the day off, to let her know that he was on the way.
She expressed interest in going for breakfast at a local diner. Selby balked, offering a counter proposal that entailed their having breakfast at her apartment.

"If you like," she said. "But you'll have to pick up eggs, butter and English Muffins. I have nothing in the house. Or, if you prefer, get some bagels, cream cheese and lox."

"Do you really want to eat that stuff?" asked the firefighter, concerned over the cost of the items, aside from their health value.

"Sure," she replied.

"You really shouldn't be eating that crap," said Selby, "it ain't healthy."

"Then what to you want to eat?"

"You still have oatmeal, right?"

"Yes. Is that what you want?"

"Oatmeal is a much better option for us. Do you have bananas?"

"I have just one."

"That works. We'll have oatmeal and split the banana."

The saleswoman refused to recognize the warning signs of excessive thriftiness. She preferred to view her lover as a health enthusiast, rather than as a cheapskate who sponged off her.

After having their oatmeal, half banana and coffee, Selby's lady friend began suggesting how they could spend the day together.

"How about we go to the zoo today, Owen?"

"What zoo?"

"The Bronx Zoo, silly. I haven't been there in years. It'll be fun."

"I thought we'd be hanging out here. I just come off work, you know."

"You'll have plenty of time to rest later."

Mentally calculating how time-consuming the zoo was going to be, the firefighter came up with an alternative that would take less time.

"How about I build that platform bed you want. You got the mattress delivered, right?"

"Yes, of course. You prefer that we work on the bed?"

"Yeah, let's get it done. It won't take long, let's go pick up the wood and whatever else we need."

"You don't mind?"

"Nah, let's get it over with. You got the money for the wood and hardware, right?"

"I have a credit card."

"Good. When we're all finished with the bed, we can break it in."

***

LOUIS PAGNETTA ROSE EARLY on the day he was planning to murder Owen Selby. The assassin didn't permit his unsavory mission to interfere with the breakfast he was having at a diner.

Dressed in all black clothing, he sat alone in a booth devouring a vegetable omelet with whole wheat toast. He washed his food down with orange juice and coffee.

After Louis finished eating, he checked his watch. Seeing that there was time before having to head over to the fireman's residence, he ordered more coffee. His plan was to ambush the fireman as he entered the lobby of his apartment building upon his return home from work.

As Louis sipped coffee, he reached down into his boot to touch the dagger he had secreted there. There was no reason for this other than to reinforce the fact that the weapon was still there. He then placed his hand inside the exterior pocket of the overcoat that rested alongside him on the seat. The gun contained in the pocket was also in place.

Since Owen Selby was a sizable man, Louis took along the handgun just in case he couldn't get the drop on the firefighter using the dagger. Believing it possible that Selby was capable of giving him trouble, the gun was a necessary lethal supplement.

At the appropriate time Louis, who was driving the less noticeable Buick he borrowed from Cosmo the Florist, took a slow drive over to the apartment house where the firefighter resided. He parked close to the entrance and patiently waited for his target to come home from work. Louis intended to piggyback behind Selby as his target entered the building.

After a couple of hours of waiting Louis came to realize that the fireman wasn't coming home. The assassin drove around in the vicinity of the firefighter's residence in search of his car. When this proved negative, he took a drive by the firehouse to look for Selby's vehicle. Not seeing the car parked in the vicinity of the firehouse caused Louis to abandon his plans altogether.

Ahh, the lucky bastard must be away someplace, thought Louis.

At this point Louis had little choice other than to put off his homicidal plan to another day. He headed over to the florist shop to update Cosmo as to their bad luck concerning the firefighter. On the way he happened to pass by Ciccarone Park. To his surprise, he spotted Selby's car. It was parked in front of a building opposite the park.

Delighted by his good fortune, Louis quickly circled the block, securing a position from which he could observe the firefighter's vehicle. After an hour or so the fireman, accompanied by a woman, got into his car. They had come out of the large building located opposite the park.

Louis followed behind at a safe distance. The pair was shadowed to a lumber yard. Twenty minutes had elapsed before the twosome emerged from the lumberyard carrying wood that was cut to the specifications of their project.

"What's this guy doing, building a friggin' house?" Louis asked aloud, as he watched the firefighter place a large square of ¾" plywood on top of the roof of his car.

The killer shook his head as he witnessed the firefighter place other specially cut pieces of wood on top of the plywood. Louis patiently waited as Selby tied the wood down with rope. The assassin correctly assumed that the paper bag being held by the target's female companion contained the hardware necessary to complete whatever project that was to be worked on.

Louis followed the couple back to Ciccarone Park, where they double parked in front of the woman's residence. The killer watched as the pair carried the wood into the house. The two seemed to be a happy couple that worked harmoniously together. To someone like Louis, their lack of bickering could only mean that the two weren't husband and wife.

*This gotta be his girlfrien*d, thought the pessimistic Louis, *and a* *new one at that.*

Selby handed the last piece of wood to his lady friend to carry into the apartment house. As she did this the firefighter, who had left his coat in the back seat of the car, parked his vehicle in a space that just opened up on the block.

Louis saw his opportunity to strike when the civil servant proceeded back to the building while carrying his coat. Since there was no one on the street, Louis got out of his car and approached Selby.

"Excuse me," asked Louis, pretending to be lost. "Can you tell me how I can get to Arthur Avenue from here?"

As the fireman turned to point in the direction of Arthur Avenue, Louis quickly bent down to remove the dagger from his boot. He swiftly came up with the dagger in hand and dug the blade into the firefighter's midsection. The force of the upward thrust buckled Selby's knees.

Selby let out a groan as he slowly sank downward. The pain attached to the steel that penetrated him rendered him incapable of warding off the second entry of the twisted tri-edge dagger. This time home was Selby's neck. The dagger entered the victim at a point even with the firefighter's Adam's apple. This cutting into Selby's carotid artery was the finisher.

After quickly looking about to see if there were any witnesses, Louis briskly walked to his car. Luckily there were no bystanders on hand to see the dastardly act committed. Had someone been close enough to interfere, Louis would have been compelled to use the handgun he carried.

After slaying the fireman Louis drove to the florist shop. Once there, he returned the car keys to Cosmo. He then briefed Cosmo accordingly on the success of the assassination. After sharing the details, the murderer asked for his payment.

"Hold down the shop," said the delighted Cosmo, "I'll go and get you your money."

After paying off Louis, Cosmo asked the assassin what he was going to do with this installment of money.

"I think I'll buy myself a new wardrobe," advised Louis.

"Don't you think you should save a little money for a rainy day?"

"What for? If my cousin Gino gets wind of what I've been doing they're gonna need a good suit to bury me in, ain't they?"

"Don't worry about that, Louis. If that comes to pass, I'll get you a nice suit. What do you prefer, black or blue?"

"Get me blue, with a black tie and white shirt. And make sure you get yourself nice sendoff clothes too, Cosmo."

"Me?"

"Yeah, you," answered Louis. "If Gino gets wise to me, he'll be on to you too." A serious look came over Cosmo as he realized the validity of the point being made. "If my ship goes down, it'll be with us holding hands, my friend," added Louis.

"I see what you mean, Louis."

"I figured you would. Now get going, I got shopping to do."

18

Big News For Gino

WHILE VON HESS AND SILVERLAKE were tied up securing a search warrant for the florist shop, Markie remained at the office. The sergeant occupied his time by reviewing reports submitted to the chief's office by detectives assigned to commands throughout the city. While the sergeant had faith in what Silverlake had told him about the use of a unique dagger in a number of Bronx County killings, he wanted to read the unusual reports for himself.

After reviewing the documents in question, it was clear to Markie that a homicide pattern did in fact exist. Due to the rare weapon involved in the murders, Markie suspected that the homicides could have very well been committed by the same person. This translated into meaning that it was only a matter of time before he and Von Hess would be instructed by Chief McCoy to involve themselves in the investigation of a suspected serial killer.

With a high-profile assignment on the horizon, Markie saw the need to move quickly on the other matters he was looking into while there was still time to do so. At this point the news of Firefighter Selby's murder hadn't reached the desk of the chief's office.

Once armed with the search warrant, the sergeant intended to promptly execute it. Markie planned to have Detective Silverlake place one final bet at the florist shop just prior to raiding it. This was to confirm that the venue was continuing to conduct illicit business. Establishing ongoing activity would likely mean that there would be gambling records on hand to recover. Most importantly, once inside the florist shop Silverlake would be able to advise the arrest team who was on hand to be apprehended.

***

GINO PAGNETTA SAT IN A BOOTH at a small family restaurant located in the Chelsea section of Manhattan. Not knowing exactly why the family underboss wanted to see him left him apprehensive. Sophisticated as to the ways of the criminal organization he belonged to, being called to a meeting could either be something good or bad.

The number two man in the family sitting across from Gino was Mario "Rooster" Savoldi. The fifty-five-year-old Savoldi was a squat barrel-chested man with an eighteen-inch neck. His ears were thick with pancake-like lobes, his lips were fleshy. The underboss had a pale face, which was attributable to his aversion to the sun.

After ordering a bottle of wine and some food, Savoldi looked over at Gino and laughed. His teeth, while perfectly aligned, were brownish due to a lot of coffee drinking.

"Relax, Gino," said Savoldi, seeing that Gino appeared nervous. "You're here for a very, very good reason."

"I'm glad to hear that, Mario," said Gino, breathing a sigh of relief. "I thought that there might be a problem."

The underboss leaned forward and whispered something to Gino in Italian. Gino's concerned look was suddenly replaced with the widest grin imaginable. The ecstatic organized crime soldier had been notified that he was being elevated to the rank of capo in the family. This promotion meant that Gino was now ranked in the family pecking order above all other soldiers.

"You have to be at Orsatti's Funeral Parlor on Park Avenue in Brooklyn tonight at 10:00 P.M. sharp," advised Savoldi. "Dress up."

"What's going on there, Mario?"

"Long John wants to announce your promotion to all the other skippers. We're also gonna be making a few proposed members tonight."

"The books are open?"

"Yeah, Long John wants you to participate in the induction ceremony."

"No problem."

"My cousin ain't one of the guys getting his button, is he?"

"Who, Louis?"

"Yeah."

"How could he be, you never proposed him. That's another one of the reasons why you're getting bumped up, Gino. Long John respects the fact that you don't show favoritism."

To Gino, being a capo meant more than just receiving money from soldiers who reported to him. A thick bankroll was something Gino already had. It was the enhanced authority that came with the title that he relished. To a ruthless egomaniac with a Napoleon complex like Gino, it was all about power. That, and the respect he was now going to command from those in his family. Money was just the icing on the cake.

***

MARKIE AND VON HESS sat in their unmarked department vehicle with Detective Silverlake. The sergeant had just finished prepping Silverlake and was about to send his detective, with his broom and standing dustpan, into the Bronx florist shop to place a bet.

Silverlake had just gotten out of the department car when he was suddenly called back. Von Hess had taken notice of a

Lincoln Continental that was backing into a parking space a few doors away from the flower shop.

"Look who it is, Sarge," said Von Hess, pointing to Gino Pagnetta, as the gangster exited his vehicle.

"It's that racketeer from last time. What was his name again?"

"Gino Pagnetta, Sarge," replied Von Hess, "and he's all spruced up like he's going to a wedding."

"That runt is a racket guy?" asked Silverlake. "He struts like a freaking peacock."

"Where is he going, Ollie?" asked Markie.

Von Hess adjusted his binoculars to gain a clearer look. "He's checking out the Vet parked in front of the florist shop, Sarge," replied the detective. "Wait a second, he just went in the florist shop."

"Do you want me to go in now and place that bet, Sarge?" Silverlake asked.

"No, sit tight. That'll hold. I want to give this guy a toss when he gets back in his car."

"Whatever you say, Sarge."

"We'll take him when he's a few blocks away from here, Ollie."

***

GINO ENTERED THE FLORIST SHOP appearing to be in a very good mood. Both Cosmo and Louis were used to seeing the mobster dressed nicely. However, on this particular occasion Gino was dressed exceptionally well, attired in a fine blue suit, gold tie and matching pocket square. He was also sporting a look that suggested that he had a reason to be happy.

"Looking good," commented Cosmo, in greeting Gino.

"Yeah, you're looking sharp, Gino," chimed in Louis.

The controlled smiles worn by Cosmo and Louis paled in comparison with the gleeful grin projected by Gino. Both Cosmo and Louis were curious as to what caused Gino to be in such a happy frame of mind.

"Who owns that Chevy Vet parked outside?" asked the newly minted capo.

"It's mine," replied Louis.

"Yours?" asked the surprised cousin. "Those are pretty slick wheels you got yourself. Good luck with it."

The gangster's good wishes were far from sincere. Gino disliked anyone outshining him in any way. It bothered him that his cousin's yellow vet stood out so prominently. The fact that the sports car was sure to draw more envy from onlookers than Gino's Lincoln Continental was disturbing enough to erase Gino's big smile. Also dimming Gino's mood was his wondering where his cousin got the money for the car.

If he made a score, I got no taste of it, thought Gino.

"Big day today, Gino?" asked Cosmo, diverting Gino's attention after sensing that there might be tension in the air. The perceptive florist was sure that Gino was wondering where Louis got the money to buy such a car. Since both he and Louis were dipping into the profits of Gino's gambling operation, Cosmo was wary for a good reason.

"This is a very big day for me, Cosmo," announced Gino proudly, his grin resurfacing. His jealous side vanished now that the spotlight returned to him.

"What's the big news?"

"Louis looked over at Cosmo and answered for his cousin. "He must have gotten bumped up," declared Louis, certain that this was the reason for Gino's elation.

"You're looking at a guy who is gonna be running things," announced Gino. "A lot of guys are reporting to me now!" he announced, pointing his thumb at his own chest.

"Congratulations," voiced Cosmo.

"Yeah, all the best," piped up Louis.

"I figured I was due," said the gangster, who picked a carnation for himself.

"Let me pin that on your jacket for you," offered Cosmo. "There, that looks great," he said, admiring his handiwork once finished.

"There is no telling how fast this baby's train will be traveling up the track," Gino boasted. "When I get to the top, you could both say that you knew me when."

"Any word on my situation?" queried Louis, who had been waiting years to be officially inducted into the family as a made man.

"It'll come, Louis. I keep proposing you for membership, but you know how it is. You can't rush these things."

"I've been waiting a long time, Gino."

"I know that Louis, and I've been pushing for you," lied the new capo. "Trust me, it'll come."

"Yeah, but…."

"Enough Louis, this ain't the time or place to talk about this," barked Gino, "especially in front of Cosmo, he's a civilian for Christ's sake."

"But you were talking about it."

"That's enough, Cosmo is a civilian I said."

"What are you talking about," challenged Louis, "what civilian? Are you forgetting that Cosmo did a piece of work with us?"

Being corrected by Louis caused Gino to explode. Whatever joy he had was now replaced by venom.

"I'm telling you, Louis, you better shut your trap right now. You're treading on thin ice." The gangster's tone was menacing, which caused concern for Louis, who knew he had pushed the envelope. Cosmo tried to break the tension.

"Let's not ruin a big day, guys. How about we have a drink to celebrate your good news, Gino? I got a nice bottle of 12-year-old Scotch for us to break open. What do you say?"

"I'm not thirsty," barked the agitated gangster. "Go have one with the asshole who works with you," he added, pointing to Louis. Gino then stormed out of the shop.

Louis knew that he was now in trouble. He looked at Cosmo without speaking. He didn't have to say a word. Both men knew that Gino would seek retribution. The form of payback was the question.

Gino got behind the wheel of his car muttering curses. Quite perturbed, he briefly considered running his car key along the hood of his cousin's Chevy Vet. Deciding that he'd do that at a future time, he drove off with a screech. As he sped away Gino's anger was further fueled when he thought about how well his cousin was dressed.

Since when is Louis wearing nice clothes, thought Gino. *Where the hell is he getting all this money from?*

***

MARKIE AND VON HESS were surprised at the reckless way Gino tore out from his parking space. He pulled out so abruptly that he narrowly escaped getting struck by a passing car who was forced to stop short.

"Something must have happened to light a fire under his ass, Ollie." commented Markie.

"I'll pull him over, Sarge once we get a few blocks from here."

"Silvie, you duck down in the back seat," said Markie, "I don't was this guy to see you."

When Von Hess had the opportunity to pull alongside the gangster he tooted his horn. Gino paid no attention. It took several more horn toots for the gangster to acknowledge the detective. When Gino looked to his left at the vehicle who pulled up alongside him, he saw Markie displaying his sergeant's badge. Gino rolled down his window.

"What?" Gino icily asked.

"Pull over and turn off the engine."

"What for?" The defiance in Gino's voice was clear.

"I said pull over and turn off the car," repeated Markie. This time Gino, with a huff, complied.

"Let me see your license and registration," said the sergeant, once standing at the driver's side door of the pulled over vehicle.

"What did I do?"

"You almost caused an accident back there," replied Markie. "Now let me have your license and registration."

"I didn't do anything."

"Are you gonna give me your shit or what?"

"And what if I don't?"

Markie looked over the hood of the car at Von Hess, who stood on the passenger side of the vehicle.

149

He let out a deep sigh before answering Gino's question. "If you don't, I'm gonna yank you out of the car
through the window."

 "No, you ain't," said Gino, defiantly. The mobster forgot that he had a small quantity of cocaine on his person and a loaded small caliber automatic in the car glove compartment.

 Markie wasted no time in taking hold of Gino's shirt collar. With one swift motion the sergeant pulled the gangster through the car window as threatened. Gino was then quickly handcuffed by Von Hess and bent over the hood of the Lincoln face down. At this point Detective Silverlake, wanting to avoid being seen, slipped out of the unmarked department car with his broom and standing dustpan unnoticed. Silverlake then made his way back to headquarters.

 Once Silverberg was gone, Von Hess placed Gino in the rear of the unmarked police car, while Markie looked through the Lincoln. Gino was subsequently transported to the local precinct where he was charged with cocaine possession, possession of a loaded gun, reckless driving, resisting arrest and misdemeanor assault. The assault charge was the result of Markie jamming his thumb during their brief scrimmage.

19

Gino Sees The Light

GINO PAGNETTA SAT HANDCUFFED to a metal chair in the precinct detective squad room. Although no stranger to being arrested, he nevertheless was simmering. He was irked that his liberty was restricted on what was supposed to be an important night for him.

Gino kept looking at the clock on the wall. When he tired of watching time move slowly, he turned his attention to Detective Von Hess, who was sitting at his desk typing arrest papers.

When Von Hess rose from his seat Gino's eyes followed the detective as he walked to a file cabinet to gather print cards. Gino, who knew what was coming next, winced as Von Hess uncuffed his prisoner.

"Okay, Gino, up we go," said Von Hess. "Time to get you fingerprinted."

It was painful for the gangster to stand alongside the tall detective as his fingertips were being inked and rolled. It was an unpleasant reminder to Gino that he was a very short man, a touchy reality for someone with a massive ego.

After being printed Gino was photographed. He was then again handcuffed to the chair alongside the detective's desk. The prisoner scanned the squad room to see if anyone had been looking at him. Glad to see that no one was, he began to look at his surroundings through a critical lens. It was all he could do in the way of striking back at his keepers.

The prisoner saw the squad room as a work area in desperate need of refreshening. The walls and ceiling both needed painting. The workstations were antiquated. The gray metal desks and chairs, while sturdy, were an uninteresting eyesore. Aged typewriters stood atop each desk. To the side of every desk sat a cheap wastepaper basket.

"How do you like working in this dump, Detective?" Gino asked, unable to resist taking a shot at Von Hess.

"It'll do," replied Von Hess, not bothering to look at the prisoner.

Not getting the reaction he hoped for from Von Hess, Gino started watching the other detectives. The prisoner felt superior to the detectives. He considered law enforcement officers, of all stripes, to be suckers that toiled in professions that, at best, provided only a living.

They don't deserve any better, thought the gangster.

Gino's greatest special distain was reserved for the sole female detective working in the squad. His animosity for her was immense. As the organized crime capo listened to the female detective speaking assertively, he turned his head away in disgust.

It irked Gino to see a woman in a position of authority over any man. He shuttered at the thought of his ever having to concede to directions put forth by a female. He was so entrenched in his sexist beliefs that he equated male compliance when interacting with a woman as being unmanly. *I'd never let her put handcuffs on me,* Gino thought as he stared at the female detective.

Being sensitive to his own stature, the female detective's tallness also played a role in Gino's harsh position. The mobster turned to address Von Hess, who continued to busy himself tending to arrest paperwork.

"I don't see how you guys can work with a skirt," declared Gino. Von Hess let the comment pass. When Von Hess refused to dignify the statement, Gino pressed on. "Anytime you put a man and woman together a fire is bound to start."

"Do you know how we extinguish fires started by prisoners?" Von Hess asked, this time replying.

"How?"

"With a smack in the puss." answered Von Hess tartly.

Gino was taken aback by this remark. He hadn't been spoken to in such a manner for many years. The prisoner took a moment to study Von Hess closer. Now seeing the detective in a different light, he turned his attention to Markie, who was on the telephone at another desk.

Gino concluded that both Von Hess and Markie were a throwback to old school policing, a time when law enforcement carried out the threats they made. The prisoner held his tongue rather than put Von Hess to the test.

I wouldn't put it past these two bulls to give me a tune up that would land me in a hospital, Gino thought. *One prick would lie and the other would swear to it.*

"Excuse me, Detective, seriously, can I ask you a question?"

"What is it now, Gino?" asked Von Hess, sounding annoyed.

"Why did you guys really pull me over? I'm curious as to why I was singled out."

"Because you were driving like an asshole?"

"I was in a bad frame of mind when you stopped me."

"Was that my fault?"

"No, it had nothing to do with you. Something pissed me off. Then you guys came along and, well, you know the rest. You guys ruined a big night for me."

"How did we do that?"

"I'm not at liberty to say."

By the end of Gino's question and answer period, the prisoner gathered more information than he gave.

"You guys ain't precinct detectives, right?" asked Gino, looking to confirm what he suspected.

"We work on cases for the chief of detectives," replied Von Hess.

"You kept harping on the florist shop. Why, what do you care about the florist shop?"

"We already explained to you, our interest is in the murder of a retired police captain," replied Markie.

"Is that the guy they found in the Split Rock parking lot?" asked Gino, fishing for insights pertaining to the murder he participated in. Von Hess wasn't fooled by Gino's pretending to be uninformed.

"That's right, so now all of a sudden you heard about it. Do you know anything about that, Gino?"

"Only what I read. The paper said that the captain was shot and found in the trunk of a car, right?"

"He was also stabbed with a twisted tri-edge dagger," pointed out Markie, who joined in the conversation.

The sergeant's statement caused Gino to blink. The image of his cousin Louis flashed before Gino's mind. "I don't remember reading that."

"There have been quite a few dagger murders occurring in the Bronx," advised Markie.

"Really? What kind of dagger?" asked Gino, thinking of his cousin Louis.

"You know, Gino, if you could give us a little guidance on these knifings, things could work to your advantage."

"What do you take me for, some kind of a snitch, Sergeant?"

"I wouldn't say that." Markie replied. "I see you as someone smart enough to know how to help himself."

"What's my advantage?"

"You get to clear yourself of the charges in this case."

"You'll shit can these charges you got against me?"

"I think we can convince the district attorney's office of making this go away in court, if we put forth a good enough reason."

"You know, Sergeant, I'm not even sure if I need help on this case you got against me. What's a little recreational cocaine today? As far as the gun charge, you had no legitimate reason to go in my glove compartment. My lawyer will get that charge thrown out."

"You're forgetting one thing," reminded Von Hess.

"What's that?"

"These assistant district attorneys like nothing better than hammering wise guys like you. You're a victim of your own fame."

"How is that?"

"Your name gets their name in the paper. It helps establish their reputation as a racket buster."

"I'll concede that," acknowledged the mob capo. "Let me give it to you straight, I don't know a damn thing about that captain getting shot. I got no idea why he was clipped."

"And he was stabbed with a dagger," said Markie.

"Look, you guys seem regular, can't we work something out over here?" asked Gino, hinting that he was willing to bribe the law enforcement officers. "Let me give you some walking around money, Sergeant."

"You can forget that, unless you're looking to add another charge to the ledger."

"Okay, I made a mistake," admitted Gino, who was fast to correct himself. "Look, Sergeant, let's try another way."

"What way is that?"

"What if I find out what I could about that captain and these dagger stabbings? Will that get me off the hook on this little misunderstanding we had."

"It would help."

"I get to walk away clean?"

"We can get your case adjourned," advised Markie. "While you're out on the street, you can work your magic. If you deliver, you'll get a play. Or I should say, the DA will probably let you off the hook."

"I ain't signing anything that says I turned rat. Do we understand each other?"

"Understood," answered Markie.

"Okay, Sergeant, we got a deal. Give me some names of who got whacked with a dagger."

"Start with Captain John Bronco and a club singer named Frankie Flamarian."

"You get me out and I'll find out something for you to sink your teeth into."

"You'll be out right after you get arraigned."

"Remember, if I deliver, this shit case goes away, right?"

"I said deal," repeated Markie. "I'm going to reach out to the DA's office now."

***

SINCE GINO KILLED JOHNNY BRONCO, that was one murder he knew all about. It was also one Gino wouldn't talk about. When it came to the other homicides, the first suspect that came to mind was Gino's cousin Louis, who Gino knew carried the unusual dagger described.

Since many of Gino's associate**s** had an interest in club venues that offered entertainment, Gino was confident that after making a few telephonic inquiries he'd get a line on Frankie Flamarian. In this he was correct. He soon learned where the Frankie Flamarian Trio performed regularly.

With what would have been surprising news to Gino's cousin Louis, the organized crime capo remembered Leaky, the uncle of Louis who was a plumber. Having met Leaky at past family functions, Gino recollected that Leaky lived in close proximity to the club where Frankie Flamarian performed. Gino decided that paying the plumber a visit would be worthwhile.

Leaky was at home watching television in his living room when Gino pulled his Lincoln Continental into the driveway. Hearing the car pull up, the plumber went to the window to see who was there. He paused for a moment, not recognizing Gino. When he opened the door to investigate, the plumber finally realized who it was.

"Gino!" said a smiling Leaky. "What the hell are you doing here?"

"I was in the neighborhood," replied Gino. "How have you been?"

156

"Getting a little old, but I'm hanging in there. I can't believe you remembered me and stopped by to say hello. I'm honored. So how are you?"

The gangster chuckled at the genuine enthusiasm expressed by the plumber. I'm doing great, Leaky."

Once the pleasantries were behind them, Gino got around to asking about a singer by the name of Frankie Flamarian. This led to Gino being advised that Leaky and his nephew Louis had taken in a Flamarian performance at a local club that happened to be a client of the plumber.

"Louis came all the way up here to see you?"

"Yeah, he came by out of the blue, just like you. What did you guys think I croaked?"

The plumber went on to explain how he and Louis spent their time together when Louis visited. Leaky had no inkling that Frankie Flamarian had been murdered. As a result of their conversation, it was now crystal clear to Gino that treachery had taken place behind his back.

On his drive back to the Bronx, all Gino could think of was that his cousin had been committing murders without his authorization. The more Gino pondered this, the more his blood began to boil.

Sure, he thought, *it all makes sense now. The car, the clothes! Somebody must have shelled out plenty to get Louis to knock off those guys. The sneaky bastard didn't even give me a taste, forget about his asking permission! Just wait until I get my hands on him*!

By the time Gino arrived in the vicinity of the florist shop he came up with additional disturbing possibilities. *Wait a friggin' minute,* thought the capo, *if Louis can start killing people without my permission, what else is he capable of?*

At this point Gino decided not to go to the flower shop to confront Louis. His alternate strategy called for a late-night visit to his cousin's apartment.

I'm gotta take my time and plan things out, thought Gino. *Louis can't be arrested under any circumstances. The stinking louse could turn informant and rat me out. He's got enough on me to have me put away for the rest of my life!*

20

Louis Faces The Music

LOUIS PAGNETTA SETTLED IN A COMFORTABLE CHAIR in front of his television set. Since his landlord wasn't stingy when it came to providing heat, Louis was able to lounge around in his light blue boxer shorts and wife beater t-shirt. Atop his stomach rested a generous bowl of vanilla and chocolate ice cream.

As he searched for a late movie to watch on television, he wolfed down his treat. He was halfway through the bowl when his phone rang. It was his cousin Gino.

"I'm swinging by your place tonight at midnight, be outside," said Gino.

The click of the phone came rapidly, leaving no time for Louis to respond to the caller. Having no choice other than to comply, Louis downed the ice cream and got dressed.

Gino's total lack of consideration was another one of the things that Louis despised about his cousin. Being a slave to Gino's whims was a primary factor in Louis wanting to be inducted into the Long John Capezzo organized crime family. Once a family soldier, Louis knew things would be different. He'd be his own man.

Louis stood outside in the cold smoking a cigarette while waiting for his cousin. Since their last interaction didn't go well at the florist shop, and his having a suspicious nature, Louis carried his dagger in his coat pocket where it would be easily accessible.

When Gino pulled up in a black Chevrolet Impala, instead of his Lincoln Continental, Louis was fairly certain that dirty work was afoot. It was Gino's routine to switch to a less attention-grabbing vehicle when up to no good.

An unsmiling Gino pressed the power button that activated the passenger side window. When the window was half down the gangster called out to his cousin.

"Get in," said a snarling Gino.

Louis could see that his cousin was still was pissed off at him. This had now become a moment of personal concern for Louis.

"What's up, Cousin?" asked the wary Louis, after getting in the car.

"We need to talk."

"No problem," said Louis, who slipped his hand in his coat pocket to take hold of his dagger.

Gino drove in silence to an area located within the confines of the massive Pelham Bay Park. Once parked, Gino turned to his cousin to confront him with accusations.

"You got anything to tell me?" asked Gino.

"About what?"

"About you knocking people off," answered Gino, being as direct as possible.

"I don't know what you're talking about," answered Louis, raising a hand in a defensive manner. He
was trying his best to appear innocent of the accusation.

"Don't lie to me, Louis. You keep bullshittin' me and you're putting yourself an inch away from making the obituary column." Louis stiffened, preparing to defend himself with his dagger at this point. "I know you've been hiring yourself out."

"Gino, wait a minute, will ya? Honest, I...."

"You want honest, Louis?" screamed the now enraged Gino, taking things up several notches. "I'll give you honest. I know for

160

a fact that you've been putting that friggin' dagger of yours out for hire without my okay. You know as well as me, that's way out of line!"

"Look, Gino...."

"No, you look, Louis," said Gino forcefully, again silencing his cousin mid-sentence. "You killed this kid Frankie Flamarian. I want to know for who, how much for, and why."

"I swear to you that I never heard of any guy by the name of Flamarian."

"Who is that over there by that tree?" asked Gino, suddenly directing the attention of Louis elsewhere.

As Louis looked in the direction of the tree, he heard a sound that could only be the cocking of a gun. Turning his attention to the click, Louis found himself looking down at the barrel of the gun that was trained on him.

Gino raised the revolver and pointed it at the head of his cousin. He then ordered Louis out of the car. Believing that he was facing execution, Louis hesitated. Hoping for the best, the confronted man shifted his body, preparing to draw his dagger. Gino, anticipating this, was a step ahead of him.

"Don't make me cap you in the car, Louis," voiced Gino. "You're my cousin, and that still rates something. I'm gonna give you a chance to come clean with me, and then maybe we can move on. Now get out of the car."

Louis paused, unsure if his cousin could be trusted. He held on to the dagger tightly as he exited the vehicle. Gino could tell that his cousin had something in his pocket.

"You ain't got a chance, Louis," said Gino, "so don't even think about it. Take your hand out of your pocket, real slow."

"You win, Gino. Don't shoot," pleaded Louis, "let me explain."

"Get that hand where I could see it and start explaining." Louis complied.

"I didn't know Flamarian or any of those guys I clipped. I took them out because I was getting paid big bucks for the work. It was the kind of money you don't say no to."

"Who paid you?"

"Cosmo the Florist. He had it in for them all." Gino was

genuinely surprised to hear this.

"What did they do to Cosmo?"

"He never told me what they did, and I didn't ask. Look Gino, for the money I was getting, you'd have done the same thing."

"How much are we talking?"

Louis conveyed how much money Cosmo paid him to commit each murder. The mob capo had to admit to himself that for that amount of money, he too would have taken on the murder contracts.

These guys must have done something really out of line for Cosmo to shell out that kind of money, thought Gino. *The florist ain't exactly the last of the big spenders.*

"I'm telling you, Gino, he wanted this done bad."

"I didn't think Cosmo had that kind of scratch. And you got no idea what these guys did wrong?"

"Not a clue, I swear it."

Gino relaxed the grip on his weapon. He looked at his cousin in a way that made it evident that he was sizing Louis up to determine if he was being truthful.

"So, that how you were able to buy that Chevy Vet and all the clothes on the money Cosmo paid you."

"That's right," answered Louis.

"And you didn't even think to give me a taste," chastised Gino. "What am I supposed to do with a selfish bastard like you?" Louis reacted by somberly looking down toward the ground. "Answer my question!" barked Gino.

"I know I was way out of line, Gino. It'll never happen again, I swear it. Look, how about I give you some of the money I got left?" This was what Gino wanted to hear.

"That's a good start, Louis," said the man holding the gun. "Just where did Cosmo get that kind of money?"

The question caused Louis to pause. He found it to be a tricky one to answer. When he finally replied, he did so without implicating himself in Cosmo's thievery.

"Cosmo has been skimming from your gambling operation."

"How do you know that?"

"I got suspicious of the way he was acting, so I started watching him."

"Why didn't you come to me with this information?" Gino asked, again fighting to control his temper.

"I was going to come to you, but I wanted to first understand exactly how Cosmo was working it."

"Did you help yourself to my money too, Louis?"

"Not a dime, Gino," Louis replied. "I swear it."

"You're a liar!"

"I'm telling you the truth, Gino. Cosmo would never offer to cut me in, he knew I wouldn't take a penny because I was too loyal to you."

"Get back in the car," Gino ordered.

Both men returned to the vehicle. Knowing that his cousin had given him a reprieve, Louis let out a sigh of relief.

"Can I smoke?" Louis asked softly.

"Yeah, go on and light up."

"Tell me what you want me to do, Gino," voiced Louis after releasing the deep drag he took in. "Say the word and I'll clip Cosmo today."

"Be quiet while I think of what to do," said the mobster. "I know for a fact that the bulls are on a mission to solve those dagger murders."

"How do you know that?"

"Never mind how I know. Just be glad that I don't want to see you pinched. I think that I see a way to wrap things up nicely."

"You do?"

"Those white aprons at the florist shop, they have names written on them, right?"

"Yeah, we both got our own aprons with our name written in red stitching."

"Here is what I want you to do. You're gonna wipe the fingerprints off that dagger of yours and then figure out a way for Cosmo to get his paws on it. Then you're gonna plant the dagger in the pocket of one of Cosmo's monogramed aprons. Do you think you can do that without messing things up?"

"Sure, I could. But why?"

"Never mind why. Just figure on doing what I said and be grateful you're getting a pass."

"When do you want me to do this, Gino?"

"I'll tell you when. In the meantime, let's go get my end of the money you made for doing Cosmo's killing for him."

***

GINO'S PLAN WAS TRULY a diabolical one. It called for his forcing Cosmo to sign over his florist business, and the building that housed it, to a designated front man that still needed to be identified. Gino saw this forced takeover of Cosmo's assets as just the first payback for the florist having dipped into the revenue generated from the mobster's gambling operation. The final curtain was to come down on Cosmo shortly after, with the law having a role prior to the ultimate retaliation.

Gino's designated front man, whoever that was to be, had to learn the workings of the florist shop, the building and the gambling operation. Cosmo was needed to do the training. Once Gino's front man was capable, papers would then be drawn up by Gino's lawyer to reflect the transfer of ownership of the business and property. After things were legally finalized, Cosmo elimination would then be addressed.

Gino's plot saw Cosmo as the fall guy. He intended to have Louis plant his dagger, with Cosmo's fingerprints on it, in the pocket of Cosmo's monogramed work apron. Once that was done, Gino was going to tip off Markie as to where the murder weapon could be found.

Gino believed that the authorities would then have the evidence they needed to identify the perpetrator in all of the dagger-related slayings. Included in this would be the Captain Bronco murder. Subsequently, the law would then look to arrest Cosmo for all of the homicides.

Gino's intention was to murder Cosmo long before the authorities got to him. Cosmo's death would mean that all of the homicides would be deemed solved and closed. The scheme hatched by Gino was one he was quite proud of.

***

GINO WENT TO THE APARTMENT of Cosmo the Florist armed with a revolver. Gino didn't mince words in telling Cosmo point blank that his days of being a business and property owner were over. When informed that he was expected to sign over his assets to Gino's representative, Cosmo balked.

"Why would I do that?"

"Because I said so, Cosmo."

"Are you serious, Gino?"

At this juncture Gino produced his gun. He pointed the weapon at Cosmo head and asked, "Does this baby look like a jokester?"

"I don't understand…."

"You understood enough to steal from me," accused Gino, "and use my cousin Louis to kill for you!"

The remark immediately quieted the florist. "You're lucky, Cosmo, that's all I can say," Gino voiced, adding, "you're only getting a pass because I need you to break in your replacement. Louis ain't got the brains for it."

"Gino, I never stole…."

"Save your breath, Cosmo," barked the gangster. "From now on you got only one job, and that's to train your replacement. As of right now you are an employee in MY florist business and a tenant in MY building. I don't even want to know why you wanted all those guys killed."

Cosmo knew that a counter argument professing innocence would be to no avail, so he endeavored to shift blame.

"I didn't mean to steal from you, Gino. I was forced into doing it," lied the florist.

"Yeah, by who?"

"It was your cousin Louis, he put me up to it. He said if I didn't go along, he'd kill me."

"You don't say."

"It's true, you have to believe me. What could I do? Louis is a very dangerous man."

165

"You're saying that Louis was stealing my money, and he forced you to do the same. Why would he want to share a good thing with you?"

"I caught him with his hand in the cookie jar," replied Cosmo, thinking fast.

"I see, so he made you a partner in order to keep you quiet."

"I was no partner. Louis threatened to kill me, Gino. All Louis ever gave me was a few crumbs."

"I think you better shut your trap while you still can, Cosmo. Quit while you're ahead."

It was obvious that Gino didn't believe a word of Cosmo's fabrication. The gangster strongly believed that his cousin Louis lacked the confidence to make such a bold play. Gino, on the other hand, saw Cosmo in a different light. The florist was smart and greedy, a combination that made his treachery plausible.

"What is going to happen to me after I train this guy?" asked Cosmo.

"You're gonna be allowed to leave this town alive. For that you should be grateful."

Gino left the florist with no alternative other than to agree to the terms he dictated. It was only after Gino returned his weapon to his coat pocket and left the apartment that Cosmo again began to breathe easily. Once alone, Cosmo began to realize he was a doomed man.

Gino wouldn't give his own mother a pass, thought the Florist. *He's definitely going to kill me!*

Cosmo was accurate in his analysis of the situation. Gino had every intention of murdering him once things were up and running.

21

The Recruitment

IT WASN'T IN GINO PAGNETTA'S NATURE to forgive and forget. Once Gino didn't need Cosmo any longer to break in a new man, he'd be history. The florist's violent end was merely postponed to a future date. As far as Louis went, Gino was on the fence as to the fate of his cousin. Gino's decision on Louis would come after the dagger was found in Cosmo's monogramed apron.

While Gino knew that the planted dagger, in and of itself, may or may not be sufficient enough to secure a conviction, he wasn't worried. Gino understood how detectives worked. As a rule, they looked to close their cases in the fastest possible way. Having this understanding, Gino was going to make things easy for all concerned.

Gino was in a rush to identify a suitable resource capable of replacing Cosmo at the florist shop. He commenced his talent search at his social club. Once the new man was in place, Gino would give Louis the go ahead to put the dagger in the pocket of Cosmo's work garment.

Gino's ideal candidate to work at the florist shop was someone who, on the surface, appeared to be reputable. Respectability would prevent eyebrows from being raised when ownership of the building and business was transferred over. Considering the clientele who frequented the social club, Gino knew that finding someone fitting his criteria wasn't going to be easy.

Standing in the center of the club, Gino looked at the talent pool at his disposal. Some were amusing themselves by playing cards at tables, others sat around drinking coffee as they swapped tales of their involvement in past crimes. A few were consuming beverages at the small bar area.

The men came in assorted shapes and sizes. Some were getting on in years. None could be considered the ideal fit. Gino shook his head at what he considered a limited candidate pool.

*I'm overloaded with leg breakers and nickel snatcher*s, lamented Gino inwardly. *How am I going to come up with somebody with half a brain among these guy*s?

Gino finally saw daylight when a man everyone knew as Davey the Fixer came into the club. Davey, a talented handyman, was carrying a large blue plastic pail containing the items he'd need to perform his work. The jack of all trades was at the club to address a roach problem. As Davey headed to the rear of the club he did so smiling, greeting those in the room he knew.

Gino was impressed by the handyman's friendly demeanor. It dawned on the mobster that Davey could be exactly what he was looking for.

The forty-one-year-old David Brazil was a happily married family man who lived in the neighborhood with his wife and children. Davey made his living by doing odd jobs off the books. Since he never took advantage of anyone by inflating the costs connected to his work, the services of the handyman were always in demand.

Oddly, while Gino preferred the company of crooks like himself, he nevertheless had a true appreciation for an honest working man. That is, as long as the working man wasn't a cop or an employee of the federal government, who he considered all to be feds.

Adding to Davey's appeal was the handyman's lack of inquisitiveness. Davey never asked too many questions. This was an admirable characteristic in Gino's estimation. A big plus was that Davey wasn't very much taller than Gino. This went a long way. It made the handyman a standout candidate for working at the florist shop.

Gino watched with great interest as the baseball cap wearing Brazil began squirting the corners of the club with an insecticide that paralyzes and kills roaches.

The mass killing of bugs was something Gino could relate to. He personally enjoyed killing ants. As a child, he blew them up with firecrackers. He also pulled wings off butterflies.

In Gino's final analysis, Davey Brazil was what he was looking for. Gino did his homework on Brazil. He learned that Brazil's brother-in-law was an International Longshoreman Association (ILA) union representative.

Gino had someone approach the union rep, asking him to feel out Davey. After being informed that the money to make was good, Davey sent back word that he was willing to learn more about the opportunity Gino was offering. A meeting was subsequently arranged at a venue away from the social club.

"I'm offering you this job because I like you, Davey," advised Gino.

"What kind of job is it?"

"A good one," replied Gino. "You'll be looking after my interest in a florist shop. Once you learn the business, we'll make a few staff changes, and you'll be your own boss with only me to answer to."

"But I know nothing about the flower business, Mr. Pagnetta."

"You'll learn what you need to know. And call me Gino, you're among friends."

"I don't know…."

"Don't worry, I ain't throwing you to the wolves. You'll learn all you need to know from the old owner. Once you got things down pat, I'll clean house and you'll be the man over there."

"Can I still do my handyman work on the side?" Gino burst out laughing upon hearing the question.

"Forget that shit, it's a dead end. You own a house?"

"I rent."

"That's what I figured. Look, I'm offering you the chance to make enough money to buy a house, a car or whatever else the hell you want. All you gotta do is get on the gravy train with me, and you can throw away your hammer and wrench for good."

Once Davey voiced that he would accept the job being offered, Gino explained the other duties that were expected of him.

"Listen, Davey, there is one other thing that we need to understand each other on. This new job ain't all petunia pushing, you're also gonna be doing other things

"What kind of things? You know, I'm a pretty straight guy, Mr. Pagnetta."

"I know that. Look, the florist shop is run strictly legit, so you can relax as far as that goes. All you're gonna be doing extra is taking bets at the florist shop. That's a victimless crime."

"Can I ask you one question?"

"What?"

"Why me?"

"Because I could tell that I could trust you. Do you want to know how much?" Davey nodded. "Enough for your name to appear on record as the official owner of the florist shop and the building that it's located in. So, what do you say, Davey?"

"I don't understand…."

"You don't have to. Just think of what the extra money is going to mean to your wife and kids."

This was the point that sold Davey. "I guess I have to say thank you. How much money are we talking about?"

"Good question."

Gino went on to explain how much money Davey stood to make. "So, are you in or do I look elsewhere?"

"Count me in, I just retired my work belt, Mr. Pagnetta."

"Hey, I said call me Gino."

***

COSMO THE FLORIST WAS PERCEPTIVE enough to know that he was living on borrowed time. He recognized that Gino was a ruthless killer who couldn't be trusted to let bygones be bygones. Under the circumstances, the only thing for him to do was buy time by playing nice in the sandbox until he figured out what steps to take.

The florist couldn't have been more cordial to Davey Brazil when Gino's designee began working at the florist shop. Cosmo correctly believed that as long as he was teaching Davey Brazil how things worked, he'd live. As a result, the florist educated Davey at a snail's pace.

The problem with Cosmo's strategy was that there wasn't all that much to learn. Complicating this further was Davey Brazil proving to be a fast learner. Davey even took to the artistic component of the florist business in relatively short order.

The onetime handyman also had little difficulty adapting to the business side of things. Customer relations, inventory and proper record keeping all came easy to him. As far as the illegal activity went, Davey was quite adaptable in that area as well.

This kid is too smart, thought Cosmo. *At this pace I'm as good as dead right now. My only chance is to get Louis behind me. If I can't swing that, I'll have a shot. If not, I'll have to make a run for it.*

When alone with Gino's cousin Louis, Cosmo shared his concerns.

"I'm telling you, Louis, your cousin can't be trusted. The guy has it in for us both. I can feel it my bones that Gino is going to kill us both someday. We have to stick together and do something."

"I'm out of the woods," advised Louis. "Gino said that I was receiving a pass." Louis had no idea that Cosmo had previously attempted to place blame at his doorstep.

"Pass my ass! Wake up, will ya? He's keeping me around only to teach the new guy the ins and outs of the business he's stealing from me. And the son of a bitch wants my building to boot!"

"Maybe that's true for you, Cosmo, but I made peace with my cousin," insisted Louis.

"You really think so?"

"I do. Look, if my cousin wanted me dead, I'd be dead already."

"I'm telling you, Louis, you're kidding yourself. You know Gino as well as I do. Nobody gets a break with your cousin. It's down to him or us."

Cosmo's remark caused Louis to pause for a second before commenting. "I don't see it that way, Cosmo. I got nothing to worry about."

Seeing the calm demeanor of Louis opened Cosmo's eyes. He now realized that Louis just might have stabilized his alliance with his cousin. Ironically, Cosmo didn't realize how effective in influencing Louis he actually was. He had gotten Louis to begin thinking.

Maybe Cosmo's right about my not trusting my cousin, thought Louis. *I've never seen Gino forgive and forget. Maybe I do need to do something or go on the lam while the going is good.*

***

THAT SUNDAY COSMO was in the bedroom of his apartment packing when he heard his doorbell ring. At the front door of his apartment was Gino Pagnetta. This unexpected visit caused the florist to think the worst. Gino could see that something wasn't right with the florist.

"What's wrong?" asked Gino, sensing Cosmo's nervousness,

"Nothing, Gino, everything is great. Come on in," invited Cosmo. "I was just gonna make myself something to eat. Are you hungry?"

"Yeah, I'm hungry," replied the gangster coldly.

"What would you like to have?"

"I think that I'm gonna have your ass fried, Cosmo."

The florist froze upon digesting the remark made. Now he knew for sure that he had a serious problem.

"I don't understand, Gino, what did I do now? If it's about Davey Brazil, I couldn't be treating him better. He practically knows all there is to know about everything."

"I know, I spoke to Davey. He told me that you're a slow teacher and that he's got nothing more to know," replied the

172

mob capo coldly. "Did you honestly think you could get away with pulling more shit on me?"

"There must be some misunderstanding here...."

"SHUT YOUR TRAP!" thundered Gino, viciously slapping Cosmo across the face. The silenced Cosmo held the palm of his hand to his stinging reddened cheek.

"Gino, your acting crazy...."

"Shut your mouth, I said!" barked Gino, who was snarling. "You crossing me is the worst thing you ever did, my friend."

Cosmo looked away in apparent remorse. He then began shaking his head to further express his regret. "I'm sorry, Gino, let me explain the situation."

"I don't want explanations," communicated the angry mobster. His tone was such that it made his inflexibility clear.

"I don't know what to say...."

"Well, let me do the saying. Monday the lawyer is coming by with the papers. You're signing those papers, Cosmo. After that, I don't want to see you again."

"Where will I go? How do you expect me to live?"

"I don't care where you go or how you live. You're lucky that I'm letting you live at all." The glaring look reflected on Gino's face caused Cosmo to hush up. "Come Monday our business together will be settled. If you know what is good for you, you'll sign those papers and be prepared to move on after we settle up."

"Settle up what? You're taking by house and business."

"A little matter of cash you owe me."

"I thought the building and business covered everything, Gino."

"Not quite. After you sign your business and building over to Davey Brazil, we're gonna settle up moneywise. If you got a problem with that, I have a permanent alternative."

"How much do you want?"

"You come up with a number, and don't be stingy," instructed Gino, who intended to immediately murder Cosmo once he received the money.

"Whatever you say, Gino."

22

Catch Me If You Can

AFTER GINO PAGNETTA DEPARTED his apartment, a panicky Cosmo hurriedly resumed packing his things. Once finished, the Florist rushed from room to room to take a quick look to see if he had forgotten anything of importance. Quick movements, along with the stress he was under, caused his heart to beat at an accelerated rate. Finding the condition worrisome, Cosmo took a seat at the kitchen table.

As he waited to normalize, the florist looked around at his surroundings. An emptiness began to set in once it registered that life as he knew it had come to an end. He began to chain smoke cigarettes as he wallowed in despair.

Each worn-down cigarette was used to light up fresh one. Before long the ashtray in the table was riddled with ashes and butts. The smoky kitchen created a gothic-like atmosphere reminiscent of the smog in old horror movies. Cosmo began to feel nauseous as the tobacco odor became overwhelming.

Cosmo rose from his chair to pour himself a large glass of cold water. He then relocated to the living room where the air was slightly better. As he cooled his throat, he concentrated on trying to figure out a way to salvage his relationship with the man who banished him. This effort was to no avail. There was simply no way to mend a fence with the likes of Gino Pagnetta.

Pagnetta, first and foremost, was a heartless murderer without a scintilla of decency. Facing the facts squarely, Cosmo the Florist knew that he stood a better chance of getting nuked than receiving a pass from Gino.

I can't be on any dreamer's holiday, thought the florist. *Gino forgives nobody. He's gonna look to whack me, and that's that.*

Believing this to be the case, Cosmo rose to his feet. The brief rest he had taken allowed him to regroup. His worry was now replaced by a determination to survive.

The florist put on his overcoat and grabbed the suitcase he packed. Absconding was his only option. It was a way to save his life and prevent him from having to sign legal papers that would see him forfeit what was rightfully his.

"I ain't sticking around for that bastard to pluck me like a chicken and then kill me," announced Cosmo aloud, suddenly finding a confidence powerful enough to spark energy. "Screw him, let him try and find me!"

Cosmo gathered whatever cash and small valuables he had in his apartment. After filling his pockets to the tune of five thousand dollars in cash, two watches and three rings, he carried his suitcase to his parked car. After locking the suitcase in the car trunk, the florist returned to his building.

Cosmo made his way up to the roof. At the top of the interior ladder, and just beneath the roof hatch was a crawlspace filled with insulation. Hidden within the insulation was a black physician's bag containing four-hundred thousand dollars in United States Currency of varied denominations. Cosmo retrieved the bag and put it in the trunk of his car.

Just before driving off, Cosmo remembered that there was something in the florist shop that might come in handy. He entered the shop and took possession of one of the aluminum softball bats that were kept in the shop for protection. He thought of emptying the cash register. He then decided against doing that.

Let Louis and Davey come to work and find everything in order, Cosmo thought. *That'll buy me more time for a good head start.*

Once he was out of the Bronx, the florist stopped to have his car filled with gas. As the gasoline was being pumped, Cosmo began looking through a Rand McNally Road Atlas. The spiral bound book contained maps of every state in the country.

After filling up, Cosmo stopped by an all-night deli to purchase something to eat while driving. He also had a large black coffee to help keep him alert during his overnight journey. Cosmo's aim was to drive through the night in order to distance himself as far as possible from his trouble.

Cosmo, who was heading to Portland, Maine, listened to the news on the car radio as he traveled through the New England states. Having visited Portland once before, the florist recollected how beautiful the coastal paradise was with its active seaport.

Cosmo envisioned taking up residence in Portland, a venue far enough away to allay any concern of being recognized. He even had thoughts of perhaps opening a small business there.

Cosmo telephoned his Bronx florist shop a few minutes after it opened for business. The call was answered by Davey Brazil. Cosmo snickered as he heard the familiar twang in Davey's voice.

"It's me, Cosmo," said the absconder. "Is Louis around?"

"Yeah, hang on," replied Davey, "we just opened up."

"Who is it?" asked Louis, taking the phone from his co-worker.

"It's Cosmo, he wants to talk to you."

"What's up Cosmo?" Louis asked.

"I'm not feeling well this morning, Louis. You guys will have to handle things."

"You ain't coming downstairs to work?"

"No, that's why I'm calling. I got the flu so I'm staying in bed. I don't want to get everybody sick down there. I'm gonna take something to help me sleep."

"Do you need anything?"

"No, I'll call you if I do. I'm gonna go to bed."

Cosmo the Florist took a room in a small motel in Portland. It was while staying at the motel that he realized he left Esther's diary behind in his Bronx apartment. There was little he could do about that. Cosmo went on to trade in his vehicle at a used car dealership for a more modest vehicle that was sure not to draw any unwanted attention.

Cosmo next concentrated on emptying both his personal and business checking accounts. He wrote checks to himself and used the money to open an account in a Maine bank that had safety deposit boxes. He rented a box and placed the money from his physician's bag in it.

With his cash now safeguarded, Cosmo contacted the various investment houses that handled his financial accounts. He notified these concerns that he relocated. Since none of his former Bronx associates actually knew how much money he had or where his accounts were held, the florist felt that revealing his current location to the investment houses posed no threat.

The only wrinkle that Cosmo saw pertained to his florist business and property ownership. While the florist shop and building remained in Cosmo's ownership, he knew that he'd have to forfeit the rental income and florist shop revenue for an undetermined length of time.

Cosmo tried to remain optimistic, believing that one day he'd be able to emerge from the shadows to reclaim his business and rental property. He felt that someone of Gino Pagnetta's ilk wasn't destined for longevity. Cosmo saw it as inevitable that the day would come when the shifty Gino would miscue and end up murdered by his own kind. When that day finally came, Cosmo would return to the Bronx and take back what was rightfully his.

To speed up Gino's demise, the florist began thinking of who he could make an anonymous telephone call to. He intended to spread the rumor that Gino was an FBI informant.

Cosmo, to blend into the Portland community, took on a part time job in a funeral parlor. Once acclimated to a work routine, he thought it prudent to open a small florist shop that was in close proximity to a cemetery.

All things being considered, this was a sound decision. The work kept Cosmo busy, allowed him to meet some nice people and he made a few bucks. Portland proved to be a suitable place for Cosmo the Florist to chill out.

***

THE CHILDLESS GINO PAGNETTA WAS a selfish man with no desire for children. This was no mystery. All who knew him were aware that he always put himself first. Be it his home life or business interests, it was all about him.

At home Gino's wife catered to him. His business interests came with minions serving him. Gino was shameless in his belief that it was the duty of others to serve him. In fact, he saw it as an honor.

The mob capo's wife was responsible for keeping their house in order. She shopped, arranged for repairs, prepared Gino's meals, washed his clothes and even pressed his underwear and handkerchiefs. Having no independent access to Gino's money, she was on an allowance. Since it was a generous allotment, she voiced no complaints.

Gino was intentionally vague whenever his wife asked where he was going. If he was going to play handball with a crony, he'd just say, "To play handball," without giving a specific location or the identity of who he was meeting. Mostly, "out" was his reply to a question pertaining to where he was going.

In someways Gino's routine was a predictable one. Two nights a week, Tuesday and Friday, Gino spent with his mistress. Their time together often entailed dinner and socializing with mob friends in similar relationships. Inevitably, whatever they did, they ended up back at the girlfriend's apartment.

Saturday nights were reserved for Gino taking his wife out to dinner. It was always Mrs. Pagnetta at her husband's side when attending weddings or family occasions.

Gino began each day by devoting several minutes to stretching exercises. This activity wasn't for the purpose of alleviating back pain or some other physical ailment. Gino incorporated this into his schedule because he read someplace that this was a way to enhance height. This, shoe lifts and the special heels he had put on all of his shoes were supplements that made him feel better about himself.

Afternoons he'd play cards at the club. In fair weather he took to playing handball in a local schoolyard. Every so often Gino might be seen playing bocce ball with non-criminal senior citizens. These social outlets were used to heighten Gino's visibility as an everyday good citizen.

The organized crime capo believed receiving attention was very important. Gino was wise in realizing that there was value in the public being made aware of both his decent and dark side. Whispers of his questionable activities were the kind of publicity that made his word law on the street. Such talk served as a reminder that Gino was someone to be on the good side of.

Gino's positive image was enhanced by his charitable donations. Gifting turkeys to the poor on Thanksgiving, toys for orphaned children and paying for church improvements, went a long way with a forgiving public.

Monday morning Gino visited the florist shop to see how Davey Brazil was making out. He was glad to see that Brazil knew everything he needed to know.

"It looks like you're an old pro around here, Davey," commented Gino.

"Just about."

"How could that be?"

"I don't know, I just find the work easy."

"Is that true?" Gino asked, addressing his cousin Louis, who was standing nearby.

"Yeah, he's even making floral arrangements like an old pro," answered Louis.

"What do you think of this, Louis? Could Davey handle the whole shooting match all alone."

"Probably, Gino," replied the cousin.

He probably doesn't even need you, the crime capo thought. "Where is Cosmo hiding anyway?"

"He's upstairs in bed," advised Louis. "He's got the flu or something. Do you want me to go get him?"

"No, get him up when the lawyer gets here. He'll be coming late this afternoon. He's got some papers for Cosmo to sign. Davey, come outside with me for a minute."

Once they were alone together Gino informed Davey of the changes that were going to be made.

"Later today, this flower business and this building is being transferred under your name, Davey. Like I said, the lawyer will be coming over late this afternoon with the papers. It'll all be done legal."

"Are you sure you want to do that?"

"Yeah, it's better for me that way. Don't worry, Davey, like I promised, you'll be well taken care of."

"What about the gambling operation?"

"You'll be handling that too."

"What's Cosmo saying about this?"

"Cosmo has no say, he's out."

"Shouldn't Louis be the one, Gino. I mean, I don't want him pissed off at me."

"I got other plans for Louis. Besides, he ain't got the gray matter you got. So, you're the guy who will be running things around here from now on. Okay?"

"Sure, whatever you say, Gino."

"Good, now go back to work and give Louis his first order."

"What order is that?"

"Tell him to get outside and see me," answered Gino, adding, "and say it just like that."

Louis, knowing that he was still on thin ice, received the news of Davey's elevation stoically. Before dismissing Louis, Gino announced that the time had come to plant his dagger in one of Cosmo's monogrammed aprons.

"Did you get Cosmo's prints on the dagger, Louis?"

"Yeah, Gino, I did that right away."

"How did you pull that off?

"I told him that I was thinking of picking up a new one. I told him the blade looked bent. I asked him to examine it and see what he thought."

"What about your prints being on the dagger."

"It was clean when I gave it to him. I was wearing gloves. Around the flower business it ain't unusual to wear gloves half the time."

"You can be pretty cute when you want to be, Louis…. but don't you ever again get cute with me."

"I learned my lesson, Gino, so you don't have to worry about that. So, what happens now?"

"All you have to know, no matter who asks, is that the dagger always belonged to Cosmo."

"No problem."

An hour later, Louis telephoned his cousin to inform him that the dagger had been planted. Their conversation was brief.

"It's done, Gino."

"Did our friend ever come to work today?"

"No, Cosmo never came down. I called him but he didn't answer the phone."

"Maybe he's still sleeping. Go get him when the lawyer gets there."

When alone, Gino telephoned Sergeant Markie. He informed Markie where the dagger used in several murders could be found. He also said the dagger belonged to Cosmo the Florist."

"How did you find this out?" asked Markie.

"A little birdie told me, Sergeant."

"Are you sure Cosmo is the owner of the dagger?"

"Trust me, Sergeant, he man you're looking for is a guy by the name of Cosmo the Florist. He lives over his florist shop."

"Why would he want to kill those people?"

"You're gonna have to ask him, Sergeant."

"What about the gun that was used in the retired captain's killing?"

This was a question that Gino wanted no part of, because the gun used to murder Johnny Bronco belonged to him. "I got no idea about no gun," replied the mobster.

"How is it you found out about the dagger but not the gun?" questioned Markie.

"You asked about a knife, not a gun. I'll have to see if I can find out more," Gino fibbed. "At what point is our friendship going to be over, Sergeant?"

"Let me know what you find out," answered Markie, ignoring the question. "I'll talk to you."

"Wait a friggin' minute, what about my pending case?"

"Don't sweat it, if the dagger is where you say it is, your case is as good as gone."

***

MARKIE HAD VON HESS INFORM DETECTIVE KIRBY, the investigator who caught the Johnny Bronco homicide, that a break may be coming in the homicide of the captain. Kirby, who had almost forgotten about the case thanks to the involvement of Markie and Von Hess, provided Von Hess with interesting news of his own.

"Thanks for the update, Ollie," said Kirby. "I've been meaning to share something with you."

"What news is that?"

"I received the medical examiner's report. The knife used is definitely a Jagdkommando twisted tri-edge dagger," advised Kirby.

"How could they know that?"

"They were able to tell by the nature of the wound I guess."

"I know that they can determine the width of the blade, the length of the knife and the angle of the assault."

"This kind of knife has a twisted blade, Ollie."

"I suppose that would help make the knife more identifiable then," said Von Hess.

"Yeah," agreed Kirby, "if we come up with it. But it would be even better if we found the gun." The investigators agreed on that point.

23

Headquarters Huddle

WHEN CHIEF OF DETECTIVES HARRY MCCOY returned to work, he called his special squad into his office for a team meeting. He wanted to be updated on recent events that occurred during his absence. He sat behind his large desk waiting for his handpicked investigators to file into his office. The detectives quietly assumed their seats on either side of the long wooden table that pressed against the center of the chief's desk. The chief favored his furniture being in this t-shaped format because it left no doubt as to who the boss was.

To the chief's left sat Lieutenant Wright, who technically was the commanding officer of the chief's special squad. Next to Wright sat Sergeant Markie. Opposite the supervisors sat Detectives Silverlake and Von Hess. All, with the exception of Silverlake, were attired in a suit and tie. The tieless Silverlake wore a navy-blue sport jacket over a white polo shirt that was buttoned to the top.

Chief McCoy, believing that it was a superior's job to be critical, opened his meeting employing the sandwich theory. The technique called for first praising his underlings for all the good work they had been doing. This was to be followed by McCoy alluding to whatever shortcomings he detected in their performance. The chief would then conclude on a high note, thus sandwiching his criticism. He'd leave off conveying how proud he was of his staff and how confident he was in their ability to excel even further moving forward.

One topic that came up during the fault-finding segment was the chief's disappointment in his crackerjack team not yet solving the Johnny Bronco homicide.

"Bronco was one of us," reminded McCoy. "You men need to step things up and figure out who killed him. It's our duty to make it clear to people that an assault on one of us, is an assault on all."

"We've made some headway, Chief," piped up Lieutenant Wright.

"You did?"

"Fill the chief in, Al," said the lieutenant, passing the ball to Markie.

"We believe that we may have located the twisted tri-edge dagger that was used in killing the captain, Chief."

"Silvie, you told me Bronco was shot," commented McCoy, while looking at Detective Silverlake.

"I think I told you he was shot and stabbed, Chief."

"Whatever," said McCoy, not recollecting. He then turned to Markie. "This is good news, Sarge. So, you have the dagger?"

"No, not yet, Chief. We haven't retrieved it yet."

"Why not? What are you waiting for?"

"We are here, Chief."

"Go get the dagger!"

Markie and Von Hess rose from their seats and left the meeting. Remaining was the chief, the lieutenant and Detective Silverlake.

"How did they get a line on where the dagger is?" questioned the chief, addressing Lieutenant Wright.

"They got the tip from a snitch."

"You signed up a new informant?"

"Not exactly, Chief," said Wright, who went on to explain the

184

circumstances that led Gino Pagnetta to cooperate. "We got no formal agreement with Pagnetta."

"How come you didn't sign him up?"

"Pagnetta is a ranking member of the Long John Capezzo crime family, Chief. He'd never go on record with us. The case we have him on isn't strong enough for that. We're lucky Markie and Von Hess got him to help us at all."

"So why is he cooperating?"

"He doesn't want the headache of a court case I suppose."

"I see. And he's definitely a made man?"

"Definitely, Chief."

"He may have his own reasons," said the chief.

"I found several other homicides connected to a similar type of knife," reminded Silverlake, wanting to show his own value. The detective's information was met with enthusiasm by the chief.

"The police commissioner is going to love it if we solve them all," conveyed the chief, who was thinking down the road.

"I even saw a guy who works in the Bronx florist shop holding a similar dagger," piped up Silverlake, again wanting to highlight his contribution.

The chief listened quietly as Silverlake explained the details surrounding his remark. The detective added that he was scheduled to place a final bet at the florist shop prior to their executing the search warrant.

"You got all the paperwork squared away on this warrant?" asked McCoy.

"Yes, Chief," answered Silverlake, "we're locked and loaded."

"Lieutenant, do you have enough people to execute the warrant?"

"Markie made arrangements with the local precinct to provide back up. The precinct is giving us two and one." This translated into two uniformed officers and one uniformed sergeant.

"Good," said the chief. "Was there any difficulty getting those bets in, Silvie?"

"A little, Chief," fibbed Silverlake. "I had to dance a bit, but I got over."

"Just don't…." began the chief, who was then interrupted by a ringing phone. "Quiet, that's the commissioner's line," announced McCoy, who sprung to his feet and straightened out his suit jacket. He reacted to the call as if the police commissioner had just physically entered the room.

"Hello, Commissioner," greeted McCoy cheerfully.

Within seconds the chief's face took on a pained look. He began to hold the phone a couple of inches from his ear, making it obvious that he was getting a tongue lashing.

"I don't appreciate being embarrassed by YOU, or anybody else, Harry," thundered Police Commissioner John Randolph telephonically. "When I say to take care of something, I don't expect to be disregarded!"

"I'm sorry, Commissioner, but I don't understand."

"You don't understand? Then maybe I have the wrong guy sitting in that cushy office I put you in!"

"What happened?"

"I'll tell you what happened! That contract over the missing girl at the Performance Club was never honored."

"I put my best people on that."

"Well, your best people apparently did squat."

Chief McCoy shifted his eyes to glare at the lieutenant seated at the table before him. "Let me find out what happened, Chief. Can I call you back?"

"You do that, Harry, and get back to me right away. I have to go back to a lawyer with some kind of a story."

Once off the phone Chief McCoy turned to Wright for answers. "How come you didn't do something about that missing girl at the Performance Club?"

"You were away, Chief," answered Lieutenant Wright.

"So, the world stops because I was away?" The chief then turned to Silverlake. "You know anything about this, Silvie?"

"Markie and Von Hess were on top of it, Chief, as far as I know. They wanted to head out to Dutchess County, on that case, but had to wait."

"Wait for what?"

"There was no one around here to give them the okay to travel beyond the city limits, you were off."

"There was nothing else they could have done to further things?" questioned Chief McCoy.

"I think they've been bouncing back and forth between the receptionist case and the captain's homicide, Chief."

"Look, I don't want you making excuses for them," said the chief. He then turned to address Wright. "This is important to the commissioner. I want you to go find that missing girl. It's the priority now."

"What about the warrant?"

"That'll keep. Right now, I want you to go find the girl."

"Then we have your authorization to send Markie and Von Hess up to Dutchess County, Chief?"

"I don't care if you send them to the moon, just come up with that girl."

Just like that, recovering the dagger was placed on the back burner.

24

Bloodhound
Bloodbath

ENZO BAFFI STOPPED TO WATCH A COMMERICAL being filmed on a street not far from his Manhattan penthouse. He took notice of a young actor appearing in the commercial. He wasn't a handsome man in the traditional sense, but there was a unique sensitivity about him that Baffi thought might click with movie viewers. The producer envisioned a place for the sandy-haired, slight built twenty-six-year-old among the battery of talented actors he gave work to. He specifically thought the man might be a good fit in the role of an introverted neighbor in a movie production he was considering.

Baffi hung around observing the shoot until he had an opportunity to introduce himself. The producer explained that he wanted to discuss a movie role with him. In this Baffi was being truthful.

Thrilled to have met such an industry bigwig, the actor readily accepted the producer's invitation to join him for dinner that evening. The actor, who was under the wrong impression, took a step closer to Baffi. Having his space invaded caused the producer to make it clear that the purpose of their getting together was purely professional.

The two men met for dinner at Benito's on Mulberry Street in Manhattan's Little Italy. After some wine the young actor grew comfortable enough to reveal himself as opinionated to a point of obnoxiousness. His weighty outlook on current events, while perhaps welcomed in some circles, fell flat with Baffi.

The guest for dinner undermined whatever chance he had with the producer when the talk turned purely political. This aspect of their conversation was an omen that suggested the young actor would be, if taken on, complicated to work with.

Realizing that he made a mistake in his selection of talent, the producer endeavored to fast forward dinner by skipping dessert and coffee. What really irked the producer came at the conclusion of their meal. The young actor instructed the waiter that he wanted to take home the leftover pasta to feed his poodle, Princess. Baffi, who had a distinct dislike for canines, cringed.

"Taking home food is rather common," voiced the elitist Baffi, unable to avoid taking a swipe at his guest. The producer's display of snobbery didn't go unanswered.

"We proletariats never let good food go to waste," said the guest, bucking his host. "Princess thanks you."

"Your dog likes pasta?"

"Why, of course. I don't believe in restricting Princess to dry foods. She deserves better."

"Yes, of course she does," agreed Baffi, putting forth a false front.

At this juncture the connection between the two men was clearly a mixture akin to oil and water. Baffi now disliked the young actor more than dogs.

"I'm glad you think so too, Enzo. I was starting to worry that you disliked animals."

"Not at all, my friend," answered the producer, who secretly took offense at being addressed with such familiarity.

"If you ever need a dog in any of your movies, consider using Princess. She's wonderfully intelligent."

"I will," stated Baffi, who was secretly thinking of how he hated his Dutchess County neighbor's howling hound. The producer became consumed in nasty thoughts of what he'd like to do to both dogs. He was so immersed in foulness that he failed to follow the conversation he was engaged in.

"Didn't you hear me?"

"What was it that you said?" asked the producer, snapping out of his far away evil thoughts.

"I asked if you would like to meet Princess?"

"Perhaps that could be arranged. Why don't we plan on you reading for my director at my estate in Dutchess County, you can bring Princess along."

"Why that would be wonderful!" said the dinner guest. "You are going to love Princess. She is always there anxiously awaiting my return home. Sometimes the excitement in seeing me results in her urinating on the floor," said the young actor with a chuckle.

*Now isn't that a lovely though*t," thought the producer. *This imbecile probably squats and tinkles alongside her.*

"Princess must love you dearly," voiced Baffi, making nice. "I'm curious about something, does the barking of Princess bother your neighbors?"

"No one has ever complained to me."

Baffi looked at his dinner guest closely as the call from his Dutchess County incinerator rang in his ears.

"You must have very tolerant neighbors."

"Not really. I mean, who in the city complains about a dog barking?"

"Yes, indeed. So, let's finalize things, my friend. You'll read for my director in Dutchess County, and if you meet with his approval, I'll make you an offer to participate in the project we intend to work on. This could be an opportunity that may be of great benefit to your career."

"I have no car, what's the best way for me to get there with Princess?"

"Oh," thought the producer. "I suppose I'll have to drive you. Let's plan on next week sometime."

***

WHEN THEY WERE A SHORT distance from Enzo Baffi's Dutchess County abode, Princess began barking. It was the dog's way of notifying her owner that she needed to relieve herself.

"What's wrong with your dog?" asked the producer, who's ears were ringing. Being confined in the car magnified the noise being made by Princess.

"Princess has to go."

"Tell Princess, we'll be there in a minute."

Jumping out of Enzo Baffi's car, Princess began arduously sniffing the ground in front of the producer's Dutchess County log cabin. Baffi looked at the dog curiously, unsure of what the animal was hunting for. The mystery unraveled once Princess began chasing her tail. After four quick circles, the animal squatted and began taking short steps while her droppings fell to the ground.

Seeing his property soiled caused the producer to crunch his mouth. Saying nothing, he forced a smile to cloak his displeasure. Baffi escorted the owner of the dog into the house. Once the cabin door closed, Baffi began to experience the sensation that came with taking a life.

"You forgot Princess," reminded the dog owner.

"Oh, yes, I'll let her in. Help yourself to a drink," said the producer pointing to his portable bar, "pour yourself a cognac, while I feed Princess."

"Feed her what?"

"I have spaghetti and meatballs in the fridge. I'll heat it up. Princess will love the sauce."

"You remembered what Princess liked!"

"Why of course."

As the young actor poured the cognac, Enzo Baffi went to the kitchen where he warmed the bowl containing food that he riddled with a toxic poison.

"Here you go, Princess," said the producer happily, placing the bowl on the floor. He then turned to address the young actor. "Pour yourself another. The director won't be here for hours."

The producer watched with a crooked smile as his guest rose from his chair to get his drink. Baffi then looked over at Princess as the canine gobbled up the doctored food. Seeing that the hound was occupied, the producer quietly snuck up behind his victim. Baffi removed the scarf from around his neck and looped it around the neck of the slight man he knew he could easily overpower.

As he was being strangled, the actor tried to jam his fingers behind the scarf that was choking him. It was to no avail. Once he lost consciousness, the producer let his victim slip to the floor. He then removed duct tape from a desk drawer. Baffi went on to tie the actor up with duct tape and seal his mouth with it.

By the time Princess was aware of her master's need for help, the dying animal was too weak to engage in a rescue attempt. Princess lapsed into a state of unconsciousness. Soon after, the dog's legs and snout were bound with duct tape.

With this done, the gratified Baffi relaxed and poured himself a drink. Afterward, he closed his eyes to take a nap. He had plenty of time. It was hours before he intended to incinerate the dog and her master.

When he awakened the producer made himself a hot cocoa. With mug in hand, he went to his bookcase to find something to read. He selected *The Picture of Dorian Gray* by Oscar Wilde. Finding the novel a fascinating tale, he began imagining himself as Dorian, a vain man with fading looks that has the ability to live on and on. Wilde's reading made the time pass quickly.

At the designated hour, Baffi donned his coat. Once again, his perverted desires were triggered at the thought of what he was going to do. Armed with a flashlight, Baffi firmly took hold of the young actor by his clothing. He dragged the body into the darkness, stopping at the outdoor incinerator located behind the cabin.

After disposing of his victim, the producer, having climaxed, returned to the cabin to fetch the hound, who was similarly treated. Baffi then returned to the cabin, showered and put on his pajamas. He poured himself a nightcap and had a bite to eat prior to turning in.

The producer's sleep was disturbed by the howling of his neighbor's dog. The barking coming from across the road was an annoyance that Baffi found impossible to ignore. Disgusted, he put on his shoes, scarf and overcoat.

Having reached his breaking point, the producer walked to the hearth and removed one of the two antique swords that were on display over the fireplace. Armed with the sword, flashlight and what was left of the remaining lethal spaghetti, Baffi went out in search of the disruptive canine from the other side of the road.

"PSST!" the producer hissed loudly as he stood in the road outside his neighbor's property line. "PSST!"

The neighbor's dog, a golden-brown bloodhound, was given much latitude by its owners. Day or night the dog was free to wander the property. Not venturing onto the roadway in front of the property was the only restriction placed on the highly trained animal.

Responding to the throaty whisper in the night, the bloodhound traveled in the direction where the whispers were coming from. When the dog reached the roadway, he was faced with the temptation posed by the waiting bowl of spaghetti that rested on the ground at the edge of the property line.

When the bloodhound spotted Baffi, the dog began to growl. Alarmed, Baffi retreated, distancing himself from the food. The bloodhound, now satisfied, ceased its fussing and proceeded to put his snout into the macaroni and gravy. After his sniffing was met with satisfaction, the dog began chomping away in earnest.

The producer waited patiently for the hound to show signs that the poison was taking hold. When it became obvious that the dog was faltering, Baffi approached the animal. As he crept forward, the producer drew the vintage sword he held behind his back. He swiftly slammed the blade down across the back of the canine's neck. The squeal of pain echoed in the night. Baffi quickly shoved the antique sword into the animal to silence him.

The producer withdrew the sword and picked up what was left of the macaroni. He then returned to his log cabin with the remaining food, which he went on to place in a green garbage bag.

Baffi meticulously cleaned the sword that was once used by Basil Rathbone when dueling Tyrone Power in the 1940 movie, *The Mark of Zorro*. Once the weapon was pristine, he returned it to its proper home over the fireplace.

Now wide awake, Baffi decided to dress and return to his Manhattan penthouse. For added weight, the producer filled the green garbage bag containing the tainted food with two bricks. On his way to Manhattan, he stopped to dispose of the bag in a body of water.

***

IT WAS 6:30 A.M. WHEN WILLIS P. OVERDEAU, a university political science professor, got around to wondering where the family dog was. The professor and the bloodhound were in the habit of breakfasting together each morning. Not having his hungry pet underfoot was indeed unusual.

After preparing his food, Overdeau sat down to have his breakfast. He was confident that the dog would appear shortly. When this didn't happen, he decided to look for the bloodhound after finishing his oatmeal and English muffin.

Overdeau donned his coat and conducted a search of the grounds. Not finding the dog led him to scour the house. When this also netted no positive results, the professor thought that the bloodhound may have wandered off his property. He again went outside in search of the dog.

Professor Overdeau was aghast at the sight of his discovery on the road. At first the gory scene led the professor to think that his pet was struck by a motor vehicle. A closer inspection of the bloodhound's injuries made it clear that the cause of death was something far worse.

Believing that a slasher was responsible for the cutting wounds inflicted on the bloodhound, the bewhiskered professor felt personally threatened. He instinctively placed his hand to his throat, his neck fitting between his index finger and thumb. He backed up a couple of steps before suddenly turning around and scurrying back to the house to inform his wife of what had occurred.

The out of breath professor entered his bedroom and proceeded to abruptly shake his wife, a successful author of a dozen novels.

"Beverly, wake up!" he shouted.

The startled spouse jumped up from a sound sleep thinking her home was on fire. When the author realized there was no fire, she didn't know what to think based on the distressed face of her white bearded husband.

"What's wrong, Willis?" she asked.

"Do you know what happened?" questioned the professor.

"How could I possibly know what happened?"

"When did you last see the dog?"

After a series of questions were exchanged, the couple jointly concluded that they were being targeted by some unhinged lunatic. They summoned the authorities.

The responding member of law enforcement interviewed the couple for purposes of preparing a police report. After the scene was examined, arrangements were made to remove the slain bloodhound from the road.

When bluntly informed that without a witness little could be done to determine who killed their dog, the couple reacted by vehemently voicing their dissatisfaction.

"Are you telling us that no detective is going to investigate this?" questioned Mrs. Overdeau.

"Do you find that acceptable?" queried the professor, supporting his wife. "What are we paying taxes for?"

I got a couple of letter writers here! Thought the law enforcement officer after listening to the couple.

The professor, a fleshy man of sizeable proportions, asked the officer if there had been similar incidents in the area. When told that there had been no other animal attacks reported, Professor Overdeau began stroking his long white beard before posing his next question.

"Can't you see the distinct possibility that my wife and I are being targeted by some maniac?"

"Anything is possible, sir," replied the officer.

"Well doesn't that warrant further investigation?"

"That's not my call. All I can do is submit my report." This answer did little to appease the husband and wife.

At this point the couple collectively put forth a series of additional questions to the officer. The professor and the author both liked to ask a lot of questions. It played into their belief that important people needed to have a voice.

In response to the pushback, the law enforcement officer thought it wise to give the squeaky wheels a little oil. He assured the couple that he would bring the incident to the attention of his superiors, adding that someone would be contacting them once he turned in his report.

Others from law enforcement followed up later that morning. By the afternoon the professor and his wife learned that their dog was poisoned, along with being viciously stabbed.

***

MARKIE AND VON HESS arrived at the Dutchess County log cabin of Enzo Baffi very late in the afternoon. They were disappointed to find that no one was at home. With the houses in the area spaced so far apart, a canvass seemed likely to be an unproductive undertaking.

A visual inspection of the grounds in front of the cabin provided the sleuths with some indication of activity. The trash pail awaiting pick up contained the remains of items that suggested that someone had been recently staying at the house. The mailbox was empty and fresh tire marks were evident.

Von Hess tried the front door and found it to be secure. He took a step back and admired the magnificence of the two-tier log cabin. They then circled the cabin and found that there was an unlocked back door to the premises.

"This back door is open, Sarge," informed the detective.

"I'm not surprised, Ollie. We're out in the sticks up here, so who's gonna be looking to burglarize the joint?"

"Yeah, I suppose. That looks like an incinerator in the back of the house. I wonder what that's there for."

"We'll have to ask Baffi that question when we catch up with him. Let's grab something to eat. We'll come back after dinner and see if anyone is here."

When Von Hess pulled out onto the road Markie noticed a man puttering around the front of the property opposite the log cabin. He was wearing boots, black jeans and a red flannel shirt beneath his sleeveless beige down vest. Most striking about him was his long hair and profuse white beard that came down to his chest.

"Let's go talk to Santa Claus, Ollie," said Markie.

Von Hess neared Professor Overdeau with his shield in his hand. "We're NYPD detectives, can we have a word with you?"

"Are you here about my dog?"

"No sir, we're trying to locate someone."

"Are you aware of what happened to my dog?"

"No, what happened to your dog?"

"Didn't anyone tell you that some madman poisoned and stabbed my dog and left him on the road?" queried the professor. "Can you believe that someone could do such a thing?"

"That's terrible," replied Von Hess, who was fond of animals.

"Why do you think…." began the professor, who was then abruptly interrupted by the sergeant.

"Let's get to the point, Ollie," said Markie. "Show him the picture."

Von Hess removed from his coat pocket the photo of Juliana Swain, the Performance Club receptionist. He then handed it over to Overdeau for examination.

"Have you ever seen this woman around here?" Von Hess asked.

The professor studied the photo for a few seconds before responding. "No, who is she?"

"Just someone we're looking for."

"Have you ever come across a man named Pascal around here? Markie asked."

"No, do you have a photo of him?"

"No, just a first name."

"Are these people supposed to be around here? Are they wanted?"

"They may be friends of your neighbor across the way," said Markie.

"Oh, you mean the man in the log cabin?" asked the professor, his negativity evident.

"You've had problems with him?"

"Why wouldn't I?"

"What do you mean?"

"Can you imagine that he had the nerve to complain about my dog barking?"

"It happens."

"Do you think that he could have killed my dog?"

"I don't really know. Did he seem like the type capable of such a thing?" asked Von Hess. "After all, he is a professional man."

"You don't think a professional man could kill a dog?"

Markie glanced at Von Hess before speaking. "All dogs bark, your neighbor should understand that," said the sergeant, making it sound as if he was siding with the professor.

The professor returned the photo of Juliana Swain that was handed to him.

"Tell us about the words you had with him over the dog," asked Von Hess.

"It was over barking, I mean, what dogs don't bark?"

"Were threats made?"

"No, I can't really say that, but wasn't his attitude enough? And what about the strange doings across the road."

"Can you be a little more specific?"

"Who has an incinerator blasting in the middle of the night?"

"Have you any idea of what he is burning?" questioned Markie.

"How would I know?"

"Does he live in the log cabin alone or does he have guests up for a visit?"

"I've seen him drive onto his property with a guest on occasion."

Markie was glad to finally get a straight answer to a question without receiving one in return.

"Men or women?"

"Both. We have never seen him pull into the driveway with more than one man or woman."

"Did he entertain often?"

"What kind of big entertaining could there be with only one other person?"

"How long does his guest usually stay for?" asked Markie.

"Who can tell when he always leaves alone?

A stern look came over Von Hess and the sergeant as they began to ponder what this information could mean.

Von Hess asked the final question. "Has he ever used that incinerator when he doesn't have company?"

Professor Overdeau stroked his beard for a second and hunched his shoulders. "My wife is a novelist and works from home, do you want to go in the house and speak to her?"

When the men arrived at the house they found the professor's wife diligently at work on her latest novel. The author was a woman of average size, attired in a purple sweatshirt with rolled up sleeves that revealed a tiny tattoo of a green whale on her thin forearm. The significance of the whale was lost on the detectives. Mrs. Overdeau's jeans were faded blue, with a slight hole at one knee. Her grayish-blond hair was worn very short.

The author was leaning forward in her chair while feverishly pounding away on the keyboard of her computer. It was obvious that her concentration was all absorbing. Her upper teeth, which were rabbit-like, were locked down on her lower lip. She never noticed that visitors had entered the room.

"Honey," her husband softly called out. "Do you have a minute?"

Surprised, the startled author jumped. When apprised of the

reasons behind the intrusion, she readily agreed to answer questions. Her responses pertaining to the neighbor across the road echoed the account offered by her husband. Beverly stated that she never heard the neighbor's incinerator going during the daylight hours. When asked how she could be so sure of this, her reply came quickly.

"How could I miss the stench, noise and smoke generated by that incinerator? I've never experienced that during the daytime, only later at night if I happen to be writing. As a rule, that's my most creative time."

"I see," said Markie, glancing at Von Hess.

At this point the investigators thanked the couple for their cooperation. Von Hess gained points with the Dutchess County duo when he promised that he would remain on the alert for the existence of any potential dog killers in the area.

25

Poop And Snoop

INSPIRED AFTER SPEAKING TO MR. & MRS. OVERDEAU, Markie decided to put off getting something to eat. He and Von Hess crossed the road for a return visit to Enzo Baffi's log cabin for a closer inspection. As the sergeant approached the dwelling he did so while looking upward at the second tier of the cabin. This took his focus off where he was walking.

Unexpectedly, Markie's foot slid forward, almost causing him to topple over. Upon regaining his balance, he immediately realized what he had stepped in. The foul odor left no doubt in his mind. He looked down at his feet with dismay.

"Damn it!" said the angered Markie, as he walked to a tree that just a few feet away.

"What happened, Sarge?" queried Von Hess.

"I stepped in dog shit."

"I guess they don't use pooper scoopers way out here," commented Von Hess. "You know what they say, stepping in it brings you good luck."

Markie began vigorously scrapping the bottom of his shoe against the tree. Satisfied that he did the best he could, he turned to Von Hess. "C'mon, Ollie, let's go around to the back and take a look see."

The detectives noticed nothing on the grounds that would indicate the presence of the missing receptionist.

"I can't get over the size of these windows, Sarge," said Von Hess. "They are huge."

Markie nodded in agreement as he pointed to the rear door of the cabin. As before, the door was found to be unlocked. The detectives looked at each other and shrugged.

"There might be burglar's inside, Sarge," said Von Hess, offering an excuse to enter the premises.

"It's our duty to check, Ollie," voiced Markie, conveying his agreement.

The detectives entered the log cabin. They were awestruck by the impressive interior.

"Wow!" exclaimed Markie. "Now this joint is something. It must have set Baffi back a bundle."

The massive stone fireplace, cowhide rug and timeless furniture were things the investigator had only previously seen in magazines while waiting in a professional office. Particularly magnificent was the double staircase that led to the second floor.

Markie noticed that two antique swords were hanging over the fireplace. On the mantlepiece beneath the weapons was a large marble paperweight with a square yellow metal plate affixed to it. The sergeant took a couple of steps closer to read what was printed on the plate. It reflected a brief history of the two swords.

Finding the weapons of interest, the sergeant removed one of the swords from the wall for a closer examination. His visual inspection made him curious. He returned the sword and then closely examined the second sword. After having seen enough, Markie returned the second weapon to its proper location over the fireplace. Markie then called out to Von Hess, indicating that the detective should join him by the fireplace.

"Take a gander at these swords, Ollie."

"What about them?" asked Von Hess, who from afar, saw nothing out of the ordinary.

"Take a closer look. One of them is clean as a hound's tooth," advised Markie, "and the other has been neglected."

"That's weird," acknowledged Von Hess. "Why would a person go through the trouble of buffing up one sword and not bother with the other?"

"Take a guess."

"I think I see what you mean, Sarge. If you're thinking about that dead dog across the road, we're on the same page."

"We may be on to something. Let's go look around upstairs."

The master bedroom, equipped with a full bath, was found to be expensively furnished. The other bedrooms, although smaller, were also impressive. One room on the upper floor was found to be locked.

"See if you could open the door without damaging anything," said Markie.

Von Hess took out a credit card to successfully slip the lock. Upon entering the room, the detectives were thrown off guard by what they saw. They had never seen anything up close like the dungeon in the sky Enzo Baffi crafted for himself.

"Jeeze, this is the kind of thing you see in a Bela Lugosi movie," declared Markie. "This Baffi must be a regular Count Alucard," declared the sergeant, ever the old movie buff.

"Who is Count Alucard again, Sarge?"

"Alucard is Dracula spelled backward," informed the sergeant, referring to author Bram Stoker's fictional vampire. "If you had watched enough of those old monster movies like I did growing up, you'd know that."

"You're right, Sarge, I neglected my education."

When they finished going through the dungeon, the detectives returned to the first floor. Once downstairs, Von Hess happened to notice an earring on the floor in the corner of the kitchen.

"Hey, Sarge," called out the detective. "Come and take a look at this."

"What have you got?" Markie asked, responding to the shout out.

"It's a heart shaped emerald earring, just like the one described by the mother of the missing receptionist. Look, it's even got the gold siding."

"Let me see that, Ollie."

After examining the earring, Markie had Von Hess fetch the binoculars from the car. The sergeant placed the earring where it was partially hidden yet could be seen from the yard through a window.

When Von Hess returned with the binoculars, Markie was standing outside the back of the cabin. Using the high-powered glasses, he peered through the window to see if the earring could be clearly seen. Once satisfied, the sergeant had Von Hess shut off the cabin lights.

The two sleuths then returned to Manhattan satisfied that they had performed a good day of work. The investigators, being old school, felt that detectives had to take whatever advantage they were afforded when in pursuit of criminals. Their justifications came with the belief that they were doing God's work.

The next step in the inquiry came the following day, when the investigative team went to see the mother of the missing Performance Club receptionist.

***

ENZO BAFFI WAS UNPREPARED FOR the stormy weather he encountered during his flight to California. The bumps that came with the extreme turbulence made no exceptions for those flying first class. So unsettling was Baffi's journey that his stomach was in knots.

The sight of nervous airline crew members fastening their seatbelts only made matters worse. It was at this time that Baffi began to wish that he had paid closer attention to the safety lecture given at the onset of the trip.

Fearing that he was on a doomed flight, the producer began praying to a God he hadn't worshipped in many years. Once repentance was behind him, the frightened passenger closed his eyes in an effort to sleep through his transition to the other side.

Unable to sleep, the producer resumed praying. Once the plane got beyond the bad weather conditions, the producer regrouped mentally. Forgotten were his promises of living a wholesome existence if spared. After ordering a cocktail, Baffi began dwelling on the forbidden earthly things that mattered most to him.

***

JULIANA SWAIN'S MOTHER was sitting alone in the kitchen of her apartment. As she stirred her coffee, she stared at the mouse trap that jutted out beneath her stove. Unable to catch the elusive rodent for days, she had to give the mouse credit for avoiding the temptation of the peanut butter she left on the trap.

He's a smart one, she thought, wondering where the elusive mouse might be.

The mouse was a diversion that temporarily took her mind off her troubles. When her interest in the mouse passed, Mrs. Swain circled back to the woe she felt over her missing daughter, who was also nowhere to be seen.

The worry over the missing Juliana came with sleepless nights, causing the mother to fail terribly in appearance.

When the doorbell rang to her apartment, Mrs. Swain rose from her chair slowly. Attired in a weathered house coat, she cared little about how she looked. Even her unkempt hair was of no consequence to Mrs. Swain. She approached the front door listlessly, dragging her feet.

The mother's heart jumped at the sight of Markie and Von Hess standing before her. A fear now consumed her as to the purpose of visiting detectives. *They're going to tell me Juliana's dead*, she thought, as tears began their descent down her cheeks.

Von Hess picked up on what Mrs. Swain was thinking. "We believe we have a lead as to where your daughter may have been, Ma'am," said the detective, trying to put a positive spin on things.

"You found her?" asked the excited mother hopefully.

"Not exactly, Ma'am."

"What then?"

Von Hess advised Mrs. Swain that she needed to accompany them to Dutchess County. When she questioned why, the detective explained that he needed her to look at something.

"You did find her!"

"Not yet, Ma-am, we're still trying to locate her. But for right now, we do need you to take that ride with us."

When they arrived at the log cabin the detectives were glad to see that there were no vehicles parked on Baffi's property. The detectives escorted Mrs. Swain to the back of the cabin. Von Hess was carrying his binoculars.

"Mrs. Swain please look through the window," instructed Von Hess. "Do you see anything on the floor?"

"Yes."

"Do you recognize it."

"It looks like a piece of jewelry, but I'm too far away to tell for sure."

"Let her have the binoculars, Ollie."

"It looks like my daughter's earring!" exclaimed the mother excitedly, as she looked through the high-powered glasses.

"Are you sure?" asked Markie.

"Yes, I'm sure. Its heart shaped and had gold all around it. What's it doing here?"

"That's something we need to find out," said Markie.

"What are you going to do?"

"We have more investigating to do, Ma'am. We'll take you home now. Ollie, take Mrs. Swain to the car."

When Von Hess removed the receptionist's mother from the area, Markie entered the log cabin through the open rear door. At this point he needed to figure out a way to prevent the earring, which was potential evidence, from being confiscated by Baffi or someone else, before he had a chance to gain legal authorization to enter the log cabin.

A solution came to the sergeant after seeing a roll of tape atop the kitchen counter. Markie taped the earring to the rear of the toilet bowl in the bathroom. He then joined Von Hess and Mrs. Swain. During the drive to the Bronx, Markie apprised the receptionist's mother of whatever information he could share.

"What do we do about that earring, Sarge?" asked Von Hess, once the mother was out of the car.

"I taped it behind the toilet bowl on the first floor. We'll reclaim it whenever we can get a warrant to search the place."

"What do we do now?"

"I think we should go find this producer."

"You want to confront him about the earring?"

"No, not yet. For now, I just want to size him up. We'll go in questioning him about Fishnet. That shouldn't raise any concerns if we make it seem that we're only concerned in finding out why Fishnet hung himself."

"And what do we do after that?"

"I figure that we're going to have to put a tail on him."

***

ENZO BAFFI WAS ANXIOUS TO return to his family on the west coast. He found that distancing himself from the atrocities he committed in New York helped ease his conscience. The presence of his wife and children kept him too occupied to dwell on his wicked ways.

Baffi recognized his deviance for what it was. However, not being one to deny himself anything when it came to self-gratification, the producer had no intention of curtailing his aberrant behavior. The only limitation he placed on himself was restricting his foul activities to New York, a venue in which he believed everything went.

Upon Baffi's return to California he learned that his wife accepted an invitation for them to attend a cocktail party at the home of a prominent west coast friend. The friend was a well-known Hollywood agent who was always pursuing opportunities for the talent he represented. Such outings were occasions that

Baffi's wife looked forward to. Part of the event's appeal was her being afforded the opportunity to dangle carrots in front of the favor seekers who sucked up to her.

The jewelry Mrs. Baffi wore at social gatherings was specifically selected for their attention-grabbing value. The smiles she displayed reflected what seemed to be amusement, rather than an actual happiness in seeing someone.

A woman of humble origin with much ambition, the producer's wife attained the prominence she enjoyed thanks primarily to her own ability and drive. Her status as the wife of Enzo Baffi, while helpful, was only a starting point. Baffi's spouse emerged from the shadow of her husband to become a power in her own right.

Through clever manipulation and access to her husband's money, Mrs. Baffi managed to build a real estate portfolio consisting of many commercial properties. She also came to be a controlling stockholder in an IT concern.

In building her own success the producer's wife saw a benefit in fabricating her history. She claimed that her mother was the first cousin of the American born British socialite, Lady Randolph Spencer-Churchill, the mother of the onetime British Prime Minister, Sir Winston Churchill. So ingrained in her mind was this fallacy that she probably could have taken a lie detector test and passed it.

Mrs. Baffi also made it a point to tell people that she was raised and educated in England. To add credibility to this she mastered speaking with an English accent, giving people little reason to challenge her claim.

In actuality Mrs. Baffi hailed from Avenue A on Manhattan's lower east side. A onetime aspiring actress, she was the daughter of a junk dealer and seamstress. She came to meet Enzo Baffi while working as a hostess in an upscale restaurant. At the time Baffi, who was substantially older, was involved in a movie that called for someone serving in that capacity. As a result of the producer hiring her for the part, a romance developed that led to marriage.

On the night of the cocktail party in question Mrs. Baffi positioned herself strategically in the room and waited for people to approach her. She purported herself as if she were a queen, holding gifts to be distributed sparingly. Enzo Baffi on the other hand moved about, mingling among the guests.

The producer was interested in a well-known gossip columnist, who worked at a major newspaper. He viewed the columnist with mixed emotions. On the one hand he found Lucille A. DeCoursey attractive enough to be worthy of romance. On the other, since she recently penned something highly unflattering about him in her *Lucy's Little Corner* column, Baffi felt a need to fire back. For the producer, return fire translated into his enjoying a sexual romp followed by incineration.

DeCoursey had written that a certain high-powered producer with the initials E.B. fancied golden showers. This was something that the producer could never forgive or forget. After having a second dry martini the producer approached the scandalmonger with the charm he was noted for.

"How are you, my dear?" asked Baffi warmly.

"I'm feeling fine, Enzo," replied the surprised DeCoursey, who hadn't expected such a civil greeting.

"You look marvelous, my dear."

"Do I?" DeCoursey asked. She was taken aback at the producer's kind remark. "How nice of you to say so."

"Are you genuinely surprised at my complimenting you."

"Well, I had heard through the grapevine that you were angry at me."

"Nonsense, my dear, you were just doing your job."

"I'm surprised to hear you say that."

"Allow me to prove my good will toward you, my dear. How would you like to meet someone who can provide you with juicy details concerning the spouse of a billionaire, who discreetly slips under the table to pleasure a talk show host whenever they dine in New York's Little Italy?"

"I'd just love it! Who are you talking about?"

"Or perhaps you'd care to hear my friend tell of the academy award recipient who hosts drug fueled orgies at his home in the Hamptons?"

Not knowing those involved in such naughtiness caused DeCoursey to begin twitching her nose in anticipation of learning more. "You simply must tell me who this person is I'm to meet."

"You'll have to come to New York for the answer to that. I assure you that the trip will be worth it, my dear. I'm heading back in a few days."

"That's no problem."

"But I must insist that we remain discreet. My involvement in this must be strictly cloaked, and kept between us. You understand, I hope."

"My lips are sealed," DeCoursey replied.

"Notify my office when you will be arriving in New York. My assistant Rochelle will make all the arrangements for you to be picked up at the airport."

"I thought you wanted secrecy…."

"I do, but that doesn't apply to Rochelle."

"You must have a lot of trust in her."

"I'd trust Rochelle with my life."

"Really?" asked the columnist, who smelled a tidbit for her column. "That says a lot."

"It does."

"What makes her so trustworthy?"

"She doesn't work for a newspaper."

26

The Ice Lady

ON THE SURFACE ROCHELLE PARRISH was a no-nonsense professional who would have exceeded the expectations of any employer. She found a home as the personal assistant/private secretary for Enzo Baffi, who greatly appreciated her. For a man like Baffi, finding someone he could trust was no simple task. He knew what he had in Rochelle and treated her well in order to hang on to her.

Parrish exemplified the corporate image. She was poised, impeccably attired and expressed herself articulately when engaging in face-to-face interactions. Her telephonic skills were also superb.

The devotion of Parrish, who worked for the producer for over a decade, was unwavering. Rochelle's allegiance to Baffi exceeded the norm. She became so entrenched in her position that she often made decisions for Baffi without prior consultation.

A decisive woman who was not above abruptness, Parrish served as an effective barrier to get beyond for those seeking an audience with the producer. Her efficiency in dismissing poor fits was well established. Her earnestness in insulating her boss garnered her the reputation of being something of an ice lady.

Working in such a capacity for Enzo Baffi came with generous compensation. Rochelle received a healthy salary, an annual bonus and many perks that came in the form of show/event tickets, invitations to premiers and so on. All this came in return for the personal assistant's loyalty and understanding when it came to the producer's philandering conduct.

As far as Enzo Baffi's darker side went, Parrish only possessed a limited knowledge. She was restricted to being acquainted with Baffi's non-criminal activities as they pertained to his romantic escapades. Parrish remained totally in the dark in regard to the producer's homicidal activities.

At times Parrish was called upon by her boss to step in and help out with potentially embarrassing situations. The personal assistant always complied without question or passing judgment. Her proficiency in cleaning up after her boss earned additional rewards for Parrish. Membership to a health club near the office and a leased car were just two of the extras Baffi provided to express appreciation when a complicated matter was handled well.

Socially speaking, the unmarried raven-haired, forty-year-old Parrish was particular when it came to dallying with inamoratos. Being an assertive woman, she had little use for men lacking confidence. For whatever reason, she was more taken with the coarse types who weren't shy about going after what they wanted. Since Enzo Baffi was perceived by Parrish to be a smooth operator, and no caveman, there was no romantic spark in their relationship.

When Markie and Von Hess arrived at Enzo Baffi's office asking to see the producer, Parrish lived up to her reputation as the no-nonsense guardian of the boss she served. When Von Hess produced his gold shield to identify himself, Parrish didn't blink. She promptly asked to see his police identification card.

"What is this in reference to, Detective?" Parrish asked, once satisfied with the credentials produced.

"It's police business," replied Von Hess.

"And the precise nature of your police business is?"

"It's a matter that your boss may not want to share with you."

"I can't think of anything that would fall into that category, Detective."

"Is he around or not, Ma'am?" asked Markie, who lost patience with Parrish running interference.

"Mr. Baffi happens to be in California with his wife and children."

"Well, now that we're making progress, how about you answer a few questions?"

"That all depends on the nature of the questions," replied Parrish.

"Go head, Ollie," said Markie, looking to avoid saying something he might later regret.

"So, Enzo isn't around today, Ma'am," Von Hess said, seeking to confirm Baffi's absence. Parrish took exception to Von Hess referring to the producer by his first name.

"I already told you that MISTER Baffi is away," she answered. Her tone of voice smacked with snobbery.

"When will MISTER Baffi be back?"

"He won't be back until next week sometime, but that could always change. It would not be unusual for Mr. Baffi to be off to Europe for a few months," she lied. "Now if you don't mind, please get to the point of you being here. I have a lot of work to do."

"Do you know anyone by the name of Fishnet Milligan? We were told that he was a business partner of Mr. Baffi."

"I know of no one named Fishnet. But I do know a Mr. Milligan. The late Mr. Milligan did have a business relationship with Mr. Baffi."

"What was the nature of their business relationship?"

"They were working on a project together."

"What kind of project?"

"Movie related. That's all I know."

"That seems kind of peculiar, Ms. Parrish," said Markie.

"What does, Sergeant?"

"That you don't know. You seem the type not to miss very much."

"I'm well versed in my duties, but I'm not privy to every aspect of Mr. Baffi's affairs, Sergeant."

"So, you are kept in the shade on some business-related things?"

"I beg your pardon?"

"Would you say that Mr. Baffi and Mr. Milligan got on well?" asked Markie, moving on.

"I know of no reason why they shouldn't have gotten along well."

"Did you have any dealings personally with Fishnet....err, I mean Mr. Milligan?"

"Indirectly, Sergeant. I assisted his girlfriend in making the arrangements for Mr. Milligan's funeral and burial."

"Isn't that a little out of your job description?" asked Von Hess.

"The woman was quite distraught, so Mr. Baffi requested that I lend a hand. Mr. Baffi is a very generous and considerate man. He paid for everything."

"Has your boss ever asked you to make such arrangements for anyone else?"

"Why.... yes, Detective," replied Parrish, who was taken aback by the question.

"Who was that for?"

"I also made the arrangements for a very dear friend of his. It was someone who Mr. Baffi knew for many years."

"The Maestro?" asked the detective.

"Why, yes, Detective," replied the surprised secretary. "How did you know that?"

"Word gets around."

"Did you know the virtuoso's pal, a guy named Pascal?" Markie asked.

"Yes, I met him when I made the funeral arrangements. He was the Maestro's life partner as I
understood it."

"Do you know where Pascal is now?"

"I have no idea."

"What about Fishnet's girlfriend? Do you know where she is now?"

"No, I don't."

"Well, do you know whether or not your boss has been in contact with either Pascal or the girlfriend?"

"I have no idea. Where on earth are you going with all these questions?"

"Fishnet Milligan was a former detective, Ma'am. We're just following up on his suicide."

"You don't suspect Mr. Baffi of doing anything wrong you?"

"Oh, no, Ma'am," lied the sergeant. "It's our job to ask a lot of questions. We just wanted to make sure
that there was nothing more to our former colleague's suicide."

"I see."

"Are you a wrestling fan, Ma'am?"

"Why, yes. Why do you ask that, Sergeant?"

"I see that you have tickets to the matches at the Garden on your desk."

"Oh, yes, of course. I usually attend the matches held at Madison Square Garden. I find wrestling to be great theater. That isn't a crime, is it?"

"Of course not, Ma'am."

After thanking Parrish the detectives left the office. As a result of their interview their suspicions were magnified. Since Enzo Baffi was in California the next step in their inquiry would have to be put on hold.

"What do you make of Ms. Parrish, Ollie?" asked Markie, once the investigators were alone.

"I think she could whip either one of us two out of three falls," replied the detective.

"Maybe so, but I find her hot."

***

ENZO BAFFI WAS TAKING THE SUN while relaxing poolside at his California home. The blue swim trunks he wore matched the blue raft that floated lazily atop the water in his built-in swimming pool. He was sucking the last drops of his cocktail through a straw when his cell phone began ringing. Seeing that

215

the call was coming from his New York City office he answered it.

Ms. Parrish wasted no time in apprising Baffi that two detectives had come to his office looking to speak to him. Baffi's initial reaction was one of concern. He had Parrish go over each detail of her conversation with the detectives.

After digesting what Ms. Parrish had to communicate, the producer believed that things may not be as bad as he initially perceived. Seeing things differently, he felt that he had gotten upset over nothing.

It's plausible that detectives would want to follow up on the suicide death of one of their own, thought Baffi.

"Did they ask for my contact information, Rochelle?"

"No, they didn't."

"Did they indicate that they'd be returning to the office when I'm back in New York?"

"They never mentioned that."

"Do you think that the detectives seemed like they were satisfied then?"

"I'd say so."

"Did they ask you exactly when I'd be back in the office?"

"No, not really. If anything, they seemed like they found out what they were after."

"I see. Be sure to let me know if you hear from the detectives again."

"I certainly will."

"And if they do call, Rochelle, tell them I'm over in Portugal on a movie project."

"I understand."

Ms. Parrish was quick to catch on that her boss didn't want to speak to the law under any circumstances. Perceptiveness was one of the attributes that the producer appreciated in his employee.

After hanging up the phone Baffi closed his eyes to think things out. Concluding that he had nothing to worry about at this juncture, he turned his thoughts to things that were more to his liking.

216

Baffi began to envision having his way with Lucille A. DeCoursey and then feeding the gossip columnist to his Dutchess County incinerator. The thought activated the producer's joy button, compelling him to dive into the pool to cool off. When he was done with his swim the producer showered and dressed. He then telephoned the gossip columnist with the intent of charming her into joining him in New York City sooner, rather than later.

"You want me to leave this week?" asked DeCoursey, adding, "I don't know if I could get away."

"Remember what Marcia said, my dear," voiced Baffi, referring to a character in Joseph Addison's 1712 play, *Cato: a Tragedy.*

"Who is Marcia?" asked the gossip columnist, drawing a blank."

"Come, come, my dear, you should know. Marcia was the wife of Cato Uticenisis."

"Oh...."

"It was Marcia who said, 'The woman who deliberates is lost, my dear."

"Yes, of course, now I recall," she fibbed.

"Are you going to hesitate and be lost? The information you desire awaits you in New York, my dear."

"When do you want me there, Enzo?"

27
The Raid And The Blade

WHEN MARKIE SAW THAT THE DOOR to the office of the chief
of detectives was closed, he went to look for Detective
Silverlake. After seeing that Silverlake was nowhere to be found,
the sergeant checked the movement log to see if the detective
signed out to go someplace. He didn't.

  Markie concluded that Chief McCoy and Silverlake were likely
in the chief's office enjoying a late afternoon libation. With the
time not right to disturb the chief, Markie returned to the office
he shared with Von Hess.

  "Did you speak to the chief?" asked Von Hess.

  "No, I'll have to go back in a little while. The chief was in
conference."

  "Is that what Silverlake said?"

  "I think Silverberg is part of the conference with the chief."

  Thirty minutes later Markie returned to Chief McCoy's office.
This time, determined to speak with the chief, the sergeant
knocked on the office door. At the sound of the knocking, Chief
McCoy looked across at Silverlake. McCoy placed a finger to his

lip, indicating that the detective should remain quiet. The two were having a mug of tea spiked with Jack Daniels.

"Who is it?" barked the chief loudly. He was annoyed at being disturbed.

"Sergeant Markie, Chief. "I have some information on that receptionist matter."

"Very well," said the chief with a frown. "Go get yourself a cup of coffee and come back in five minutes."

The chief then finished his drink and instructed Silverlake to do the same. Once done, McCoy placed the bottle of Jack Daniels under his desk. He then removed a package of breath mints from his desk drawer. After placing several mints in his own mouth, he offered some to Silverlake. The detective took the mints, after which he set out to wash out the mugs he and Chief McCoy drank from.

"Leave the door open, Silvie," said the chief, as he sat back in the chair behind his desk.

When Markie returned to the chief's office he explained the situation in Dutchess County to the chief, noting that Enzo Baffi was currently believed to be on the west coast.

"So, where does this leave us?" McCoy asked.

"When Baffi gets back, I think that we should put a tail on him."

"When will that be?"

"I don't really know."

"Do you know where he is on the west coast?"

"Supposedly he's in California with his wife."

"Did you call the police out there and ask them to check if the girl is with him?"

"If he's with his wife, that could get sticky, Chief," pointed out Markie. "Besides, if he gets spooked he'll never come back."

"Maybe you're right. The commissioner isn't going to like the delay, but it can't be helped I suppose. I can hear him now."

"Let's hope the girl is alive."

"Do you really think she may be dead, Al?"

"I don't know, Chief. Time will tell. In the meantime, are you okay with us executing that warrant at the Bronx florist shop?"

"You might as well. How many arrests do you figure to make at the florist shop?"

"We should be looking at three perps, Chief," advised Markie. "We got Cosmo the Florist and two other guys who work in the flower shop."

"I placed bets with all three, Chief," reminded Silverlake, who reentered the chief's office with their now clean coffee mugs.

"And you're confident that these arrests will get us someplace on the Johnny Bronco homicide?"

"We're hoping to come up with that dagger, Chief," replied Markie. "I'm gonna need Silvie again."

"To put in another bet?"

"Yeah, this will be the last one, Chief."

"Okay," said McCoy, nodding approvingly. The chief then turned to Silverlake. "Go saddle up, Silvie." The detective complied as quickly as a trained dog performing for a treat.

***

DETECTIVE SILVERLAKE, BY NOW, had gotten comfortable assuming his sanitation worker role. Even wearing the soiled sanitation department uniform was no longer an issue. He, Markie and Von Hess sat around the corner from the florist shop in their unmarked police car. Parked not too far away from them was a precinct radio car containing their back up.

"Go have a look see, Ollie," said Markie.

"Righto, Sarge," voiced Von Hess, who then walked onto the block for a quick visual of the florist shop. He returned a few minutes later to advise that there was nothing out of the ordinary going on.

"Go to it, Silvie," directed the sergeant, sending Silverlake into the florist shop to place his bets.

The undercover detective was told by Markie to place his bet(s) with whoever was working in the florist shop. The currency to be used had been photocopied and the serial numbers on each bill pre-recorded. This was for evidentiary purposes.

Silverlake, who was carrying a broom and standing dustpan, had entered the florist shop with the confidence of someone who belonged. He nodded his acknowledgement as he approached Louis Pagnetta, who was stationed behind the counter. Louis, who wasn't the warm and fuzzy sort with those placing bets, returned the nod without speaking. Standing alongside Louis was a much warmer Davey Brazil, who smiled pleasantly.

Silverlake placed a wager with Louis without incident. He then turned to the exit. At the exit door he paused for a few seconds. The detective then turned around and placed another bet, this time with Brazil.

"What happened?" asked Brazil, with a chuckle. "Did you have an inspiration?"

"I feel lucky," said Silverlake, as he handed money over to Davey, who wished the bogus sanitation man luck after accepting the bet.

Silverlake then returned to where Markie and Von Hess were parked. After hearing how things went, Markie asked Silverlake if Cosmo the Florist was in the shop. Silverlake reported that he hadn't seen the florist.

The authorities entered the florist shop and promptly arrested Louis and Davey. The two perpetrators were then handcuffed and transported by the uniformed officers to the local precinct.

Markie and Von Hess remained behind to search the premises. As a result of their search, the detectives confiscated gambling records, and the pre-recorded buy money that Silverlake bet with. Also recovered was the dagger with the twisted blade. As expected, the deadly weapon was found in a work apron that belonged to Cosmo the Florist.

"I hope the forensic team can lift a fingerprint off this dagger," said Markie. "And let's hope that this was the dagger used on the captain."

"Maybe we can squeeze information out of one of the guys we pinched."

"That's the plan, Ollie. Let's go upstairs to Cosmo's apartment. Maybe we'll find him hiding under the bed."

When they arrived at Cosmo the Florist's apartment, they were surprised to find the front door unlocked.

"Doesn't anyone lock a door anymore?" asked Markie, remembering how the rear door to Enzo Baffi's log cabin had been found unlocked.

The detectives entered the apartment for a quick look around. What they saw was totally unexpected. The furniture drawers were all open. The clothes closet was practically bare.

"It looks like this joint was either burglarized or Cosmo took off," stated Von Hess.

"I don't see any signs of a forced entry, so this guy may have flown the coop."

"What do you think made him skip, Sarge?"

"I don't know. Maybe there was a falling out among thieves. Let's look around."

In looking around the apartment, Von Hess came across Esther's diary. Out of curiosity the detective began leafing through the journal. It wasn't long before the pieces started to come together. The detective let out a low whistle as he read the contents of the diary.

"What have you got there, Ollie?" asked Markie.

"The mother lode, Sarge," replied Von Hess. "Take a look."

"The names in this book match the names of the stabbing victims!" declared Markie, after reading several pages. "Even Captain Bronco's name is mentioned in the diary, Ollie. This baby made the rounds."

"Do you want me to put a want card out on Cosmo, Sarge?"

"Call Detective Kirby, fill him in and have him put the want card out. After all, he was the one who caught the Johnny Bronco homicide, let him do something."

"Righto. Are we about ready to head to the precinct and question the prisoners?"

"Definitely."

***

DETECTIVE VON HESS photographed and fingerprinted both prisoners. Research on Davey Brazil indicated that Davey had no criminal history. His lack of a record and overall cooperative demeanor gave the investigators the impression that Brazil wasn't much of a criminal. Louis, on the other hand, was a different story. He looked the part of a man with a record and one who had served time in a penitentiary.

After locking Davey in a cell, Markie and Von Hess began grilling Louis after he received his Miranda Warnings. As expected, at first the ring-wise criminal refused to provide any information.

"I got nothing to say to you guys," Louis stated firmly.

"I understand, Louis," said Markie. "I wouldn't say anything either."

"Then why are you asking?"

"Our interest is in finding out who clipped Johnny Bronco."

"Never heard of him," answered Louis, pretending not to have heard of the retired NYPD captain.

"Have it your way, Louis. But just for your own edification, Johnny Bronco was found in the trunk of a car with bullet holes in him....and a very peculiar stab wound that was made by a dagger with a twisted blade."

"Just like the one we recovered at your flower shop," injected Von Hess.

"It's not my place, I only work there, Detective," pointed out Louis with clear agitation. "And you can't put that dagger on me!"

To seasoned detectives like Markie and Von Hess the upset reaction of the organized crime associate was as good as his confessing involvement in the killing of the onetime captain. Markie was the first to capitalize on this observation.

"When the forensic people and the medical examiner get through with that dagger, they'll be able to match it up to past homicides, Louis," pointed out the sergeant. "I've been told that you've been spotted handling that very same dagger."

"Whoever said that was seeing things!" Louis shouted. "They ain't finding my prints on any dagger, you can bet your life on that."

"You never know about them things, Louis," conveyed Von Hess. "A tiny hair, a drop of blood or any other small thing is enough to link a person to that dagger." This remark caused Louis to panic.

This bull bastard could be thinking of framing me, thought Louis. "I want my lawyer," he announced, now more visibly agitated than ever.

"Are you sure you don't want to talk to us, Louis?

"Look Sergeant, I ain't talkin' to you! I just want my lawyer."

"Sure, Louis, you can call your lawyer in a minute. I'm wondering where Cosmo is," declared Markie. He was looking away from Louis when he said this.

"How should I know?"

"That was something about the diary," said Markie, again looking away from the prisoner. The sergeant was careful to make only statements, not ask questions.

"What diary?"

"Are you speaking to me?"

"Yeah, Seargeant, I'm speaking to you. What diary?"

"A diary that belonged to a young woman named Esther, who killed herself. The people who got knifed, including the captain, were all mentioned in that diary. It seems like they all broke the poor girl's heart."

"I don't know nothing about that."

"I didn't ask you if you knew. Tou said you wanted a lawyer."

"I heard that there is a connection is between Cosmo and Esther, Sarge," chimed in Von Hess. "They are supposed to be father and daughter."

This comment spurred an interest in Louis, who began to wonder where the detectives were getting their information from.

"That's news to me," said Louis.

"So, now you want to talk all of a sudden?" asked Markie.

"That depends on what we talk about."

"Let's put the cards on the table, Louis," said Markie. "Cosmo took off, leaving you to hold the bag, pal."

"I ain't taking about anything like that!" Louis blurted out. His composure now shattered. "I said that I want a lawyer! Are you guys deaf? I'M ENTITLED TO MAKE A CALL!"

Markie knew that he could go no further with his bluff. Louis wasn't going to budge. When finally allowed to make a telephone call, Louis reached out to his cousin, Gino Pagnetta

"What's up?" asked the mob capo.

"They raided the florist shop, me and Davey both got pinched."

"What about the potted plant? Did you put it where it belonged?" Gino, speaking cryptically, was referring to the dagger he had Louis put in Cosmo's apron pocket.

"Yeah, it's where you wanted. Me and Davey need a lawyer."

"Relax, if all they're charging you with is gambling, you don't need any lawyer. Once you go before the judge, they'll let you guys out."

"The bulls are talking a lot of shit over here, Gino."

"Let them talk, they're playing you. As long as all they're charging you with is gambling, they're just on a fishing expedition. All you and Davey gotta do is keep your trap shut. As long as you do that, you'll both be out tomorrow. Did they pinch Cosmo too?"

"No, Cosmo's in the wind. The bulls went to his apartment and…."

"That's enough," interrupted Von Hess, taking the phone from Louis. "You made your call."

After the abrupt ending of the telephone with Louis, Gino telephoned his lawyer to find out if Cosmo had signed the legal papers that transferred ownership of the florist shop and building.

"I got there after the cops raided the place," said the attorney. "The florist shop was closed down, so I went right to Cosmo's apartment. Nobody was home."

"What do you mean nobody was home?"

"I'm telling you, nobody was in the apartment," advised the lawyer.

"Cosmo was supposed to be sick. Are you sure he wasn't sleeping?"

"The door to the apartment was open, so I went in. Nobody was there. I think he cleared out from the way things looked."

Cosmo's not being around was worrisome to Gino. The absence of the florist meant that Cosmo left a sick bed to avoid the police, or he wasn't sick at all and absconded. Not taking any chances, Gino decided that he had to move quickly.

The gangster now saw himself in a race with the authorities. Cosmo had to be eliminated before the detectives were able to get to him. Alive and in police custody, Cosmo was a sure bet to roll over and cooperate with law enforcement, thus placing Gino in the crosshairs of the authorities. The pressure was now on for the mob capo to get to Cosmo before the law did.

28

Eliminating Risks

GINO WAS FORCED TO ADMIT that he had misjudged Cosmo's nerve. Verifying that Cosmo had in fact absconded rather than sign over the assets demanded, fostered an awakening in Gino. Fearing that the police may get to Cosmo before he could, made Gino desperate to find the florist.

I'm gonna find Cosmo and make him sign those papers. Then I'm gonna collect whatever money I can off him. Once he's drained, he'll get his payoff.

Gino next turned his thoughts to his cousin. *If Cosmo had the guts to cross me, what would stop Louis from taking the same chances?*

Gino now saw Louis as a danger to him. Gino knew that his cousin, a proven killer, would murder to advance himself. He'd probably even cooperate with the authorities if cornered by the law.

I ain't giving Louis the chance to filet me, thought Gino. *I don't know how I didn't peg him and Cosmo from the beginning.*

***

AS GINO PREDICTED, BOTH HIS COUSIN LOUIS and Davey Brazil were cut loose after their court arraignment. They were released without having to post a serious bail. The court instructions called for both defendants to return to court on an adjourned date. Their court appointed attorney was optimistic that the defendants would likely just face a fine in return for a plea of guilty. The release of Brazil and Louis, for differing reasons, was good news for Gino.

Gino arranged to meet privately with Davey Brazil. The purpose for this meeting was for Gino to ascertain Davey's ability to manage the florist shop and his gambling operation unassisted. Davey assured Gino that he was capable and willing.

Davey's affirmation freed Gino to concentrate on eliminating both Cosmo and Louis. Since Cosmo was in the wind, Louis became Gino's first target. The mob capo understood why his cousin Louis betrayed him. The money paid to Louis for doing Cosmo's bidding was seen as an understandable temptation to a poor earner like his cousin. Gino's receiving a taste of that money wasn't enough to soften him. Louis had to die.

Gino contacted Louis telephonically, informing him that they needed to meet at a secluded area in Pelham Bay Park at 11:00 P.M. Curious as to why, Louis questioned their need to meet in such a remote area at such a time. The answer he received was an abbreviated one.

"Just be there," Louis was curtly told.

"Should I come dressed?" asked Louis cryptically, wanting to know if he should take along a gun.

"Not necessary," answered Gino, conveying that there was no reason to take a weapon. The mob capo ended the call without bothering to say goodbye. Louis, who was distrustful of Gino, found security by arming himself with a handgun.

Louis was the first to arrive at the designated location in the park. When Gino pulled up in a vehicle other than his Lincoln. Louis saw this as a red flag. Gino, who left his engine running, got out of his car and walked over to his cousin's Vet. He opened the passenger door and took a seat alongside Louis

"You like a flashy car like this?" asked Gino.

"I always wanted a Vet."

228

"What car did you use when you were out clipping those people?"

"I used Cosmo's car for that. So, what are we doing here?"

"We're gonna turn the lights off on somebody who was violating the rules."

"That's something that comes with a big consequence," said Louis, not thinking of his own rule violations.

"Do you know what else comes with a big consequence, Louis?" Gino asked, placing his hand in his pocket to take hold of his gun. "Crossing me." Gino's tone was chilling, causing Louis to tense up.

"I thought all that was behind us, Gino," said Louis nervously.

"You got a break because I needed you around. Now I'm not so sure." Louis, now sensing danger, discreetly began to inch his hand toward the gun in his pocket.

"C'mon, Gino, we're blood for God's sake…."

"Relax, Louis," advised Gino, who noticed his cousin's hand moving toward his pocket. Gino now spoke with his gun trained on Gino. "I got you covered."

"Look, Gino…."

"I said relax," interrupted the gangster. "I'm looking to find Cosmo. You got any idea where he went?"

"I ain't got a clue. I swear it."

"Yeah, well wherever he is, I'm gonna find him."

Louis remained quiet, not wanting to add fuel to the fire within his cousin.

"How much do those bulls who pinched you know?"

"They said that they found a diary in Cosmo's apartment that contained his hit list."

"Cosmo kept a diary?" Gino asked, now sensing a new vulnerability.

"The diary belonged to a tenant of his, some girl named Esther. All I know is that something in that book caused Cosmo to want those guys knocked off."

"How many guys are we talking about again?"

"Four guys, and that includes Johnny Bronco."

"Cosmo never told you why he wanted those guys rubbed out?"

"He never said a word about why, and with the kind of money he was giving me, I never asked."

"I get that," conceded Gino. "Those detectives found the dagger you put in Cosmo's apron, right?"

"That's right. They thought it was mine at first. But once they found out that the only prints on the dagger belonged to Cosmo, they changed their tune.

"That's just what I figured," admitted Gino. "Once the bulls get their man, that'll put an end to their nosing around."

"That was smart thinking, Gino."

"So, Cosmo and you must have had a good laugh making a chump out of me," commented Gino, switching topics.

"Cosmo was set up good, Gino," complimented Louis, trying to get off the topic that inflamed his cousin. "Like you figured, now that the bulls have their evidence, they won't bother us any further."

"You should have never crossed me, Louis."

"Why do you have to keep rehashing it, Gino? You said that my mistake was forgiven."

"Sure," said Gino. At this point the mob capo removed a pack of cigarettes from an interior pocket of his coat. "Let's have a smoke, Louis."

As Louis took out his own pack of cigarettes, his cousin watched him closely. Gino waited for Louis to occupy both his hands. His moment came when Louis struck a match to light up. At this point Gino fired his snub nose .357 Magnum. The round entered his cousin's chest. The smoke inside the vehicle generated by the gunshot was thick. The odor of gunpower was strong. The subsequent ringing that developed in Gino's ears came right away.

The unpleasant smoke and deafening noise of the gunshot discouraged Gino from firing a second shot. The assassin didn't believe another bullet was necessary, thinking that the round he dispatched struck the heart. This later proved to be a careless error.

"Nobody makes a fool of Gino Pagnetta!" declared the assassin with satisfaction. As he closed the door to the Vet, Gino announced before returning to his own car, "So long, cousin."

***

THE POLICE OFFICER ASSIGNED to the Pelham Bay Park post treated herself to a big breakfast. It was something she did when she was assigned to foot patrol. Having several hours ahead of her to walk off the food she consumed caused her to be guilt free of straying from her diet.

While strolling along her post, the officer was drawn to something that stimulated her curiosity. *What's that Chevy Vet doing illegally parked in such an isolated area*? This thought required investigation. She approached the vehicle with her summons book in hand. As she neared the Vet, she saw that the driver's head was resting on the steering wheel.

Thinking that he was sleeping off a drunk, the officer slapped the back of the vet with her hand to awaken the man. When the person behind the wheel remained motionless, the officer approached the driver's side of the car. The unexpected sight of claret inside the Vet made things clear that foul play had occurred.

When the officer opened the driver's side door to check the driver's body for vital signs, she was able to ascertain that life still existed. The officer immediately requested the response of the patrol sergeant and that a rush be put on the responding ambulance.

The consensus among those who arrived at the scene of the shooting was that the incident was not a robbery gone bad. This determination was reached because there was no sign of the victim's pockets being tampered with. Further supporting this was the presence of the dead man's wallet and jewelry. Also found was the gun Louis took to the meeting with him.

The victim was identified as Louis Pagnetta based on the identification in his wallet. The responding law enforcement officers speculated that Louis was shot due to a romantic late-night pickup gone sour or an argument with someone over a business dealing of some type.

Louis proved to be a man who didn't die easy. For someone shot in the chest with a bullet from a .357 Magnum, he was somehow miraculously clinging to life. In the ambulance on the way to the hospital the shooting victim drifted in and out of consciousness. When with it, Louis was actually able to feel a jarring sensation that began at his feet and worked itself up in the direction of his head.

Louis hung on long enough to make it to the hospital operating room. To the surprise of everyone, including the attending doctors, Louis lived through the removal of the bullet. Once Louis was in the recovery room, the odds of his surviving were deemed to be less than fifty-fifty.

Several hours later Louis began speaking in a low voice. A nurse placed her ear closer to his mouth in an effort to understand what was being communicated. The words of Louis lacked structure.

Louis always had a selfish slant when it came to death. This came through while on his death bed. He had lived his life a callous man with no qualms about ambushing his murder victims without any thought of giving them a chance to make peace with their maker. Yet, he demanded such time when it came to his own life. Due to his uncertainty about heaven and hell, Louis wanted to leave this world with a clean slate. This meant repenting. Somewhere in his psyche this need surfaced while on his deathbed.

As he babbled, the shooting victim spoke of his remorse for the wicked life he led. A nurse notified the detectives who promptly responded to the hospital with a pad and pen in hand. They began writing down whatever Louis said.

"I'm sorry…. repentance, that's the ticket," Louis voiced. "Why, Gino, why? We're cousins…. all was to be forgiven," he said seconds later. This was followed by a period of quiet, and then the ranting resumed.

"Forgive me, Father…. it was me…. Cosmo tempted me."

"What did you do?" asked the older detective who stood over Louis.

"I put the dagger in the apron…no more killing, I swear it. Righteous is the way…."

"This guy is delirious," said the younger investigator, who stood next to his partner.

"Dear God…. have mercy….it was the money," continued Louis, "money tempted me to kill."

"Who did you kill?" pressed the older detective.

Again, the silence came. The younger detective looked at his partner and commented. "This guy is in another world."

"Shhhh," spat out the older investigator. "This guy is making a dying declaration." He then turned to the man on his death bed to again ask, "Who was it that you killed, fella?"

Louis responded with agitation. "The captain, the singer, the pharmacist, the fireman….and so many others…. FORGIVE ME, LORD!!!" shouted Louis.

"Who shot you?"

"Gino…. I can't help that I'm tall!" Louis now murmured.

"Did Gino shoot you?"

"Forgive me!" Louis said softly, his voice now difficult to hear.

"Take it easy, pal. You're forgiven," said the older detective.

"I think he's finished," said the younger detective.

"Shhh, listen," said the other law enforcement officer.

"Markie and Von Hess…. lay off me…. I'm answering to God," Louis' voice seemed to strengthen. "Save me, Lord," voiced the dying man with a sudden final burst of energy. Then came silence. Louis was gone.

The precinct detectives memorialized the last words of Louis in their report. They then notified Sergeant Markie. In the end, thanks to what was called the dying declaration of Louis, sufficient grounds existed to close the dagger homicides with positive results.

As far as the law was concerned, Louis admitted to being the killer, end of story. There was no need for a further probe into the executions of Johnny Bronco, the singer Frankie Flamarian, the pharmacist Georgie Pride and the fireman Owen Selby.

Gino Pagnetta's lucked out. The last words of Louis, as gathered under the circumstances, fell short of being enough to prosecute Gino. Further spared of murder charges due to a lack of evidence was Cosmo the Florist, who also managed to slip through the net.

Markie and Von Hess believed that the motive for the murders rested in the diary of Esther, the daughter of Cosmo the Florist.

***

MARKIE SAT IN THE OFFICE OF the chief of detectives briefing Chief McCoy on the details of the Johnny Bronco homicide. The sergeant explained that the captain's murder was committed by Louis Pagnetta, who also admitted, via a dying declaration, to perpetrating several other homicides.

"The dagger used in those other homicides was recovered?" asked Chief McCoy.

"Yes."

"Did the dagger match up to the wounds?"

"It did, Chief. Silverlake identified it as the same dagger he saw Louis Pagnetta with in the florist shop."

"So that's that."

"Do you want us to stick with this and try and figure out who killed Louis?"

"Don't bother. Nobody is going to give a rat's ass about who took out a low-level hood. The big interest was in Johnny Bronco's murder and the other dagger killings. All that is behind us now. Let it rest."

"Very good, Chief. Any other fish to fry?"

"The fish I want you to concentrate on is that girl who disappeared from the Performance Club. Figure out what happened to her before the Police Commissioner starts calling me on that bat-phone."

"We'll get right back on it, Chief."

"Was the old man happy, Sarge?" queried Von Hess, who was seated at his office desk waiting for the sergeant.

"He seemed happy enough, Ollie."

234

"What now, Sarge?"

"The chief wants us to go back to finding the missing receptionist."

29

The Magic Of
Cologne

MOST WOULD FIND IT A GOOD POLICY to refrain from sticking their nose in the business of others. Such was not the case for Lucille A. DeCoursey. As a gossip columnist of no small notoriety, DeCoursey made her living by circulating rumors. Scandalous tidbits of tattle were her lifeblood. Her appetite for malicious whispers was voracious.

DeCoursey's ardor in leaking embarrassing information went beyond earning a living. Her poisonous pen was a weapon she used to avenge an old grudge.

The columnist started out with the ambition of being a successful model/actress. Failure to capture the attention of those who could launch her career, she grew bitter. With rejection came an inner need to strike back in as vicious a way as possible. DeCoursey found muckraking to be a powerful vehicle in accomplishing that end. Her venom was directed at the entertainment field in general.

DeCoursey managed to land a job on a newspaper. Once on salary, she worked hard, eventually attracting a following among readers. In time, DeCoursey's success afforded her the opportunity to have her own column. Her dishing dirt on notable people evolved into the columnist acquiring a massive readership.

Once armed with the power to publicly humiliate, the playing field was now leveled. Invitations to social gatherings came her way by those wanting to remain on DeCoursey's good side. Feigning a close friendship was a way to avoid the sting of a career damaging item in DeCoursey's column.

The strength of the column could only be sustained by having resources that could keep the flow of information coming DeCoursey's way. Having someone like Enzo Baffi feeding her leads was akin to hitting the long ball. The producer was a surefire high-level pipeline to America's most celebrated people. Baffi's invitation to join him in New York was a dream come true for the unmarried columnist.

Baffi's personal assistant/secretary arranged for DeCoursey to fly into New York City's Kennedy Airport, where the producer was to personally pick up the invited guest at the airport. The two were to then drive to Baffi's Manhattan offices. DeCoursey couldn't quite fathom why Baffi would want to extend himself to this degree. She found it odd that the producer didn't just send a car for her or allow her to make her own way to Manhattan.

DeCoursey, who was carrying a pink suitcase, smiled broadly when she spotted the waving producer in his car. As she made her way to his vehicle, Baffi visually studied her. He approved of the navy business suit she wore, finding it becoming. DeCoursey's black shoes and the long wool tweed coat that covered most of her body were also beyond criticism. From what Baffi could tell, the columnist's legs seemed thin, causing him to think of a wishbone. The producer felt his body reacting when Dutchess County and wicked thoughts entered his mind.

The columnist was not without her own impressions. As she zoned in on Baffi in the daylight, she was able to detect that the producer had some cosmetic work performed on his face. DeCoursey was unsure when it came to the producer's hair.

I wonder if that's a hairpiece, she thought. *Now that would make for interesting reading!*

"How was your flight, my dear?" Baffi asked once they were on the road in his chocolate-colored Bentley.

"It was marvelous, Enzo," she replied, inhaling deeply. "You're looking quite handsome, as always." The producer smiled in answer to this compliment

The aroma of the producer's powerful cologne permeated the interior of the Bentley. It was a familiar fragrance that tickled DeCoursey's nose. She found that the perfume triggered the memory of a former lover who was in the habit of liberally dousing himself in the same liquid.

"That's wonderful, my dear. Sometimes the flight can be bumpy."

"You really didn't have to pick me up. I could have found my way to your offices."

"Why, I wanted to pick you up. Do you like the color of this car? Its new."

"I love it, Enzo."

The two continued with their small talk until DeCoursey realized that Baffi wasn't taking her to his Manhattan office. "Aren't we going to your office in Manhattan?" she inquired.

"I've taken the liberty of changing plans. We're off to my log cabin in Dutchess County. It's quite private there and the drive will give us time to get better acquainted. I hope you don't mind."

"Oh, well that's fine with me. Am I to stay over?"

"But of course, my dear."

DeCoursey reacted to his assurance with a straight-line smile that accompanied her thoughts. She was wondering if the producer had romantic intentions up his sleeve.

"You simply mustn't keep me in suspense, Enzo. Who is this big mystery person I'm to meet?"

"Alright, my dear, I'll tell. Alfredo DeMar is meeting us at the cabin this evening."

"The restaurant owner?"

"None other."

"People die to get an invitation to his restaurant. Is it true that he's opening an Alfredo DeMar in Las Vegas?"

"Yes, that's true. Alfredo is a shameless chatterbox. With some wine, Alfredo becomes quite loose at the tongue. He'll provide you with all the juicy subject matter you'll need for awhile."

"Do you really think he'll talk in front of me?"

"My dear, I can assure you that this will be a most interesting evening for you."

"I don't know how to thank you. Enzo."

"We'll think of a way, my dear," said the producer. His reply caused the columnist to do a double take.

Remaining silent, DeCoursey now strongly suspected the producer's graciousness was going to come with a price. The seduction effect of the cologne worn by Baffi couldn't be ignored. The fragrance brought back erotic memories that caused DeCoursey to think that she'd likely cave in to the producer's advances if put forth.

I'll bet that he just used Alfredo to lure me into his bed, she thought. Having no small ego, DeCoursey didn't find it surprising that Baffi would find her desirable.

What are you thinking, my dear? Baffi asked, noticing that his passenger seemed to be deep in thought.

"I was thinking of how long it's been since I last visited New York," she lied.

He's definitely older than he appears," the columnist thought, *but he's certainly not too far along to be cut from the lineu*p.

* * *

PROFESSOR WILLIS OVERDEAU WAS SITTING NEXT to the fireplace in the library of his home. The heat emanating from the burning logs kept him comfortable as he re-read *The Communist Manifesto* by Karl Marx. The political science professor, an avid reader, often refreshed his mind with previously read material.

The professor paused for a moment to fill his pipe with tobacco. He favored smoking a pipe because he saw the pipe as perfect for intellectuals. Overdeau equated cigars with capitalistic fat cats. Those opting to smoke cigarettes he considered to be low-brow types. The pipe, he felt, suited him perfectly.

Shortly after lighting up, the smell of the burning cherry blend tobacco reached his wife who was in another room working on a new novel. The scent irritated her nostrils. All smoke, with the exception of marijuana, adversely affected her. Mrs. Overdeau wasted no time reminding her husband that smoking in the house was in violation of the rule they agreed on.

"Didn't we say that only smoking marijuana in this house was permissible, Willis?"

The startled professor, who was approached from the rear, jumped in his seat at the sound of his wife's voice. This knee jerk reaction resulted in Overdeau's pipe falling from his mouth.

"Why would you sneak up on me, like that, Beverly?" barked the agitated professor, as he feverishly began to pat down his whiskers.

"You're going to put you're beard on fire one day with that pipe," said Beverly. "You need to go outside if you insist on smoking that thing."

The political science professor donned his winter coat, woolen scarf and furry dark brown Russian trapper hat with long ear flaps. Once on the porch he again fired up his pipe. As he was doing this, he heard the sound of a running engine on the road in front of his home.

Curious, the professor walked in the direction of the road. Concealed behind a tree, he saw a car pull over on the opposite side of the road. He watched closely as his neighbor, Enzo Baffi, slowly pulled into the driveway that led to his log cabin.

That's some fancy-schmancy car, thought the professor, who disliked having an affluent neighbor with enough money to own such a luxury vehicle.

Seated next to Baffi in the Bentley was a female passenger. When the vehicle pulled into the property, the woman was seen exiting the vehicle carrying a piece of pink luggage. When the pair entered the log cabin the professor turned around and hurried to his own home. He was anxious to inform his wife of what he observed.

"What did I say about that pipe?" his exasperated wife asked in a scolding way.

"Not now with the pipe, do you think that I should call those detectives?"

"What on earth are you talking about?"

"Sorry, I got ahead of myself," answered the professor. He then explained to his wife what he saw.

"Why bother, Willis?"

"Well, why not?"

"Do you really think we should get that involved?

"The cop gave me his cell phone number to call him when someone was home across the way, didn't he?"

After a volley of back-and-forth questions, it was finally agreed that they should mind their own business and not telephone the authorities.

**

THINGS PROGRESSED IN SHORT ORDER for Enzo Baffi and Lucille A. DeCoursey once they were alone together in the log cabin. Reflections of the masterful lovemaking of a former cologne wearing paramour triggered a receptiveness in the columnist, who would eventually welcome Baffi's advances.

"I love this place," declared DeCoursey, after placing her luggage down on the living room floor. "I've never seen a log cabin of such magnificence."

"I had this place specially built to my specifications, my dear. Would you care for a tour? The fun rooms are upstairs." Baffi, an experienced seducer, could tell by the columnist's expression what she was thinking.

"Would you really like to show them to me?" she asked coyly, stepping closer to him. She fell just short of invading the producer's space. The close proximity made her willingness clear.

"Why of course, my dear."

"When is Alfredo expected to be here?"

"We have plenty of time before he is expected."

Baffi's request for a golden shower as a part of their bedroom intimacy wasn't totally surprising to the columnist, who had heard the rumors. Not the inhibited type, DeCoursey complied with his kinky wish.

"Would you care to experience my special room?" Baffi asked calmly, referring to his dungeon.

"Your special room?"

"I think you'll find it quite unique."

"By all means then, lead on," answered the columnist.

Baffi removed a small orange vial containing pills from his pants pocket. He then popped a pill.

"What was that you took, Enzo?"

"Viagra, my dear, I wouldn't want to disappoint you."

The utter depravity that came next was far more than the columnist bargained for. DeCoursey's resistance to Baffi's deplorable wants resulted in his suffocating her. As he snuffed the life out of his victim he did so with a singular thought in mind. *You'll never again write anything about me, my dear.*

With the columnist dead, all Baffi could do now was wait for the wee hours to arrive. When they came, the producer would once again experience another of his demented pleasures.

After feeding DeCoursey into his incinerator, Baffi took time to reflect on his life. He realized that if he continued on with his murderous ways he'd eventually get caught. Yet, although armed with this awareness, he nevertheless remained incapable of resisting his foul urges. In answer to this dilemma, he devised an exit strategy.

242

30

Too Late For A
Date

BEVERLY OVERDEAU'S WAS IN HER home working on her novel at her workstation. Her creative juices were flowing, so she found herself writing well into the wee hours of the morning. Engaged in the development of a character, she was forming the character's personality traits. As she collected her thoughts, she began hearing the low-pitched growling that was emanating from the bedroom. The distraction of her husband's snoring prevented her from continuing on.

Her concentration disrupted by the raspy blasts of air caused the author to abruptly rise from her chair. Annoyed, she proceeded to the bedroom to put an end to what caused her to lose focus. Finding the bedroom door ajar only added to her irritation.

Seeing her husband sleeping on his back led Beverly to briskly shake his shoulder. Once aroused, the professor, as instructed, rolled over onto his side. This adjustment curtailed the snoring, at least temporarily.

Beverly went to the kitchen to fix herself a hot cocoa before returning to her work. As she prepared the cocoa, she pondered creating a new book centering on a man with obstructed sleep apnea, who is subsequently murdered by his spouse. The thought was invigorating.

As the author poured milk into her cocoa, she happened to glance out the kitchen window. Noticing that the lights were on in the log cabin across the road caused Beverly to be curious as to why her neighbor was up so late. With cocoa in hand, she rushed to wake her sleeping husband.

The professor, now grumpy, got out of bed and donned his slippers and bathrobe. He went to the kitchen window to investigate. Seeing the lights on across the road caused him to dig out a vintage hand telescope that had been in the family for decades. Thanks to the telescope, the professor was able to see movement in his neighbor's house.

The professor watched with curiosity as his neighbor emerged from the log cabin carrying the pink suitcase the professor had seen a woman carrying earlier. The neighbor placed the suitcase in the trunk of his car. With no woman in sight, the professor and his wife decided that a telephone call to Markie was warranted, even at such an hour.

***

MARKIE WAS DRINKING at Fitzie's bar when he received the telephone call from Dutchess County. Due to the time, the sergeant was reluctant to answer the call. He correctly assumed that the caller was Professor Overdeau.

Since he had just entered into his swing, Markie was afraid that by answering his cell phone he'd be running the risk of interfering with his days off. Putting the pleasure that came with inebriation aside, the sergeant decided to put duty first. He took the call.

Professor Overdeau apprised the sergeant that his neighbor across the road was home, having arrived the day prior with a female companion carrying a pink suitcase. He informed Markie of what he had seen just a few minutes earlier. The sergeant thanked the professor for the heads up without revealing what he intended to do. He was undecided.

Markie was torn between continuing to quench his thirst or pursuing what could be a hot lead. While his yen for drink was strong, the sergeant put duty first. He wanted to get to the bottom of the missing receptionist matter.

Markie finished what he had been drinking and told Fitzie that he was heading out. Fitzie looked at the sergeant and merely nodded slightly. The bar owner seemed to act as if he didn't recognize his friend. This was very concerning to Markie because Fitzie had been acting strangely as of late. The sergeant feared that Fitzie was showing signs of dementia.

At first, Markie thought Fitzie was just joking when the two were standing side by side at the urinal in men's room earlier in the evening. Markie had glanced to his side only to notice that Fitzie paused, seeming to be confused. When the bar owner dropped his pants, Markie laughed, thinking he was being ribbed. Markie took things more seriously when he later saw Fitzie jotting down drink orders in a notepad. Forgetting what people drank was something Fitzie never did.

Although Markie was concerned about his friend, duty took precedence. Due to the hour, the sergeant decided not to telephone his superiors. He and Von Hess would go to Dutchess County without authorization.

Von Hess was watching an old war movie on television when Markie called. Seeing that the caller was Markie, the detective lowered the television to answer the call. Mrs. Von Hess could tell by the seriousness on her husband's face that he was being called in to work.

"Righto, Sarge," said Von Hess, "I'll pick you up in half an hour."

"You have to go to work, Ollie?" asked Mrs. Von Hess when her husband got off the phone.

"I have to take a ride to Dutchess County with Al," replied the detective.

"All the way up there at this time? What on earth for?"

"We're following a hunch, it probably won't even payoff. But, you never know."

"Do you want to eat something before you leave?"

"No time, I have to get ready."

***

THE PROFESSOR WAS unable to go back to sleep. His wife was unable to return to her work. The two were having toast and tea when they noticed, through the kitchen window, a car stop on the road in front of their home. The car then turned into their driveway, stopping close to the porch.

The professor and his wife were relieved to see that it was just Markie and Von Hess. The professor invited the detectives in.

"We saw your lights on, and wanted to thank you for reaching out," said Markie. "Is there anything else doing?"

"There is only one light on across the road now, but that incinerator just went on a few minutes ago," explained the professor. "I don't know what's going on over there."

Markie asked if they could leave the unmarked police car on the professor's property for a few minutes. Once permission was granted the two detectives proceeded to the log cabin on foot.

Professor Overdeau and his wife Beverly were both curious enough to want to see what the detectives were going to do. The couple quickly changed into warmer attire. Once appropriately dressed, the couple went outside to watch what was happening across the road from their car. To attain a clear view the professor brought along his telescope. Once positioned, the couple began conversing in their usual inquisitive fashion.

"Why don't you put the heat on?" Beverly asked.

"Can't you see that I'm doing that?" replied the husband. "It'll take a few minutes for the car to warm up." The professor then raised the telescope to his eye.

"What do you see?" Beverly asked.

"Don't you see that only one light is on in the log cabin?" questioned the professor. "What more can I see?"

"I'm freezing, how long is it going to take for the heat to come up, Willis?"

"Don't you feel it getting warmer? It's coming."

"So is News Years, isn't it? How about turning that heater up to full capacity?"

While not happy over wasting gas, the professor nevertheless complied.

"Do you mind if I smoke my pipe, Beverly?"

"Since when is smoking in the car okay?"

"Why can't I just leave the window open and smoke?"

"How about we do something that we both enjoy?"

"Like what?"

"Why don't we smoke some weed?"

"Do you want me to go in the house and get some, Beverly?"

"Do you expect me to go?"

***

MARKIE AND VON HESS, who both carried flashlights, quietly crept in the dark toward the log cabin. They followed the foul odor which led them to the back of the cabin. When they reached the rear of the log cabin, they noticed someone at the incinerator.

"That stink is the smell of burning flesh!" whispered Von Hess, who was familiar with such an unpleasant odor.

Markie drew his revolver. "Let's see what this asshole is up to," he said.

Hearing the approach of the detectives caused Enzo Baffi to turn his flashlight on them. The two investigators, guns drawn, moved in briskly. Von Hess flashed his light in the producer's face, blinding Baffi.

"POLICE, DON'T MOVE!" Von Hess announced authoritatively. "GET THOSE HAND UP!" Baffi, taken by surprise, hesitated. "I SAID HANDS UP!" repeated Von Hess. This time the producer complied.

Markie flashed his light on the ground around Baffi. The sight of a woman's shoe at the producer's feet left little doubt in Markie's mind about what was being cooked in the incinerator.

"Put your hands behind your back, you sick bastard," ordered the sergeant.

Baffi allowed himself to be rear cuffed without putting up any resistance. To the surprise of the detectives, the producer cooperated fully, accepting the fate that awaited him.

The dog and pony show that followed involved the Dutchess County Sheriff's Office, local prosecutors, forensic investigators and search warrants. During the execution of the search warrant at the log cabin, Markie retrieved the earring of Juliana Swain that he previously hid. He placed it on the first floor where Juliana's Swain's mother had seen it. This evidence would later be identified by the mother as belonging to her daughter.

***

THE OVERDEAU'S SPENT THE NIGHT SITTING in their car taking turns looking through the telescope at
what was going on across the road. It turned out to be something akin to a movie night at the drive-in for the couple, who got high as they took in the show. The arrival of the crime scene truck and the various responding agencies each represented a new attention-grabbing scene.

As a result of their cannabis use, the Overdeau's developed the munchies. The couple made a party of it. They chomped on popcorn, opened a bottle of red wine and continued to smoke weed. The pair only returned to their home after Enzo Baffi was seen being taken away in handcuffs.

"Why didn't we go across the road to find out exactly what was going on?" asked the novelist.

"I don't know, why didn't we?" asked the professor.

"Do you think there is a reward being offered?"

"Do we even know what the guy did?"

"Do you want to do another joint, Willis?"

"We can't. We're all out, aren't we?"

"What about my cookies?"

31

Endzo for Enzo

SURPRISINGLY, ENZO BAFFI APPEARED TO TAKE his Dutchess County apprehension in stride. After being given his Miranda Warnings, the producer agreed to answer the questions put forth by the authorities. It was astonishing to the Dutchess County Sheriff's Office, and the local prosecutors, that a man of such affluence would waive his right to legal representation.

Although a Dutchess County homicide investigation, Markie and Von Hess were invited to sit in on the interrogation of the producer.

Baffi's confessed to the gossip columnist homicide, thus making his prosecution airtight. The producer also admitted to the other murders he committed, in both Dutchess and New York City. Markie got the sense that confessing his sins relieved the producer of a great burden.

In articulating his motives for the murders, Baffi concealed the sexual gratification aspect connected to the homicides. His fessing up to having such a deviant perversion was the one thing he was too ashamed to admit to. Regardless of his adamance in this regard, the producer wasn't fooling anyone.

When queried specifically about the dungeon in his log cabin, Baffi offered a feeble explanation. He explained the room as being a temporary storage area for equipment he intended to use in his upcoming cinema project. After making this claim the producer looked at the law enforcement officers surrounding him. He wondered if they bought his assertion. They didn't.

Markie took great personal satisfaction in being proven correct in his belief that the rogue detective Fishnet Milligan did not commit suicide. Baffi's confession made it clear that he and two associates, Maestro and Pascal, murdered Fishnet. In the Fishnet homicide the producer provided the true motive behind the killing. Baffi went on to further admit to his role in the later homicides of the Maestro, Pascal, Fishnet's girlfriend and the others.

Of all the murders Baffi perpetrated, it was the death of the young Performance Club receptionist that bothered Markie the most. Deep within the sergeant rested the urge to beat the producer. Although it was never discussed, this feeling was shared by Von Hess.

Markie couldn't help but wonder what was going on in Enzo Baffi's twisted mind. It was a question he sought an answer to.

"What made you decide to waive legal representation?" asked the sergeant.

"I'm fully aware that there is no hope for me, Sergeant," voiced the prisoner. "I'm not one to pursue paths of futility."

"You're a very cool customer, considering the circumstances."

"I've always been a successful man, Sergeant. To be successful, one needs to set realistic goals and prepare for the landmines. I've always known that someone like you would eventually catch up with me at some point. I'm prepared for the consequences I face."

"You've prepared yourself?"

"I think so. Is there anything else you have to ask me, Sergeant?"

"I'd like to ask you something," injected Von Hess, "what caused you to run off the track?"

"I bore easy," answered the prisoner. "Perhaps I've had too much fame, perhaps too much of everything. Having lots kept me needing something new, something more." The investigators remained stone-faced as they processed the words being spoken. "I suppose that's the curse that accompanies genius."

"I'll say this for you, you're a humble man," said Markie, being sarcastic. At this point the sergeant really wanted to backhand the producer.

The serial killer smiled at Markie's comment. His unusual composure was attributable to his having prepared an exit strategy. Baffi knew that no lawyer in the world would be able to successfully defend him against charges of murdering and incinerating people, so he masterminded a B-plan for his day of reckoning.

The notion of wearing an orange prison suit, being subjected to public ridicule and a lifetime of mixing with an unsophisticated criminal element while incarcerated was simply out of the question for the producer.

Baffi kept three-hundred thousand dollars in cash in his office safe. This was the kind of money that could buy many ringside seats for his wrestling loving personal assistant/secretary, Rochelle Parrish. Also, in the safe was an envelope addressed to Parrish that contained specific instructions.

"I am entitled to a phone call, aren't I?" asked the prisoner.

"You said you didn't want a lawyer," reminded the arresting Dutchess County law enforcement officer.

"I'm not calling a lawyer."

"Who do you want to call?"

"I want to call Rochelle Parrish. She works for me."

When Baffi got Parrish on the line he explained to her that he was arrested without revealing the charges. Expressing concern, she offered to contact a well-known criminal lawyer for the producer. Baffi assured her this wasn't necessary.

"What can I do for you?" asked the upset Parrish, who was at a loss as to why her boss wouldn't want representation.

"I'm being held in Dutchess County. I want you to come to where they're holding me and collect my things from them, my dear. They have my watch, ring, money and so on. I'd like you to give these things to my wife. Will you do that for me, my dear?"

"Of course, I will, Enzo. Where exactly are you?"

252

After providing Rochelle Parrish with his exact location, the prisoner instructed her to be sure to open his office safe, advising that there was travel money for her contained within the safe. After getting off the phone with the producer, Parrish went to the safe, where she found a package addressed to her. Contained within the package was money and a pill inside a tiny plastic bag. There was also a printed letter:

My Dear Rochelle,

I want to first thank you for your unwavering loyalty to me over the years. As you know, I've never been perfect. What you don't know is that I've lived a Jekyll-Hyde life. I am a murderer. Some details I'm sure will be chronicled in the tabloids no doubt. The field day they will have at the expense of me and my family is unfortunately unavoidable. Let the bastards have their fun. With that said, there is no need for me to expand upon my inexcusable behavior in this communication.

Money is all I have to offer in return for the favor I now must ask of you, my dear. You must not fail me in my time of need, Rochelle. I know I can depend on you to see me through. All will work out if you strictly adhere to my instructions as detailed below:

1. The three hundred thousand in cash is yours. It's my thanks for your years of devotion to me, my dear.
2. The pill contained in the small plastic wrapping is for me. It's a deadly poison.
3. You must secrete the plastic containing the pill in the side of your mouth when you come to see me wherever the authorities are holding me captive.
4. When we meet, you must kiss my lips and pass me the plastic.
5. Do not fear getting in trouble. I'll leave a note stating that the pill was hidden in my anus all along.

6. Burn this letter, take your money and after our final parting, don't look back.

I implore you to do what I ask, my dear. To abandon me means that I'm doomed to spend the rest of my life a disgraced man behind bars among creatures too detestable to endure. As for my wife and children, my last will and testament will leave them well taken care of.

As I exit the stage, all I can say is thank you, my dear. I remain confident that you will not let me down.

Affectionately and with much love,
Enzo

Rochelle Parrish had difficulty digesting what she read. After reading the letter several times she shook her head in disbelief. The whole affair seemed too impossible to be real. But yet, it was.

Without knowledge of the heinous crimes perpetrated by the producer, Rochelle wanted to believe that Baffi was over-dramatizing his problem. Confused at first regarding how to proceed, the money left for her was the deciding factor. Her devotion to a man who had treated her so well over many years also swayed her, blurring right and wrong.

He needs me, thought Parrish. *I don't care what crimes he's being charged with, how can I possibly let him down?* She fell short of admitting to herself that the money left for her also impacted her decision.

As the executive assistant/secretary gathered her things she began to further justify her commitment to comply with the wishes of her boss. She likened herself to an athlete performing in one of the wrestling matches she so enjoyed. In this respect, Enzo Baffi was her tag team partner. The producer was being battered in the corner by their opponents, who in this case was the law. *What else is there for me to do,* she thought, *but jump into the fray!*

Parrish took the clear plastic containing the kill pill and placed it in the side of her mouth to get the feel of it. Once the foreign object was in a comfortable position, she began practicing how to roll it out of her mouth with her tongue and into her hand. After some practice she was confident that she'd be able to transfer the cyanide to Enzo Baffi's mouth as requested.

By the time Parrish arrived at the facility where the producer was being held, Markie and Von Hess were no longer there. Parrish signed for the prisoner's belongings and was given everything except Baffi's cell phone, which was being held for further investigative purposes.

Parrish was permitted to exchange a few brief words with the producer before it was time for her to be escorted out of the facility.

"Goodbye, my dear," whispered the producer.

"Oh, Enzo…."

"May we kiss goodbye?" asked Baffi, addressing one of his keepers.

"This isn't the Honeymoon Hotel," came the tart reply.

"I've cooperated with you fully, isn't that worth such a small consideration?"

"Okay, but keep it decent."

When their lips met Rochelle Parrish passed the plastic containing the cyanide orally to Enzo Baffi. The transition of the pill from one mouth to another went unnoticed.

Rochelle Parrish headed back to Manhattan feeling sorry for her former employer. When through with her pity, she began to dwell on the money she came into. The funds she received provided a cushion substantial enough to give her the time necessary to find another job to her liking.

While gaining employment was not an immediate concern, Parrish turned to the wrestling magazine she purchased at the newsstand before getting on public transportation. In short order her attention was devoted to the wrestling star who sported an Indian headdress whenever he entered the ring.

***

MARKIE AND VON HESS learned the following day that Enzo Baffi was found poisoned in his Dutchess County cell. The detectives were at a loss as to how that could have happened.

"Can you believe this, Sarge?" asked Von Hess.

"That son of a bitch said that he had prepared himself," voiced Markie.

"This is one for the books. It reminds me of that snitch, Kid Twist from Brownsville. He went out the window of the Half Moon Hotel in Coney Island years ago. He was under police guard when that happened."

"You're talking about Abe Reles, the guy from Murder Incorporated."

"That's right."

"Whatever the story is up there in Dutchess County, it's not our problem, Ollie. Actually, this is probably the best thing that could have happened."

"How do you figure, Sarge?"

"All the homicides, including the girl from the Performance Club, are cleared with positive results now....and without any wear and tear on us."

"I see your point."

"Plus, we don't have to support that murdering psycho for the rest of his life. If he got life in jail, he could have lived to be a hundred!"

"How do you figure he got the poison?"

"That's a question for those guys in Dutchess County to figure out. Oh, that reminds me of something, Ollie. I want you to give Professor Overdeau a call. Let him and his old lady know that it was Enzo Baffi that whacked their dog."

"No problem, Sarge. They'll be glad to know that."

***

THE CHIEF OF DETECTIVES, after speaking to Markie, reached out to Police Commissioner Randolph to ask him if any extra attention needed to be given to the mother of the murdered Performance Club receptionist. The commissioner indicated that it wasn't necessary, noting how pleased he was with how everything turned out.

"Pinching Enzo Baffi on all those murders gave us a million bucks worth of good publicity, Harry," said the commissioner energetically. The top cop used the term *us*, but what he really meant was *me*.

"Yeah, John, that was terrific press we received, and they'll probably be more to come. It looks like Sergeant Markie was right all along on Fishnet Milligan's death. He smelled a rat from the onset."

"Yeah, he did a good job, Harry. Do you want me to give him the special assignment money?"

"He already has it. Markie's been making lieutenant's money for a while."

"Oh, that's right, Harry, I forgot. What about the German detective he's always with?"

"Von Hess already has first grade."

After getting off the phone with Chief McCoy, Commissioner Randolph dialed Fred Klein, the labor lawyer for the Performance Club. He wanted to make sure Klein knew how things turned out with the receptionist investigation.

"This Enzo Baffi turned out to be a real sick puppy, Fred," advised the commissioner.

"I can hardly believe it, Commissioner," stated Kelin after being apprised of the facts. "I suppose you never know about people."

"Well, I just wanted to make sure you knew, Fred. I guess the heat is off the club now."

"In a sense, yes. I intend to put together a training session on workplace violence for the club employees. We don't want to see a reoccurrence of something like this."

"Good idea. The girl's mother must be a basket case."

"That's another thing, I'm determined to find a job for Juliana's mother, something a little better than what she is currently doing."

"That's nice of you, Fred," said Commissioner Randolph. "You know my daughter will be graduating from college soon, she'll be job hunting."

"What did she major in?"

"Accounting."

"Keep me posted, Commissioner. Maybe I can help her."

"You're a good man Fred," said the commissioner before hanging up the phone. The commissioner's comment made the labor lawyer feel good.

Finding an accounting firm that would want to hire the police commissioner's daughter shouldn't be very difficult, thought the attorney.

32

Davey Makes Gravy

NOW THAT GINO PAGNETTA'S cousin Louis was removed from the equation gangland style, Gino knew that he'd have to deal with Long John Capezzo, the family boss. Long John would undoubtably want to know who was responsible for the murder of an associate in his family. It was the duty of the boss to avenge an unsanctioned hit on one of his people. If identified, the assassin(s) would be dealt with in the harshest of ways, so that an example could be set.

Gino never sought family approval to murder his cousin because he knew he'd run into resistance. Louis, while not an earner for the family, was nevertheless a valuable resource to have on staff. Gino's cousin had long proven himself as a capable enforcer and killer for the family. The two cousins collectively contributed to the muscle that kept Long John in power.

When queried by Long John regarding the fate of Louis, Gino claimed total ignorance. He attributed the murder of his cousin as likely the work of some unidentified renegade with an axe to grind. Since Gino's track record as a generous earner who passed thick envelopes to the family boss, Long John accepted this explanation. The family boss instructed Gino to conduct an inquiry on the matter. Gino gladly welcomed this assignment because this enabled him to control the outcome.

Having to deal with Cosmo the Florist was Gino's priority. He reached out to his vast array of connections to let it be known that he was looking for Cosmo. This notification came with a reward for anyone who could provide Gino with Cosmo's whereabouts. Those who had been put on alert didn't need things spelled out. The message was clear to them that Cosmo, who had no official status in the crime family, was a marked man. Those less attuned to mob ways remained unaware of Gino's nefarious intentions.

Once Cosmo was located, Gino's plan was to strong arm the florist into signing the documents that transferred full ownership of the florist shop, and the building that housed it, to Davey Brazil. Gino then planned to kill Cosmo in a way that gave the impression that the florist was the victim of a hit and run accident. It was to be the kind of death that could happen to anyone, thus drawing minimal media attention.

On the hunch that Cosmo might go into the florist business someplace, the organized crime capo had Davey Brazil reach out to the vendors that did business with the Bronx florist shop. Once the word was spread, all alerted agreed to notify Brazil if they came into contact with Cosmo.

Gino had no choice other than to be patient at this point. It was only a matter of time before he would receive a word from one of the many recruited to serve as his eyes and ears. He could only hope that the authorities were trying too hard to find Cosmo. Gino briefly considered notifying Markie that he heard that Cosmo was in Mexico someplace. He came to dismiss this notion, thinking that it may be best to just let matters rest.

***

IT DIDN'T TAKE LONG FOR Davey Brazil, who was working unassisted, to have the Bronx florist shop doing a brisker business than ever. It turned out that Davey was a diamond in the rough who exceeded expectations. He was diligent, innovative and possessed a creative talent for business development. These attributes were beneficial to both the floral and gambling businesses.

Gino, thanks to his elevation to capo, was now the recipient of an enhanced bankroll. Being a master at knowing how to protect himself politically within the family, he put some of the extra money to good use. The tribute envelopes Gino kicked upstairs to the family boss were fattened up. Also taken care of financially was Davey Brazil, who was now recognized as a rainmaker.

Gino kept Davey in the dark as to what he had planned for Cosmo. The mobster led Davey on, leaving him to believe that Cosmo was remaining in the business mix for the time being.

***

LONG JOHN CAPEZZO WAS A LANKY MAN who towered over most of his underlings. Sensitive to his thinning hair, few ever got to see the few remaining strands that sprouted from his skull. The solution to the gangster's embarrassment over his hair deficiency rested in the straw hat he always wore. Be he indoors or outdoors, the family boss was never without the head covering.

Long John's nose was long and hooked. His arms and legs were extended beyond average, as were his fingers and toes. It was whispered that Long John probably had other lengthy parts.

After a conversation the family boss had with his underboss, Long John began to rethink what happened to Louis Pagnetta. The more the two men discussed the hitman's murder, the greater Long John's concern became. The underboss advised that there was the possibility of a conflict brewing with another organized crime family. Unable to dismiss this observation, Long John summoned Gino Pagnetta to his New Jersey home.

"What do you think really happened to your cousin, Louis?" asked Long John, being direct.

"It's like I already told you before, John, I really got no idea," Gino lied, trying his best to appear sincere.

"Have you made any headway in your inquiry to find out?"

"Of course I did, John. I got nothing concrete for you though."

"What do you have?"

"I'm hearing talk that my cousin had money out on the street," lied Gino. "I had no idea that he was shylocking money behind my back."

"How much did he have loaned out?"

"I guess it must have been enough to get him whacked. Louis could have loaned money to somebody who didn't want to make good on what he borrowed."

"That's happened before," acknowledged Long John. "It's an often-used way to escape an obligation."

"That's about all I can figure, John."

"Who bankrolled Louis to start him off in that business?"

"All I know is that it wasn't me." Long John began shaking his head after hearing this comment.

"Has there been issues with any of the other families?"

"No. John. Everyone's been getting along fine."

"Okay, Gino, now listen to me. If you ever find out who killed Louis, I want his death avenged in a way that draws a lot of attention. Like I told you before, I want an example made."

"No problem, John."

The conversation Gino had with his boss put to rest any further questions pertaining to his cousin for the time being. Gino hoped that Louis would eventually become a distant memory.

***

THE NEWLY MARRIED COUPLE left their New Jersey residence to embark on a two-week honeymoon. They were driving to Canada. The groom, a longtime bachelor who married late in life, worked for a floral supply house with a national footprint. While traveling to Canada the couple thought it might be fun to spend a day in Portland, Maine. Their plan was to take a walking tour of the city sights.

As they strolled, the newlyweds window shopped. They stopped in front of a small florist shop. The husband peered through the window glass, deciding whether to buy his wife a red rose as a token of his love. To his surprise he saw a familiar face standing behind the cash register. It was a client from the Bronx who he had known for many years.

"Look who it is," said the husband to his wife.

"Who?"

"That's Cosmo the Florist behind the counter."

"Who is he?"

"He's an old client. C'mon let's go in and say hello."

Cosmo's mouth dropped open when he realized he had been recognized. With no place to hide, he had little choice other than to engage the visitors in conversation. After hearing all about the couple's matrimonial bliss and their plans to go to Canada, the florist gifted the bride the red rose the husband wanted for his wife. At this juncture Cosmo was hoping that his customers would be on their way. The florist had no such luck.

"You own this place, Cosmo?" asked the husband, seeing an opportunity to drum up new business.

"No, this is my cousin's place," lied Cosmo. "I'm just holding down the fort for him this week. He's on a cruise."

When pressed for more information, Cosmo conveyed that he was only spending a couple of more days in Portland, before returning home to the Bronx.

"Does your cousin use my firm?"

"I'm not sure."

"If not, have him give me a call. Maybe I can save him some money."

"I'll do that."

When the newlyweds returned to Patterson two weeks later, they did so with fond memories and numerous photos taken during their trip. The happy husband was showing co-workers the places he had captured on film. Among these was a photograph of Cosmo the Florist pinning a small red rose on the lapel of the bride's jacket. A co-worker instantly reacted upon hearing the husband refer to the man in the photograph as Cosmo the Florist.

"What did you say this guy's name was?" asked the co-worker.

"Cosmo the Florist."

"From the Bronx?"

"Yeah," confirmed the newly married man.

"Did he say what he was doing in Maine?"

"He's filling in at a florist shop for his cousin who was on a cruise," replied the newlywed. "What's the big interest?"

"People from the Bronx have been calling over here asking if we knew where Cosmo the Florist was."

"What people?"

"Important people," said the coworker, who then pressed his index finger against his nose. This was his way of indicating that mobsters were looking for Cosmo without actually having to voice it.

"Really? Is he in trouble?"

"All I know is that there is a bounty on his head."

"No kidding."

"What's the name of that florist shop in Portland?"

"I don't remember, but it's across the street from O'Dell's Pub. I remember that because my wife and I had lunch there."

"What do you say we make a call and let people know where Cosmo is," said the co-worker.

"Why do you want to do that to the guy?"

"Didn't you hear what I said? There is a bounty for us to split."

"Maybe we should," agreed the newly minted husband, thinking of the cost of his honeymoon.

***

TO ASSURE THAT DAVEY BRAZIL remained happy, Gino compensated him well. Davey was instructed to pay himself a minimum wage salary on the books. This legitimate wage was supplemented with a substantial cash payment under the table. This was a classic way to bypass the taxman.

Davey had much success in expanding the Bronx florist shop. His natural aptitude for preparing floral arrangements was a big help. Those projects beyond his scope were farmed out to friendly competitors who were amenable to working with Davey. Their agreeability was primarily due to Gino being the neighborhood's most prominent gangster. Davey quickly grasped the value of Gino's reputation.

As a rule, dropping the name of a gangster without permission was a social no-no in mob circles. Violators ran the risk of penalties that could range from tongue lashing to physical violence. In Davey's case, with money pouring in, Gino had given Brazil carte blanche to use his name. Armed with this influence, Davey wasn't shy about maximizing the advantages he held over those he dealt with. He did this in a non-threatening way.

Since there was nothing thuggish about Davey, business development became one of his key talents. He possessed an uncanny ability to make friends. His charm led many gamblers to get comfortable gathering at the florist shop. This led to greater business.

Early morning betters coming off overnight work shifts began to stop by the florist shop to unwind for a couple of hours. Some of the regulars would bring along coffee and bagels. The men would eat, place wagers and chat about sports until it was time to return home to their wives and children.

Hanging out at the florist shop led gamblers to wager more, inevitably leading to a depletion of their funds. This created the need to borrow money from Gino, who via Davey, was more than willing to front cash at inflated interest rates. This criminal usury proved to be another lucrative revenue stream enhanced by Brazil.

Davey, with the aid of Gino, went on to expand the business being conducted at the florist shop. They began stocking the back room of the shop with untaxed cigarettes, fireworks and various items of swag. To the delight of all involved the revenue flow increased substantially.

In terms of legitimate business, everyone began coming to the affable Davey to meet their floral needs. He had evolved into the neighborhood go to man when it came to weddings, funerals, graduations and similar flower worthy occasions. Aside from Davey's worth as a business asset, Gino appreciated that Brazil was strictly above board in terms of integrity. Davey's honesty made him a rare gem among those in the questionable circles Gino traveled.

As Davey's pool of flower shop patrons steadily multiplied, Davey became innovative. He began converting many of the regulars into salesmen. These financially strapped gamblers appreciated the compensation they received for the business they drummed up.

Things got so good that Davey hired additional part time helpers to support the needs of the florist shop. There came a point where Davey considered asking Gino if he could rent the adjoining storefront so that the demand for goods and services could be accommodated. The hecticness of all this became too time-consuming for Gino, who considered bringing in someone to stand between himself and Davey.

Occasionally Davey would ask Gino about Cosmo. The mobster assured Davey that all was fine with Cosmo, adding that the florist was off somewhere on an extended vacation. Davey accepted this as truth.

As far as Long John Capezzo went, the family boss didn't get to the top by not paying attention to those earning money for him. He was well attuned to how instrumental Davey Brazil was in generating revenue for his capo. The hefty envelopes Long John was receiving from Gino, since boarding Davey, was proof of Brazil's value. Since things were going well, Long John sat back, content to embrace the rewards.

**

WHEN WORD REACHED Gino Pagnetta that a New Jersey supplier spotted Cosmo the Florist in Portland, the mobster was delighted. *Finally*, he thought.

266

33

Jackie The Lackey

GINO PAGNETTA WAS THE sort of man who was often miserable to be around. Even when things were breaking his way, he was never happy. The news of Cosmo the Florist's whereabouts was a short-lived joy. The information was dampened due to his own doing.

Gino had become obsessed with the thought that Davey Brazil was doing too good at his job at the florist shop. This came about after Long John Capezzo mentioned to him how pleased he was with what he had been hearing about Brazil.

Davey's being praised by the head of the family caused Gino, who coveted such recognition, to feel diminished. He was of the opinion that he, as Davey's boss, should be the recipient of the accolades. Having his thunder stolen was so upsetting to the egomaniacal Gino that he decided to do something about it.

To put things in its proper perspective Gino entered into a subtle campaign to trim Davey's relevance. He had his lawyer redraft the legal papers that transferred ownership of Cosmo's florist shop and building. With Davey's name being removed, Gino set out to find a replacement to front for him before heading out to Portland to even the score with Cosmo.

The organized crime capo intended to install someone in a position of authority over Brazil. His objective in doing this was to blur any future accomplishments of the high achieving Brazil. The employment adjustment would enable Gino to attribute a portion of future successes, to the collaboration between himself and his new appointment. Gino turned to his social club to find an appropriate candidate for the newly created position.

***

JACKIE LANNO FIRST BEGAN hanging around Gino Pagnetta's social club at 15 years of age. The fatherless Jackie lived with his mother, an alcoholic who drank heavily to combat depression. The mother's drinking adversely impacted Jackie's only sibling, an older half-sister, who turned to drugs for relief.

His sister's death due to a drug overdose and his mother's increased alcohol dependance left Jackie in need of money to support himself and his mother. Jackie dropped out of high school and found limited relief running errands for the men who hung out in Gino Pagnetta's social club, located beneath the apartment the Lanno family resided in.

At first Jackie made do on the tips he earned. Once he became a familiar face around the club, he was sent out on the street to sell swag, fireworks and untaxed cartons of cigarettes. Being referred to as "a good kid" by the men who frequented the club was viewed as an honor by the impressionable youth. Before long the misguided teenager was nicknamed Jackie the Lackey. It was a handle that stuck.

Gino, who was heartless in most things, was compassionate when it came to Jackie. Aware of the youth's hardships, the gangster felt it was his responsibility to take Jackie under his wing. As a result of Gino's questionable mentoring, Jackie grew wise to the ways of the street. In this respect he was advanced far more than others his age. Being the capo's protégé caused Jackie to model himself after Gino.

Jackie soon began emulating the gangster by assuming some of his traits. He adopted Gino's cocky strut, which gave him an arrogant look. The teenager's temperament was also altered to where he exhibited, like Gino, an explosiveness when angered.

Perhaps most significant was how Jackie began to express himself with confidence.

Lacking the financial wherewithal to project himself as the fashion plate Gino was, Jackie had to make do with what he could afford. He settled on wearing button-down shirts with dark jeans. The top two buttons of his shirt, regardless of temperature, were left open to expose the silver cross that was attached to a chain around his neck.

This look was classic Gino, who wore his shirts the same way. The only difference was that Gino's cross was made of gold, and the matching chain thick.

Jackie, now nearing twenty, maintained a routine of lifting weights. This earned him an athletic physical appearance. He was considered to be ruggedly handsome. His light brown hair was always clean and cut stylishly. One of Jackie's muscular arms was decorated with the tattoo of a broken heart that bore the word mother.

In a strange way, Gino Pagnetta saw Jackie as a part of his legacy. The childless organized crime capo loved having someone look up to him with respect that was coming from the heart. The homage Jackie afforded Gino resulted in his receiving additional opportunities to make money via various illicit undertakings.

Jackie the Lackey was in the habit of waiting for his idol to arrive at the social club. Gino came to the club around the same time each day. Jackie moved to the curb when he saw the diminutive gangster's black Lincoln Continental approaching.

There was no mistake about who was behind the wheel of the car. The little head appearing over the steering wheel could only be that of Gino. The mobster slowly pulled up in front of the social club and double parked. Jackie rushed to open the car door for the man he longed to be.

Gino exited the Lincoln with a genuine smile that made it evident that he had a soft spot in his heart for the young man. Jackie was so well liked by Gino that the gangster overlooked the fact that Jackie was tall. Perhaps the age difference made Jackie seem smaller to Gino.

The mob capo was dressed sharply in a blue suit, white shirt and black tie. His beige double-breasted overcoat remained on the passenger seat of the vehicle. The shine on Gino's black loafers was brilliant. On Gino's wrist was a watch with a solid gold band. The expensive timepiece was something Jackie coveted almost as much as the handgun he so badly wanted.

"What do you say, Jackie?" voiced Gino, as he slipped the kid the double sawbuck. "How's your mother feeling?"

"She's fine, Gino," Jackie replied, as he stuck the twenty-dollar bill in his pocket. "She really appreciates you going to bat for her with that landlord."

"The prick got what he had coming to him. Is she getting enough heat now?"

"Plenty, Gino, I can walk around the apartment in my underwear now."

Jackie got behind the wheel of the Lincoln and parked it by a nearby fire hydrant. Jackie's job was to sit in the car and wait until Gino emerged from the club. While waiting Jackie listened to the singer Jimmy Roselli's emotional warbling of Italian favorites. Not understanding the language, Jackie wondered what the lyrics meant.

Jackie took pride in the way people looked at him when sitting behind the wheel of the Lincoln. He believed that they thought he was somebody important. All Jackie could think of was the day that he would actually be somebody of importance like Gino.

***

GINO PAGNETTA ENTERED THE MAIN ROOM of his social club hoping to find something different going on. He let out a sigh in reaction to seeing the usual. *Nothing ever changes with these guys*, thought the mob capo. *I'm saddled with dependents who don't know how to earn!*

Among those seated at the card tables were men focused on games of either knock rummy or pinochle. Other than an occasional profanity uttered by someone who was dealt a poor hand, the card players remained silent as they studied their cards.

Those not gambling at the tables could be heard discussing current events, sports and assorted acts of crookedness they either once participated in or heard of. None spoke of future moneymaking schemes, criminal or otherwise.

A few of those present watched Gino to see what he was going to do or say. There was a plausible explanation for this. Since Gino could be volatile, people anxiously waited to see which side of Gino they were going to have to deal with. Luckily, today Gino was relatively docile. As Gino made his way to the rear office he nodded his greetings. The absence of a scowl was another good sign.

A few minutes after entering his office, a serious looking Gino emerged to look out at the main area of the club. He began nodding slowly. It was as if he knew a secret that no one else did.

I wonder if he's capable, thought Gino, looking at a man everyone called Brute.

While Brute wasn't too bright a minion, he did do what he was told to do without question. Gino raised his hand and pointed at Brute. He then wiggled his index finger inward, summoning Brute to him. Brute didn't procrastinate in answering the call. The fifty-four-year-old squat man with the broken nose promptly rose from his chair and followed Gino into the private office.

Brute's appearance was his strong suit. His muscular arms and thick neck scared people, thus making him effective as a debt collector. Upon closer inspection Gino realized that Brute was the wrong fit.

The guy is all muscle with limited brains, finally admitted Gino to himself. *Long John isn't ever gonna believe that Brute is the idea guy, and not Davey Brazil. I can't put him in over Davey.*

An idea then suddenly came to Gino out of the blue. *Why not the kid? He's young, but he's got brains and balls*, thought Gino.

"Go outside and keep an eye on my car," said Gino abruptly, dismissing Brute. "And tell Jackie I want to see him right away."

271

"You don't need me, Gino?" asked The Brute, who saw a potential payday disappearing.

"Not today, I'll find something for you to do tomorrow, Brute. Just go get Jackie for me."

Jackie entered the office nervously. He was wondering if he had done something wrong. Gino could see the anguish in the face of his protégé. He immediately put him at ease.

"Relax, kid. You ain't in any trouble."

"Oh, I'm glad to hear that...I thought I screwed up."

"Nah, you did nothing wrong. In fact, I got good news for you."

"You do?"

"I'm going out on a limb for you, Jackie. You're getting a big push up, one that nobody your age gets. Are you ready to play in the big leagues?"

"I definitely am, Gino," answered Jackie enthusiastically.

"All you have to do is stay loyal and do what I say. I'm gonna lay the groundwork that will get you your button one day, kid."

"You think so?"

"If I didn't, I wouldn't be wasting my time with you. What do you think I've been grooming you for?"

"Thank you," voiced Jackie, not knowing what else to say.

"What I'm trying to convey here, is that I'm bringing you along with me as I move up the ladder. I know that's something you want, right?"

"Definitely, I'm honored."

"Okay, then. The first thing you gotta do is clean yourself up. You need to start by shaving every day. You can't go around looking like some wolfman. The important people in the family notice such
things," advised Gino.

"No problem."

"To advance you have to do a piece of work, Jackie. Do you understand what that means?"

Jackie bit his lip before answering. He knew that doing a piece of work meant that he'd have to commit murder. "I'm up for it Gino," he finally replied, feeling that he really had no choice.

"Good. I got a job for us to do right away. When that's done, we're gonna go shopping and get you some good clothes. You gotta look like somebody, if you want to be treated like somebody. Remember that, Jackie. Nobody wants to be around a slug."

"I know," commented Jackie. "Whatever you need me to do, I'll do it."

"I know you will. Here is the deal, we're gonna go out of town to do a piece of work. There is this guy who made a big mistake in thinking he can cross me and get away with it."

"What did he do?"

"I caught him with his hand in the cookie jar."

"He must be crazy to steal from you."

"Crazy ain't the right word for it, kid. He's suicidal!" Jackie shook his head in disgust. "After we do this job, as long as you do good, I'm giving you a position of responsibility. You'll be overseeing some of my interests and be answering only to me. How does that sound?"

"Great, Gino!"

"You're gonna be fronting for me in a business and building I own, kid."

"No problem."

Gino scribbled the address of Funzi's Auto Salvage, in Greenpoint, on a matchbook cover and handed it to Jackie.

"Have Brute drive you there in my car. When you get there, ask for Funzi. He'll give you wheels to take home. Drive carefully, the car ain't gonna be legit. Park it close by here."

"No problem, Gino".

"And remind that moron to bring me my car back."

Jackie was later instructed to pack a bag for a three-day trip. He was told to be at Gino's house at 5:00 A.M. with the vehicle he received from Funzi. The plan was for Jackie to follow his mentor, who would be driving his black Lincoln, to Portland, Maine.

"You're taking the Lincoln?"

"Yeah, it's too long a drive not to be comfortable. You'll be staying at a hotel in Portland," advised Gino.

273

"What about you?"

"I'll be checking in at a different hotel. I don't want us seen around together up there."

"Can I ask what's doing there?" Not understanding the cloak and dagger, Jackie was clearly apprehensive at this point. Gino understood the young man's concern.

"I already told you, you graduated, Jackie. We're gonna go do a piece of work together." Jackie gulped, as the reality of taking part in a murder sunk in.

"Oh, okay." Gino sensed the lukewarm response.

"This is gonna help build your reputation, Jackie," assured Gino. "Once people start seeing you dressed sharp and standing with me, they're gonna take notice. Wait and see how you're treated then. Your rep is what gets you respect, kid. Do you want to know the fastest way to a solid rep, Jackie boy?

"Yeah...."

"Get a couple of notches under your belt. That's what causes people to fear you....and it don't get any better than that, kid. Are you with me or what?"

"I'm definitely with you, Gino."

"Good, you had me wondering there for a minute. I spoke to my lawyer; he's drawing up the papers I want you to sign."

***

JACKIE TOOK GINO'S words of wisdom to heart. From the perspective of the impressionable young man, the advantages of having people fear you were obvious. When it came to proof, Jackie looked no further than the success attained by Gino and other powerful men of his ilk. Members of the secret society ruled over those without underworld affiliations, of that there was no doubt.

Now having set a dubious standard for himself, Jackie willingly entered into the dark side of the life he chose to live. If gaining membership to the Long John Capezzo family demanded his having kill(s) to his credit, so be it.

Jackie convinced himself that he was fortunate to have such an apt tutor as Gino mentoring him.

With Gino behind me, I can't miss getting my button, thought Jackie, who could only see the upside of induction into a mob family.

Jackie was filled with nervous energy the morning he and Gino set out for Portland. He wondered if Gino was going to give him a gun to take along. Unsure, it crossed his mind that perhaps he was expected to bring along his own equalizer. Finally, he inquired.

"Should I be carrying a piece, Gino?"

"No, you don't need a gun on this job. For right now all you need to do is a couple of small things."

"Like what?"

"I want you to wipe down the car so there are no prints. Then you have to wear gloves whenever you get in the car."

"Got it. But what about money? I don't have much."

The statement caused Gino to chuckle. "Don't worry about that, I got you covered. Now look, Jackie, I don't want you to talk to anybody about this. Remember, whenever you do a piece of work, mum is the word. Once a piece of work is done, it's done. You never ever talk about it to anyone, even me. AND you never admit what you did to anyone. Do you understand that?"

"I got it, Gino. But if it's a secret, how will I be able to build my reputation?"

"Don't worry about that. Trust me, Jackie, people are gonna see how you're being treated by the people who count. They'll all know. Word will spread that you're a serious man."

"I see."

"You still got that phony ID I got for you, right?"

"Yeah, of course I do."

"Make sure you use it when you check in at the hotel in Portland."

As planned, both men checked into their respective hotels without incident. The following day, traveling independently, they met for lunch at a restaurant in Kennebunkport to discuss their nefarious mission. Gino felt it safe for them to meet openly in Kennebunkport, which was a 35-minute drive from Portland.

Once settled in the privacy of a booth inside the restaurant, Gino explained to Jackie how the hit was going to go down. The plan was for Gino to first check out the Portland flower shop to make sure that their target was still there.

"While I do that, you stay put in the hotel and be packed. Wait until you hear from me," instructed Gino. "Once I'm sure he's there, I'm going to confront our man and make him sign these documents I got with me. After I get his John Hancock on those papers, I'll notify you."

"Got it."

"For now, go pick up a bottle of whiskey and pour half of it out. When I call you, you drive to the florist shop. When our boy closes up, we'll make it happen. You'll run him over and then jump into my car. All the cops are gonna find is a dead man on the street and half a bottle of whiskey in an abandoned car at the scene."

"Do I know who the mark is?" asked Jackie.

"You may," replied Gino. "It's Cosmo the Florist. Do you know him?"

"No, I never met him."

"It makes no difference if you know him or not, kid. In this racket friendships don't mean a thing. When the order comes to do a piece of work, you just do it. If you don't, somebody else will, so you might as well just go and do it."

"I understand, Gino."

"Now listen, this is important. You gotta make sure Cosmo's dead," emphasized Gino. "If you gotta run him over a couple of times, you do it. At the end of the day, Cosmo's gotta croak."

"And I get away with you, right?"

"That's right. And don't worry, I'll be right there to take out anybody who gets in the way. We'll grab our bags and head home without looking back."

"Do you figure we take him out tomorrow?"

"That's hard to say. I got to see if he has people with him and what time he leaves work. Once I size things up, we make our move."

"What if he's lives right there and don't leave, Gino?

"What do you mean?"

"You know, maybe he lives above the florist shop or something?"

"Stop with all the questions, Jackie," said Gino, abruptly. "Let me do the thinking."

The following day Gino surveilled Cosmo's Portland flower shop. To his good fortune he was able to see Cosmo standing in his shop through the front glass. Parking was available on the opposite side of the street. *This is gonna be a piece of cak*e," thought Gino.

34

Cosmo The Fox

COSMO THE FLORIST COULDN'T get over his lousy luck. The absconder thought he was out of danger after establishing himself in Portland. Cosmo's every move had been made with an eye toward caution. He assumed an alias when settling down and used it for opening his small business. He made a serious effort to maintain a low profile. This included refusing to be photographed when offered the opportunity to have his new business featured in a Portland newspaper. Now, with all going well, everything collapsed.

Being recognized by a salesman working for a supplier Cosmo had done business with was an unforeseeable setback. The interaction, however brief, put the florist at risk. With his future in Portland now iffy, Cosmo knew what he had to do. His only option was to relocate because Gino Pagnetta was a gangster who lived for revenge.

Cosmo needed time to tie up loose business ends in Portland before picking up stakes. During this period, he fretted over being ambushed. Cosmo, now forced to remain vigilant, never took more than a dozen steps without looking over his shoulder when outdoors. The florist took to carrying an aluminum softball bat wherever he went.

278

Cosmo's cash register in the flower shop was located next to the shop window. This was good in that it afforded him the opportunity to see if any suspicious characters were lurking about. It also enabled Cosmo to spot vehicles that he knew were favored by mob types. Anyone operating a vehicle with New York or New Jersey license plates immediately came under suspicion.

The downside of Cosmo being near the shop window was his being visible from the street. This was a chance he believed that he needed to take. It was a good thing he felt that way.

Cosmo's heart jumped after noticing the black Lincoln with New York Plates that was parked in the vicinity of his florist shop. He immediately recognized the little man behind the wheel of the Lincoln as being Gino Pagnetta.

*The son of a bitch wasted no time in getting her*e, thought the florist. *I stayed here too lon*g. *What the hell was I thinking*!

Cosmo suspected that Gino would likely enter the florist shop at some point and look to shoot him dead. Either that, or the mobster would wait for Cosmo to close the shop at the end of the day and look to take him out on his way home. The florist decided that he wouldn't give Gino any chance to get off a clear shot at him. Without delay he locked the door to his shop. Prior to pulling down the shades Cosmo hung a sign on the front window that conveyed that the store was closed.

The florist thought it wise to wait until dark before making his way to his car. He took refuge in the storage room in the rear of the shop, where he locked the door and waited for nightfall. Feeling safe, Cosmo closed his eyes and tried to sleep his troubles away.

***

GINO PAGNETTA, ARMED WITH LEGAL PAPERS in need of Cosmo's signing, nonchalantly exited his vehicle and approached the front door of Cosmo's business. To Gino's dismay, he read the posted sign that indicated that the business was closed. Seeing that the lights inside the premises were now off, gave Gino pause.

The organized crime capo assumed that his prey had to have seen him pull up to the location. Gino believed it more than likely that Cosmo locked himself in his shop.

He'll have to come out sometime, thought Gino, deciding to wait his man out.

***

BEING ALONE IN THE STORAGE ROOM gave Cosmo the Florist time to think. Feeling cornered, he reached the conclusion that he had to do something proactive in order to survive the situation he faced. While he disliked the thought of having to partake in murder, he saw no other way out of his predicament.

I can't run forever, he thought.

It was well after midnight when the florist decided to make his move. Crouching down low, Cosmo crept to the front of his shop to take a peek out of the front window. From his vantage point he was able to see that Gino's black Lincoln was parked a good distance in front of his own car.

I'll beat this bastard at his own game, thought the pursued man.

Armed with his softball bat, Cosmo slipped out of the rear door of his shop. Taking a long way around, he made his way to his parked car undetected. Cosmo rested the bat on the passenger seat and got comfortable. *Now I'm the one doing the hunting*, he thought as he looked at the Lincoln in the distance.

I could run, but if I do that it'll never end with this guy. I have to finish him off and be done with him.

***

DUE TO THE NIPPINESS of the weather, and in part out of boredom, Gino had been helping himself to the cognac that he kept stored in the glove compartment of his car. As the time passed, the contents of the flask disappeared. Travel weary, the gangster's alcohol consumption caught up with him to where his alertness had become diminished.

280

The mobster entered into a struggle to stay awake. He began dozing off, only to wake up a minute or two later. Finally, he succumbed to the call of slumber. After a forty-five-minute sleep his eyes slowly opened. After wiping his eyes with his fingers, Gino gazed at his surroundings. When he saw the florist shop he remembered the purpose for his being there. He cursed himself for falling asleep.

"Shit," voiced Gino aloud, as he checked his watch. "Cosmo could have left." At this point Gino thought it made sense to abandon his mission for the time being. *"The hell with this, tomorrow is another day,"* he said to himself.

Gino took a slow ride back to his hotel. He struggled to keep his eyes open as he drove. Although hungry, Gino decided to forgo stopping off someplace for food. Concentrating on the road before him, Gino neglected to look in his rear-view mirror. If he had, he may have realized that he was being shadowed.

Since Cosmo was familiar with the Portland area, he knew that the road he and Gino were traveling on led to a dead end. This meant that Gino could only be going to one destination.

"Unless he's lost, he's gotta be staying at the old hotel at the end of this road," said Cosmo aloud.

Excited with anticipation of what was to follow, the florist was hunched forward with both hands on the steering wheel of his vehicle. With whitened knuckles he pursued Gino in earnest.

When Cosmo noticed that Gino's Lincoln was swaying, it became obvious to the florist that the gangster was either drunk or dozing at the wheel. At this point Cosmo decided to take a chance. He passed the black Lincoln and took the lead. Gino, who was fighting to stay awake, never noticed.

Cosmo pulled into the parking lot of the old hotel. After parking, he shut off his car engine and exited his vehicle carrying his bat. Since there was renovation work underway at the hotel, there were several large green dumpsters stationed in the corner of the parking area. Cosmo took a position behind one of the dumpsters and awaited Gino's arrival.

When Gino pulled into the lot, he parked his car in a way that took up two spots. Unsteady on his feet, the gangster's awareness was below par. All he could think of was getting to bed.

Gino was just steps from his vehicle when he was felled by a crashing blow to the back of his skull. The only noise was the dull thud of the bat striking Gino's head. Cosmo's sneak attack grounded Gino, leaving him dazed, but still alive. All that the gangster could distinguish was a hazy figure of someone standing over him. The mobster's feeble reach for the gun in his pocket was thwarted by the additional blows he received to his crown.

The last thing Gino saw in life was the maniacal look of Cosmo standing over him. It was a look that came complete with tightened teeth and bulging eyes. When Cosmo completed his battering, he used the bloodied weapon to poke at the torso of the fallen Gino. Seeing no reaction to the jabs, Cosmo was convinced that his victim was gone.

Cosmo looked around the parking lot at the completion of his dirty work. He was relieved to see that there was no indication of any activity. He gazed at the exterior of the hotel itself. Except for the light coming from the lobby entrance, all appeared dark.

Satisfied that he drew no attention, the florist was about to make his way to his car when he suddenly paused. He thought to rifle Gino's pockets to give the impression that a robbery had taken place. In doing so he came across the papers drawn up by Gino's attorney. Cosmo took charge of the papers.

When Cosmo reached his home, he let out a satisfied sigh of relief. The florist opened up a bottle of Old Grand Dad to celebrate his liberation from the wrath of Gino. The double he poured was something he actually needed.

As Cosmo sipped the intoxicant, he began reading the documents he confiscated from the man he murdered. The notarized papers reflected the sale of his business and building to someone he didn't know. The name Jackie Lanno was a mystery to him. The florist could only suspect that Jackie Lanno, AKA: Jackie the Lackey, was the accomplice of the man who had planned to murder him.

Cosmo rested the papers on his lap. Putting his head back in his chair, the florist took a moment to self-reflect. Justification for killing Gino came easy. *I had no choice*, Cosmo though*t. It was him or me.*

The florist closed his eyes and contemplated his options. Cosmo doubted that Gino would have told anyone that he was on a mission to murder in Maine. The only one who could accuse him of killing Gino with some credibility was Louis. Since Louis was no fan of his cousin, Cosmo felt certain that he could come to an understanding with Louis as long as a financial upside existed. The florist had no idea Louis was dead

Now free of Gino, Cosmo believed that he could return to the Bronx to reclaim what was rightfully his.

Cosmo knew that a member of organized crime would step in to assume control of Gino's gambling empire. He also knew that Louis, as a family associate, would have the ear of whoever that person was. The florist believed that, with the cooperation of Louis, an amicable arrangement could be made with whoever was awarded the gambling operation.

35

A Surprise For
Cosmo

COSMO ARRIVED BACK IN the Bronx just before daybreak. Unaware of the changes that had taken place since his absence, he was in for a few surprises. The first came when he entered the apartment he abandoned. Based on the condition of the digs, it appeared that someone was using his apartment.

The florist noticed a pile of mail that was neatly stacked atop the kitchen table. As he perused the correspondence, he noticed that there were no outstanding bills. A spiral notebook rested on the table. When Cosmo opened the notebook, he saw entries that reflected rent payments received from the several tenants who resided in the building. To the far right of each entry was a red check mark. Cosmo could only assume that this meant that the money had been turned over to someone, likely Gino.

*Whoever is doing this bookkeeping is very efficien*t, Cosmo thought, as he rubbed the stubble on his face. *It can't possibly be Louis. That idiot doesn't have the discipline to keep good records.*

Cosmo picked up the telephone to see if it was working. It was. He then looked inside the refrigerator. He found that it housed a container of unexpired milk, cold cuts, mustard, mayonnaise, beer, soda and several other newly purchased items. Atop the refrigerator there was lots of bread. Cosmo then entered his bedroom, where he found his bed made. The only clothes in the closet were the threads he had left behind. There was no indication that someone was using the apartment for overnight lodging.

The florist looked for the diary he had forgotten to take with him. He found it odd that the journal was nowhere to be found. "Now who the hell would want my daughter's diary?" Cosmo asked himself aloud.

Although weary from his travel, Cosmo couldn't bring himself to climb into bed due to the puzzling situation. He eventually dozed off while sitting in a comfortable recliner. A few hours later, he was awakened by the presence of a teenage youth who noisily entered the apartment. The visitor was as startled as Cosmo. After Cosmo revealed who he was, the teenager indicated that he worked in the florist shop downstairs for Davey.

At this juncture Cosmo realized that the florist shop was open for business. The florist quickly freshened up and went downstairs to announce his return.

The activity encountered in the florist shop confounded Cosmo. He was awed by the number of people lingering inside the premises. Cosmo was only accustomed to people entering the shop for brief periods. They'd either purchase something or place a bet, then they'd depart.

The florist looked at the half dozen men who were seated at a newly installed table in the corner of the store. They were drinking coffee as they chatted. Some were making notations in the Daily Racing Form, as they handicapped their race selections.

They turned the place into a hangout, thought Cosmo.

Cosmo watched as Davey Brazil monitored the gamblers and directed the several teenagers who were working at the florist shop.

"Joey, go take care of Mrs. Baker," said Davey, addressing one of the youths, "she needs a floral arrangement made up." Davey then turned to another worker and instructed, "Butchie, go get Tommy and start moving those shoe boxes to the back room. They can't be left out front. Stack them in the back between the radios and the cigarettes."

"I'm going out for bacon and eggs, Davey, you want something?" asked one of the gamblers at the table.

"No, thanks, I'm good."

When Davey Brazil noticed the open-mouthed Cosmo, his face broke into a welcoming grin. He seemed to be sincerely glad to see the florist. At this point no papers were signed transferring ownership, and Gino led him to believe that Cosmo was still involved in the business.

"Welcome home, Cosmo!" greeted Davey. "Gino never mentioned that you were coming home. He had been looking for you." It had now become obvious to Cosmo that word hadn't yet reached the Bronx that Gino was no longer among the living.

"Well, I'm back now. What's all this?"

"Business is great, Cosmo," advised Davey, who was proud of the strides made. "Gino gave me carte blanche to do what I wanted to in order to drum up more business. He said you were okay with it. We've been making plenty of money in both businesses, as you know, Cosmo."

"As I know?"

"Gino's been sending you your money, right?"

"Oh…. sure." The thought of Gino keeping his money made Cosmo glad he killed the gangster. "Who has been upstairs taking care of my apartment?"

"I've been on top of things. Gino told me to look after the mail, pay the bills and hold the fort until you got back. The apartment was kind of messy, so I straightened things out."

"The refrigerator is filled with food and beer. Who is that for?"

"I have the kids working here make sandwiches for themselves when they're hungry. By the way, how was Maine?"

Cosmo was taken aback by the question. "I was never there, I was in Florida," lied Cosmo. "What made you think that I was in Maine?"

"Gino wanted to send you your money. He wasn't sure where you were vacationing, so he made me reach out to all the venders to see if anybody knew where you went. One of them said they saw you in Maine, so I assumed that's where he sent you your money."

"The guy must have been seeing things. I was in Florida."

"Oh, Gino never mentioned that he was sending money to you in Florida."

"Whatever," said Cosmo, not wanting to continue on that conversational road. "What about my rent money, Davey?"

"I turned all the money over to Gino. He said he'd send it on to you. Didn't you get it?"

"That's right, I forgot. I got it in Florida. What else did you implement around here, Davey?"

"All the tenants are paying their rent in cash now, at a slightly discounted rate of course. Gino wanted it that way, he said you were all for it."

"That was Gino's idea?"

"Actually, it was mine. I figured that you guys didn't really need Uncle Sam as a partner."

"That was very thoughtful of you."

"Gino said you would appreciate it."

"So, where is Louis?"

"Oh.... you didn't hear?" asked Davey, his face turning grave.

"Hear what?"

"Louis is dead.... he was murdered."

"Dead?"

"We were all shocked when we heard."

"What happened?"

"Gino said some deadbeat killed him to avoid paying back a loan."

"When did Louis is go into the loan shark business?"

287

" I don't know anything about that, Cosmo. I guess Gino can fill you in when he gets back."

"I suppose he will," said Cosmo, while thinking, *that son of a bitch Gino was cleaning house!* "So, it looks like you've been pretty busy around here, Davey."

"Yeah, the money has been pouring in."

"What's the story with all these guys hanging out in here?"

Davey explained in detail how he grew the florist business and the gambling operation. This impressed Cosmo, who now saw the value in Davey. However, concerns remained.

Without Louis being around, Cosmo now needed someone to represent him in dealing with the Long John Capezzo organized crime family. It was clear to the florist that Davey was limited in terms of his connection to the mobster element. Then there was another issue.

I'm not gonna be able to skim money off the gambling operation with Brazil having such an active role in things, thought Cosmo.

Cosmo now would need time to determine if Davey Brazil was receptive to being compromised. In this the florist wasn't overly optimistic. The florist knew that inevitably someone from the Capezzo family would come around to collect their end of the money being pulled in from the gambling business. That was the way things worked. All Cosmo could do was sit tight until Gino's replacement made his presence known.

"Were you dealing with anyone else from the Capezzo family besides Gino?" asked Cosmo, fishing for information.

"No," replied Davey, "the only person I ever dealt with was Gino, that is, aside from his cousin Louis. Let me show you what we got going in the back, Cosmo."

After seeing all the swag in the backroom Cosmo had a question. "Who brings in all this stuff? You got fireworks, untaxed cigarettes and everything but Aunt Millie's red underwear piling up around here."

"I don't know much about that end of things, Cosmo. Guys just come in with the items."

"They can't be just dropping stuff off on their own. How do things work, Davey?"

"I get a call from Gino telling me what kind of delivery to expect," explained Davey. "When the delivery arrives, I inventory what we received and then later sell everything off piecemeal or in bulk. Gino sets a ballpark price, but I have a lot of latitude in that."

"You line up the sales?"

"I take care of the piecemeal transactions. When it comes to bulk transactions, I first clear the deal with Gino before going ahead."

"I see, Davey."

"You should really talk to Gino, he could fill you in on everything," suggested Davey.

"I'll have to do that," replied Cosmo, not letting on that Gino was gone.

The florist felt that since he held full ownership in the florist business, it was reasonable for him to assume that any illegal money generated off the back of his florist shop entitled him to a taste of the profits. This was another reason why negotiations with the Capezzo family needed to be entered into.

36

Post Gino

JACKIE THE LACKEY HARDLY TOUCHED the Chinese takeout his mother had ordered for them. He sat at the kitchen table poking at the General Tso's Chicken with the white plastic fork that came with the delivery.

"What's wrong, Jackie?" asked the mother, sensing something was troubling her son.

"Nothing, Ma, I'm just thinking about something," replied Jackie. "Have some more tea."

"Are you worried about me?"

"No, Ma."

"I haven't had a drink in months," advised the mother defensively.

"I know, Ma."

"Then what are you thinking about?" questioned the mother.

"Nothing, Ma," said Jackie, smiling softly. He was proud of his mother who had been doing well in her battle against depression and drink. "I'll finish this later, I'm just not hungry now," voiced Jackie, rising from the table.

After retiring to his room, Jackie locked the bedroom door to avoid being disturbed. While resting in bed he reflected on the evening he sat in a Portland hotel room awaiting word from Gino Pagnetta. It was a memory he'd never forget.

"Unbelievable!" said Jackie aloud, when thinking of the law enforcement officer who finally answered Gino's cellphone that fatal night. Jackie immediately hung up when asked who the caller was. At that point Jackie had assumed Gino had been arrested.

Feeling thirsty from the food he consumed, Jackie reached for the water bottle that rested atop the end table next to his bed. After taking a healthy swig, he returned the water bottle to where it was. His need for water reminded Jackie of his thirst in Maine. He recollected going to the soda machine in the lobby of the hotel for something to relieve his dryness. It was there that Gino's protégé first learned of his mentor's murder. The stack of newspapers that sat on top of the lobby desk told the story. More specifically, it was the shocking headline that remained etched in Jackie's recall. The large black print on the front page reflected:

NEW YORK MAN FOUND MURDERED!

Jackie remembered rushing back to his room to read about the homicide. As he digested the reported details, he came to learn that a man was found murdered in the parking lot of the hotel where Gino was staying. The newspaper account neglected to include the victim's name.

Jackie remembered how he hastily checked out of his room and drove to the hotel where the homicide occurred. His conversation with a hotel employee of about his age was informative. He learned that the murder victim had been staying at the hotel. The description provided by the employee was further enlightening. Only Gino Pagnetta could have been the very short man who drove a big black Lincoln Continental with New York license plates.

"Did anybody see anything?" queried Jackie, at the time.

"No one saw a thing," replied the hotel employee. "People are scared to death that there may be some kind of madman on the loose. Killings like this just don't happen here."

"What makes you think it's a madman that done it?"

"The man was beaten to death with a bat or something. Now, what normal person would do that? The killer has to be some kind of a crazy nut."

Or a florist, thought Jackie.

Jackie believed that Cosmo the Florist had somehow gotten the upper hand on Gino. This led to a disturbing question that lingered within him as he rested in his room. *Did Cosmo know that I was there to support Gino in killing him?* Jackie asked himself.

Ingrained in Jackie was the things taught to him by Gino. What stuck most was the mobster's emphasis on never squealing or fessing up to any wrongdoing. Taking this advice seriously, the young hood was firm in his belief that it was in his interest not to breathe a word to anyone about his role in the mission to murder Cosmo in Portland. If a discussion were to ever arise as to what occurred in Maine, he'd remain adamant in his silence.

After another swig of water, Jackie thought of what he did after returning to the Bronx. He disposed of the car he had been using by dumping it on a dead-end street in a depressed section not far from where he lived. The vehicle with the altered VIN number fit in nicely with the other discarded car that had worn out its usefulness.

Jackie's loyalty to Gino remained unwavering. Determined not to forget the murder of the man he looked up to, he saw it as his duty to one day avenge the death of his mentor. Jackie staunchly believed that Gino would have wanted him to retaliate. In this regard Jackie was dead right. Gino would never have wanted his protégé to remain idle and not provide an answer to his assassination.

Jackie knew that the absence of Gino would change the dynamics for him at the social club. It had always been clear to him that some of those jealous of his close relationship with the boss resented him. Such ill will was bound to manifest itself once it became known that Jackie's mentor no longer lived.

"They will never treat me like some errand boy again!" said Jackie aloud with definiteness.

JACKIE WAS AT THE SOCIAL CLUB when he became aware that Cosmo had returned to his Bronx florist shop. He overheard someone at the club say that he saw Cosmo when putting in an order for a floral arrangement with Davey Brazil.

While Jackie immersed himself in figuring out a way to kill Cosmo, he heard that an organized crime powerhouse assumed control of the gambling empire that once belonged to Gino Pagnetta. This resulted in Jackie putting a temporary hold on things.

LONG JOHN CAPEZZO WASN'T HAPPY after learning of the death of Gino Pagnetta. Having lost Louis, and now Gino, left the family boss feeling threatened. He summoned his underboss to his Hoboken, New Jersey home. Long John sat in a leather burgundy armchair in the library of his home waiting for his guest to arrive. When the family boss heard the doorbell ring he reached for his cup of espresso. He sipped the beverage as he listened to the footsteps of his wife going to the front door to let the caller in.

Long John was warmly dressed in a chocolate cardigan sweater, a wintertime favorite of his. Beneath the sweater was a beige collared shirt. His creased slacks were black. On Long John's feet were powder blue tasseled suede loafers. On his head, tilted to one side, sat his ever-present straw skimmer.

The scent of the Anisette flavored cigar in the ashtray, although unlit, made its presence known. Capezzo's long thin leg draped lazily over the other one as he awaited his visitor. When the mafia chief saw Mario Montana standing at the entrance of his library, he waved his underboss in.

After greeting his superior, Montana took a seat opposite the family boss. The second highest ranking member of the crime family was a stubby man with a round face. His thick white hair was buzzed on the sides and back well over his ears, leaving just a patch of hair in the center of his head. This gave him the look of an aging rooster. Montana sat in silence, waiting to be addressed. He could only speculate as to why the family boss requested his presence.

On the table next to Capezzo's chair rested a copy of *The Devine Comedy* by Dante Alighieri, a tale of encounters during a trip through hell, purgatory and paradise. Beneath this classic was what the mafia don considered to be his bible, *The Prince by Niccolo Machiavelli*, a political tutorial he adhered to when it came to leadership and power. Capezzo took Alighieri's work, lifted the book and uttered, "The inferno, the purgatorio and paradiso."

The underboss, not sure of how to respond, just nodded as if he understood what Long John meant by referencing fire, purgatory and paradise.

"You don't understand?"

"I don't follow you, John," said the underboss.

"There are three destinations we have to think of in life, Mario."

The underboss maintained his look of bewilderment. Without bothering to expand on his remark, the family boss went in a different direction.

"I want a full investigation conducted on the death of our captain," said the boss, finally making sense to Mario. "I want to know exactly what happened to Gino Pagnetta up there in Maine. Gino was a big earner for the family. I want you to look into this personally, Mario."

"I'll handle it, John," assured the underboss. "Who do you want to step into Gino's shoes?"

"For the time being, you take charge of things. Whoever I ultimately decide on will come in time."

"Sounds good," said Mario, who was appreciative of receiving a new revenue stream. "I know Gino had a lot going. Right, John?"

"Plenty," answered the mob boss, producing a piece of paper from his wallet. "What he had going is listed here," said

Capezzo, handing the paper to Montana. "Head over to Gino's social club and inform everyone as to the change. They must know that you are running things for now."

"No problem."

"There is this young kid over there who Gino was grooming. Talk to him, see if he knows anything about what happened to Gino."

"What's the kid's name?"

"Jackie."

***

MARIO MONTANA ARRIVED at the social club with his driver. The men were about the same age. Each wore turtleneck shirts, dark slacks and black overcoats. The black single-breasted overcoats they wore were identical. Not surprisingly, they came off the back of the same hijacked truck.

What made Mario memorable was the dark gray fedora he sported and the large unlit cigar that protruded from his mouth. The driver, Jiggs Tuminaro, was distinguished by his chiseled looks and the nasty scar that ran across his left cheek.

The buzz in the social club faded after Jiggs, who made his way to the center of the room, quieted everyone down. Both he and Mario Montana were known as no-nonsense powerful members of the Capezzo crime family. Mario, as the family underboss, was particularly impressive to those in attendance.

"Everybody, listen up," announced Jiggs in a commanding voice. Everything about the sloped shouldered six-footer, with the scarred face and permanent scowl, conveyed tough. "Mario's got something to say."

"Gino ain't around no more," declared Mario, taking center stage, "so I'll be running things over here now." The cigar chomping underboss continued without mincing words. "It'll be this way until I tell you different." A hush fell over the room. "So, from now on consider me your skipper. You guys are all reporting to me. If you got questions, take them up with Jiggs." Those in the room nodded their understanding.

"And don't forget this," injected Jiggs, "remember your place. I'm the only one who gets to talk to Mario directly."

"That's right," confirmed the underboss.

"Now, where is this kid Jackie?" Jiggs asked.

"He went to pick up some sandwiches," informed one of men seated at a card table.

"Is there a private room in this joint?"

"It's in the back."

"When Jackie gets back tell him Mr. Montana wants to see him. We'll be in the backroom."

When Jackie the Lacky returned to the club with the sandwiches, he was told that the underboss of the Capezzo family was in the office waiting to see him. Jackie stiffened. He figured that an audience with the family underboss meant trouble.

Surprisingly the meeting started off rather well with Jiggs explaining why he had been called into the office. As Jiggs did this, Mario sat quietly in silence. Finally, the underboss stated that he was aware of Jackie's close relationship with Gino Pagnetta. He noted that Gino must have seen something special in Jackie for him to bother with someone so young.

"You heard about what happened to Gino?"

"I heard," said Jackie.

"What exactly was it that Gino liked about you?" asked Mario.

Jackie stammered for a moment as he struggled to find the right words. "I think Gino knew that I looked up to him," he finally answered.

"That's it?"

"I was very loyal to Gino."

"Why is that?"

"Gino knew I didn't have it easy at home. He was there for me."

"What was the problem at home?"

"My father was killed in a freak accident. My sister overdosed and my mother got depressed and began drinking. I had to drop out of high school to help support me and my mother."

"Did you ever do time in a protectory?" asked Jiggs.

"No, I never got busted."

"I did, and let me tell you, the things that went on there was as bad as any prison I was ever in."

"That's a story for another time, Jiggs," said Mario to his driver.

As the three continued to talk Jackie became comfortable to a point where a part of him wanted to tell all he knew about the plot to kill Cosmo the Florist in Portland. Mario, who was quite astute at reading people, sensed that Jackie was holding something back.

"C'mon open up. Get whatever it is off your chest," said Mario. Jackie began to squirm in his seat, another telltale sign that he was concealing something.

"Talk to us," said Jiggs. "You ain't in any trouble."

"I idolized Gino," Jackie finally said, starting to open up. "I mean, I wanted to be just like him, so whatever he told me to do, I did without question."

"There is nothing wrong with that," voiced Mario. "What did he ask you to do?"

"I even took up his mannerisms to be more like him."

Jackie's statement got a reaction out of Jiggs, who remarked, "What's the matter, kid, Jack the Ripper wasn't a good enough role model for you?"

"This is nothing to joke about over here," chastised Mario, "so be quiet before I start sending you out for the sandwiches."

"Sorry, Mario," apologized the driver, raising his open hand defensively.

"Listen Jackie, tell me the truth and you will have gained a good friend. But if you start jerking me off, then it'll get ugly for you really quick. Which way is it gonna be?"

Jackie could tell that Mario was someone not to be trifled with. Rather than risk his wellbeing, Jackie decided to tell all he knew. He began by explaining to Mario how he and Gino went to Portland with the intention of murdering Cosmo the Florist.

"Gino took it upon himself to do this without permission?" asked Mario, who found this surprising.

"I don't know the answer to that, Mr. Montana."

Mario looked at Jackie suspiciously before concluding that he was being told the truth. "I suppose you probably wouldn't know about that," said Mario. Being called Mr. Montana went a long way in impressing the underboss. "Why did Gino want to clip the florist?"

"Cosmo was skimming money."

"That would do it," voiced Jiggs.

"What made things really bad, Mr. Montana, was that Cosmo involved Gino's cousin in the skimming."

"What cousin is this?"

"He's talking about Louis," chirped in Jiggs. "So, it must have been Gino who whacked Louis," concluded the driver.

"Nobody asked you to play Sherlock Holmes," barked the underboss nastily, addressing Jiggs. "We don't know a thing for sure yet about what happened to Louis."

"Listen to what the kid's saying, Mario."

"Did Gino clip his cousin, Jackie?" queried the underboss.

"He never told me anything like that," answered Jackie. "All I really know is that Gino is dead, and Cosmo is alive and kicking here in the Bronx."

"You know, Cosmo could have killed Gino in self-defense," pointed out Mario, looking at his driver."

"What difference does that make?" asked Jiggs. "Gino was still a made guy."

"You're right," acknowledged Mario. "There is only one answer for that."

With Mario's statement came a brief pause. The quiet was broken by Jackie, who saw an opportunity to prove himself to the mobsters.

"Mr. Montana," said Jackie. "I'd like to even the score."

"What are you talking about?"

"I'd like your permission to kill Cosmo. I feel like I owe that to Gino." Mario and Jiggs exchanged glances upon hearing this. "Allow me to do this work, Mr. Montana," continued Jackie, "I promise not to let you down."

Jiggs Tuminaro found Jackie amusing. "We got a junior Al Capone over here, Mario," scoffed the driver.

298

The underboss found Jackie's willingness to murder in a positive light. To Mario, Jackie represented the strength necessary to ensure the future of the family.

"I like your loyalty and balls, Jackie," said Mario. "This family could use more of that."

Jiggs Tuminaro now viewed Jackie cautiously. *I'm gonna have to keep an eye on this little shit,* Jiggs thought. *The little bastard will be after my job one day!*

"Gino taught me the meaning of loyalty, Mr. Montana."

"Is there anything you forgot to tell us, Jackie."

"No, Mr. Montana."

"I still can't see how this florist could ever get the drop on Gino," voiced Jiggs. "It just doesn't make sense."

"Maybe Gino had things to talk about with Cosmo before clipping him," speculated Mario. "Do you know if he did, Jackie?"

"I know that Gino wanted Cosmo to sign some legal papers."

"What kind of legal papers?"

"He wanted Cosmo's house and business signed over to me. I was going to be Gino's front man."

"Gino sure had a lot of faith in you, kid, declared the underboss. "Tell me something, how does a kid with your balls allow these guys to send you out for sandwiches?"

"I'm just biding my time, Mr. Montana. Every dog has their day."

"I suppose Gino taught you that."

"Yes, Sir."

"Sit tight, Jackie. Don't do nothing crazy. I'll be getting back to you."

37

The Ruling

ON THEIR WAY TO THE Bronx florist shop Mario Montana expressed to his driver that he thought highly of Jackie the Lackey. Jiggs Tuminaro listened, but he wasn't of the same opinion. Jiggs was a hard person to impress, especially if he saw the potential for competition.

"I think that kid Jackie has what it takes, Jiggs," said Mario. "I can see why Gino saw something in him."

"He's still wet behind the ears, Mario," commented Jiggs, derisively.

"You didn't like him?"

"It's not that I don't like him, I just think the little prick is green," voiced the driver.

"Why are you calling him a little prick?"

"C'mon, Mario, I don't know. That kid just underwhelms me."

"You'd be underwhelmed by a successful exorcism. Do yourself a favor and put a cork in criticizing the kid, I'm getting behind him."

"You are?" asked the surprised Jiggs.

"Yeah, and that's something I want you to do," advised the underboss. "That kid knows the meaning of respect, something some people around here forgot."

"I don't deserve that, Mario," said Jiggs, who got the message. "I've been nothing but loyal to you."

"Then stay that way and help me boost the kid up. It's the guys like him that's gonna keep our thing going when we get too old to be effective.

"Whatever you say, Mario. But can I speak plain?"

"Go ahead, say what you gotta say."

"I'm just saying that you need to be careful with this kid, he's untested."

"So now you think I'm stupid, Jiggs?" asked the underboss, who was growing more confrontational.

"I never said that...."

"This kid said that he is willing to go out and do a piece of work. Can't you see what that says about him? What it means long term?"

"Not really."

"Let me draw you a diagram," replied Mario. "Our family doesn't have any young guns willing to pull the trigger."

"I'm ready, anytime, anyplace," chirped up Jiggs.

"I'm talking young guns, not antiques. We aren't kids anymore, Jiggs. The only way for us to protect the prestige of this family is by continuing to show strength. Right now, we got enough talent to carry us, but we need to think of tomorrow when our old age catches up with us."

"You see this kid as strength?"

"Absolutely! If we can get a few like him in the family, we won't have to worry about our income
drying up down the road. Gino probably knew that. I know Long John does."

"Okay, Mario, I get the point," conceded Jiggs. "But, there is another way of looking at it."

"What way is that?"

"When I hear a kid like that talking about clipping people, I see a cowboy who might clip you and me one day."

"C'mon, don't be paranoid. That's nothing new. Getting whacked is an occupational hazard that can happen to any of us."

When the gangsters arrived at the florist shop, it didn't take them long to see that Davey Brazil was a workhorse. The efficient way Davey oversaw the legal and illegal business being conducted out of the florist shop was impressive.

"This joint is humming," announced Mario, as he watched workers performing shop chores and servicing customers. He then pointed to several men who were seated at a corner table diligently studying the daily racing form.

Although Davey was never formally introduced to Mario or Jiggs, he recognized them as ranking members of the Capezzo organized crime network. Unsure of their purpose in visiting the florist shop, he waited for the visitors to speak first.

"You're Davey, right?" asked Jiggs. Davey humbly nodded his acknowledgement. "Do you know who we are?"

"I think so. Gino's not here. I'm not sure when he'll be back."

"Haven't you heard the breaking news? He ain't coming back. We're in charge now."

Davey's mouth dropped open. After the initial shock he began to wonder what was coming next. His concentration was broken when a school bus driver entered the florist shop. The driver asked to speak to Davey privately. Davey looked at the two mobsters and asked if they minded his speaking to the visitor.

"Go ahead," said Mario, see what he wants." Davey and the driver stepped away to talk.

The bus driver's business had to do with his need to borrow money. After a couple of minutes, Davey could be seen nodding. When Davey returned to Mario and Jiggs, he was asked what his conversation with the bus driver had been about. He told it pertained to a shylock loan.

"Are you putting money on the street?" asked Mario.

"I would for Gino, but under the circumstances, I told the driver that he'd have to come back tomorrow."

"You can continue making loans," approved Mario. "Just keep Jiggs here abreast of what you got on the street. Who does your collecting?"

"With Gino, we never really had a need for a collector. Everybody has been paying."

"Well, you let Jiggs know if you run into a deadbeat."

"Where is Cosmo?"

"I think he's upstairs in his apartment."

"We'll talk to him later," said Mario. "For right now, bring us up to speed about what we got going here."

Both the underboss and soldier were impressed when learning that Davey used gamblers as salespeople.

"You're a pretty bright boy," said Mario. "Show us the rest of this dump."

"Yeah, sure."

When Mario and Jiggs saw all the swag stored in the back room, they were taken aback by the inventory there.

"You're cooking on all cylinders over here," voiced Jiggs.

Davey was queried as to the breakdown on how much illegal money was being generated out of the flower shop. Brazil, who knew the numbers off the top of his head, provided the requested information without hesitation. This further impressed the mobsters.

"Who you been turning all the money over to, Davey?" asked Mario.

"I always gave everything to Gino, but now I guess I'll turn it over to Cosmo."

"You guessed wrong," injected Jiggs.

"Have you already given money to Cosmo?" questioned Mario.

"Yes."

"Who pays you?"

"Gino always did. A lot of times he would give me the okay to pay myself."

"Gino gave money to Cosmo? Is that how it worked?"

"Yeah, that's my understanding."

"How much?"

"I'm not privy to that information."

"What did you do with the last money you collected?"

"I took my salary for running the florist shop and the gambling, paid bills and held the rest of that
money for Gino."

"You still have that money?"

"No, I turned it over to Cosmo.

"Why?"

"I gave it to Cosmo because he asked me for it," explained Davey. "He said that he'd give the money to Gino when he sees him again."

"Tell us about Gino's relationship with Cosmo," said Jiggs. "Were there any problems between them?"

"I don't think so. But honestly, I wouldn't want to know about any problems."

"Don't you care?"

"I get paid really well, so I don't mind being in the dark when it comes to a lot of things. I make it a point not to stick my nose in where it doesn't belong."

"I guess that is a healthy way to operate," said Jiggs.

Mario looked at his driver and said, "That's enough for now." He then tossed his head in the direction of the door, indicating that it was time for them to go."

"Don't you want to talk to Cosmo?" asked Davey. "He's probably upstairs in his apartment."

"We'll see him later," advised Mario. "You're doing okay over here, Davey," said Mario, "you got nothing to worry about. We'll be back."

"What do I do about turning in money?" asked Davey. "Should I keep giving it to Cosmo?"

"For now, just keep doing what you're doing."

When Davey Brazil later informed Cosmo that they were paid a visit by high level representatives of the Long John Capezzo crime family, Cosmo displayed no overt reaction that suggested concern. Cosmo had been expecting such a visit. With the success of the businesses being run out of his florist shop, Cosmo felt that he was in a fine position to negotiate a reasonable arrangement with the mobster(s) who were replacing Gino. This was wishful thinking.

***

LONG JOHN CAPEZZIO sat quietly in his home library with his underboss. The two were having espresso and Italian pine nut Pignoli cookies. Jiggs Tuminaro was having his eats in the kitchen with the don's wife.

Long John displayed no emotion upon learning that Gino Pagnetta plotted to kill Cosmo the Florist. Like his underboss, he too formed the opinion that Cosmo likely murdered Gino, who was a big earner for the family. The loss of a money machine didn't make the family boss happy.

Long John began rubbing his chin after having heard Mario's full report. With a raised index finger, he began speaking.

"So, as far as this Davey Brazil goes, he's a good fit for us over at the florist shop, correct?"

"Definitely. The guy implemented all kinds of ideas that are making money over there."

"That's what I was led to believe. We'll leave him in place."

"This Davey ain't no gangster though, John. I think that he's a safe bet for us because he doesn't seem the type to look to branch out and go in business for himself," advised Mario. "As long as he's making money, he's content getting paid and turning the money over to us."

"Who have we got to replace Gino over at the florist shop?"

"I can handle it."

"No, you're there on a temporary basis. I need you free for other things. Do you have anyone in mind who could fit in Gino's shoes?"

"As a matter of fact, I do. Do you know who I see as a real comer with a future John?"

"Who is that?"

"That kid you told me to talk to, Gino's boy, Jackie the Lackey. I know he's young, but I see in him what Gino saw in him."

"He's promising?"

"Exceptionally, John. If groomed right, he could be the muscle of tomorrow, a good protector of the family."

"You would be willing to sponsor him and propose him for membership one day?"

"I think that I would."

"And you feel that Jackie could oversee Davey Brazil at the florist shop?"

"With the right grooming, I think so."

"So, Jackie could be trusted to collect money, turn it over to us and be loyal?"

Mario replied, "I think so," after the slightest hesitation.

"So that settles it then," said the don. "As far as Cosmo goes, I want you to settle up with him for what he did to Gino. Give that work to Jiggs."

"I'll let him take Jackie along with him. Okay?"

"Do that, it'll be a good test for the kid. Do you have anything else for me"

"Yeah, one other thing. Before I remove Cosmo, how about I make him sign ownership of his florist shop and the building to Jackie. We can have the kid front for us as the owner. That's what the kid said Gino was going to do."

"Gino was a smart boy. Go ahead and do that, Mario. Talk to Testa the lawyer, he'll care of it."

"Which Testa do you want me to use, John, the father or the son?"

"The father, he'll know what to do. The son is an imbecile." Long John's remark caused Mario to shake his head and chuckle.

"You're laughing? It took the son three shots to get his license to practice law?"

"I didn't know that, John."

"That's why I'm glad I have no children, Mario. It's too much of a crap shoot. You never know what you're gonna end up with."

"I hear you."

"One other thing. Make it clear to Davey Brazil that from now on he answers to Jackie. He's to give all the money he takes in to Jackie."

"Right. How do you want to whack things up, John?"

"I'll take forty-five percent; you get thirty percent and Jiggs gets twenty percent. Give Jackie the remaining five percent."

"Just five percent?"

"Let it go at that. Jackie's big payoff will come when you get around to proposing him for membership into the family."

"Got it."

"So, are we done here?"

"One last thing, what do you want me to do about Gino's crew over at his social club?"

"They will answer to you and Jiggs until Jackie proves worthy. Once he gets his button, we'll give him the club."

"Do you think that we're putting too much stock in this kid, John."

"You said he was worthy," voiced the don, lowering his face. "Did you not?"

"I did."

Long John's lips formed a downward curl that pronounced his hawk nose. The mob kingpin now gave the appearance of the vulture he was. "Then don't worry. Like you said, we need the young to protect us in the years to come, so let's keep this young man happy. Take a pignoli for the road, my loyal friend."

38

Raccoon Eyes

THE SECOND TIME MARIO MONTANA and Jiggs Tuminaro walked into the Bronx florist shop they found Cosmo the Florist behind the counter. Based on appearances, Cosmo had no difficulty in pegging the men to be who they were, organized crime family mobsters.

Cosmo understood that the gangsters were entitled to take over Gino's illegal enterprises. He saw that as being only right, as long as he received compensation for the use of his labor and florist shop as a venue for their crookedness. Cosmo was under the impression that he'd be able to once again skim money as he did with Gino. In this, Cosmo was greatly mistaken. The florist took a deep breath as the gangsters approached him.

"Good afternoon, gentlemen, what can I do for you today?" asked Cosmo, politely, treating the men as he would an ordinary customer. The mobsters weren't impressed by Cosmo's polite greeting. If anything, they viewed such cordiality as a sign of weakness.

"You can do plenty if you're Cosmo the Florist," announced Jiggs. "Are you him?"

"Yes, that's me," replied Cosmo, who now noticed the long scar on the face of Jiggs. The florist found the harsh lesion to be intimidating. The distinct cicatrix was further proof that he was talking to a hood. "Can I help you?" he asked, feeling uneasy.

"Do you know who we are?" asked the stone-faced Mario icily. The look of the underboss exuded anything but warmth.

"I'm sorry, no. Have we met before?"

"Does that name Mario Montana ring a bell to you?" Jiggs questioned. "If not, it's time you take your head out of your ass."

Cosmo recognized the name at once. While he anticipated a visit by someone from the crime family, he never dreamt that he'd be confronted by the family underboss. This suggested to the florist that he and his shop were more valuable to the mobsters than originally thought.

"I'm sorry I didn't recognize you, Mr. Montana."

"So, you do know who I am?"

"Of course, a dear friend of mine often spoke of you fondly."

"Who is that?"

"Gino Pagnetta."

"Alright, skip the bullshit," said Mario curtly. "Let's cut to the chase. Do you know why we are here?"

"I think I have an idea."

"Explain, Jiggs."

"We're here to tell you that we're taking over for Gino."

"Did something happen to Gino?" Cosmo asked, feigning ignorance as to Gino's end.

"Don't get cute," warned Jiggs. "You ain't fooling anybody. Just cough up the money we got coming."

Cosmo was taken aback by such aggressiveness. He had envisioned this meeting with people not to be trifled with to be more cordial. Now unsure as to how things were going to unfold, the florist instantly complied.

"I have Gino's money in my apartment upstairs. I'll go get it if you want."

"We'll go with you."

Cosmo nodded in agreement. He then called out to one of the helpers, instructing him to fetch Davey Brazil, who was in the back room. "Go in the back and tell Davey to come up front keep an eye on things," said the florist.

Once in the apartment Cosmo produced a medium-size brown paper bag that contained cash. He handed the money to Jiggs, while advising, "This is the money made from the gambling. I've been hanging on to it for Gino."

Jiggs took the bag of money without saying anything. He then passed it to Mario after the underboss held his hand out.

"What about the take from the back room?" asked the underboss.

"It's all in the bag lumped together. What should I tell Gino when I'm see him?" Cosmo asked, still pretending that Gino was alive.

"Tell him to save you a bunk," coldly voiced Jiggs.

The remark caused Cosmo's mouth to drop open. He turned his confused face to the underboss for clarification. Mario responded accordingly.

"You got nothing to say to nobody anymore, pal," said Mario flatly, his face reflecting pure evil. "You're out of the equation altogether," he declared.

"How could I be out?" asked the appalled Cosmo, adding, "I mean no disrespect, but you guys are operating out of my place of business."

"Wise up," injected Jiggs, "this ain't your place of business anymore, it's ours. We're doing you a favor."

"What do you mean?"

"You're signing the florist shop over."

"And the building too," pointed out Mario. "See, that's where the favor we're doing for you comes in."

"I don't understand…."

Cosmo's voice was silenced when Jiggs pushed the barrel of his gun into the florist's throat. After a few choice words, Cosmo the Florist understood the favor being extended. He was being permitted to live in return for the florist shop and the building that housed it. Having no choice in the matter, Cosmo reluctantly agreed to sign his assets over to Jackie the Lackey.

"Put the gun away, Jiggs," said Mario. "Our friend gets the point. Go outside and tell the lawyer to come with the papers."

By the time the lawyer arrived at the apartment Cosmo knew he was a beaten man. The papers were signed with minimal conversation.

"Can I ask a question?" Cosmo asked timidly. He was addressing Mario.

"What?"

"What did I do to warrant this type of treatment?"

"You don't want to go there," replied the underboss after dismissing the attorney.

"What happens to me now?" asked Cosmo, testing the waters to make sure he wouldn't be assassinated. Mario looked at Cosmo offering nothing in the way of a reply.

"Our business is over," said Jiggs, answering for the underboss. "You got forty-eight hours to clear out. Got it?"

"I have to move?"

"What am I speaking Chinese? You're through here, so start packing."

"I understand," said Cosmo weakly.

They know I killed Gino! Cosmo thought. *First, they come over here to pluck me like a chicken and then they give me a deadline to take a walk. I know their game. I'm a doomed man!*

Cosmo realized that he was now in a worse position than before. With his business and building signed over to another, there was no longer anything for him in the Bronx. As the bitter florist thought about it, he realized how hopeless his situation was.

Even cooperating with the authorities made no sense. Cosmo felt that he knew too little about those belonging to the secret society to be of value to law enforcement. What he actually knew he could never reveal. Fessing up to having a role in the Johnny Bronco homicide, and the others he incentivized Louis to commit, was out of the question.

They'd lock me up and throw away the key, Cosmo thought.

The circumstances, being what they were, didn't require very much further consideration. Cosmo strongly believed that someone from the crime family would be dispatched to assassinate him. He knew what he had to do and the little time he had to do it in.

***

COSMO DUG OUT THE BLUE DUFFLE BAG that contained his cash from the bottom of his bedroom closet. He then hastily gathered up whatever money he had in his apartment and stuffed the money into his pockets. Cosmo gathered a few travel things and packed them into a black suitcase. Without procrastination he left his apartment with no intention of ever returning.

Undecided as to what part of the country he would ultimately settle in, he proceeded to a hotel located just outside the Bronx in Yonkers. He made the drive without ever looking back. He should have checked his rearview mirror. Had he done so, he might have noticed that he was being followed.

Cosmo did his best to hide his car from view by parking in an unlit section of the hotel parking area. He checked into a room that left a lot to be desired. Since he was only staying one night, it mattered little. Famished, he felt the need for a solid meal. The florist, with his money stuffed duffle bag in tow, went to the hotel lobby to ask the clerk where he could get something to eat. He was directed to a small steakhouse within walking distance of the hotel.

The florist asked to be seated at the far end of the restaurant where he couldn't easily be seen. Once at a table, Cosmo ordered a bottle of red wine. As he drank his wine Cosmo came to see himself journeying across the county to Colorado Springs early the next morning. He hoped that was a destination far enough away that he wouldn't run into anyone who knew him. To further protect himself from recognition the florist intended to grow a beard. Cosmo was fortunate in one respect. He had what he believed to be sufficient cash to last him.

Eventually they'll forget about me, he thought. As Cosmo got deeper into the wine, he began to get onery. *Those bastards know I killed Gino, but they wouldn't even give me the satisfaction of saying they knew. They must think I'm stupid, like I'm not gonna know they had no choice but to come after me.*

"Now I gotta get in the wind all over again," he said aloud. The frustration in his voice was clear. He then gulped his wine and quickly refilled his glass.

"What did you say?" asked the raspy voiced waitress, who had just approached Cosmo's booth. She seemed gruff. Her hands were large for such an average sized woman. Her red fingernails were clipped short and needed touching up.

"I said get me another bottle of wine," answered Cosmo.

"Don't you want to order your food?"

The florist, now paying attention, looked at the gum chewer. "Yeah, let me have a T-bone steak medium rare."

"Mashed potatoes and broccoli?"

"Yeah, that fine. And hurry up with that wine."

"Should I put on roller skates for you, honey?"

"No, why don't you just jump on your broom."

Cosmo's nasty remark actually got a crooked smile out of the middle-aged waitress with tattooed eyebrows. She let the customer's reply go unanswered. She could tell he had worries by the dark circles under his eyes and his urgency for wine.

* * *

AS COSMO WAS DROWNING HIS TROUBLES, Jackie the Lackey sat waiting in his car a short distance from the restaurant. He had been tasked with following Cosmo on the order of Jiggs. He wasted no time notifying Jiggs that Cosmo was settled in Yonkers.

"What the name of the place where he's staying, Jackie?"

"He's staying at the Mercury Capital Hotel."

"He's there now?"

"He's in a steakhouse down the street from the hotel."

"He's probably gonna be there awhile. Does Cosmo know you, Jackie?" asked Jiggs.

"No, we never met."

313

"Good. Go into that restaurant and get the lay of the land. Make sure there are no cops inside eating. After you do that, call me."

"He's sitting in the back drinking a bottle of wine," advised Jackie, reporting back. "It looks like he's gonna have dinner."

"Is the restaurant a big joint?"

"No, it's a small place."

"Where exactly is our boy sitting?"

"He's sitting in the far corner of the restaurant."

"Where is this place again?" Jackie provided Jiggs with the exact location of the restaurant. "Stick with him. I'm on my way."

* * *

COSMO MANAGED TO CONSUME most of the food he had ordered. Polishing off the second bottle of wine went far in alleviating his surliness. After letting out a loud belch, Cosmo waved his hand, signaling the waitress over.

"Let me have the bill when you get a chance."

"Don't you want coffee?" she asked.

"No, just the bill,"

"How did you like the steak?" she asked.

"It was good. Did you cook it, sweetheart?"

"Yeah, and I stomped the grapes for the wine too."

Seeing that her customer softened, the waitress walked off smiling. When she returned with the bill, Cosmo paid in cash. Delighted at receiving an exceedingly generous tip, the waitress was profuse in expressing her thanks.

"Be sure to come back in again," she said flashing a broad smile, now wanting to know her customer better.

Cosmo nodded as he rose to his feet. Protecting his money, the florist held his duffle bag tightly to his chest as he walked. Staggering due to the wine he drank, the cool outdoor air seemed to bounce off Cosmo's face. He turned to walk in the direction of his hotel.

A man was seated alone at the bar having a drink with his back to the restaurant's front glass. He
turned to face the street after hearing what sounded like firecrackers going off. Peering through the glass he observed a man dressed in black running off with a gun in his hand. He also saw the man who had just exited the restaurant lying motionless on the sidewalk. It all happened so fast that the man was unable to get a good look at the shooter's face or the vehicle he fled in.

"CALL THE COPS," bellowed the man at the bar to the bartender, "A GUY JUST GOT SHOT OUTSIDE!"

The drinker then jumped from his seat to render assistance to the victim. He was followed by two waitresses who had been in the area of the bar ordering drinks for their customers.

"I saw the gunman sprint off like his ass was on fire!" exclaimed the witness, who bent over the shooting victim.

"He was a customer, I just served him his dinner!" said the waitress who serviced Cosmo.

"Is he dead?" asked the second waitress.

"I think he's gone," voiced the man who had been at the bar.

"He left me a hundred-dollar tip," said the first waitress.

"A hundred dollars!" exclaimed the second waitress. "He was all alone. Nobody alone ever left me that kind of a tip. He must have had a thing for you."

The waitress frowned at the remark. "At first I didn't think too much of him, he had eyes like a raccoon."

"For a hundred-dollar tip, I wouldn't care if he had eyes like a zombie! The man must have had money to leave that kind of tip."

"I'm going inside to make sure the bartender called the cops," said the man from the bar, who remained focused on the dead man.

"Yeah, do you know something, you're right about one thing," agreed the first waitress. "He must have had money."

The waitress who served Cosmo now stared at the duffle bag alongside the dead man. She bent down and opened the bag.

Seeing that the bag was filled with cash, she quickly zipped the bag closed, announcing to her co-worker, "We hit the jackpot!"

"What do you mean?

"The bag is filled with money."

"What are we going to do?" asked the second waitress.

"Go back inside the restaurant and stall people from coming outside," said first waitress, thinking fast.

"How am I supposed to do that?"

"Fake a heart attack and collapse in the doorway so no one can come outside. Make it good, so I have enough time to run across the street and hide the duffle bag in one of the factory trashcans. The place is closed, we can come back for it later."

"Out of the way, I'm having chest pains."

39

Lackey, Wacky And Lucky

WHEN THE BOSS AND UNDERBOSS of the crime family commended Jiggs on a job well done, they were astounded to learn that it was actually Jackie the Lackey who pulled the trigger on Cosmo. They were impressed to learn that the execution took place before Jiggs even arrived at the scene.

"The kid did the work unassisted?" asked Mario.

"Yeah, I was making good time until there was an accident on the highway," explained Jiggs to his bosses. "I couldn't believe that the kid took care of business all on his own. I have to hand it to you, Mario. You were right, and I was wrong. That kid has what it takes."

"Do you two want to propose him for membership, Mario?" asked Long John.

"So soon?"

"Rewarding this kid will incentivize the others in our family to work harder for us. Our people need to see an attainable goal. Boosting Jackie will give the others something to shoot for and make them work harder for us."

317

The news of Jackie being elevated to the rank of soldier spread like wildfire within the family. His meteoric rise at such a tender age came with mixed results. Some, who had been waiting for years for their button, were bitter at being passed over. Others, as the family boss predicted, saw Jackie's rise as inspiring.

Everyone agreed that Jackie must have done something unique to earn his push upward. Since there were no indications that Jackie was a big earner, the consensus was that he must've fulfilled a murder contract. It was the only palpable assumption to make.

As the recipient of all the benefits afforded to a made man in an organized crime family, Jackie had a license to commit whatever crimes he wanted to with the exception of drug dealing. Even murder was within bounds as long as he received permission from the higher ups in the family.

Having been mentored by Gino Pagnetta made transitioning to soldier status relatively easy for Jackie. He had seen firsthand how Gino used his power as a soldier. The dead gangster's formula was one that Jackie intended to emulate.

Jackie's promotion came with responsibility and some income. Aside from overseeing the goings on at the florist shop and the property for his superiors, he was receiving a share in the profit.

Jackie was also assigned to run the crew of men who frequented the social club that once belonged to Gino. These associates were expected to turn in a portion of their ill-gotten gains to their skipper, who in this case was Jackie. This was sweet revenge for someone who was once sent out for sandwiches.

Once revenue began coming in, Jackie made sure to kick money upstairs to the family boss and underboss, just as Gino had done. Jackie eventually began to branch out businesswise. His success was obvious. He started to dress well, as his mentor once did. The car he now drove was impressive. And, like the late Gino, he was continually on the lookout for opportunities that would enhance his bankroll.

Jackie came to befriend a woman from Central America who worked in a restaurant he frequented. She was a few years older than he was. This friendship blossomed into a lasting romantic relationship. Aside from the physical benefits, this union gave Jackie access to a drug trafficking network that the girlfriend's brother belonged to.

With the availability of a cocaine supplier before him, Jackie made the decision to capitalize on what he saw as a golden opportunity. Drawing on the assistance of those his own age who were willing to work for him, Jackie eased into the drug business. He did this with full knowledge that he was in violation of the rules of the crime family he belonged to.

Jackie evaluated the risk he was taking. His belief was that a sufficient amount of money passed up to the family higher ups would result in their putting blinders on, thus neutralizing the enforcement of any restrictive rules.

Jackie's calculation proved right. There was no questioning as to the origin of the money entering the pockets of Long John and Mario Montana.

Jackie's business model was hardly a new one. He armed each of his worker bees with beepers and product. Their instructions were to develop a client base of recreational cocaine users.

Customers were found in bars, schools and various other establishments that attracted people with an eye for partying. These hand-to-hand transactions involved the seller driving to where the purchaser awaited delivery of the product.

The narcotics business was not one that came without competitors. When faced with territorial problems, Jackie found himself in need of support. To meet this need he sought out the muscle of Jiggs Tuminaro, who for the right price agreed to assist Jackie in purging the field of competition.

The Jackie and Jiggs combination was something similar to what was once the Gino Pagnetta-Louis Pagnetta relationship. The difference was that since both Jackie and Jiggs were family soldiers, no one was getting abused.

Jackie murderous path made the moniker of Jackie the Lackey no longer applicable. Behind Jackie's back the ambitious homicidal young upstart was now referred to as Jackie the Wacky.

Jackie developed into someone of great daring. With enhanced confidence came big thinking. Jackie convinced his girlfriend's brother that they should embark on a bold, dangerous mission. With inside information provided by the brother as to the scheduled deliveries of large narcotic shipments into the country, Jackie saw great opportunity for tremendous wealth that came with less labor intensiveness.

When Jiggs Tuminaro was approached by Jackie to back him up in ripping off the drug traffickers, the Capezzo soldier initially balked at the idea. His hesitation lasted until he learned of the magnitude of the money to be netted if all went well. The gain to be made after a few successful rip-offs involving serious weight, convinced Jiggs to throw in with Jackie. It turned out to be a chance well taken.

Jackie used some of his money to purchase a home on City Island. The residence was large enough to comfortably house himself, his mother and his girlfriend, who Jackie made resign from her job at the restaurant. Thanks to the efficiency of Davey Brazil, there was no heavy lifting for Jackie at the Bronx flower shop other than to collect money and distribute it accordingly.

Jackie came to forge a friendship with a real estate agent, Henry Alvarez, who lived in the house next to him on City Island. The two saw the advantage of their uniting to form a construction company. From Jackie's perspective, this newly formed business was a way for him to explain away what he had accumulated and also make more money.

The success that followed caused Jackie to evolve into something of an egomaniac. Jackie thought nothing of being photographed with celebrated people at the trendiest locations. His public image didn't sit well with Long John Capezzo, who began to hear rumors that bosses from the other families were questioning how he allowed his capo to draw such attention. The embarrassment Long John felt surpassed his greed. He decided that something had to be done.

***

LONG JOHN CAPEZZO WAS in his home library when his underboss arrived. The mood in the library was grim. There was no espresso, no cookies and no Jiggs Tuminaro invited into the kitchen to jaw with Long John's wife. Jiggs was told to remain outside in the car.

"I can't permit such talk coming from the other family bosses about my leadership to go unanswered, Mario," declared the boss.

"What can you do, people are always gonna talk, John," answered the underboss, trying to downplay things. The comment made by Mario caused the top mafioso to explode.

"THE BOSS OF YOUR FAMILY IS BEING MOCKED AND YOU SAY LET THEM TALK?"

"I didn't exactly say that...." said Mario, before being abruptly cut off.

"JACKIE CREATED A CLIMATE THAT HAS LED TO A MOCKERY OF ME!" Long John thundered. "I WANT THIS CANCER YOU BROUGHT TO ME REMOVED. DO YOU UNDERSTAND ME, MARIO?"

"Take it easy, John. If you want me to clip Jackie, I'll clip him."

"I want his body found in a way that sends a message. He's to be found with a syringe stuffed up his ass."

"Whatever you say, John. But you do realize that by taking out this kid we're giving ourselves a big haircut," reminded the underboss.

"If I lose my prestige with the other families, we're losing more than money," explained Long John. "We can always make money, but a damaged reputation is not that easily repaired."

"You're right, John," said Mario, appeasing his superior. "I'll get it done right away."

"And I don't want to see Jiggs anymore either, Mario."

"But Jiggs is my man...."

"He should have done more to control the situation. He too will represent an excellent example for the others."

When Mario returned to his waiting car, he told Jiggs of the order he received from Long John concerning Jackie.

"Is he crazy, Jackie is making all of us a fortune," said Jiggs.

"I know, but the old man is pretty sore over people in the other families talking about him. You know how he is about his reputation. He thinks he's the second coming of Giuseppe Garibaldi."

"Did you tell him that I could talk to Jackie and tell him to tone it down?"

"It's beyond the talking stage. The old man wants Jackie dead and that's it." The silence in the car lasted two minutes before the lull was broken.

"I suppose you want me to do it," said Jiggs, who was unhappy about the death sentence he would have to execute.

"Don't count on that, Jiggs."

"What do you mean?""

"Long John wants you buried alongside Jackie."

"WHAT!"

"Easy, Jiggs, if that were going to happen, we'd never be having this conversation."

"You know something, Mario, if you were the boss this could all be avoided."

Mario turned in his seat to face his driver. "I had the same exact thought. It wouldn't be the worst thing if Long John had an accident."

A small smile crossed the face of Jiggs. "An unfortunate accident would solve the problem. They do happen," he said.

"Yes, they do, and it would remove any questions put forth by the other family bosses who sit on the commission."

***

ONCE MARIO MONTANA BECAME THE new boss of the family, he appointed Jiggs Tuminaro as his underboss. Jackie walked away from the death sentence imposed by Long John with nothing more than a verbal reprimand that in effect ordered him to stay out of the public eye. Jackie offered no resistance to this demand. He continued to see that Mario, and now Jiggs, got a percentage of whatever money he made.

Jackie's soaring career finally ran into a snag when he was asked to enter into a new venture with Alvarez, his construction company partner who lived next to him on City Island. Jackie liked the opportunity presented by Alvarez so much that he asked Mario and Jiggs if they wanted to go in with him on the deal. They did. Soon after, a corporation was formed.

The partners purchased 96 acres of land in Pennsylvania and developed Glad Pine World, a bustling lake community. The 60 acres of developed land was soon occupied by happy families who enjoyed their newly built homes, and the amenities that came with ownership in the development. Visitors to the property could easily see that there was fun to be had by all at the lake, clubhouse, game rooms, pools, tennis courts, bocci courts and various events held at the site throughout the year.

The scheming partners formed a second corporation that was used to purchase the remaining 36 acres of land for a pittance, with full knowledge that these acres were unsuitable to build homes on. The new corporation then sold this land, in one-acre parcels, to people seeking affordable vacation homes. The scam showed up on the radar of the FBI after two acres were purchased by the sister of a Supreme Court Justice.

Things didn't go well for the partners once the feds discovered that the entity principles included members of organized crime. The subsequent examination of the land by the feds was something the fraudsters hadn't counted on. The law unearthed the remains of two criminals who had mysteriously disappeared. When all was said and done, those involved in the swindle received lengthy prison sentences with the exception of Alvarez, who cooperated with the authorities.

Mario Montana, being a mob kingpin, entered jail with what would have to be considered a healthy attitude. He remained positive by looking at the bright side of things. He met cronies affiliated with various mob families from around the country. These associations would present opportunities on the outside, which would keep him relevant with the new bosses who took over the family.

In prison Mario smoked his cigars, played cards and lived happily among friends while doing what most would refer to as a soft stretch for a senior citizen doing time. He was also alleviated from having to live with his wife, who he had long lost love for. The visits he received from his grown children were infrequent, which suited him because they always asked him for money.

Mario's tranquility was upset during a prison sanctioned baseball game. While the team he wagered on came from behind to rally, he began rooting wildly. Amid the excitement of winning a carton of cigarettes, he suddenly keeled over. Mario was dead from a heart attack before any medical assistance was rendered.

Jiggs Tuminaro, a heavy smoker, was diagnosed with lung cancer shortly after his conviction. He was housed in a prison hospital when the end came. When asked by someone how he was doing shortly before the final curtain came down on his life, his answer was to the point. "Ahh, it's the friggin' ballgame," he replied, just before signing out.

Alvarez, Jackie's City Island neighbor, received a reduced sentence for cooperating with the authorities. He sold his home on City Island and moved out of the Bronx after entering the witness protection program with his family. He was never seen again in the tri-state area.

As for Jackie, he ended up serving his full sentence. Upon regaining his freedom, Jackie returned to the Bronx florist shop to reestablish himself. He found that recapturing his former status was easier said than done.

The florist shop that remained in his name had expanded substantially. There was now an interior spiral staircase leading to the second floor. The several unfamiliar faces who were working in the shop looked at him suspiciously, giving him the impression that they didn't know who he was. Jackie, after identifying himself, was told that Davey Brazil could be found at the social club.

Upon arriving at the club, Jackie was quickly able to see that things had changed drastically. The club itself was immaculate.

The walls were freshly painted, the furniture upgraded, and the bathroom was new. Even the small bar received a makeover.

Jackie found Davey in the rear office that was once his. Davey, who was attired in a charcoal custom made suit, sat in a leather chair behind a nice desk. Most stunning to Jackie was not the physical appearance of things, but rather the news that Davey Brazil had been elevated to the status of capo in the crime family.

"You got made a capo, Davey?" asked Jackie after the pleasantries were exchanged. "I never even knew you got made."

"The powers to be thought that since I made them all a lot of money, I needed a title so that people would listen to me better. It wasn't something I was looking for. But you know how it is, you just can't say no."

"I never saw you as the type to do, you know, to do any dirty work," said Jackie, putting things delicately.

"Sonny exempted me from any of that rough stuff. I was told that all I had to do was just keep earning."

"How is he as the boss?"

"He's been very protective of me. He even put one of his men driving me."

"Did he say anything about me, Davey?"

"Sonny knows you're out. He told me that if I saw you, to tell you that you should go see him," advised Davey.

"What's he gonna tell me?"

"I think they want you to retire."

Jackie had no ill will toward Davey Brazil. He understood that things were now being run by a new family power base. Jackie could do only one thing, make his case to the new family boss. The meeting took place after hours in an East Harlem funeral parlor. Present for the meeting with Sonny was the family underboss and a capo.

At the onset of the meeting Jackie reminded everyone of his history with the family. Seeing no heads nodding agreeably suggested that reaching an understanding was going to be problematic. Jackie spoke of the work he did on behalf of the family and the money he generated. When he received no positive feedback, he finally spoke straight out. He bluntly made known what he believed that he was entitled to.

"You're entitled to shit," said Sonny, the new boss of the family. He was an emotionless man of middle age who wore thick black tinted glasses. "Where do you get off coming in here and making demands?"

"That florist shop and the building are still in my name, so technically they both rightfully belong to me."

"Yeah, well we're gonna fix that," said the family boss. "You don't fit in anymore, Jackie. Your trigger-happy ways are dangerous to the family, my friend."

"I've modified," stated Jackie.

"I doubt that. You've been conditioned to the old way of doing things. And you're a drug dealer to boot. That shit doesn't fly under this regime."

"So where does this leave me?" asked Jackie, realizing the futility in offering a rebuttal.

"I'm putting you on the shelf."

"Why am I being shelved?"

"Look, Jackie, you either willingly walk out of here officially retired or you don't leave here alive."

"Those are my choices?" asked Jackie, refusing to flinch.

"Look, we know you got plenty of money," injected the underboss. "Why don't you just go along with the program and go live someplace nice and enjoy spending your money in retirement."

Jackie knew that he was in an unwinnable battle, so he accepted the offer. He left the funeral parlor agreeing to sign over the florist shop and building.

With his mother now gone, Jackie sold his house on City Island. He moved to Florida, settling in a Fort Lauderdale condo complex. Being alone caused him to often think of how things turned out for him. It depressed him to consider the murders, serving time in jail, his sister's self-destruction and his mother's passing during his imprisonment. The double homicide of his girlfriend and her brother, at the hands of betrayed narcotic traffickers was further cause for gloom. He knew that the only reason he escaped assassination himself was because of his being incarcerated. Luckily by the time Jackie was once again a free man, the drug dealers were either dead or incarcerated themselves.

As things turned out, living in Florida served Jackie well. His good fortune came after he offered to assist a tenant in his building while the two were riding the elevator. The daughter of a retired Boston civil court judge, the tenant had been carrying packages. Taken by Jackie's act of chivalry, the tenant was amenable to his offer.

Once at the woman's apartment she invited Jackie in for a cup of coffee. Finding his neighbor attractive, he readily accepted her invitation. As they conversed Jackie came to learn that the woman, who was in her late 30's, was an accountant who had never married. Her being a woman of education impressed Jackie, who appreciated her refined way of speaking. As their conversation deepened there came a point where their eyes began locking. This was surefire proof to both parties that a mutual attraction existed.

Once interest became clear to Jackie he extended a dinner invitation for that evening. The offer was instantly accepted. The two went on to enjoy the company of each other over a six-hour meal. The time flew by as Jackie spoke of what he could about his days in the Bronx. His highly interested dinner guest sat riveted as she listened to Jackie talk of his having once owned businesses that made it possible for him to retire and live off his investments.

Meeting his accountant neighbor turned out to be the first step in Jackie's reformation. The influence of the CPA transformed him in a way no rehabilitation professional could. Jackie began to regularly attend Mass with the new woman in his life, participate in feeding the down and outers on holidays and came full circle to adopt a do-gooder mentality. Once he grew acclimated to living an ethical law-abiding life Jackie came to like it well enough to propose marriage.

Being wedded to a judge's daughter kept Jackie on the straight and narrow. When the accountant gave birth to Jackie Jr. the former criminal embraced being a devoted stay-at-home dad who tended to household affairs while his wife worked. Setting Jackie apart from many others in a similar arrangement was his willingness to pitch in with the cooking and housework. Even his father-in-law was impressed by this. The former civil court judge developed a genuine fondness for a son-in-law who treated his only child well.

The union of the accountant and the former mobster worked. The accountant finally met her ideal. In Jackie she found a man of means who proved to be a caring husband and a family man. From Jackie's side of the equation, his feelings for the woman who didn't probe deeply into his past evolved from lust to love. Being able to leave his sordid history buried far in the past, coupled with having a family, made Jackie a contented man beyond temptation to return to his past ways.

40

Doors Close, Others Open

AS FAR AS HIS PRIVATE LIFE WENT, Markie was content with Karen. Although she was a single working mom with small children, she came with relatively little baggage. She and her children lived in her retired father's house, so she had help. There was also her student sister who was there to pitch in.

From Karen's perspective, in Markie she connected with someone compatible. They were of the same faith, meshed well behind closed doors and the sergeant got on well with her children. She also liked the fact that Markie saw his ex-wife and his own children, who were older, infrequently. As far as Markie's drinking went, that was something Karen was willing to accept.

Having Sunday dinner with her family, movies and time alone for intimacy was something that worked well for both. Markie was fine when it came to attending weddings, birthday parties and the like. He even went apple picking with Karen's children.

Over a bowl of rice at a Japanese restaurant one evening they began discussing taking a holiday together over Easter week. Karen thought that Disney World would be a fine destination, adding that her children have never experienced Mickey Mouse and the gang.

"You want to take your kids to Disney?" asked the startled Markie, who didn't see this coming. He had been thinking more along the lines of the two of them escaping somewhere for a few days without the children.

"Why, of course," replied Karen. "Is that a problem?"

Markie cleared his throat before answering. "I suppose not," he said, in a clipped response.

As they worked on their soup, Karen began to get sentimental. She expressed her affection, capping off her talk with how her kids loved the sergeant. Feeling cornered, Markie began to squirm in his seat as he anticipated what was coming next. When the conversation turned to marriage the sergeant felt as if he was being choked. While Markie cared for Karen, he wasn't prepared to entertain any talk of marriage.

Markie's attempt to shift the conversation elsewhere was to no avail. Karen remained fixated on hearts, flowers and a trip down the aisle. As Karen rambled on about how wonderful their life together would be as a family, Markie felt as though he was inches away from quicksand.

The sergeant looked at Karen's lips as she spoke. He saw her open mouth as a trap ready to pull him down deep into the quicksand's saturated granular material. The notion of a steady diet of schoolbooks, swimming meets, youthful drama and miscellaneous expenses had now become an intolerable nightmare.

For whatever imperfections Markie had, leading someone on wasn't one of them. The time had come to reach an understanding. Finding it difficult to arrive at the kindest way to express his feelings, the sergeant had several false starts. Finally, he abandoned all hopes of cushioning his unpleasant message.

The words, "I ain't ever getting married again," devastated Karen, who hadn't anticipated such an adamant response. The bluntness of the words ignited a flow of tears that proved embarrassing to both Karen and the sergeant. Uncomfortable at the attention being given to his table by those seated nearby, Markie took a stab at damage control by making light of the situation.

"C'mon, Karen, the soup is watery enough," said the sergeant.

"Why did you lead me on?"

"I never led you on," corrected the sergeant. "That's unfair of you."

"You met my kids, my father! How could you?"

"How could I what? I'm sorry, but you took a lot for granted and now you're overreacting."

"So that's it? Your final word is we'll never marry?"

"I'm sorry, Karen. But I'll never marry anyone again."

The remark made by Markie strengthened Karen's resolve to go on the offensive. She sat up straight in her seat. Her shoulders were pulled back and the tears were now under control. Karen suddenly rose to her feet defiantly. Before walking off she poured her cooled off soup on Markie's lap.

Surprisingly Markie wasn't overly upset. He calmly called the waiter over and asked for the bill. On his trip home a sense of relief came over the sergeant. He felt free.

Once at his apartment Markie cleaned up. He was a proponent of the philosophy that claimed the cure to one woman, was another. Since it was still early, he decided to drive over to Manhattan in the hope of getting lucky. His destination was Mustang Harry's. There was usually a good crowd on hand thanks to the events held at the nearby Madison Square Garden.

***

THANKS TO THE WINDFALL OF MONEY SHE received from Enzo Baffi, Rochelle Parrish spared no expense when it came to pursuing her passion for professional wrestling. Already a familiar figure sitting ringside at Madison Square Garden, she now began attending matches in out-of-state arenas to see her favorite performers.

Rochelle usually went to the Garden exhibitions accompanied by her sister, who also enjoyed the matches. On this particular evening Rochelle's sister was sick at home with the flu, leaving Rochelle to attend the Garden show alone.

As an avid wrestling fan, Rochelle enjoyed the histrionics exhibited by the burly men as they manhandled each other. The grunts, groans and gestures of agony expressed by the bodies being tossed around the ring provided great entertainment.

Rochelle would watch with fascination as the grapplers pounded each other with intensity enough to redden their chests. She was usually seated close enough to the ring to see sweat accumulate on the bare-chested grapplers. This caused Rochelle to imagine herself entwined with the slippery men in the privacy of her boudoir, where baby oil would substitute for sweat.

Rochelle interpreted every applied hold as a struggle for dominance, with the victor of the match proving that strength overcomes weakness. Perhaps this was why Rochelle was attracted to men of power. Her unwavering loyalty to Enzo Baffi, her former employer, was largely attributed to his extensive sway over others.

Rochelle, as usual, stopped by Mustang Harry's prior to attending the matches. She enjoyed having a cocktail or two prior to walking over to the House that Tex Built, a name that referred to the promoter Tex Rickard, who built the third Madison Square Garden back in the day. When she sat at the bar, she was immediately met by the bartender who recognized her as a regular customer.

"The usual, Rochelle?" asked the bartender.

"Yes, please."

"Where is your sister tonight?" he asked, as he put Rochelle's cocktail down in front of her.

"She's feeling under the weather this evening."

"Sorry to hear that, send her my regards."

The man working the stick wasn't the only one who noticed Rochelle. Markie, who was seated at the middle of the long bar had taken notice of the attractive woman in business attire.

Rochelle, who was between jobs, had been spending lots of time working out at a Westside fitness club. The results of her efforts were obvious to someone on the prowl, as Markie was.

There was something about the woman on his radar that looked vaguely familiar to the sergeant. He stared as he tried to place her. His inability to recall where they may have met led Markie to ask the bartender if he knew the woman's name.

"Are you talking about the woman in the black pants suit?"

"That's right, she looks familiar to me. I'm trying to figure out from where."

"That's Rochelle," advised the bartender."

"That's right, Rochelle," said Markie, "now I remember. Does she come here much?"

"She stops in when she goes to the Garden."

"Do me a favor, move my drink to where she is. I'm gonna go say hello."

"Hello, Ms. Parrish," said the sergeant softly, taking a seat next to Enzo Baffi's former personal assistant/secretary. "Remember me?"

Recognizing Markie as the law, Rochelle grew nervous by his presence. She feared that his visit may have something to do with the cyanide she orally passed to her former employer. Her reply was polite, but distant.

"Yes, I remember you," she answered, turning away from the sergeant.

As Markie continued to engage Rochelle, it became obvious that the sergeant was coming on to her. Once realizing that she was not under suspicion for committing a crime, Rochelle got nasty.

"Go away, I don't want to talk to you!" she barked.

"Okay, have it your way," said the sergeant, shrugging his shoulders. Rejected, Markie turned to his drink.

"Are you still here?" asked Rochelle loudly. "Go away!"

"If you don't want to talk to me, that's fine," voiced Markie.

"I DON'T!"

"Look, if you're trying to embarrass me, then I'm going to embarrass you," threatened Markie. His tone was serious, making it clear he wasn't bluffing. Markie's abrupt turnaround seemed to thaw Rochelle, who became more receptive to chatting. There even came a point where Markie got close enough to Rochelle for their knees to touch.

Rochelle began to see something in the sergeant that made him attractive. Perhaps it was because she now noticed that Markie had a tough side to him. She also appreciated his broad shoulders. Despite his fondness for drink, the sergeant maintained a workout routine that preserved a good deal of the muscle of his younger days.

"You seem to be a man who takes care of himself," said Rochelle.

"I manage to keep in shape," said the sergeant, holding up his arm for her to feel his muscle. "Take a squeeze."

Rochelle took the bait and massaged the hard ball between Markie's elbow and shoulder. "I'm impressed," said Rochelle, displaying what loosely could be referred to as a smile.

Markie felt confident that he was gaining traction in drawing Rochelle into his web. In actuality, he was the moth being drawn to the flame. While Markie was no wrestler, he was definitely the sock-em in the eye sort that Rochelle preferred.

Markie's profession opened the door to an assortment of fantasies for Rochelle. The fact that he packed a gun, and handcuffs, worked in the sergeant's favor. She accepted the sergeant's drink offer.

"Yours is a rather dangerous profession," said Rochelle, as she locked eyes with Markie.

"It can be at times."

"Doesn't that concern you?"

"I went into it with my eyes open, so I got nothing to cry about." This type of talk was gaining Markie points.

"What brings you to Mustang Harry's?" she asked.

"I come here when I'm lonely."

"I see."

"What brings you here?"

"I'm going to Madison Square Garden," she replied.

"What's doing there, a concert?"

"No, wrestling. Do you find that strange?"

"No, Ma'am, I love wrestling myself," he lied.

"Really? That is fortuitous. I have an extra ticket; would you care to join me as my guest?"

"Tonight?

"Of course tonight. I usually go to the matches with my sister, but she couldn't make it this evening."

"Count me in!"

Markie and Rochelle were seated close enough to the action to see the physical toll taken on the wrestlers. Markie watched in awe as the welts and bruises began to appear on the torso of the wrestlers as they worked each other over.

"Jesus, these guys really do a number on each other," commented the sergeant.

"Yes, they do," agreed Rochelle. "I find it all so fascinating." Markie looked at Rochelle twice after hearing this. At this point he didn't quite know what to make of her.

When a man attired in an Indian headdress came running down the aisle making his way toward the ring, Rochelle reacted with great enthusiasm. "It's Chief Red Hawk!" she said excitedly. "He wasn't listed on the program. He's my all-time favorite!" Markie chucked at Rochelle's childlike reaction.

As the Chief's match intensified Rochelle began to loudly root for her hero as he began his war whoop. Whenever things were going against her favorite, Rochelle took hold of Markie's forearm and tightly squeezed. As the tide eventually changed in favor of the chief, Rochelle eased her grip.

"He has him in the Indian Death Lock!" shouted Rochelle with great enthusiasm. "It's a submission hold, the chief has it won now!"

*This one could be nut*s, thought Markie, as he watched Rochelle wildly applaud the grunt and groaner as he went into his victory dance.

The sergeant was hoping that Rochelle's good spirits would last through the remainder of the card. If yes, he believed he stood a decent shot of spending the night at her place. As things turned out, he wasn't disappointed.

41

The Big Surprise

SINCE THERE WERE NO FIRES to put out, Markie and Von Hess had time on their hands. They sat in their headquarters office chatting about current events. Once they finished weighing in on what appeared in the newspaper headlines, Markie got around to mentioning the incident with Karen at the restaurant. Von Hess, as a rule, was always a good audience. So good that the Sergeant went on to communicate his chance encounter with Rochelle Parrish at Mustang Harry's.

Detective Silverlake happened to be walking past the ajar office door just as Markie began speaking of baby oil. These words piqued Silverlake's curiosity, causing him to circle back a minute or so later. This time he assumed a position behind the ajar door where he'd be able to listen in on the conversation. Silverlake, as Chief Harry McCoy's pipeline, was expected to pass gossip to his boss.

Von Hess was seated at a desk that faced the office entrance. He heard what sounded like a shuffling coming from outside the office door. He rose from his desk and looked though the open slit between the door and the hinges. Seeing someone there, Von Hess pointed at the door, signaling Markie that someone was outside listening in.

"So, she likes wrestling," said Von Hess.

"Yeah, Ollie, she's nuts for it. As it turned out I was in the main event."

Von Hess suddenly slammed the office door shut, causing it to swiftly swing into the side of Silverlake's head. The impact caused Silverlake to cry out in pain.

"What was that?" asked Markie, pretending he didn't know what happened.

"I don't know, Sarge," replied Von Hess, sounding innocent.

Silverlake didn't stick around to answer questions. He scurried off without looking back.

"It was Silverlake, Sarge. I got a look at him as he scooted off down the hall."

"Surprise, surprise, Ollie."

"So, finish your story, Sarge. What happened with you and the woman?"

"Ollie, I have to tell ya…. she almost drowned us both in baby oil."

"That's kind of messy, ain't it?"

"Messy? I slid off her twice before I was able to pin her shoulders for the count of three. To tell you the truth, I think she let me win."

"That's pretty wild," commented Von Hess. "Are you going to see her again?"

"I don't know, if I do it won't be right away. I still got aches and pains."

***

A FEW DAYS AFTER THE SILVERLAKE incident, Markie received a certified letter addressed to him at his
headquarters office. The return address indicated that the communication was from a Manhattan based law firm.

"Now what the hell is this," said Markie.

"What's wrong, Sarge?" asked Von Hess.

"I'm not sure, Ollie," said Markie as he began to open the letter.

As Markie read the contents of the letter he was shocked to a point where he needed to grasp the top of a chair for support. He slipped slowly into the chair and again read the notification to himself, this time more slowly.

"Sarge, is everything alright?" Von Hess asked, thinking that Markie must have received troubling news.

Too stunned to talk, Markie remained quiet. He held out the letter that was wedged between his thumb and index finger for Von Hess to take. After reading the letter from the law firm, Von Hess needed to find his own seat to sit in.

***

VON HESS ACCOMPANIED MARKIE to the Madison Avenue law offices of Weston, Jones, Salak and Loubet. On their way there the sergeant voiced his bewilderment at being remembered in Fishnet Milligan's will.

"For the life of me Ollie," said Markie," I don't get this. Why would Fishnet put me in his will?"

"You got me, Sarge."

"He was a rogue when on the job and even worse when he retired. I'm only sorry I didn't get to put him in jail before he died. So why me?"

"What do you suppose he left you?"

"His dirty underwear probably," quipped Markie.

The fact was that Fishnet had much more to leave than most people were aware of. Markie knew that Fishnet had come into a substantial amount of money after getting away with the murder of his celebrity spouse, but he had no idea of the exact magnitude of that inheritance.

After Markie identified himself to the law office receptionist, she telephoned a partner of the firm, Walter P. Salak. A few minutes after she hung up the phone the detectives were met by the attorney's secretary who escorted them to a conference room.

"Would you like coffee, tea or bottled water?" asked the secretary.

"Nothing, thank you, Ma'am," replied Markie.

"Mr. Salak will be with you in a minute."

When the seventy-year-old Salak entered the conference room both detectives immediately sized him up as someone in poor health. His face was pale and deeply lined. The partner's sparse hair was gray, with a trace of red remaining here and there.

Salak gave the appearance of someone tight with a buck. The knot on his thin black tie, which hung low, looked like it hadn't been untied in years. The top button of his shirt was open to give his fleshy neck breathing room. Red suspenders held up blue pinstripe pants that long needed a dry cleaning and pressing. The watch on his wrist was pricy, but aged. Salak's classic black wingtips, although polished, came with rundown heels.

Well established in the area of trusts and estates, Salak represented a client base of high net worth individuals. One of his clients was Fishnet Milligan. As the executor of Fishnet's fortune, Salak was tasked with notifying Markie of the windfall bequeathed to him by Fishnet. Also present at this meeting, aside from Salak, Markie and Von Hess, was the attorney's stepson, a young financial advisor.

Markie was astounded when he learned how much money Fishnet bequeathed him. He could hardly believe his ears when informed that $250,000 was left to him by the man he wanted to put behind bars. The sergeant looked at Von Hess, who was smiling broadly after hearing about Markie's good fortune.

"Are you joking?" asked the astonished sergeant.

"I assure you I'm not," replied the lawyer, who seemed inconvenienced by the question.

There came a point in the meeting where the attorney introduced the services of his stepson. The attorney, who was aware of Markie's occupation, assumed that the sergeant was limited when it came to investment strategies. Salak described his stepson, who was just starting out as a financial advisor, as a valuable resource when it came to managing money. Since the sergeant was used to having an anemic bank account, the amount was too large a sum to take any chances with.

"Of course there is no obligation, but he could guide you accordingly," voiced Salak, referring to his stepson.

"Keeping it in the family, huh?" said Markie, who easily recognized that he was being hustled.

"Mr. Milligan also wanted you to have this, Mr. Markie," advised the attorney, who abruptly ceased pitching his stepson. He handed the sergeant a sealed envelope.

"What's in this?" asked the sergeant, as he took possession of the envelope.

"Mr. Milligan didn't share that with me. My instructions were to just give it to you in the event something unfortunate should ever happen to him. My client was peculiar in some ways."

"Yeah, I know. How about we just wrap up what needs to be done here."

When his business with the lawyer was finished, Markie accepted the financial advisor's business card out of politeness. Before leaving the office, Markie posed one final question to the attorney."

"Mr. Salak, I have a question. Who did your client leave the rest of his money to?"

"Mr. Milligan made no other provisions before his unfortunate death. Quite frankly, I could never understand why he would kill himself without first planning for his vast estate."

"Does the State end up with his bankroll?"

"I'm afraid so."

What a dumb ass, thought Markie. Von Hess had the exact same thought.

That evening Markie treated Von Hess to a steak dinner at the Ruth Chris Steak House in Midtown. Over drinks Markie produced the sealed envelope given to him by the lawyer. He opened the envelope to read aloud the undated letter. Fishnet had penned the following communication, using a format favored by the police department:

To: Sergeant Al Markie

From: Bruce "Fishnet" Milligan

Subject: Easy Money

If you're reading this, Sarge, it means that my number came up. Since I got no use for money now, I decided to give you a small bite of the apple I leave behind. I didn't leave you the works because a guy like you wouldn't know how to enjoy the money anyway.

I just want you to know that I never really hated you. You did what you had to do, and I did what I needed to do. To be honest, there were times that I enjoyed the challenge of outfoxing you.

As I write this I do so with pride knowing that you never got to lay a glove on me. I do hope you drop dead before I do so I get the final decision over you in our little scrimmage.

One thing I'll give you though, you never flaked me. In that respect you were probably a chump. Had the positions been reversed, I'd have framed you sure as shit. I guess that was the difference between me and you, Sarge. You let opportunities slip by, I never did.

Just so you know, I left you the money in appreciation for what you did for me when I shot it out with Red Harris. You did right by me on that. Anyway, now with a quarter of a million bucks in your pocket, I figure we're even.

On the remote chance that you ended up killing me, all I could say is what a laugh on me. Anyway, go do what you want with the money and give a few bucks to Ollie, he was always a good guy.

See you in hell asshole,
Fishnet

"What do you make of this, Ollie?" asked Markie, putting down the letter. "Was this guy out of his mind or what?"

"Fishnet was always a little off, Sarge," replied Von Hess. "What are you gonna do with the money?"

"Well, I guess I'll buy a new car. What are you gonna do with the fifty grand I'm giving you?"

Von Hess was taken aback at the thought of receiving fifty-thousand dollars. "Well, I guess I might do the same," he finally said, smiling broadly.

42

The Dream Of The Hunt

HAVING COME INTO SOME MONEY, Markie was definite in his plans for a new car. Since he never owned a sports car, he considered that an option. He dismissed that idea altogether after factoring in the cost of insurance. Thinking about how effectively to manage the cost of his new car, he decided to talk to Von Hess before doing anything. It occurred to him that collectively, they would strike a better deal with two purchases, regardless of what car they purchased.

Markie felt obligated to give some money to his children. He decided to give five thousand dollars to each child. As far as his ex-wife was concerned, she didn't come into consideration. Once Florence married her dentist boss, Markie closed the iron gate on her. *Let that tooth plucking putz take care of he*r, was the sergeant's final thought on the ex-Mrs. Markie.

Bolstered by a nest egg to fall back on, and with the pension he'd receive upon retirement, it began to cross Markie's mind that he was now in a position to move on from police work.

I could pack it in and get a private investigator's license, he thought, *and try going into business for myself. Maybe I can even convince Ollie also to retire and come in with me.*

Preventing the sergeant from pursuing entrepreneurship at this time was his lack of knowledge on how to proceed. All Markie really knew was that he'd have to secure a private investigator's license. Incidentals such as insurance, contracts, finding an office and business development were a mystery to him. He found these so daunting that he abandoned the notion, at least for the time being.

Once rainy evening Markie stayed home to watch an old movie on television. Rather than being antiquated, *The Most Dangerous Game*, based on a short story by Richard Connell, remained an exciting adventure of survival. The movie was so enjoyable to the sergeant that he went on to dream about it with himself in the lead role. The irony in this was that Fishnet Milligan once had the very same dream.

Markie's mental cinema featured Rochelle Parrish. Despite her knowledge of how to execute spinning toe holds and hammerlocks, she was cast as a vulnerable protagonist. The sergeant's role was that of the hero. Both had been lured onto an isolated island by an insane big game hunter, played by Fishnet Milligan, who was determined to hunt them down overnight.

With only a knife for protection, Markie and Rochelle must survive in the jungle while being hunted by an armed madman and his team of hounds. Markie ultimately triumphs, saving the life of himself and Rochelle. When Markie later awoke, he continued to have Rochelle on his mind. His dream fantasy created a romantic desire that left Markie wanting more of Rochelle. In answer to this calling the sergeant dialed Rochelle to ask her out. She was receptive.

Markie kept checking his watch at work one afternoon. He was anxious for the time to pass. He did this often enough for Von Hess to notice.

"You got plans tonight, Sarge?"

"Yeah, I got a date."

"With who?"

"Dick the Bruiser," answered Markie flippantly, referring to a popular wrestler of days past. Von Hess knew he meant Rochelle Parrish.

"You've getting kind of tight with her," said Von Hess.

"Yeah, Ollie, I suppose I am. I haven't felt this way about a woman since Alley Cat."

"Really...."

"You know what the best part is?"

"The baby oil?"

"There is something to be said about that too, but the best part is that Rochelle comes with no baggage."

Shortly before the end of his shift Markie closed his office door. He stripped down to his undershirt and removed the shaving kit he kept in his desk drawer. Von Hess watched as the sergeant headed off to the men's room humming the Elvis Presley tune, *Are You Lonesome Tonight*? When the clean-shaven Markie returned to the office the scent of his cologne was noticeable.

He must really dig this woman, thought the first-grade detective. Von Hess was quite correct in his observation.

***

MARKIE AND ROCHELLE arrived early at Madison Square Garden. Sitting at the ringside caused Markie to reminisce of when he attended Garden wrestling matches in his youth. It was a time when slipping the ticket seller ten bucks got you cushioned seats close to the ring.

Markie looked all around the huge arena as people began to slowly file in. His attention was drawn to the area where the wrestlers made their entrance. He noted that the security person assigned to this entry point was an off duty, moonlighting cop he knew. Markie took Rochelle by the hand.

"Come with me, baby," said the sergeant.

Markie flashed his sergeant's shield to gain access to where the wrestlers congregated prior to their performances. When queried by the wrestlers themselves as to what they were doing backstage near the dressing room, Markie again produced his shield. He explained that his girlfriend was a rabid fan. Being a detective sergeant in the NYPD went a long way in making the intrusion acceptable.

After a few minutes of polite talk with several grapplers, it became apparent to the wrestlers that
Rochelle was not your typical groupie. She was well spoken, sophisticated in manner and attractive in appearance. She was also underestimated in her boldness, particularly by Markie.

Rochelle's eyes danced happily as she conversed with the wrestlers. Markie, who was engaged in his own conversations, neglected to see how Rochelle was thrilled at meeting her all-time favorite bone breaker, Chief Red Hawk.

When not entertaining in the squared circle, Chief Red Hawk, minus his headdress, returned to being the thrice divorced Ed Oster from Newark, New Jersey.

A charmer, the ruggedly handsome Oster knew his way around women. In Rochelle, he recognized an infatuated fan. Prior to their parting the wrestler discreetly passed his business card to Rochelle. After the Chief walked off, Rochelle looked at the nameless card, which reflected only a tomahawk, a telephone number and the words, "call me." Parrish smiled softly and placed the card in her purse.

When Chief Red Hawk entered the ring to wrestle that evening Rochelle couldn't cease imagining what time spent with him would be like. While she appreciated Markie, the sergeant paled in comparison to the appeal of the musclebound Chief Red Hawk. The invitation posed by the bogus Indian proved to be too great a temptation for Rochelle to resist.

At the conclusion of the matches Markie took Rochelle to his favorite drinking haunt, Fitzie's. Rochelle got a kick out of Fitzie, a former old school professional boxer. While boxing wasn't quite wrestling, it was close enough for Rochelle to find it appealing.

Rochelle particularly liked the photos that decorated the walls of the bar. Some of the celebrated people she recognized and some she didn't. She was particularly impressed by the large image of the legendary heavyweight champion Jack Dempsey that hung prominently behind the bar.

Markie's conversation with Fitzie gave the sergeant the impression that his friend was repeating himself. This was an indication that his friend's mental health might be declining. Fitzie had forgotten that he had previously met Rochelle. After the re-introduction, Rochelle questioned Fitzie why there were no photos of wrestlers hanging off the walls.

"What are you talking about, I got wrestlers hanging in the corner by the men's room," advised the bar owner.

"You do?"

"Sure, go look."

Rochelle rose from her seat to look at the hanging photographs. In her absence Markie ordered the drinks. When Rochelle returned, she indicated to the sergeant that she didn't recognize the two men with the cauliflower ears that decorated the wall. Markie got up to look at the photos himself. One man he recognized to be Argentina Rocca, a barefoot acrobatic wrestler he recalled watching on television in his youth. The other person was unknown to the sergeant.

"Excuse me, Fitz who are the wrestlers next to Rocca?" Markie asked, addressing the bar owner from the distance of a few feet.

"Ahh, that's ahh...I forget their name," answered Fitzie, failing to recall the names of long forgotten Strangler Lewis and Jim Londos, The Golden Greek.

"I'm a little worried about him," whispered Markie to Rochelle, referring to Fitzie.

"Why?"

"Fitzie's slipping, the guy never forgot a thing before. Now his long term and short-term memory is shot."

Markie concluded that Fitzie was showing definite symptoms of having taken too many punches to the head. Doctors would later call it chronic traumatic encephalopathy.

43

Headlocks and Heartbreaks

NOT SINCE THE TRAGIC DEATH of his girlfriend Alley Cat had Markie been so smitten with a woman. With Alley, it was her honesty that captured his affection. There were no hidden agendas with Fitzie's onetime bartender.

Another thing that endeared Alley to the sergeant was her affinity for the underdog. Her loyalty was unwavering to those she viewed as being at a disadvantage. Markie respected that about her.

Alley's death was a setback that the sergeant never fully recovered from. He liked to think that she was the yardstick he used in measuring all women. However, this wasn't always the case. His ex-wife was a very different sort.

It had taken years for Markie's relationship with his ex-wife to unravel. The two had married early in life, which in retrospect, the sergeant realized was probably a mistake. Yet, even though divorced, an emotional attachment remained. Down deep it bothered Markie that Flo married the dentist she worked for.

What does he have other than money? Markie would often think.

Even though the affair with her boss had begun after Markie separated from his wife, the sergeant still resented the new man in Flo's life. Markie's bitterness was fueled by the feeling that something had been taken from him.

Over time Markie's children grew more aligned with the dentist, an affluent man who was able to provide much. This reality distanced the sergeant from his kids. The situation was an unfortunate one that now seemed unfixable. Relief came when Markie met Karen. He was quite smitten with his new romance.

Markie was immediately attracted to Karen. The fact that she came with a family mattered little. However, although fond of Karen's children, his feelings fell short of love. Up until this point in Markie's life, the only true kindred spirit he felt true affection for had been Alley. Then, Rochelle Parrish came along.

Rochelle was a complex study who ran hot and cold. This characteristic kept Markie on his toes in that she posed a challenge. Rochelle could be embracing or aloof, depending on her mood. Success with Rochelle came with a great sense of self accomplishment for the sergeant. It boosted his ego to get someplace with someone who he saw as being difficult to get close to.

The only thing Markie found odd about Rochelle was her inclination to follow professional wrestling. The extent of her devotion to bone bending was something Rochelle kept under wraps when among professional people. She feared disapproval. While her former employer, Enzo Baffi, was well aware of Rochelle passion for wrestling, he impressed upon her not to air her sporting preference to those he did business with.

Seeing Rochelle at the wrestling matches rooting her head off for Chief Red Hawk was insightful for Markie. Her enthusiasm revealed that behind Rochelle's refined persona was someone like himself. Beneath the veneer that seemed to favor wine and caviar, was a like for beer and pretzels. This made Rochelle the new Alley in Markie's mind. He could see himself one day painting Rochelle's toenails red while in bed as he used to do for Alley.

***

ROCHELLE STARED AT THE TELEPHONE NUMBER on the wrestler's business card. Without hesitation she began dialing the number of Chief Red Hawk. The fact that Rochelle was involved romantically with Markie served as no deterrent in her quest to know the grappler intimately.

Rochelle began seeing the wrestler behind Markie's back. The time spent with Chief Red Hawk further educated her concerning wrestling. Rochelle found the inner workings of the business to be of particular interest. She thought being a part of such entertainment would be something she'd like.

Whenever the married Chief Red Hawk was on the road fulfilling obligations out of town, Rochelle began hanging out with the new friends she made in wrestling. Chief Red Hawk had no objections to this. As far as he was concerned, Rochelle was just another ring rat, a term the wrestlers used when referring to the groupies who pursued them.

The rotating talent on the promoter's roster performing at the Garden provided Rochelle with access to wrestlers from other territories. Regardless of their professional gimmick, villain or baby-faced hero, Rochelle was open to knowing them better. This fast and loose lifestyle was one that Rochelle embraced.

When Markie felt himself being placed on Rochelle's back burner he began to wonder why. Rather than having a conversation with Rochelle he decided to shadow her. It wasn't very long before the sergeant realized where he stood in the pecking order of Rochelle's romantic preferences.

The devastated Markie was so distraught that he couldn't bring himself to face Rochelle. Alone in his apartment he turned to drink as an outlet to ease his heavy heart. With each ounce of whisky consumed Markie grew angrier.

Staring at a photograph he had of Rochelle triggered Markie's rage. It was a picture of the two of them with Chief Red Hawk. Seeing the toothy smile on Rochelle's face was enough to cause

Markie to totally lose it. He took a pair of scissors to the photo, cutting it into little pieces.

A second photograph of Rochelle was a framed headshot he kept atop the end table next to his bed. Markie removed the picture from the frame and drew a mustache on Rochelle with a black ink pen. He then further marred her image by darkening her eyebrows, adding lines to her brow and widening her nose. He finished his artistic handiwork by giving Rochelle a droopy mouth and placing horns atop her head. Still not satisfied, Markie stabbed the photograph with his scissors several times prior to cutting it into pieces. When done, the sergeant resumed his drinking.

Markie entered into a drinking spree that lasted through his regular days off. His binge drinking caused him to not just forget about Rochelle, but also about eating, moving his car for alternate side parking and going to work. He was unresponsive to the ringing of his phone. At this point people were beginning to wonder where the sergeant was.

As far as Rochelle was concerned, she was too occupied learning the wrestling business to think about the law enforcement officer. The fun she was having with the gladiators also consumed much of her time.

44

Duty First

DETECTIVE VON HESS LOOKED up at the clock that hung off the office wall. It was almost noon, and Markie still hadn't arrived at work. Von Hess knew there was something to worry about because Markie was never late. Whenever delayed, the sergeant always called.

"Where is the sergeant, Ollie?" asked Lieutenant Wright.

"I don't know, Loo," replied the detective honestly.

"What do you mean? Look at the time."

"I haven't heard from him."

"Did you try calling him?"

"I've been calling him, Loo."

The lieutenant looked at his watch to double check the time. He then pointed to his wrist as he remarked, "Could he have overslept?"

"Do you want me to go out and look for him?"

Wright let out a sigh that suggested disgust. "Maybe you better. The chief is talking about sending you guys out on a new job. Go find him."

When Von Hess arrived at Markie's apartment he rang the bell. Receiving no answer, he decided to speak to the landlord who owned the two-family residence. They were an elderly retired couple who hadn't raised the sergeant's rent since he had moved in several years prior.

Once Von Hess identified himself and apprised the couple of the situation, the landlord agreed to accompany the detective to Markie's apartment. Armed with a pass key, the senior citizen gained access to the apartment. Both were shocked at what they saw. The unshaven Markie was sprawled across his bed fully dressed. Beside his body was an empty quart bottle of Irish whisky. Several empty beer cans were scattered about the apartment.

"Oh, my God!" exclaimed the landlord. "Is he dead?"

Von Hess checked the sergeant's vital signs before answering. Seeing that the sergeant was alive, Von Hess turned to the landlord and announced, "No, he's not dead. He's just sleeping one off. I'll stick around until he pulls himself together."

"This is the first time anything like this has ever happened," voiced the landlord. "Al has always been a perfect tenant. He helps me shovel the snow in the winter and everything. Something terrible must have happened to cause this."

"Yeah, maybe. Why don't you go back to your wife, I'll take care of things here."

"Do you want me to put on a pot of coffee?"

"Don't bother, I can take care of that from this end. Thanks."

After the landlord left Von Hess looked around the apartment. Seeing Rochelle's destroyed photograph told the tale. Von Hess called his office to advise Lieutenant Wright that Markie was sick in bed.

"Why didn't he call in sick, Ollie?"

"I think he took some old medicine he had around. It must have knocked him out."

"What's wrong with him?"

"He ate some bad food, Loo," lied Von Hess. "He won't be in for a couple of days."

"Okay, I'll put him in for two sick days. He should be in shape to go to work after that, right?" asked the lieutenant.

"I think so, Loo. You better give me the rest of the day off so I can play nursemaid over here."

It took some doing but Von Hess managed to bring Markie around. Once the sergeant began to think clearly, he felt a great embarrassment over his falling to pieces over Rochelle. In the world of cops and robbers, displaying emotion over a broken romance was hardly considered manly.

"What happened, Sarge," asked Von Hess.

"I don't know, Ollie. I guess I just overdid it this time. I didn't eat anything, that was probably my mistake."

"That was probably it," agreed Von Hess, letting things go at that.

Von Hess, like Markie, was old school. Both men felt that any cop requiring support in dealing with any form of trauma, let alone grief over some romantic setback, was in the wrong business. Since admitting to a broken heart was totally out of the question, there was no therapeutic solution.

"How are you feeling now, Sarge?" asked Von Hess once he began to see improvement in Markie's condition later that evening.

"I'll be okay," replied the sergeant. Based on his appearance, Markie looked anything but okay. "I guess they were looking for me at the office."

"Only Lieutenant Wright was looking for you. I spoke to him for you, he's putting you out on administrative sick for a couple of days."

"What did you tell him?"

"I told him the truth."

"Which was?"

"I said that you got food poisoning." Markie slightly smiled, as he nodded weakly.

Later Von Hess received a telephone call from Lieutenant Wright. After inquiring how Markie was feeling, the lieutenant explained that the detectives had a new homicide to work on involving someone friendly with Father Fiorello St. Denis, a police department chaplain. Wright added that the chaplain was close to Chief of Detectives Harry McCoy, who ordered the matter immediately looked into.

"I don't know about that Loo," said Von Hess when Wright asked him if Markie could go to work the following day. "He's still pretty sick."

"Well talk to him, see what he says. He may feel better by tomorrow. Let's touch base in the morning."

"Alright, Loo, I'll get back to you."

"What's the story, Ollie?" Markie asked, after hearing the detective's end of the conversation.

"The chief has a new case for us to work on."

"What kind of case?"

"Some friend of a department chaplain was found murdered. The chaplain is tight with Chief McCoy."

"Which chaplain?"

"Father St. Denis."

"St. Denis is a good man, one of best they got. That guy is also a psychiatrist. There are a lot of mixed-up cops St. Denis straightened out."

"I know," said Von Hess. The detective couldn't help but think that Markie could probably do with a few sessions on the chaplain's couch. "Wright said that the chief expects us to get right on it."

"What did you tell the lieutenant?"

"I said you weren't up to it. I have to call him in the morning. I'll tell him the same thing again when I
speak to him tomorrow."

"Call Wright back, Ollie."

"What for?"

"Tell him we'll get on it first thing in the morning."

"Are you crazy?"

"I need to get busy, Ollie. I want to get my mind off something, and work is the answer. Call up Wright."

"Are you sure?"

"I'll be okay. I'm feeling better already."

"Whatever you say, Sarge. How about, just to be sure you're up to it, I call him in the morning."

"That works."

"I'll be back, Sarge," said Von Hess as he put on his coat.

"Okay, Ollie, I'll see you in the morning. Thanks."

"I'll be back in an hour. I'm just going home to get a couple of things. I'm staying here with you tonight."

Markie didn't say no to this. He was too fatigued to argue.

The following morning Von Hess telephoned the Lieutenant to inform him that he and the sergeant were prepared to go to work on the new case. Lieutenant Wright provided Von Hess with the details on the matter requiring investigation. After hanging up the phone the detective informed Markie that they were all set.

"Was your wife pissed off that you stayed with me all night, Ollie?"

"No, she was okay with it. She's not the type to give me grief over things."

"You're a lucky man."

"I know. Do you want to know what the real shame is, Sarge?"

"What?"

"We were having skirt steak last night."

The detectives then embarked on an investigation that was destined to go down into the files as *The Case of the Missing Sole*.

THE END